BRAVELY AND FAITHFULLY

Bravely and Faithfully

EDWARD HOCHSMANN

Dedication

This book is dedicated to my parents, who successfully managed to raise a son in challenging times and become a good friend to him after he left home to join the service. It is also dedicated to the Coast Guard, the oldest continuous seagoing service of the United States, and its complement of supremely skilled, committed, and courageous professionals. They stand the watch and lay their lives on the line every day to save others, defend the homeland, protect the environment, and promote maritime commerce. Finally, it is dedicated to Coast Guard Senior Chief Boatswain's Mate Terrell Edwin Horne III, killed in the line of duty on 2 December 2012 while on a drug interdiction mission.

Semper Paratus

Main Characters

Haley Reardon, Lieutenant, U.S. Coast Guard. Haley is a superbly competent, hard-charging young officer offered her dream job—command of a patrol boat on the front lines of Coast Guard operations. Easier said than done. Haley must find a way to win over the elite crew of the Coast Guard cutter *Kauai*, replacing a beloved commanding officer promoted out of the job.

Benjamin "Ben" Wyporek, Lieutenant Junior Grade, U.S. Coast Guard. Ben is the executive officer or second in command of the Coast Guard cutter *Kauai*. He is a young but experienced and heroic officer, holding the complete trust of the crew. He must overcome the challenge of the departure of his commanding officer and best friend and help Haley fit into her new role as his commanding officer while managing his courtship of Victoria Carpenter, the love of his life.

Victoria Carpenter. Victoria is a neuro-diverse mathematical genius, formerly an analyst with the Defense Intelligence Agency, who met Ben during a joint operation almost a year ago. Her condition makes some ordinary life activities challenging. She is deeply in love with Ben, who helped her leave her safe but sheltered and unfulfilling existence. She struggles with her fear for Ben's safety when he is out on missions.

Arthur "Art" Frankle, Senior Case Officer, Defense Clandestine Service, Defense Intelli-

gence Agency. Frankle is a veteran field officer, instructor, and mentor to many younger agents. He is approaching retirement age and considering moving from the field to a less "kinetic" post as an instructor or administrator.

Technical Terms

1MC	Ship's internal announcement system
252 Syndicate	Transnational Criminal Organization
BRI	Belt and Road Initiative—a global infrastructure development strategy adopted by the Chinese government
CAC	Common Access Card
Captain	The title for a commanding officer when aboard their ship, regardless of nominal rank. Also, a Coast Guard and Navy rank at paygrade O6—equivalent to a Colonel in the Army, Air Force, and Marine Corps
CO	Commanding Officer
Conn	Position controlling operation of the ship
DIA	Defense Intelligence Agency
EO	Electro-Optical
EPIRB	Emergency Position-Indicating Radio Beacon
FC3	Fire Control/Command and Control system
Gitmo	Nickname for Naval Base Guantanamo Bay, Cuba
Helm	Position or station controlling the ship's rudder
Knots	Nautical Miles per Hour
"Light Off"	Start or activate an engine or device
Main Control	Control station for the ship's main engines
NVG	Night Vision Goggles
OOD	Officer of the Deck
PB	Patrol Boat
Port (side)	To the left, when facing the bow aboard a ship
RHIB	Rigid Hull Inflatable Boat
SAMC	Sino-American Mining Corporation
SFB	Space Force Base
Starboard (side)	To the right, when facing the bow aboard a ship
UAV	Unmanned Aerial Vehicle
WILCO	Brevity code for "Will Comply"
XO	Executive Officer—second in command of a ship

Contents

Prologue

It started as a wobble in the African Easterly Jet, a river of air flowing across the continent of Africa from east to west just north of the equator between the scorching Sahara desert and the relatively cooler rainforests adjoining it. The disturbance created an area of unstable air, which allowed the formation of thunderstorms as the disturbance drifted westward across Cameroon and southern Nigeria. The persistence of the thunderstorms, fed by enormous amounts of evaporated water from the forests, eventually created a narrow trough of low pressure drifting off the coast into the Gulf of Guinea. A tropical wave was born.

Tropical waves often dissipate as they move over the slightly cooler environment of the Atlantic Ocean. Still, it was just past the autumnal equinox, with the sun almost directly overhead at noon, and the water was warm enough to sustain the thunderstorms within the system. It was being tracked and observed by this time, with computer models churning through terabytes of weather observational and simulation data, trying to forecast the risk of development. As the wave drifted west-northwest and away from the equator, it started drawing in air from its surroundings. But the system was large enough that Coriolis force began pulling the inflowing air to the right. Eventually, an equilibrium between the inward draw of the low pressure and the outward pull of the Coriolis force created a circular spin of the atmosphere. The weather satellites noted this change, and the wave was officially labeled Tropical Depression number 16, or TD16 for short.

The meteorologists at the National Hurricane Center, or NHC, in Miami, Florida, were very interested in the system by this time. They hoped that the moderate wind shear suppressing the deeper convective thunderstorms in TD16's center would persist long enough for the system to hook on to a low-pressure trough crossing just north of its track and be pulled safely northward into the open Atlantic. It was not to be. The trough passed without connecting, and TD16 moved slowly out of the area of wind shear. The thunderstorms in its center were now free to build to great heights, the condensation of water vapor releasing vast amounts of heat trapped by the spinning air around the storm. A convergence and lifting of warm, moist air releasing energy into the closed circulation created a positive feedback loop, steadily decreasing the air pressure in the center and pushing the spinning winds above the threshold of thirty-nine miles per hour. When the satellite data revealed that the sustained winds had reached this next stage of cyclogenesis, system TD16 acquired a name; the tenth issued that season. Tropical Storm Jacob had arrived.

Jacob plodded steadily westward, carried along by the easterly trade winds like many Cape Verde storms. Unfortunately, this kept it above some of the warmest water in the world, and the storm hungrily fed on the energy released as the converging winds lifted the moist air aloft in its center. After two days over the warm water, with little wind shear or other environmental impediments, Jacob charged past the seventy-four miles per hour sustained wind threshold and became the season's sixth hurricane.

The meteorologists at the NHC issued hurricane warnings for the Lesser Antilles Islands, Puerto Rico, and Hispaniola. The consensus of the myriad storm models was firm on this point: these islands would take a hit. From Hispaniola on, things got crazy—several forecast weather effects in play could send Jacob anywhere from straight west over Cuba, the Yucatan Peninsula, and the Gulf of Mexico to curving north into the Atlantic east of the Bahamas. Jacob continued to build, surging through Category 2 to reach Major Hurricane, Category 3 status a few hours before its first landfall on the island of Antigua. After battering that unfortunate land and the neighboring islands of Monserrat, Nevis, and St. Kitts, Jacob roared onward toward the Virgin Islands and Puerto Rico.

As Jacob penetrated the Caribbean basin, the meteorological picture became less uncertain. A turn to the north was now forecast—the average of the models predicted a path somewhere between Florida's gulf coast and the Atlantic just east of the Bahamas. The cities in the dead-center of the prediction cone, from Miami to Jacksonville, began emergency preparations with the evacuation of people, aircraft, and ships. In the meantime, recovery vessels and personnel converged on the areas damaged in the storm's wake.

The amount of energy powering a Category 3 hurricane almost defies belief. The largest explosion ever triggered by man released the energy equivalent to the detonation of fifty million tons of TNT—the condensation of water vapor rocketing upward in Jacob's core released an equivalent amount of heat energy into the storm *every hour*. Jacob delivered the worst pummeling Puerto Rico had experienced since its direct hit by Hurricane Maria and then began skirting the northern coast of Hispaniola. Here, finally, Jacob faltered.

Free of the trade winds, Jacob slowed, allowing the mountains of the Dominican Republic and Haiti to disrupt the airflow into Jacob's core. The storm lost some of its intensity and enough forward speed to "sense" a low-pressure trough coming off the Carolinas and begin a northward turn. Jacob's eye passed between the Turks and Caicos and Great Inagua, then skirted the eastern islands of the Bahamas before curving north and east into the center of the Atlantic after another close brush with North Carolina's Outer Banks. As it passed over the cooler waters north of the Bahamas, Jacob's energy supply was cut off, and the storm rapidly de-intensified into an extratropical cyclone headed for Europe.

With dozens of deaths and billions of dollars worth of property damage, Jacob was a tragic disaster for the areas it touched in the Caribbean and the Bahamas. Yet, it could have been worse if the storm ranged up Florida's east coast as a strong Category 3 storm. The citizens of Florida and the meteorologists of the NHC breathed a sigh of relief as people, aircraft, and ships returned from their exile. On the other hand, there was little sense of comfort for those caught in the storm's path—only a fight for survival.

Dear God, be good to me;
The sea is so wide,
And my boat is so small.
Breton Fisherman's Prayer

Part I - Preliminaries

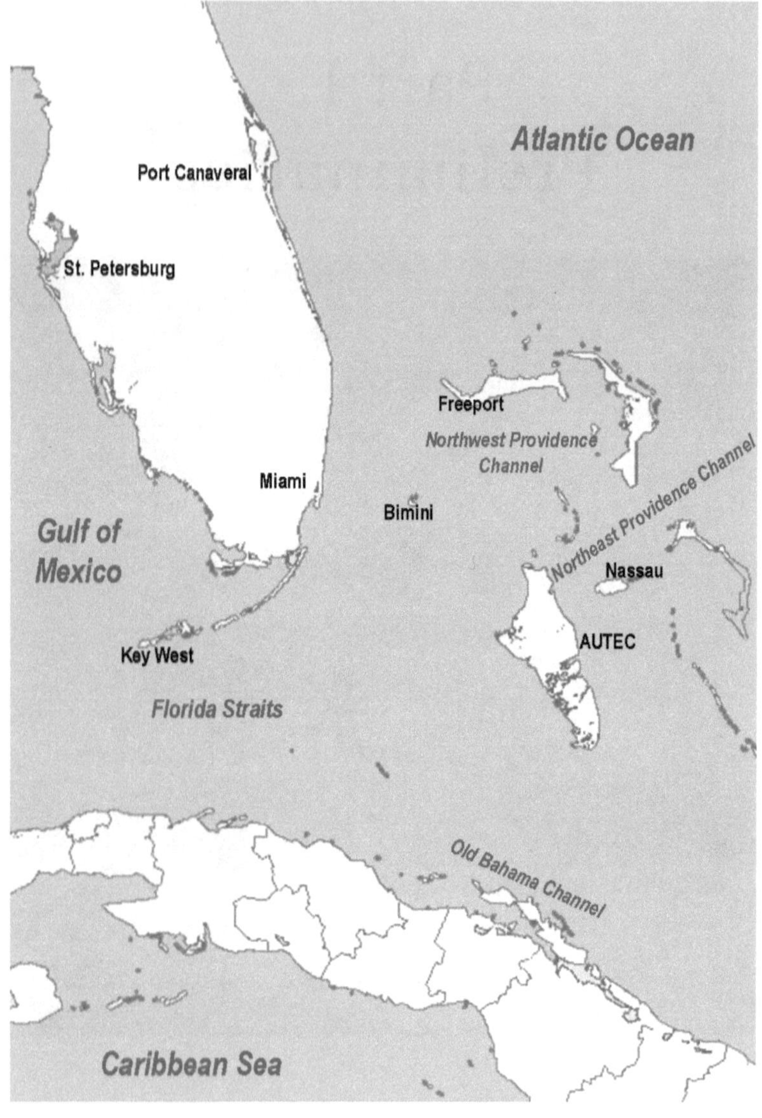

Atlantic Ocean
Port Canaveral
St. Petersburg
Freeport
Northwest Providence Channel
Miami
Northeast Providence Channel
Bimini
Nassau
Gulf of Mexico
AUTEC
Key West
Florida Straits
Old Bahama Channel
Caribbean Sea

Chapter 1

From the Jaws of Death

Sailing Vessel Aurora Mist, Northwest Providence Channel, thirteen nautical miles south-southwest of Freeport, Bahamas 15:42 EDT, 29 September

Murray

Phillip Murray had just murdered his family.

Well, perhaps not murdered. They were still alive at the moment. But tied down in the sealed cabin of the rolling, pitching, and heaving remnants of the once beautiful sailing yawl *Aurora Mist*, they were as good as dead. His lawyer's logic also objected technically—there had been no Malice Aforethought, not even the reckless negligence that would have qualified as Depraved Indifference Homicide back in New York. *Is that a thing in the Bahamas? What is the correct crime for a series of decisions that puts your wife and two little girls in the path of an intense hurri-cane with no hope of escape?*

A particularly violent combination of pitching and the roller-coaster heaving of the *Aurora Mist* wrenched his mind from these feeble professional distractions, and his stomach roiled again. Murray was breathing through his mouth now, in a desperate but vain attempt to remove one sense contributing to his nausea in the sealed, vomit-soaked cabin. He desperately wanted to open the cabin hatch or a window to at least get some fresh air in, but doing so would admit the angry sea and sink them in a heartbeat. Leaving the cabin for any reason would be certain death, as the loud thuds of wave impacts and the shrieking of the wind through the remaining deck fittings reminded him.

He directed his bleary gaze at the clock across the cabin—3:43 pm—seven and a half hours since the masts went by the board. He turned to Gemma, his wife of fourteen years strapped down four feet away. Dull, red-rimmed eyes gazed back, her face set in a gray mask of despair. Gemma was a sailor too, and she knew quite well the desperation of their situation. Her arms held their daughters tightly, faces buried in her chest. The girls had passed out from the exhaustion of vomiting and holding on against the boat's chaotic motion. It was a small blessing that he did not have to look them in the eyes anymore as they pleaded, in words unspoken,

Do something, Daddy!

It was not supposed to be this way. Murray had been an avid sailor since he was a child and had crewed for a contender for the America's Cup a decade and a half ago. He was not one of the lubberly imbeciles who thought reading Richard Henry Dana or watching a season of *Below Deck* made them expert seamen. He knew boats and respected the sea.

He could have continued sailing. But he had met, fallen hard for, and soon married Gemma Langton, a beautiful college classmate who shared his passion for the law and, to a lesser extent, sailing. The demands of school, the bar exam, and building a law practice in one of the most litigiously competitive locations in the world reduced their sailing time to summer day trips in rentals on the Long Island Sound. Then the kids came. When he held his newborn daughter Jamie in his arms, he knew he had too little time as it was to spend with his family. He would sacrifice none of it to indulge himself, regardless of how much he missed the challenge and exhilaration of bending the wind and sea to his will. Gemma appreciated this and promised that when the girls were old enough and he had a big case under his belt, he would take them all on a sailing sabbatical.

That day had come last March. He was the attorney of record for a class action that netted a nine-figure settlement. Now forty-five million dollars richer, Murray decided this was the time to live his and Gemma's dream of a sailing cruise around the Caribbean. Taking a few months to close out his remaining cases while Gemma put together a home school curriculum, the family traveled to Miami at the end of June. Everyone fell in love with the *Aurora Mist*, a beautiful fifty-three-foot yawl with a fully decked-out cabin and two bedrooms. Murray bought the boat, and the family set sail for the Yucatan Channel and Cozumel the next day.

The following three months were idyllic, with exotic ports, gorgeous beaches, lush tropical islands, and the wonders of the sea. The girls' excitement at seeing their first flying fish brought Murray the greatest joy he had experienced since Lydia was born. Like their parents, the girls took to the sea and were soon standing their own helm watches as Murray pretended to doze on the long sails between destinations.

Hurricanes were a genuine threat in the area throughout the trip. Murray was no fool—he knew what would happen if the *Aurora Mist* was caught at sea by one of those monsters. Thus, he gathered the National Hurricane Center's updates twice daily and tracked any systems that popped up with an almost religious fervor. He had even altered their voyage plan twice as a precaution when systems appeared to have a chance of reaching them.

Jacob had vexed Murray as much as it had the NHC forecasters. The *Aurora Mist* was in the Northern Bahamas, ready to run to the East or West as needed to stay clear, but Jacob stubbornly refused to commit, and the track uncertainty "cone" remained broad. Finally, the track guidance firmed away from the Florida coast and through the Eastern Bahamas. Murray set the course to the south-west around Great Abaco Island, through the Northwest Providence Channel just south of Grand Bahama Island. They would have to use Jacob's winds to help run clear, but Murray expected no problems.

But Jacob had other ideas.

The track unexpectedly jogged back to the west and picked up speed as a low-pressure trough moving off the East Coast had reached down farther than expected and tugged at the storm. It was now a race between the powerful hurricane barreling northward and the sailboat carrying progressively more reefs in the mainsail as the wind velocity increased. The Murrays and the *Aurora Mist* were winning. With Grand Bahama Island limiting the fetch, the term for the distance over which the wind could push on and build up the waves, the seas were moderate, allowing the winds to sweep them along at close to eighteen knots. Then it happened.

The boat had been running and riding well with a thrice reefed mainsail in a steady wind of twenty-five knots when a sudden gust of twice that speed took down the mizzen mast. Absent the balancing force of the mizzen sail, the boat immediately fell off from close haul, exposing the full breadth of the mainsail. The resulting strain was too high: the windward mainstays and the mast snapped in quick succession. In seconds, the *Aurora Mist* transformed from a racing thing of beauty to a wallowing wreck. The only good news was that no one was hurt—Gemma and the girls were in the cabin, and the flailing booms and stay wires somehow missed Murray at the helm.

Murray was a careful man and had prepared for this, the worst eventuality. It took a few seconds to overcome the shock of the quick sequence of events, but then he launched into action. The first step was to cut away the wreckage of the masts held alongside by the leeward stays. Then to the bow to cast the sea anchor—essentially a parachute attached to three hundred feet of reinforced line. The drag would keep *Aurora Mist*'s bow to the wind and seas and hopefully keep her from capsizing or pitch polling in the ever-building seas. As the gyrating boat swung into the wind, Murray crawled aft to the cabin, fastened the hatch cover, manually activated the Emergency Position Indicating Radio Beacon or EPIRB, and then turned to help Gemma secure herself and the children in the cabin. The girls were already seasick before the mishap. Now that there was no alternative to continuous pitching and heaving, shut tight in the airless cabin, things would get much worse for all of them.

"Phil?" Gemma asked pleadingly over Jamie's and Lydia's quiet sobs.

"The EPIRB's on, honey. It will just be a matter of time before they come for us." He was lying, of course. The rescue capabilities of the Royal Bahamian Defense Force were rudimentary at best, and they were over sixty miles from any U.S. Coast Guard station. The chance that a ship large enough to attempt a rescue would be in these narrow waters with a hurricane bearing down was vanishingly slight. *But not zero.* Despite the dread he felt inside, he smiled to encourage his wife.

The following seven and a half hours were a descent into Hell. The boat was riding well to the sea anchor, all things considered. But the wave heights were progressively increasing along with the fetch as they were pulled toward Jacob's center and away from the shelter of Grand Bahama Island. The constant strain of holding on against the motion and the throwing up from the seasickness exhausted everyone. Murray was becoming increasingly listless, no longer caring about what could be causing the lurches and what bumps and thuds could be heard over the howling wind.

There was a lurch, somehow different from what Murray had been feeling in the boat's motion, followed almost immediately by a loud thud from the overhead. He wondered what could have broken loose or collided with the *Aurora Mist* when the hatch suddenly opened with a roar of wind. Murray turned in panic and reached for the release on his strap—the hatch had somehow broken loose, and if not secured immediately, waves breaking over the boat would soon swamp the cabin. He had grabbed a secure handhold when a man wearing a white helmet, goggles, and an orange life vest appeared in the opening.

Shouting to be heard over the screeching of the wind, the man said, "Howdy, folks! Petty Officer Juan Lopez, U.S. Coast Guard! Would anybody like a ride in my boat?!"

Murray blinked at the apparition and, unable to reply, nodded vigorously.

"OK!" the young man said, ducking as a wave broke over the boat. "This is going to take careful timing! We have to take you off one at a time! Our boat can only hang alongside for a few seconds, so I will hand you off to my shipmate in the boat, understand?!"

Murray nodded again.

"Sweet! OK, sir and ma'am, this is important! When I push you off, the only thing you grab is the man in the boat! You grab at anything else, and it won't go well, clear?! I need a thumbs up from each of you!"

Murray gave a thumbs up with his free hand and turned to see Gemma wearily doing the same.

"Alright! Ma'am, can you pass the first child to the gentleman here while I call over the boat?!"

Gemma nodded and unhooked Jamie's strap, then released her once Murray had a firm grip and pulled her over. The child was listless with fatigue, mumbling something Murray couldn't hear over the wind. He leaned over to speak in her ear. "I know it's hard, honey, but it will be over soon. Go with the Coast Guard man now."

Jamie looked fearful and then nodded, turning to Lopez and reaching out. Lopez quickly pulled the child into the crook of his arm, and then they disappeared from the hatch. After what seemed an eternity to Murray but couldn't have been more than half a minute, there was another perceptible lurch in the boat and several thuds on the deck. After a few more seconds, Lopez reappeared in the hatch opening.

"OK, folks! She's safe on board the boat!" Murray stifled a cry of relief while Lopez continued, "Let's take the second child, please!"

Murray and Gemma repeated the transfer process, but Lydia was frantic. "No, Daddy! No!"

Murray held her close and spoke in her ear. "I know it's scary, sweet pea, but you have to go with the Coast Guard man to be with Jamie. Mommy and I will be there with you before you know it."

Lydia was still sobbing, but released her grip on Murray as Lopez took her under his arm. As the two disappeared through the hatch, Murray reached over and drew Gemma over to him, hugging her tightly. Lopez soon reappeared at the hatch.

"Both girls are safe and secure in the boat! Let's take you now, ma'am!"

Gemma looked into Murray's eyes and gave him a quick kiss and hug, then followed the young petty officer out of the hatch. After they were clear, Murray grasped the handhold and released his strap, then squatted in the hatchway. Before long, Lopez reappeared.

"OK, sir, just you and me now! We'll be going over together! What we're going to do is hang out right outside the hatch! You'll see the boat coming, but don't move until I pull your arm! When I do, you jump for the boat with everything you've got, copy?!"

Murray nodded exaggeratedly and shouted, "Yes! Let's do it!"

Lopez nodded and then pulled Murray through the hatch. He could barely hold on as the roaring wind gripped him, immensely strong even in the partial lee of the cockpit. The scene on deck was surreal. In all directions, from what he could see in the limited visibility, was a gray sea and waves at least twelve feet high with spray blowing from the tops. A solid overcast of clouds whipped overhead at unbelievable speed. A white vessel with a Coast Guard red racing stripe gyrated a hundred yards off the starboard side, dipping and slamming into the oncoming waves each ten to twelve seconds. He turned aft to see a small orange boat approaching, disappearing from sight as the *Aurora Mist* crested a wave and dipped, reappearing a couple of seconds later. The boat approached slowly, briefly held in position about ten yards away while another wave passed, then shot forward. Lopez leaned over, shouted, "Let's go!" and yanked his arm.

Murray leaped with every ounce of strength he had. As soon as he cleared the lee of the cockpit, the wind seemed to slap him in midair. He was falling and turning as he collided with a soft object, the crewman in the boat, then slammed onto the hard deck. A large hand gripped and dragged him to the side, where Gemma and the girls were already lashed in.

The big crewman placed his hand on a grab handle and shouted, "Hold this, stay down, and keep your arms inside the boat!" Once Murray had a firm grip, the crewman pulled a strap across his lap, fastened it to a ring fitting on the deck, and cinched it. The small orange boat pitched up as it climbed another high wave, and the strap across Murray's lap bit into him as they seemed to come near to vertical. Then the bow abruptly pitched down for yet another sickening drop to a tremendous splash.

"That's it! We're done for!" Murray thought as wind and water tugged at his body. But the boat came up again, the deck cleared, and from what he could see with his spray-fogged eyes, everyone was still there. He looked toward Gemma, sitting beside him with her free arm stretched across Jamie's and Lydia's chests, and placed his free hand over hers on the grab handle. They rode out two more monstrous wave events before reaching the cutter, which provided little shelter from the gale for the tossing boat.

Murray had turned to look at the nearby cutter when a gunshot rang out, followed by the thump of a line on the bow. Murray surmised the winds were too high for a standard heaving line, so the Coast Guardsman used a rifle to pass a line to the boat. The big boat crewman was hauling in a thin line that Murray knew was attached to the hook used to crane the boat aboard. This was the time of maximum risk—with the cutter and boat writhing in the wind and seas, attaching the hook would be a nightmare. He leaned over to cover Gemma's head with his body and closed his eyes.

And then he prayed.

The boat suddenly jolted upward after two clangs, audible even over the shrieking wind. Murray opened his eyes to see the big crewman kneeling on the deck, gripping handles on either side of a metal block attached to the boat frame. He looked over his shoulder to see they were even with the cutter's deck, which receded as they rolled to the left, then came on with a bone-jarring crash.

"Heave in, goddammit!" the big crewman shouted at several men on the cutter's deck. The small boat drifted out again with another roll, but far less than before. The boat stayed snug on the cutter's side on the next roll. The big crewman shouted, "Get ready!" The crewmen on the deck moved to the side of the boat, squatted, and seized grab handles. The cutter pitched upward, then down with a tremendous splash that inundated the scene with rushing water. It had not yet cleared when the big crewman yelled, "Take them!" Four pairs of hands released the Murray family's straps and hauled them onto the deck, moving briskly to and through an open door in the superstructure.

The room they entered seemed to be some sort of dining area. There were two tables with chairs bolted to the floor in the center and what appeared to be a stove with two large refrigerators in the corner. The oven and refrigerator doors were secured with straps, and perforated mats covered the entire deck. The crewmen who had escorted them inside were busily seating Gemma and the children against the wall and connecting them with new safety straps, while Murray's crewmen did the same for him. Even inside, the wind's howling was very loud, but conversation was possible, at least. The motion of the cutter was still quite violent—the crewmen were essentially climbing from one location to the next. Finally, one of the crew pulled off his goggles and spoke into what looked like a thin headset, "Conn, Deck Party secure and ready for maneuvers."

Murray looked up as a voice came over the loudspeakers in the room. "Attention, everybody. The good news is the ride is about to get a lot smoother; the bad news is we will have to turn beam-on. Stand by."

The crewmen all kneeled and seized railings on the wall with both hands, and the one with the headset looked at Murray and said, "Hang on tight, folks. We will run with the wind and seas to tamp down this motion, but we have to turn broadside to get there."

Murray nodded, then turned to gaze at his family across the room and locked eyes with Gemma. The cutter pitched down, plunging into the wave trough with a thundering crash, followed by the muffled roar of running water. Then, after a few seconds, the cutter began another rapid pitch up and climb up the next wave. At the crest, instead of plunging downward, the cutter rapidly yawed to the right, accompanied by a brief roll to the left so deep he felt like he was hanging off the side in his harness. The cutter then rolled back to vertical and plunged forward, the engines below the deck on which he sat roaring above the sound of the wind. He could feel the difference in the motion as the cutter picked up speed—instead of colliding with the water in the next wave, she rode through the trough, then pitched more slowly as the wave slid by. Murray released the breath he was holding. The danger was not past by any means, but running with the wind and seas now, they were hurrying away from the storm's center.

In minutes, the motion steadied to a slow roll of twenty degrees to each side, with a pitch of about ten degrees. The voice came over the loudspeakers again. "Alright, guys, the worst is behind us, and we are making thirty knots over the ground in the best direction. Normal movement is OK, but a big one can come along at any time, so remember, one hand for the boat at all times. All weather decks remain secured until further notice. Well done, everybody!"

The crewmen kneeling around the messdeck stood and removed their helmets. Crewmembers, Murray corrected himself—the shortest among them was an African American woman. Murray was astonished as they started chatting and laughing, as if this heart-stopping experience was just another day at the office. A tall, youthful crewman with the single silver bar on his uniform that marked him as an officer came over and released his harness. Murray took his proffered hand and stood unsteadily.

"Sir, were you the Master of the *Aurora Mist*?" he asked.

Murray had never thought of himself in those terms, but supposed that was the correct formal usage. "Yes, I am, or was, I guess. I'm Phillip Murray."

"How do you do, Mr. Murray? I'm Lieutenant Junior Grade Ben Wyporek, Executive Officer. Welcome to the Coast Guard Cutter *Kauai*. Are these people your family?"

"Yes, sir. My wife, Gemma, and daughters Jamie and Lydia. Thank you for coming for us."

"We're glad to have you aboard. Right now, we are going to move you to one of our berthing areas where you can rest, and our Health Services Technician can check you out."

"Thank you, sir." It was entirely inadequate for the emotion he felt for the deliverance of his family from what he believed was certain death, but it was all his exhausted mind could muster. He smiled at Gemma as she and the girls were released from their harnesses and helped to their feet. The young officer led them forward through a passageway to a tiny room almost filled with two pairs of bunk beds and four narrow lockers. A corridor barely two feet wide between the bunk pairs provided the only floor space in the room. "I'm sorry it's so cramped in here, but it's the best we can offer you right now," the officer said.

"Lieutenant, considering where we just came from, this is heaven."

"Good. I think putting the children in the top bunks is best, and there is no risk of their falling out—as you can see, we have retention rails installed."

"Yes, I agree," Murray said as he looked closely at the bunks.

"Right then," Wyporek said and kneeled to speak to Jamie. "Miss Jamie, my name is Ben, and I'm going to help you into the top bunk. Is that OK?"

"Yes. Ben, I feel sick."

"I know, honey. My friend Mike will be here in a minute to get something to help you with that."

"Thanks," Jamie said as Wyporek lifted her so she could climb into the bunk.

He then turned and kneeled by the other child. "Miss Lydia, I'm Ben. I'm going to help you into the other top bunk, OK?"

"Yes, Ben," Lydia said as she put her arms around Wyporek's neck. He lifted her to the bunk and then turned to Murray after the child climbed in.

"OK, sir. Do you or your wife need help?"

Murray turned to Gemma and got an exhausted smile and a head shake. He turned to Wyporek. "No, Lieutenant, we'll be fine."

"Right. This is our Health Services Technician, Petty Officer Mike Bryant," Wyporek said, gesturing to a shorter crewman with close-cropped blond hair and wire-rimmed glasses. "He needs to do a health check on you and the children."

"We'd be grateful," Murray said. "I'm glad to meet you, Mr. Bryant."

"Likewise, sir," Bryant replied. "XO, I've got this."

"Roger that," the officer said. Then he left the room.

Bryant closed the door and said, "I'd like to start with the children. Could you and your wife get into the lower bunks, please? I need room to work here."

"Yes, certainly," Murray said. After helping Gemma into her bunk, he climbed into his own. Under normal circumstances, he would have been mildly claustrophobic in the tight space, but he was too tired and worried at present. After a few minutes, Bryant kneeled.

"Folks, both your children are OK. They have mild dehydration and are still experiencing motion sickness. With your permission, I would like to give them an oral solution. It is Pedialyte with a small dose of ondansetron to knock out nausea and help them rest."

Murray nodded to Gemma, and she said, "Yes, please. Go ahead."

"Thank you."

Bryant finished with the children within a few minutes and kneeled again for the adults. "Ma'am, your turn." Five minutes later, Bryant had completed his examination on both adults. "Folks, same diagnosis for you two. I want you each to drink a bottle of Pedialyte, and I have a dimenhydrinate pill for you if you're still nauseous, but it might make you sleepy."

"Dimenhydrinate?" Murray asked.

"The trade name is Dramamine."

"That sounds like an excellent prescription to me," Murray said.

When Bryant turned to Gemma, she said, "Yes, I would like both, please."

"Coming right up."

The drink was not as unpleasant as Murray expected, and the pill soon eliminated his remaining nausea. Gemma was also returning from the dead, and she gave a grateful smile to the young medic. Bryant excused himself, saying he would be just a shout away if they needed anything. After he had left, Murray got up from his bunk to check on Jamie and Lydia—both were sleeping peacefully and securely in their bunks. He then kneeled beside Gemma's bunk, cupped her cheek gently with his right hand, and kissed her warmly. He then pulled back and smiled. "My dearest, I think we'll stick with daysailers on the Sound from here on out."

Gemma smiled in return. "An eminently sound legal strategy, counselor."

Murray returned to his bunk, then reached across the space between the bunks to lay his hand on Gemma's arm. Between the cutter's gradually moderating motion, the ordeal's exhaustion, and the Dramamine's narcotic effects, both were asleep within fifteen minutes.

Chapter 2

Part of the Job

***USCG Cutter Kauai, Straits of Florida,
twenty-one nautical miles southwest of
Freeport, Bahamas
16:29 EDT, 29 September***

Ben

Lieutenant Junior Grade Benjamin "Ben" Wyporek wearily climbed the ladder leading to *Kauai*'s Bridge. Every muscle ached from fatigue after the hours-long fight through wind and seas to reach the stricken sailboat, followed by the harrowing ordeal on the main deck during the recovery of the survivors. Ben and the two others in the deck crew had nearly gone overboard in that last wave when the cascading water had swept their legs from under them. All three men would be dead now if it had not been for the safety belts connecting them to the deck railing. He looked aft through the port bridge door window—the cutter's Rigid Hull Inflatable Boat, known as "the rib" for its acronym RHIB, was still there, snugged into the side with tie-downs on every available fitting. His internal mariner objected to the situation, but the risks of injury while cradling the RHIB were too high with a thirty-knot tailwind and these seas. The RHIB was replaceable, the crewmembers were not, and they had already pressed their luck too far on this trip.

They had sortied three days ago from their Port Canaveral homeport when it looked like Jacob might impact Florida's east coast. While the last place on Earth you wanted to be in a patrol boat when a major hurricane hit was in the open sea, being moored to a pier subject to storm surge was a close second. Better to get some sea room and scurry out of the way. When the storm had finally settled on a northerly course through the Bahamas, they turned back for home in relief. Then came the call from the Rescue Coordination Center in Miami.

One satellite in the Copas-Sarsat constellation had picked up an emergency signal from an EPIRB registered to the sailing vessel *Aurora Mist.* The signal was localized to a spot about eleven nautical miles south of Freeport in the Bahamas, thirty miles from their position. The owner-operator had filed a sail plan listing four people on board, two of them children. The risks of responding to the distress call were considerable for *Kauai* and her crew. If they lost control in those seas and narrow waters, whether from the storm's effects or some mechanical problem, their only achievement would be adding the names of sixteen Coast Guard men and women to Jacob's death toll.

Even if they could get to the scene and find the boat, odds were long against the successful launch and recovery of the RHIB. But when you knew there were lives at stake, particularly children, you went if there was any chance of rescue. This time, luck was on their side.

Ben was the Executive Officer, referred to as XO, the second in command of *Kauai*. A lean five-foot-ten, with close-cropped sandy brown hair surrounding a lightly tanned, chiseled face and startlingly blue eyes, he was among the younger members of the crew at twenty-five years of age. *Kauai* was his second tour of duty after graduating from the Coast Guard Academy in Connecticut three years previously.

Ben made his way to the captain's chair in the Bridge's center, moving from handhold to handhold as the deck rolled and pitched beneath him. He stopped beside the chair, fired off a crisp salute, and said, "Survivors are secured in the Port Non-rate Berthing Area, Captain. Doc says they're OK, and he's treating them for dehydration and seasickness."

Lieutenant Samuel "Sam" Powell, commanding officer of *Kauai*, returned Ben's salute. By tradition, he was addressed as "Captain" on board his ship, despite his nominal rank. About an inch taller than Ben but equally lean and tanned, Sam had dark hair, a friendly round face, and soft brown eyes. At thirty-six, he was the second-oldest member of the crew. Unlike Ben, he had been commissioned from the enlisted ranks after attending officer candidate school as a chief petty officer. Despite the differences in background and age and their positions, the two men had become best friends since their arrival on board *Kauai* nearly two years previously. "Thanks, XO. That was a hell of a job on the main deck in that mess. If I had known it would be this bad, I think I might have turned it down."

Ben smiled in return. "I don't think you would, sir. And if you have any lingering doubts about whether it was worth it, I suggest you peek in on that family we picked up when you get a chance."

"I'll do that once things calm down. Now, for real: how are *you*? I about had a heart attack when I saw you guys go down in that wave."

"No worries, Captain. Just another bruise or two."

"Just the same; I want you to have Doc give you a head check as soon as we're done here."

Ben's smile vanished, and his stomach flipped at the reminder that he was still under scrutiny for his injury during a secret mission six months previously. Ben had been shot in the head by a crazed drug cartel assailant, and though his helmet kept the bullet out, the impact caused a hematoma that nearly killed him. His continued service in the Coast Guard was contingent on special neurological evaluations in each annual physical and check-ups after any mishaps that could have caused head trauma. "Captain, I didn't hit my head, so there's no...."

"Uh-uh," Sam interrupted, shaking his head. "You know the deal. You go down, you get checked. End of story." He reached over and gave Ben's shoulder a friendly shake. "Don't worry. It will be strictly routine if you haven't cracked your bean again. Now, how's everything else holding up?"

"I went from stem to stern on the inside, sir: no leaks or engineering issues. I'm sure the lifelines are trashed, and I don't want to even think about the gun right now," Ben replied. Seawater weighs nearly sixty-three pounds per cubic foot and is almost incompressible. Waves impacting at over thirty miles per hour would wreak havoc on anything exposed topside. Lifelines, the wires strung along stanchions on the periphery of the deck to prevent personnel from falling overboard, and the main gun on the foredeck were the usual casualties when any cutter, particularly a small one like a patrol boat, encountered heavy seas.

Sam said, "Yes, I suppose I'll have some 'splaining to do when we get back. They can't ding me too hard with four lives saved."

"God, I would hope not, sir. I'll start the RHIB's crew's writeups if you don't object. Can't let a good rescue go to waste."

"Thank you, XO. That will be *after* your head exam, of course."

"Yes, sir," Ben replied.

"Buck up, son! Remember, we could all be dead now."

"Yes, sir, there is *that*. By your leave, sir?"

"Carry on, XO."

Ben turned and stepped over to Chief Operations Specialist Emilia Hopkins, scanning the horizon with binoculars in her role as the officer of the deck. Hopkins was the best shiphandler on board and was the go-to person for OOD in a sticky situation like the recent rescue. The tall and fit thirty-four-year-old widowed mother of twelve- and ten-year-old sons, Hopkins shared a house with her mother, who looked after the boys when she was at sea. While not friends in the strictest sense, as the Coast Guard did not permit such relationships between officers and enlisted members, Ben respected and admired her professionally and as an individual. He knew Sam felt the same. Hopkins was one of those most trusted voices who would give it to you straight in private, but had your back at all times. "How goes it, Chief? Do you need some relief here?"

Hopkins, who overheard Ben and Sam's conversation, returned a grin. "Sorry, XO, I can't help you. Now that I'm not puking my guts out every five minutes, I've found my second wind."

"Right. You know *I* am always here for *you*," Ben said with a mock huff, drawing a chuckle from the chief petty officer. Ben's bonhomie concealed a genuine worry that nagged at him as he departed the Bridge to find Bryant. He *had* hit the deck hard after that wave—he was sure he would have a substantial bruise on his right hip from the impact. An event like that, even one not involving a direct blow to the head, could bring the career he loved to a close.

He found Bryant in the ship's dispensary, monitoring the Murray family as they slept in the adjacent compartment. Health Services Technician Michael Bryant, known as "Doc" among the crew, cut an unimposing figure at a thin five-foot-seven with round wire-rimmed glasses. Ben knew this concealed a calm dedication to his shipmates' well-being, his courage proven with the Silver Star and Purple Heart medals he earned as an army combat medic before his transfer to the Coast Guard and his service aboard *Kauai*. He had received special training and equipment to conduct neurological assessments in the field to monitor Ben's recovery. "I need a quick check under the hood, Doc," Ben said in greeting.

"On it, XO," Bryant replied.

The assessment comprised inspections of his ear canals, pupillary responses, and general balance, not a simple task on a pitching and rolling patrol boat. He followed up with a check of Ben's right side. Ben exhaled in relief when Bryant finished and said, "Neurologics are normal, sir. You'll have a helluva bruise by tomorrow, but nothing's broken."

"Good to hear. How are our passengers doing?"

"Fine, sir. They'll be sleeping for a while between the exhaustion and anti-nausea drugs I gave them. I was a little concerned about the kids at first—they were both close to passing out from dehydration. But they took the Pedialyte well."

"Good. Let me know when they wake up, please."

"Will do, sir."

Ben nodded and then made his way to the messdeck, where Chief Machinery Technician James Drake shared coffee with two of *Kauai*'s boatswain's mates. Drake was the senior enlisted and oldest member of the crew at forty-three. He was also the tallest at six-foot-four and had a muscular build and graying hair, cut short like all the other males on board. Drake was the senior engineer aboard *Kauai* when Ben and Sam arrived. He remained with the unit even after her conversion to a diesel-electric powerplant called for a change in the senior enlisted to the Electrician's Mate rating. Drake was an old-time chief in the sense of resolving problems before they came to the officers' attention. He operated a network of "connections" from fellow chiefs to senior officers for scrounging and "intel." Ben and Sam had learned quickly not to dig too deeply into how some of the seemingly intractable problems were being handled; they just had to sit back and enjoy the results.

Boatswain's Mate First Class John Bondurant sat across the table from Drake. Bondurant was almost as tall as Drake at six-foot-three, but even more powerfully built. His great strength came in handy, particularly today—he was the large crewman in the RHIB who manhandled the passengers aboard and seized and hooked up the chaotically whirling hoist block. He was a quiet and even-tempered man, with a wife and two sons in high school.

Bondurant's subordinate, Boatswain's Mate Second Class Shelley Lee, sat to his right. Lee was a full foot shorter than Bondurant, but had the athletic build of a gymnast. She was the most skillful small boat operator Ben had ever known and was the coxswain of the RHIB during today's rescue. Lee and Ben were close in age, temperament, and interests, and they shared the same mutual admiration and respect Ben had with Hopkins. Lee was the most courageous individual Ben had ever known, as evidenced in her jumping on today's rescue sortie and the mission in which Ben was injured six months ago. In that action, a towline was hit and broken, and she ventured into the open in an environment alive with automatic weapons and rocket fire to single-handedly cut away the wreckage and save the boat.

Drake turned on Ben's arrival and said, "Pull up a seat, XO." After Ben was seated, he added, "So, I presume the head exam went OK?"

Ben's mouth dropped open, then he replied, "Shit, Chief, is there anything you don't know about?"

"Oh, sir. There are so many things. For instance, how much longer will we be buttoned up?"

"The center has already passed us to the east, and things should calm down in a couple of hours. Not sure if we will open up before we hit PC, though, if the lifelines are as chewed up as I expect them to be."

Lee piped up immediately. "Hey, sir, I don't like leaving my boat hanging off the side like that. It was bad enough to leave her there to begin with."

Ben smiled. *My boat.* "Well, Shelley, if nothing has happened to her yet, I don't think anything will. However, I will present your protests to the skipper—I'm sure he wouldn't want to let anything happen to *your* boat."

"Damn straight. What's the point of being the Boatswain Diva if you can't get your way!" Even the taciturn Bondurant joined in the chuckles on that one.

Ben excused himself after some more light banter, but as he stood, a sharp pain from his injured hip made him pause with a grimace. A look of genuine concern instantly replaced Lee's smile. "Are you OK, sir?"

Ben waved in dismissal. "Just a reminder of the need to set your feet properly when in swift water. I may not be sleeping on my right side for a few days, that's all. Please, don't worry about it."

"OK, sir. Take it easy, will ya?"

"Roger that," Ben replied as he made his way forward. He was surprised and embarrassed by Lee's reaction. *Have to be a little more poker-faced from now on.* Ben's stateroom was a short walk from the messdeck. The officers and chiefs each had their own room aboard *Kauai*, but they were tiny, and Ben's was just big enough for his bunk, desk, locker, and file cabinet. The other crew shared rooms like the one currently occupied by the Murray family. As Ben sat down and opened his laptop to jot down his notes of today's action while they were fresh in his mind, he glanced up and then fixed on the pictures of Victoria mounted on the wall above his desk.

Victoria Carpenter was the love of Ben's life. They had met in January when *Kauai* had been pulled off her regular duties to support a Defense Intelligence Agency team on an operation in the Florida Keys. The mission was so secret that only a handful of people in the world were aware of it. Ben had come ashore to serve as liaison, while *Kauai* remained offshore in support. Victoria was the protégé of Ben's DIA teammate, Peter Simmons, who warned him before their meeting that Victoria was mildly autistic and that he should expect some unusual behavior. Expecting to meet some geeky neurotic, Ben was surprised to find a beautiful, extraordinarily charming young woman who made him feel like the most exceptional person in the world during their first conversation. The interest was mutual, and although separated by their duties, Ben's in South Florida with *Kauai* and Victoria's in Washington, DC with the DIA, they shared the details of their lives on the phone each night when Ben was not out on patrol. With each passing day, these conversations became more precious to Ben, and he chafed at the operational pace that kept them apart.

Finally, *Kauai* was taken offline for a major upgrade, and Ben was assigned to an intense course of special operations training in Quantico, Virginia. During his training, they had the chance to meet for two short dates, resulting in the pictures. The first picture was of Victoria in an elegant pose from their first date, with her auburn hair up rather than pulled back into her usual ponytail. She was wearing a stunning jade green cocktail dress, a perfect match for her large aquamarine-colored eyes. Ben was so stunned at the sight of her that evening that he was speechless at first, then could only stumble through some inanities before she came to his rescue.

The second picture was a candid shot of them in jeans and jackets walking arm-in-arm on the Washington DC Mall, looking at each other happily. Ben followed the man who'd taken the picture and purchased an electronic copy. This one remained his favorite. Ben thought Victoria looked every bit as alluring in these casual clothes as she did in the green dress, and it reminded him of the night they spent together afterward. The night he knew he was in love with her.

Ben kept his feelings to himself for about a month afterward. While he knew Victoria was physically attracted to him and enjoyed their conversations, she had given no sign she was interested in anything beyond friendship. She was a mathematical genius and polymath, and Ben knew her intellect was on an entirely different level from his—although he could keep up to a certain degree on the math thanks to his studies at the Academy. Ben finally shared his feelings via satellite phone on the eve of the mission on which he was wounded and was astounded to find that Victoria felt the same about him.

It was ironic that hours after sharing their feelings, Ben was hit in the battle with the drug cartel. As he fell unconscious in the makeshift surgery on *Kauai*'s messdeck afterward, his last thoughts were of his first sight of Victoria in her beautiful green dress. A couple of days later, as Ben revived in the intensive care unit of a Miami hospital, he saw what he took to be a hallucination: Victoria asleep, sitting next to him with her head on the bed next to his hand. He reached out tentatively and brushed her lovely auburn hair back—she was real. He continued to stroke her forehead lightly, and she smiled in her sleep at his touch, then suddenly bolted awake.

His mouth was so dry that he could not talk until Victoria got him a drink of ice water from the table by the bed. He wanted to say something clever or romantic under the circumstances. But, still fuzzy-headed from the anesthesia, the only thing he could think of was the greeting he always used at the beginning of their phone calls:

"Hello, Victoria. How was your day?"

From Victoria's reaction, he could not have made a better choice.

She remained with him through his recovery, driving him to his physical therapy and checkup sessions while he recovered his balance and mobility. As she neared the end of her stay, she expressed regret at leaving behind what she referred to as "Ben's world" of welcoming and supportive friends, having never experienced such a thing. Ben saw an opening and took it, inviting Victoria to move in with him. She was uncertain—her condition had proven to be a relationship-killer in the past when her eccentricities evolved into annoying tics in the perception of her would-be partners. Ben was undeterred and pressed his case. Victoria was persuaded to try living together and quickly secured a position with a government contractor in Melbourne. They picked out an apartment together and moved in.

Like all couples, they had some collisions that they worked through, easier than most since neither was particularly ego-bound. The quirks associated with Victoria's condition, which she was convinced would drive Ben away, endeared her even more to him. He was in awe of Victoria's vast knowledge and intelligence, and the fact she needed help with some fundamental things in life made her more human to him. He loved listening to her talk. She had a surprisingly deep voice for someone so petite. Her precise elocution, even in casual conversations, was an appealing contrast to his previous girlfriends, who all seemed compelled to say "like" at least once in every sentence. Victoria never used contractions or diminutives; even at the most intimate times, he was "Benjamin" to her.

Victoria genuinely and openly appreciated his company and affection and understood the demands and separations that went with his job from her experience with the DIA. Several of Ben's earlier relationships had foundered on that issue, and her cheerful acceptance provided him with considerable relief. His worry that Victoria might have difficulty fitting into the insular community of the ship's crew and their families dissipated quickly. Although she knew her intelligence and eidetic memory were well outside the norm, to her, it was not a mark of superiority, just another personal characteristic like the color of her eyes or hair. Victoria was careful not to use her intellect to show up someone she was talking with, and her natural curiosity and openness were quite disarming. His coworkers and their families took to her at once.

Ben shook off his reverie and bent to the task on his laptop. As *Kauai*'s motion had calmed from the violence they had experienced when driving straight into the wind and seas to a still disconcerting but much more slow and tolerable pitch and roll, his seasickness had passed, and he was starving. He was due on the Bridge to relieve Hopkins for the second dog watch at 17:45 and needed to wolf down a microwave meal before that. He glanced at his laptop's system clock—17:04—and began typing furiously. After ten minutes, he was satisfied he had captured the basic details of the action and saved and closed the file. As he stood, he pulled and pocketed his Common Access Card, commonly known as a "CAC," from the computer's card reader, grabbed his cap, and headed back to the messdeck.

As Ben walked, his thoughts went back to Victoria and how he would describe today's activities to her when he returned. He knew she worried about him when he was underway, and events like today's rescue did not help. Ben did not want to add to those worries but could not gloss things over, much less lie to her—she would see right through it. He had sought advice from Sam's wife Joana on this subject shortly after he and Victoria had moved in together. Joana was a close friend of his in her own right and did not pull any punches.

"Sailor, you're on your own with that one. You and Victoria have to work out your own system. Sam gives me the details, I ask questions, and we deal with it. She *is* going to worry about you, that's the way it is, and nothing you can do short of quitting will change that. But she's smart enough to know that this is part of the package, and she's willing to pay the price to have you as you are. All I can say is never bullshit her—if she loses trust in what you're telling her, it's all over."

Ben had found that framing his descriptions in terms of calculated risk helped—Victoria enjoyed quantitative thinking and was comforted by the knowledge that something as amorphous as danger could be rationally bounded. Joana was right: Victoria never stopped worrying, but she seemed to come to terms with it. Ben smiled as he walked. Echoing his captain, Ben would have some 'splaining to do, particularly with the large bruise forming on his right hip. But the safe outcome and the rescue of a young family would help.

And Ben always looked forward to the aftermath of these "debriefings."

USCG Cutter Kauai, North Atlantic Ocean, twenty-two nautical miles east of Vero Beach, Florida
07:09 EDT, 30 September

Murray

Murray thought these were the tastiest omelet and home fries he had ever eaten, and it wasn't just the fact that he had not had a bit of food since their nightmare began over a day ago. Gemma and the girls were also digging in heartily, without conversation. A crewman working the stove in an apron and *toque blanche* had met and seated them when they arrived on the messdeck and prepared omelets for him and Gemma and banana pancakes for the girls. Ben showed up a couple of minutes later and sat with them to consume some oatmeal and coffee.

"Will we be pulling in soon, Lieutenant?" Gemma asked.

"Yes, ma'am, and you can call me Ben if you like."

"Thank you. Please call me Gemma. 'Ma'am' makes me feel old."

Ben smiled. "Well, we can't have that. We will pull into Port Canaveral about nine o'clock, Gemma. I'm sorry, it's a little off the usual beaten path, but it's our homeport, and we'll be nailed to the first dock we tie up to until our lifelines get fixed."

"Completely understandable. You've done so much for us already, and we're grateful for wherever you put us ashore," Gemma said.

"Yes, there's no way I can repay you all for what you've done, but I'd like to try," Murray added.

Ben shook his head firmly. "You can't do that, sir. For starters, it's illegal for us to accept any gifts or gratuities, and if you tried, we'd just have to turn it over to the Treasury." Then he smiled, "Besides, this is the sort of op we all signed up for, and the CO and I will make sure everyone gets recognized."

Ben was about to add to that when he stood and said, "Attention on deck!"

"As you were, please!" was the reply from another officer entering the room, who smiled and walked over as soon as he saw Ben. This officer was older; Murray guessed the new arrival was around his age and wearing two silver bars. *What is the naval rank? Oh yes, lieutenant.*

Murray and Gemma both stood as the officer reached the table, and Ben introduced him. "Folks, this is our commanding officer, Lieutenant Powell. Captain, this is Phillip Murray, Gemma Murray, and their daughters Jamie and Lydia."

"I'm pleased to meet you. Please sit, everybody." He turned to the cook and said, "Mornin', Chef. What are the chances of a Western and Homies this day?"

"Pretty near one-hundred percent, Captain."

"Sweet!" He turned and said, "You folks have everything you need?"

"Captain, your crew is killing us with kindness," Murray replied. He recognized the voice as the one on the loudspeaker immediately after they were brought aboard. "Not least of which is this meal. Did I hear you say Chef?"

The officer's face brightened. "That's our nickname for him. More properly, he is Culinary Specialist Second Class Thomas Hebert, although he *was* working up to Chef back in Naw'lins when he signed on with us instead."

"A good deal for you and us today," Murray said.

"Every day for us."

"Agreed." Murray nodded. "Is there a possibility of getting a tour of the ship? We would all be fascinated by a look around."

The officer shook his head sadly. "I'm sorry, but I can't permit that while we are underway. Space is tight, and there's a lot going on everywhere; we can't risk you being hurt. I'm afraid I have to ask you to remain here on the messdeck until we are moored. It will only be a couple of hours. After we are secure, one of us can take you on a tour if you care to hang around."

"That would be wonderful, thank you," Murray said. The light conversation continued until the captain completed his meal.

"Folks, you'll have to excuse us," Ben said as he stood. "The captain and I have to complete preparations for entering port. Chef can help you out if you need anything."

"Thank you, Ben, Captain, for everything," Gemma said.

"Our pleasure," the captain said.

✳ ✳ ✳ ✳ ✳ ✳ ✳ ✳ ✳ ✳ ✳ ✳ ✳ ✳ ✳ ✳ ✳ ✳ ✳ ✳

The rest of their stay was uneventful, although rather dull. The girls watched children's shows on the messdeck television that Hebert had switched to local broadcasting while Murray and Gemma looked out the windows at the passing port sights. Murray longed to be on the Bridge, or at least on deck, to watch the activity as *Kauai* entered port. Still, as an attorney, he understood completely the liability considerations that kept them quasi-confined.

A few minutes after Murray felt *Kauai* bump into the pier, the engines below them ceased their rumbling hum, and a voice on the loudspeaker announced, "Secure the Special Sea Detail, set the in-port watch, section three on deck."

Murray looked over at Hebert, who said. "Give them a couple minutes to square away all the classified gear, folks. Then we can sashay on up to the Bridge—you can see most everything from there. After that, we can get you a ride off base."

"A ride off base? I thought we pulled into the port," Murray said.

"No, sir. We have a berth and warehouse in the East Basin. It's on the Cape Canaveral Space Force Station, so you can't exactly get a cab. We'll have someone drive you to Melbourne where you can rent a car, or fly out, or what-ever."

"I see, thank you."

The phone rang, and Hebert answered. "Messdeck, Hebert. Right. Thanks, Chief." He hung up the phone and said, "Follow me, please, folks!"

The tour was fascinating. The Bridge was far more mod-ern than he expected, with a three-seat console in the middle equipped with keyboards and joysticks at each station in front of large, single-panel screens, now dark. A single seat was positioned behind and above the con-sole seats. Hebert explained that this was the captain's chair, placed to have a clear view of all the screens and the rest of the Bridge. Typically, three people were on the Bridge monitoring the operations when the craft was underway, but every station was manned during special evolutions. Murray shook his head. It was no wonder the captain didn't want him on the Bridge—there would not have been room for them to turn around.

As they were nearing the end of the tour, Gemma nudged him and pointed out the window at the area ashore between the pier and a parking lot. Ben and a pretty, petite young woman with her long red hair pulled back into a ponytail were trotting toward each other. The woman threw her arms around Ben's neck, and he picked her up off the ground in one of the most passionate kisses Murray had ever seen. He felt Gemma's arm around his waist and pulled her close while they watched.

Kauai was home from the sea.

Chapter 3

The Journey of Four Billion Miles

§ 165.T07-0450 Temporary Security Zone; Atlantic Ocean, Cape Canaveral, FL.

(a) Location. The following area is a safety zone: All waters of the Atlantic Ocean, from surface to bottom, encompassed by a line connecting the following points beginning at Point 1: 28° 36' 51.88" N 80° 35' 57.33" W, thence to Point 2: 28° 34' 0.00" 80° 25' 0.00" W, thence to Point 3: 28° 14' 0.00" 80° 13' 0.00" W, thence to Point 4: 28° 12' 0.00" N 80° 23' 0.00" W, thence to Point 5: 28° 16' 0.00" N, 80° 26' 00.00" W, thence to point 6: 28° 26' 31.81" N, 80° 33' 8.02" W.

(b) Definitions. As used in this section, designated representative means a Coast Guard Patrol Commander, including a Coast Guard coxswain, petty officer, or other officer operating a Coast Guard vessel, and U.S. Air Force range safety personnel, and a Federal, State, and local officer designated by or assisting the Captain of the Port Jacksonville (COTP) in the enforcement of the safety zone.

(c) Regulations.

(1) Under the general safety zone regulations in subpart C of this part, you may not enter the safety zone described in paragraph (a) of this section unless authorized by the COTP or the COTP's designated representative.

(2) To seek permission to enter, transit through, anchor in, or remain within the safety zone, contact the COTP Jacksonville by telephone or the COTP's representative via VHF-FM radio on channel 16. Those in the safety zone must comply with all lawful orders or directions given to them by the COTP or the COTP's designated representative.

(d) Enforcement period. This section will be enforced from 13 October through 15 October, during times when a Broadcast Notice to Mariners informs mariners that space vehicles are being launched in a direction resulting in a southerly trajectory.

Signed: D. L. Hemmings, Captain, U.S. Coast Guard, Captain of the Port.

USCG Cutter Kauai, North Atlantic Ocean, four nautical miles south-southeast of Cape Canaveral, Florida
11:18 EDT, 14 October

Ben

The situation was tense on the Bridge while *Kauai* kept pace seventy-five yards from the eighty-two-foot motor yacht *Bon Temps,* heading north at eighteen knots. The cutter was at Law Enforcement Stations with the Bridge's command console fully manned and operating. Hopkins was conning the ship while keeping a close watch on the *Bon Temps*'s movements—at this speed and close range, a collision was a definite risk. Ben was fully outfitted in law enforcement gear and would head to the boat deck to lead the boarding when the vessel had stopped. Sam was overseeing everything from the command chair.

Kauai was doing her "day job" on this sortie—enforcing range safety for large payload research mission launches from the Cape. It was a perfect day for a launch, with a high-pressure area over the Cape bringing clear skies, a comfortable temperature of eighty-two, and light winds out of the east. The two boats rolled gently in the three-foot seas coming out of the east as they sped northward.

Launches at Cape Canaveral occurred at a rate of one every month and a half, on average, a mixture of commercial and government research payloads. The military payloads and reconnaissance satellites were usually launched from Vandenberg in California or Wallops in Virginia, which eased the security burden at Cape Canaveral. The launches here drew excited spectators looking for the anticipation and thrill of a giant rocket liftoff rather than geopolitical activists.

Not today.

The Galle-Adams-Le Verrier spacecraft, known as GALV, was scheduled for liftoff at 13:27 local time atop a Delta IV Heavy launch vehicle on the first dedicated mission to explore the planet Neptune and its satellites. GALV would be the heaviest interplanetary probe ever launched, weighing slightly over three-and-a-half metric tons. Like the earlier *Voyager 2* mission, GALV would make close approaches to Jupiter and Saturn and use their massive gravity to slingshot to the vicinity of the Solar System's outermost planet, approximately 4.6 billion kilometers from the sun.

To complete a journey of over a decade and still have the power to conduct scientific observations and reliably transmit data the four and a half billion kilometers back to Earth, the spacecraft needed the most long-lived and durable power source available. Solar power was not an option with the dim sunlight available in Neptune's orbit. The ship would require solar panels larger than those of the International Space Station to meet the 2.5-kilowatt system demand. This left nuclear power, provided by eight Radioisotope Thermoelectric Generators, using the heat released in the radioactive decay of their plutonium-238 fuel to generate electricity. It was an elegant balance of space, weight, power, and longevity.

And like anything else incorporating the words "nuclear" and "plutonium," it drove some people batshit crazy.

An amorphous collective of environmentalists, with anti-big government activists and religious fanatics thrown in, had banded together to oppose the launch for various reasons. The issue for the environmentalists was fear of the release of the vehicle's highly radioactive and chemically toxic plutonium into the atmosphere. The few who believed that GALV was actually a world government-enabling weapons platform or that it was an offense to God made excellent copy for Internet journalists but were hardly representative of the majority. After failing in Congress and the courts, several thousand people converged on the area in an effort of civil disobedience self-titled Occupy Cape Canaveral. But Florida was not New York City—protesters who tried to disrupt traffic outside Space Force Station Cape Canaveral were immediately arrested and removed by state police and national guard troops deployed to assist. Those who scaled the station's perimeter fence were instantly scooped up and incarcerated by federal law enforcement personnel.

The seaborne element of OCC fared no better against the Coast Guard and Florida Marine Patrol, deployed in force in the near-shore area. After a few arrests and the threat of Asset Forfeiture against any boats involved in security zone violations, both sides lapsed into an uneasy stalemate. The *Bon Temps* was the last gasp. A leased yacht contributed anonymously and staffed with fifteen activist grandmothers, aging nonconformists, and radical college students excited for the cause. The FBI had infiltrated the group and relayed intelligence of their intention to dash into the security zone and tie up the Coast Guard long enough to abort the launch.

The vessel was tracked from the moment it sailed from West Palm Beach, both by the federal authorities and the public, via an embedded Internet journalist named Austin

Childress. He published regular podcast updates to his employers at the Global Multicast Network, GMN, which were breathlessly relayed to the public. As the *Bon Temps* approached Canaveral Bight, *Kauai* moved to be able to intercept if it crossed the boundary line into the security zone.

The *Bon Temps* had penetrated the perimeter of the security zone five minutes ago, heading for the inner prohibited area. This was the no-go area directly downrange of the launch complex along the flight path, into which fragments of the launch vehicle were likely to fall in the event of a mishap or post-liftoff abort. If this area were not clear, the launch would have to be scrubbed for safety. A two-billion-dollar mission was at stake—the launch had been delayed three times already because of weather and technical issues. The launch window, constrained by the movement of three giant planets and the Earth, was rapidly closing.

The yacht occupants knew this and that they would risk substantial penalties, including prison terms, for this act. They were gambling their lives that the U.S. Government would not use deadly force just to enable the launch of a peaceful scientific mission. They were right—the Coast Guard would not use gunfire to stop them, and the yacht was too large to risk a shouldering maneuver by the patrol boat. What they did not know was *Kauai* had a non-lethal ace up her sleeve: a projector firing nets that entangled a boat's propellers and disabled it.

The action was recorded in real-time, both by *Kauai's* powerful electro-optical camera on her mast and a smaller camera mounted in an RQ-20 Puma drone orbiting the two vessels. The full-motion video feed captured by the cameras was displayed on screens in the command console and relayed digitally by radio to the Seventh District Command Center in Miami. Sam was awaiting a "Statement of No Objection," essentially a permission slip from the District Commander to employ non-lethal force to stop this target. *They had better pull their thumbs out of their asses and decide,* Ben thought as he looked at the navigation screen. *This sucker will be in the prohibited area in about fifteen minutes!*

"Williams, switch to targeting on EO and warm up the Squid," Sam said. "Squid" was the nickname for the entangling weapon, essentially a three-barreled recoilless cannon shooting encapsulated nets that popped open at the end of their flight and landed in a pre-set pattern. The launcher, mounted on the foredeck forward of the main gun, took target and environmental data from Williams's console and adjusted the firing bearing and elevation to deploy the nets in a pattern a speeding boat could not avoid. The boat would overrun a net, foul the propellers, and be stopped without using lethal gunfire.

Electronics Technician First Class Joseph "Joe" Williams, sitting at the Fire Control Station in the center of the command console, pressed two buttons and said, "EO in targeting mode and locked on. All systems are feeding the Squid, sir." The Electro-optical camera was now tracking the yacht automatically and pinging it with a laser rangefinder to deliver precise bearing and range information to the Squid. The system's artificial intelligence combined the bearing and range information with GPS and environmental data to generate and update an optimal firing solution for the launcher. As long as they were within two hundred meters and the relative motion was stable, a launch would almost certainly result in the *Bon Temps* running afoul of at least one net.

Chief Avionics Electrical Technician Erich "Fritz" Deffler sat to Williams's left at the console, controlling the Puma's flight and camera operations. Deffler was not part of *Kauai*'s standing crew, but was assigned to the Coast Guard's aviation deployment center in Jacksonville. When *Kauai* needed UAV support, Deffler usually led the aviation team, allowing him to be together with Hopkins. They had met in his first deployment on *Kauai* last January and had built a romantic relationship since. When onboard the boat, they were consummate professionals—when they were off duty, well....

Operations Specialist Third Class Natalya Zuccaro, sitting to Williams's right at the console, completed the command-and-control crew. She monitored navigation and communications and kept the ship's electronic logbook. She was a relative newcomer to the crew, assigned last March after *Kauai* had completed her bridge systems upgrade. Zuccaro suddenly sat upright and turned. "Captain, incoming SIPR chat message from D7. D7 Commander has no objection to the use of non-lethal force to stop motor vessel *Bon Temps* if the subject is still within security zone 165.T07-0450."

Sam nodded. "Thank you, Zuccaro." He turned to Ben. "XO, give him a final warning."

"Aye, aye, sir," Ben said, grabbing the microphone and switching to the VHF-FM radio. "Motor Vessel *Bon Temps*, this is the U.S. Coast Guard on Channel 16. Stop your engines immediately for boarding, or we will use force to compel compliance. Repeat, stop, or we will use force. This is your final warning." He then switched the microphone over to the loudhailer and repeated the message through the powerful speakers on the mast. Ben hung up the microphone and looked at the EO camera display. There was no question that the dozen people visible on the Bon Temps's deck heard and understood the message. The reaction was a mixture of bewildered looks, laughing, waving, and middle fingers up. After a moment, Ben turned to Sam. "No joy, Captain."

Sam nodded back. "OK, they had their chance. Petty Officer Zuccaro, log the time, our position course and speed, and the *Bon Temps*'s position, course, and speed. I am employing non-lethal force to stop this vessel for violation of security zone 165.T07-0450, as authorized by D7 Commander's SNO."

After sounds of furious typing in the electronic log, Zuccaro said, "Log entry complete, sir."

Sam said, "Very well. Williams, surface action port, target Squid on the *Bon Temps*."

With the targeting data continuously updating, Williams had only to push a single button on his console. Within a second, the amber "Target Solution" light came on. "Targeting solution achieved, Captain."

"Match generated bearings and shoot."

"Aye, aye, sir," Williams replied, then pressed the "Set" button. On the foredeck, the projector came alive, pivoting to a bearing pointing slightly forward of the speeding yacht and then trained upward around fifteen degrees. The Target Solution light turned green, and Williams said, "Firing." Then he pressed the "Fire" button.

Three loud "bangs" erupted from the foredeck. The canisters sped over the yacht, tiny fins spinning them at fifteen revolutions per second to stabilize them in flight and disperse the nets on detonation. Immediately after the third bang, Hopkins brought the thrust levers back to a ten-knot setting as she ordered, "Right full rudder!"

Seaman Pickins, standing in front of the helm console, replied, "Right full rudder, Chief!" After putting his helm lever fully to the right and noting the rudder position showing a swing over to the "30" mark on the right side, he added, "Chief, my rudder is right full."

"Very well."

The reaction on board the *Bon Temps* to the Squid firing was a universal shock. Some people on deck instinctively ducked or cried out, and others caught sight of the canisters and stared in fascination as they arced overhead. The twenty-year-old college student manning the helm watched in confusion as *Kauai* suddenly swung away to the right in its clearing maneuver after the bangs and did not attempt any course change. Even if he had, it would not have made any difference.

As the canisters reached the end of their three-second flight, explosive charges popped them open. Small weights on the periphery instantly spread the nets to their full fifteen-meter diameter, and they dropped into the water in an overlapping pattern thirty meters in front of the *Bon Temps*. The yacht ran over the left-hand and center nets, drawing them into both its spinning propellers, wrapping them in a fatal embrace. The engine safeties noted the dramatic spike in torque and instantly tripped, declutching the propeller shafts and rolling the diesel engines back to idle. The *Bon Temps* coasted to a stop within half a minute, adrift a good three and a half nautical miles short of the prohibited area boundary.

As *Kauai* came through and completed her right-hand circle, Hopkins brought the thrust levers to stop and ordered, "Rudder amidships."

"Rudder amidships," Pickins repeated. As the rudder angle approached zero, he said, "Chief, my rudder is amidships."

"Very well. At all stop, Captain."

"Thank you, Chief," Sam said. "Petty Officer Williams, report on the target and nets, please."

"Captain, the target is stopped bearing three-four-nine true at two hundred ninety yards. Nets one and two are fouled on the target, and net three is at three-five-two true and one hundred forty yards." A small buoy with a radar reflector in the center of each net allowed *Kauai* to track it. Now that its primary function had been served, the third net was just a hazard to navigation that *Kauai* needed to recover. For now, they needed to keep track of it while they completed the boarding on the *Bon Temps*.

"Very well. Petty Officer Zuccaro, log our position and that of the *Bon Temps*. Record vessel successfully stopped using non-lethal entanglement system, initiating boarding. Pass that to the command center using SIPR chat when you're done."

"Aye, aye, sir," Zuccaro replied.

"Chief Hopkins, maneuver to clear net three and put the *Bon Temps* fifty yards off our starboard beam."

"Very good, sir," Hopkins said as she pushed the thrust levers out of the stop detent to a slow forward setting.

"Chief Deffler, keep the UAV over the *Bon Temps*. I need continuous overhead EO coverage through the boarding."

"Very good, Captain," Deffler said, then made some adjustments using the console controls.

Sam reached over and gave Ben's arm a soft squeeze. "You're on, XO. Any questions?"

"No, sir," Ben replied. They had briefed thoroughly before the *Bon Temps*'s arrival. This would be one of the most complex boardings Ben had ever conducted—these were ordinary citizens, not drug or human smugglers, and emotions were running high. With his boarding team outnumbered three to one and use of force options pretty limited, it would take a lot of luck and patience to prevent a disaster. *Piece of cake*, he thought ruefully.

"Right. Good luck," Sam said with a nod.

As Ben turned and departed down the bridge ladder, he heard Williams begin the broadcast over the loud-speakers. "On the Motor Vessel *Bon Temps*, this is the U.S. Coast Guard. You have been stopped for violation of the United States Code of Federal Regulations, Title thirty-three, Section one-thirty-five. Standby for boarding by federal officers. If you are carrying any weapons, place them on the deck and stand away from them. For your own and our officers' safety, do not approach the officers unless told by them to do so...."

Ben reached the main deck and approached his boarding team, grouped beside the RHIB positioned for launch at the rail. Bondurant would be his assistant boarding officer on this one. Besides being a cool customer, his great size might give any hotheads on the *Bon Temps* pause. Lee was included instead of driving her beloved RHIB because of the presence of females on the target. Maritime Enforcement Specialist Third Class Lopez and Seaman Mitchell Harris completed the boarding team, and Boatswain's Mate Third Class Brian Jenkins would be the RHIB coxswain. With the entire deck force absorbed by the boarding, Chief Drake would work the boat crane for the operation. Ben decided to get a jab in as he approached. "Good to see you in the sunshine, COB. Are you sure you can operate this thing?"

"I think I can muddle through, *sir*," Drake replied with a mock scowl.

"Well, my insurance is paid up anyway," Ben quipped. He turned to the rest of the crew. "OK, folks. Things are going pretty much as we expected so far, so no change in what we briefed. Anyone have questions?" Seeing nothing but head shakes, Ben continued. "Right, the watchword is to play it cool and courteous. Let me do the talking. Remember there's an Internet *journalist* on board, so don't say or do anything you don't want the entire world to see." Ben turned to Bondurant and said, "Boats, if it looks like I'm going to throw him overboard, please do an intervention."

Bondurant grinned and said, "If you say so, XO. Personally, I'd pay real money to see that."

The rest of the gathering chuckled. It was not an entirely facetious comment. While Ben understood the need for journalism in principle, he had a spectrum of dislike for journalists in practice. He thought the print and local news reporters were alright—a little loose with facts, but they tried. Ben regarded the national network news as just a bunch of clowns starring in another TV show. But he despised the cable and Internet news for their lack of integrity and thought their employment of information warfare techniques to boost ratings and "clicks" to be borderline treason. He had to concentrate on maintaining his objectivity today.

They remained on deck during *Kauai*'s slow approach. As they pulled abeam from the *Bon Temps*, Ben could feel and hear Hopkins slowing *Kauai* and then goosing the engines to maintain position and orientation. Finally, Ben's headset crackled. "LE One, *Kauai*, cleared for launch."

"Alright, let's do it," Ben said, leading his crew into the boat. They launched from the port side, opposite from the *Bon Temps,* and after releasing the crane hook, Jenkins took the heavily loaded RHIB in a wide left-hand turn off *Kauai*'s stern. The *Bon Temps* had a boarding port and ladder on her transom, and Jenkins headed for that point. As they approached, Ben could see that a half-dozen people had gathered on the yacht's upper deck, and three men stood near the boarding ladder. Ben turned to Jenkins and said, "Coxswain, park us ten feet off the stern until I clear those people back."

"Aye, aye, sir," Jenkins replied, his face a mask of concentration.

Ben scanned the three men standing near the ladder as they pulled to a stop behind the *Bon Temps*. One was a white, forty-ish man with long hair, wearing a stern expression with his arms folded. One was another white man, more youthful, in his twenties maybe, pointing what looked like a small camera in their direction. Ben recognized the third man as the Internet journalist, Childress, giving directions to the cameraman. Ben looked at the older man and said, "Fellas, you need to go on the upper deck so we can come on board."

"Why do I need to do that? This is my boat, and I'll stand where I want," the older man responded.

"You need to comply with our instructions, sir," Ben said coldly.

"Or what, you'll arrest me? You're going to do that, anyway."

"True, but there's an easy way and hard way. Let's assess the situation. Whatever you intended with this stunt, it's over, and that rocket will launch regardless of what happens with your folks and my folks. So, the decision before you now is: do you want to be charged with trespassing in a security zone, or do you want to add interfering with a federal officer and resisting arrest to that charge?"

The man stared without replying for about ten seconds, then turned and climbed the ladder to the upper deck. The cameraman and Childress watched him leave, then turned to look at Ben.

Ben stared back coldly. "Was I unclear about something, gentlemen?"

"I don't think you know who we are, officer," Childress replied.

"No, I know exactly who you are, sir. You are two men suspected of trespassing in a security zone, about to become two men in custody on that big white boat over there for trespassing in a security zone, interfering with a federal officer, and resisting arrest. This is your last warning. Rejoin the others, NOW."

The cameraman stopped filming and immediately turned to climb the ladder to the upper deck. Childress watched with a disgusted look, and after one last glare at

Ben, turned and followed. Ben turned to his crew and said, "Well, that was fun. OK, Coxswain, let's move in."

Jenkins brought the RHIB close, and Ben grabbed on the ladder rail and boarded, followed by Bondurant and the rest of the team. When they were all on board, Ben turned to Jenkins and said, "Stay close. We might need a quick getaway."

"Understood, sir," Jenkins replied, then backed the RHIB away about ten feet.

Ben led the way up the ladder, followed by his team. Word had apparently been passed around—the people on board were gathered on the forward part of the deck, leaving plenty of space around the ladder. Once his team had followed and positioned themselves behind him, Ben addressed the crowd. "Ladies and Gentlemen, I and these people behind me are United States Coast Guard officers. The Coast Guard is impounding this vessel for trespass within security zone 165.T07-0450, and will tow it into Port Canaveral for disposition. You will be detained on board for questioning until otherwise advised. Please remain here unless you are directed otherwise by one of us."

A young man, barely out of his teens by the look of him, stepped forward and said, "We don't recognize your authority to detain us without charge!" There were murmurs and looks of alarm among others in the crowd, particularly among the older people.

Great, the undergraduate law expert makes his appearance. Ben was careful not to show any emotion. "That would be a mistake, sir. As things stand right now, depending on your level of participation in the chartering and operation of this vessel, you *may* be cited for trespassing—a misdemeanor." He paused and looked meaningfully over the crowd. "Or not.

"On the other hand, if you fail to comply with our directions or attempt to interfere with us in any way, you *will* immediately be placed under arrest and charged with a violation of title eighteen, section one-eleven, United States Code. *That* charge could result in a felony conviction. Do you have any questions about this?"

The young man kept his mouth shut and sullenly stepped back into the crowd.

"Does anyone else have questions?" There was more murmuring and head shakes, but no one in the crowd spoke out. Ben nodded and continued, "Thank you. Now, is there anyone who needs medical help or any special accommodations?" There was visible relief among the crowd at Ben's solicitude, particularly among the older members, but no one called out. Keeping his eyes toward them, Ben whispered, "Lope, take Harris and do a security sweep for any holdouts. Call me when it's complete."

"On it, sir," Lopez replied, and then Ben heard their steps on the ladder behind him. After three minutes, which seemed like three hours, Ben's headset crackled again to Lopez's voice. "Sweep complete, XO. Nothing found."

"Very well, head to the bow."

"WILCO, sir."

Ben then switched his headset from intercom to radio and keyed his microphone. "*Kauai*, LE-One."

"LE-One, *Kauai*. Go ahead."

"*Kauai*, we have completed a sweep and detained all POB without incident. Standing by."

"LE-One, roger. *Tarpon* is in sight now and should be alongside in twenty mikes."

"*Kauai*, LE-One, roger, out." Ben let out a sigh of relief and whispered, "Stand easy, guys, but keep your head and eyes in the game."

"Roger that, sir," Lee muttered from behind him.

Just as the tension seemed to wane, Childress and his cameraman stepped from the crowd and walked toward Ben.

Great, Ben thought. *Here we go.*

"Officer, I'm Austin Childress, Global Multicast Network. Now that things have calmed down, I wonder if I can ask a few questions," he said with a smarmy smile.

"I don't have any information I can provide you, Mr. Childress," Ben said. "I suggest you contact the Seventh Coast Guard District public affairs office when you reach port. They are best equipped to handle these..." he gave Childress a contemptuous scan from head to foot. "*Things*."

"Can I get your names for my report?" Childress asked. The boarding team's nametags were concealed by their survival vests.

"No."

"Well, fine. My viewers would like to hear your comment about the Coast Guard's firing on an unarmed civilian vessel."

OK, there it is. "Now, Mr. Childress, you know that is a lie. The *Bon Temps* was not fired upon, and no Coast Guard member has employed any firearm in this operation. The operators of the *Bon Temps* knowingly violated a lawfully established security zone. After they ignored repeated warnings to stop, the Coast Guard deployed a non-lethal device that safely brought the *Bon Temps* to a stop with no harm to the vessel or anyone on board."

"And what was the nature of that device?"

"No comment."

"I can find out, you know."

"Knock yourself out."

Childress turned to Bondurant and asked, "Would you care to comment, officer?"

"You must be joking," Bondurant replied.

Childress said, "I see." He turned to Lee. "And you? Any comment?"

Lee returned a scowl. "I'd like to say screw you and your viewers, but that would be unprofessional. So, I'll settle for no comment."

Childress turned to Ben and said, "It's a shame you and your people won't cooperate. It would be in your personal best interests to get ahead of this story."

For the first time, Ben smiled. "In our *personal* best interests? Really? Someone might take that as a threat." Ben leaned forward, and his expression grew intense. "Are you *threatening* federal officers in the course of their duties, sir?"

Childress reflexively took a step back. "No, of course not."

"Very well. Neither my crew nor I have any answers for you. So, you and your assistant need to rejoin the group." When Childress seemed to hesitate, Ben said firmly, "Now!"

After Childress and his cameraman turned and returned to the crowd, Bondurant whispered, "Real money, XO."

Ben turned and gave him a warm smile. "Knock it off, Boats. I'm having a hard enough time holding back as it is."

The remaining wait was tense, but uneventful. Ben and the two boatswain's mates maintained a steady, friendly demeanor while the crowd relaxed and chatted amongst themselves. The Coast Guard Cutter *Tarpon* arrived fifteen minutes later. It conveyed over two FBI agents and four more Coast Guard Maritime Enforcement Specialists to whom Ben was glad to turn over custody of the *Bon Temps* and her passengers.

After picking up Ben's team, the RHIB retrieved the last net used in the operation and returned to *Kauai*. Ben had just stepped aboard when a roar from the northwest caught his attention. He looked over and watched as the two hundred fifty-ton rocket carrying GALV lifted into the azure blue sky atop three pillars of flame. After a minute, it had faded from sight, leaving a dissipating white contrail behind. Ben smiled—he always enjoyed the view of those beautiful and powerful machines as they launched, and this one was particularly meaningful to him. *Godspeed, GALVI*

Chapter 4

Bittersweet

***USCG Cutter Kauai, North Atlantic Ocean,
six nautical miles east of Cape Canaveral,
Florida
18:07 EDT, 14 October***

Ben

Kauai was marking time offshore to return to her home-port in darkness. With the rocket launch complete, there was little chance the Occupy Cape Canaveral crowd would be determined or even interested in exacting any retribution. However, the District Commander was hard against crowds grabbing pictures of the victorious cutter returning to port.

FBI agents in *Tarpon*'s boarding party seized the cell-phones and the GMN video camera onboard the *Bon Temps* and scrubbed any footage of the encounter with *Kauai*. Here, the media ululations that usually followed such perceived government high-handedness were conspicuously absent. This curious lack of reaction led Ben to speculate later that the FBI had uncovered some interesting media involvement in the *Bon Temps*'s fruitless sortie. The Squid projector was dismounted once the *Bon Temps* was out of sight, and it was stored in an innocuous case on the boat deck to be removed to the warehouse after they moored. It was not a classified piece of gear, but the Coast Guard still had an interest in not revealing it to casual onlookers and people inclined to develop countermeasures.

Ben completed supper and stretched out in his stateroom for rest before the port entry evolution when his desk phone rang. He sighed, reached over, and grabbed the receiver. "XO."

It was Hopkins. "XO, could you come to the Bridge, please? There's something you need to see."

Ben straightened. "I'm on the way, Chief. You want me to grab the skipper?"

"No, sir. Just you."

"Right." He grabbed his ball cap, hastened to the ladder, and climbed to the Bridge. Bondurant, who had the watch, smiled as he entered the Bridge and nodded to Hopkins sitting at the console. Ben said, "What's up, Chief?"

Hopkins patted the seat on her right and said, "Have a seat and get a load of this, sir."

Ben sat and looked at the screen in front, which displayed an official Coast Guard message. He skipped past the message header and began reading:

ALCGPSC 093

SUBJ: ADPL LIEUTENANT COMMANDER SELEC-
TION BOARD RESULTS

A. Officer Accessions, Evaluations, and Promotions,
COMDTINST M1000.3(series)

1. The Secretary, acting for the President, has approved
the report of the Selection Board convened on 2 August,
which recommended the following officers on the active-
duty promotion list (ADPL) for promotion to the grade of
lieutenant commander. Officers selected are listed below
in ADPL precedence order:

Ben scrolled down through the names, and one
jumped off the screen.

16. POWELL, SAMUEL J. CGC KAUAI

Ben blinked, looked again, and a smile spread across his
face. "Holy shit! The skipper wasn't in the zone! I didn't
know he was even eligible!" Officers in the Coast Guard
were selected by annual promotion boards who considered officers within a window that moved down the list
of officers ordered by precedence. The board could also
choose an officer eligible for a promotion by virtue of
time holding their rank but not yet within the window,
but these selections are extremely rare. That the board
reached past so many eligible below-zone officers to pick
Sam was an immense complement to his performance.

Ben was delighted for this man, who had become his
closest friend. *Deep selected, as deep as you can get! Not
only that, advanced to the top of the list!* Each event was
rare in the Coast Guard; it was unheard of for both to
coincide. It meant that Sam would get promoted several

years ahead of what was usually expected. He turned to grin at Hopkins and saw the sad look on her face. At that point, the reality hit home, and his face fell.

Sam was Ben's CO, but although there was a very formal Superior-Subordinate relationship between them set forth by the Coast Guard, they were more like partners in the practical sense. Ben regarded Sam as his closest friend and the finest officer he ever knew. He was definitely not looking forward to parting company with him on top of getting a new boss. But there was no getting around the basic fact.

"Yes, we really will lose him now. They can't keep him on board as a lieutenant commander." He turned to look at the screen again, and his smile returned. He sent the message to the bridge printer and grabbed an envelope from the cabinet below the console. "C'mon, Chief, let's grab COB."

A couple of minutes later, Ben knocked on Sam's cabin door.

"Come in."

Ben opened the door and entered, followed by the two chiefs. Sam looked at the three and then put on his best Anthony Hopkins as Captain Bligh impression. "What's this, Mister Christian? A mutiny?"

Ben waved his hand dismissively and replied, "No, no, Captain. I put down today's mutiny hours ago."

After the laughter subsided, Ben continued, holding out the envelope. "We have something for you, sir."

Sam took the envelope with a puzzled glace at his guests, opened it, and started reading. His eyes opened wide, and he looked at Ben. "Is this a joke?"

Ben beamed back. "Not a chance, sir."

Sam rechecked the page and said, "Wow!"

"We wanted to be the ones to tell you, sir, and the first to congratulate you," Ben said.

Sam stood, shook Ben's hand, then pulled him into a hug. After doing the same with Hopkins and Drake, he said, "Thanks, guys. As awesome as this is, it's much more amazing coming from you."

"Thank you, sir," Ben said. "By your leave, Captain? We need to start preps."

Sam looked into his eyes again and said, "Yes, thank you."

After pulling the door closed, Ben turned to the other two and said, "Well, I guess we'd better get on it."

Drake smiled, patted him on the shoulder, then turned and walked down the hallway. Hopkins reached over and gently squeezed his upper arm, then turned to the bridge ladder and climbed. Ben paused for a minute, glanced at Sam's door, and then turned to follow Hopkins to the Bridge.

3532 Slidergate Drive, Rockledge, Florida 20:52 EDT, 14 October

Victoria

Victoria Carpenter put the phone down and breathed a sigh of relief. Benjamin was safe—*Kauai* had moored, and he called to say he was leaving for home and ask if she needed him to pick anything up on the way. She knew she shouldn't have been worried. This was a low-risk sortie, or so Benjamin told her. But, given the increasing tensions and violence associated with the anti-launch demonstrations, Victoria feared the *Kauai* would land in some sort of conflict. She knew of the *Bon Temps*'s voyage from the news feeds and dreaded the confrontation they seemed determined to force on the Coast Guard.

Victoria watched NASA's live stream of the launch from her office that afternoon, anxiously awaiting the final moment when the rocket cleared the pad. She usually enjoyed watching the rocket launches. Like Ben, Victoria appreciated the aesthetic beauty of the machine and the precision required for a successful mission across vast distances. Today, she felt only a brief sense of relief. The launch occurred on time, so Benjamin and his crew must have prevented the *Bon Temps* from interfering. She knew that the lack of any other news was probably a good sign, but she could not help worrying about it until Benjamin's call.

Victoria sat at her desk and picked up the picture of Benjamin from their day on the DC Mall back in March, taken by the same photographer of the photograph on Benjamin's wall on *Kauai*. Victoria persuaded him to take this solo shot of Benjamin after agreeing to sell them the other picture and was delighted with the result. The photo was comprehensively perfect in her mind: the lighting, venue, composition, and the ideal subject. It was also a tangible mark of what she regarded as her most perfect day, followed by the perfect night when she and Benjamin made love for the first time in her apartment.

Benjamin had been as much a surprise to Victoria as she was to him. They met by chance on the only occasion Victoria had gone into the field from her office job with the DIA in the Washington, DC, suburb of Bethesda. She'd appreciated the challenge of processing UAV imagery data in the austere environment of a hotel room. The location of the Florida Keys was also agreeable, particularly in January. Even the journey was tolerable—because of their sensitive and highly classified equipment, they traveled on a government plane, avoiding the horror of the commercial airport terminals with their crowds, confined spaces, noise, and all those people *touching* you.

Later in the week, her mentor, Peter, notified her he was coming ashore and bringing one officer, Benjamin, with him as a liaison. Victoria had pulled Benjamin's record for Peter's review before the operation, and she was decidedly unimpressed. Benjamin was a mediocre performer at the Coast Guard Academy, had an uneventful tour of duty aboard USCG Cutter *Dependable* in Little Creek, Virginia, then was assigned to *Kauai* as second in command. There was something unusual—he had been awarded the Coast Guard Commendation Medal for heroism in saving three lives after a traffic accident. She noted this with approval as she pulled his official photo, which was also unimpressive. All official military photos looked the same to her, like instead of "say cheese," the photographers said, "Now, give us your most menacing scowl!"

The young man who arrived with Peter for the team meeting that first night was nothing Victoria expected. Some height, but not overly tall, with a slim, athletic build and the most captivating blue eyes she had ever seen. Benjamin was not the militaristic buffoon Victoria took him for after reading his personnel file, but a modest, almost shy, intelligent young man who provided fascinating conversation. She suspected he was also attracted to her—she caught glimpses of him looking at her while she worked at her computer during the team discussions.

After the team meeting, they had a long conversation, mainly with Benjamin describing and answering her questions about his life aboard ship. The next morning Victoria had to return to Bethesda, but she spoke to him that evening after he completed the search activity for the day. This time Benjamin was the receiver, and Victoria was talking. It thrilled her he was interested in what she did, and although she suspected he did not quite understand it all, he still seemed to hang on to every word. Several days passed before they spoke on the phone again after

Benjamin returned home. Something had happened during the mission, but he could not discuss it. Working in the world of classified information and secrets, she understood. Whatever happened must have been extraordinary, for he and Samuel received the Coast Guard Medal, a top award for heroism.

They settled into a routine of nightly phone calls whenever Benjamin had the connectivity. They were a welcome distraction at first, becoming an increasingly important part of her day as she got to know him. He was interesting, charming, and funny all at once, and unlike anyone she had ever met, she could discuss anything on her mind with him. Given this, she was puzzled that he was not married or had a steady girlfriend. When she finally asked why that was, he went silent, and she quickly tried to withdraw the question.

"No, it's OK, Victoria. I've asked myself that a few times. The only answer I can come up with is I haven't met anyone who needed what I could provide." Then he quickly changed the subject, and she was careful not to raise it again. Benjamin's answer created a paradox for her. She often could not connect with people she liked and felt much closer to him, knowing he shared this experience of loneliness. On the other hand, it made her even warier of making any blunders. It was a specter hanging over their early conversations, fading over time as she became more comfortable with him.

Between the distance and the relentless demands of Benjamin's job, the conversations were all they had. Benjamin had hoped they could get together when he was close by in Quantico while completing his combat training in February and March, but the short time and large volume of training requirements extended through the weekends. During his course, the only free time allowed was just one evening that served as a somewhat awkward first date and one other full day together, and they seized on those opportunities.

Their first date had been a maelstrom of emotion for Victoria. Fortunately, her coworker friend Debbie, knowledgeable about such things, helped her select a suitable dress and put on the appropriate makeup. Benjamin's stunned reaction to her appearance made things awkward at first, but they quickly recovered their usual banter over an excellent meal at a lovely restaurant. It ended up an excellent first date.

For the second, Benjamin had driven up from Quantico early on a Sunday morning and picked her up at her apartment. Although they had a lovely day touring the Mall and Smithsonian, the outing was marred when Victoria suffered a panic attack on the crowded Metro train on their return trip. Benjamin escorted her off the train to safety once he realized what was happening, but she was sure this stark presentation of her affliction would drive him away. Her fears seemed well-founded when they returned to her apartment, and he made to leave. It was one of the most emotional moments of her life, and she often replayed the memory of it like one replayed a favorite song:

He took her hands and said, "Victoria, I, um...." He gazed longingly at her, then looked down. After another moment, he held her eyes again. "I had a great time today. Thank you."

"Yes, I did too." She had willed herself not to cry. "I hope I can see you again soon."

"Yes. Definitely. As soon as possible. Goodnight, Victoria."

"Goodnight, Benjamin." She kissed him fully on the lips. After a few seconds, Victoria pulled back, then stepped inside the apartment and closed the door. She sat on the floor, oblivious to the fact that you are not supposed to sit on the floor, pulled up her legs, and put her chin on her knees. *OK, this is how it ends. He was just being kind to me today because he feels sorry for me. I will not cry!* And then, of course, she cried. About half a minute later, a knock on the door startled her. She stood slowly, reeled to the door, and looked out the peephole. She gasped and fumbled with the lock and wrenched the door open. "Benjamin!"

He stood in the doorway with a serious expression on his face. "Victoria, I'm sorry, but I can't leave it like this. I want to be with you. I know it's unfair to lay this on you so late at night and then run out at oh-dark-thirty tomorrow. But after today, I want to have every moment I can with you. If you don't feel the same, I'll understand, and I'll go, but I had to tell you."

She stepped up to him, put her arms around his neck, and pressed her head onto his chest, listening to his deep breaths and pounding heart while blinking away her tears. After a minute, she hugged him tightly, then took his hand, led him inside, and closed the door. They did not talk again until the morning, but neither did they sleep. When they embraced the last time before Benjamin left to return to Quantico, Victoria wanted to tell him she loved him, but the old fear returned, and she could not say the words. Instead, she smiled warmly at him, gave him one last kiss, and said simply, "Goodbye, Benjamin."

Benjamin had no other opportunity to visit during his training and had to return immediately to Florida once it concluded. They resumed their routine of the nightly phone calls whenever Benjamin had the connectivity. Victoria longed for these calls all day, hoping he would say something or give her some sign that it was safe to reveal her love for him.

Victoria caressed Benjamin's picture—she remembered how she had been holding and looking at this picture when he told her he loved her for the first time—a surprise call on a satellite phone before he went into action at Barbello. The call was like a dam bursting, each admitting they had been in love with the other since the night of Benjamin's last visit and lamenting the lost month they kept the truth to themselves. She went to bed that night with the most joyous feeling in her life.

Victoria woke up the following morning with the same excited joy, only to have it crushed when she arrived at work to learn Benjamin had been grievously wounded and evacuated by helicopter. His survival was in doubt, and

Victoria knew nothing she could bring to bear would affect that outcome, but she was determined to be with Benjamin through whatever was to come. Fortunately, she had plenty of help.

Her coworkers helped her arrange a flight to Miami, where Benjamin was transported for emergency surgery. One of the original January team agents went along to help her cope with the airports and transport to the hospital. She arrived just after Benjamin went into surgery and was greeted in the waiting room by Joana Powell, Samuel's wife and a close friend of Benjamin. Joana stayed with Victoria and comforted her through the operation.

Although the operation was a success, the nature and severity of Benjamin's injury left doubts about whether he would recover consciousness or even survive. Victoria stayed with him, speaking and reading to him during his coma and sleeping fitfully in a recliner the hospital staff set up for her. She had dozed off from exhaustion late the following day with her head on Benjamin's bed and dreamed about their day on the Mall when his light touch awakened her. The intensity of her relief at finding him awake and able to talk rivaled her joy at finding out he loved her.

Victoria stayed with Benjamin for the two days during his post-op recovery at the hospital and then at his apartment during his two-week convalescence, helping him while he recovered his coordination and balance. Victoria cherished the time they had together and the chance to meet and talk with Benjamin's shipmates and their families. As the time approached for her to return home, Victoria's sadness at the thought of leaving grew, culminating at a small dinner party Joana put on for her and Benjamin with Emilia Hopkins and her beau, Erich Deffler. Victoria had a grand time, particularly in what Joana called the "girl talk" session involving the three women. She discovered she fit right in with the discussion and laughter and felt a sense of belonging she had never before experienced. Benjamin sensed her sadness on the way home—he was wonderfully good at that—and asked her about it when they got to his apartment. To Victoria's shock, after she explained her pensiveness, Benjamin asked her to consider moving in together.

The surge of emotions created by that request was overwhelming. Victoria had settled into a steady existence of home-work-home in a government position with the DIA and known no other reality. She feared leaving this safety for the uncertainty of a private-sector job with different people and working in a whole new place. On the other hand, she could be with Benjamin every day, going to sleep and waking in his arms, enjoying meals, outings, and the other pleasures of life in his company. Victoria had also grown to love Joana and wanted to spend time with her. She was warming to the idea when the reality of her condition reasserted itself. Victoria was realistic—she knew her many behavioral anomalies concealed at work or on short dates would show themselves when living with someone. The thought of these coming between her and Benjamin filled her with dread, and she told him as much. Benjamin was undeterred, pointing out that he was sure he had quirks she would find abnormal, suggesting that they could work through them.

In the end, Benjamin prevailed, but only after Victoria extracted a promise from him not to propose marriage until they completed a six-month trial co-habitation period. She was not convinced they could work through the bugs and did not want the pressure to commit to what might be the disaster of a failed marriage. They were approaching the six-month point, and looking over it now, her demand seemed rather silly. She could never return to her earlier "safe" existence—despite her recurring worries about Benjamin's safety, she had never felt happier or more alive.

The sound of a key in the front door jolted Victoria out of her reverie, and she carefully placed the picture on her desk as she stood to go to the door. Benjamin was stepping inside as she came into the room. He put his backpack down, gathered her in his arms, and they shared a warm kiss.

"Hello, my love. How was your day?" Benjamin asked. "I have been on the edge of my seat waiting for the outcome of those test runs," he added, referring to a new machine language algorithm she was struggling with at her workplace, Vectorsonds, Inc.

"That can wait, Benjamin. I want to hear about your encounter with the *Bon Temps*. I was worried about you."

"You really shouldn't, you know," he said. "They were a bunch of well-meaning people amped up by a slimeball journalist. The worst that could have happened to me is them throwing me overboard, and I had John and Shelley along to keep that from happening. It all worked out. The rocket launched, nobody got hurt, and I'm home with you tonight."

"I know I should not worry, but I cannot help it. You know how I am about these things." Victoria smiled. "Now, please tell me what happened."

Benjamin provided the narration of the intercept and seizure of the *Bon Temps* he knew Victoria wanted to hear. With a crowd of civilians and a journalist already involved, there were no secrets to be filtered. She laughed at Bondurant's comment about Benjamin throwing the journalist overboard, but only smiled on hearing of Shelley's ribald answer to Childress's impertinent question. Despite Benjamin's assurances that the job would not permit any relationship between them, even if Victoria were not in the picture, Shelley was an attractive woman who had a great deal in common with him. Even Victoria was human enough to be a little jealous of her.

"Oh, and the big news is happy and sad at the same time," Benjamin said.

"Bittersweet?"

"Yes, that's the word. Sam has been selected for promotion to lieutenant commander."

"Surely that is excellent news, Benjamin. What could possibly be sad about that?"

"It *is* excellent. He was selected years ahead of normal, which is a huge deal for an officer. Naturally, I think he deserves it; even so, it is nice to see the Coast Guard do right by him. The thing is, they can't leave him on *Kauai* as a lieutenant commander. I guess he would have had to rotate next summer anyway, but I had hoped they could use our special status to keep the band together."

"Oh, I see how that could be sad." In fact, the news was alarming to Victoria. She knew if Samuel left, Joana would follow, and she could no longer hang around with the woman who had become her closest friend. Benjamin picked up on her thoughts at once.

"I know Jo is an important part of your support system here. Will you be OK?"

She hugged him again. "Yes. I am coming to terms with it. Of course, we can still talk and text, but it has been wonderful to visit with her, particularly when you are gone. You warned me this sort of thing is part of military life."

"Yes, hails and farewells. But hey, it will be months before we have to deal with the bitter part. Let's celebrate Sam's good fortune. Do we have any of that cabernet you like? We're both off tomorrow, so we might as well enjoy tonight."

"We do indeed."

"Super. How about I crack a bottle of that while you regale me with your tale of adventure in machine language land?"

Victoria snuggled into Benjamin three hours later as he lay soundly asleep and turned on his left side. It had not been a night of lovemaking, just talking about Samuel,

Joana, their work, and their future together. She caressed Benjamin's upper right arm lightly, careful not to awaken him. Like most patrols, this most recent one allowed little time for sleep, and Benjamin had been exhausted when he arrived. *Still, you stayed at it, making sure I was alright at work and with the news that Joana and Samuel were leaving us.* She softly kissed and then rested her forehead against Benjamin's shoulder. *Sleep, my love. I have the watch now.*

Chapter 5

Next Generation

***State Route 528, eleven miles east of
Orlando, Florida
10:02 EDT, 23 October***

Haley

Lieutenant Haley Reardon, U.S. Coast Guard, was halfway through the final hour of the two-and-a-half-hour drive from her duty station at the Coast Guard Sector Office in St. Petersburg to a meeting on Patrick Space Force Base just south of Cape Canaveral. The order had come down yesterday from the Seventh District Office—she was to report to a building associated with the 45th Operations Group in her tropical blue uniform at 12:30. There were no other details, and Haley's mind whirled at the possibilities as she drove her blue Miata along the flat and straight four-lane through the alternating open fields and pine woods of the Tosohatchee State Preserve. The oppressive heat and humidity of the

Florida summer were finally showing signs of breaking, and she longed to have the Miata's top down in the bright, warm sunshine. But she had spent enough time getting her shoulder-length black hair into a tight regulation bun before leaving the apartment this morning, and she did not want to deal with it again at her destination.

Just past her twenty-ninth birthday, Haley was a taller-than-average five-foot-eight with superb all-around fitness. She had been an all-state track and field star in high school in Rhode Island with scholarship offers from Brown, Bryn Mawr, and Princeton. But she loved competitive sailing growing up. After a visit to Newport by the Coast Guard's "tall ship" *Eagle*, Haley had opted instead for military service via the tiny Coast Guard Academy, to the mild disappointment of her well-to-do father and absolute fury of her socially climbing stepmother. Still, the passion for fitness stuck with her, and, short of being at sea or flat on her back sick, she was at the gym for one to two hours every day.

Haley was two years into her tour in the Law Enforcement Section in the Response Department at Coast Guard Sector St. Petersburg. It was her first ashore job since graduation from the Academy seven years ago, having been assigned first to the large National Security Cutter *Wasche* out in Alameda, California, for two years, then as Operations Officer of the Fast Response Cutter *Joseph Napier* in San Juan, Puerto Rico, for three years before coming to St. Petersburg. Haley appreciated the need for diversity in assignment experience, and, as she freely admitted after two afloat tours, it didn't suck to be ashore on liberty almost every night. But, like most junior officers, she longed for the opportunity of her own afloat command with its associated excitement and a career boost. Haley had been quite successful in her assignments and had plenty of confidence in her abilities. Still, she was anxiously awaiting the Junior Command Screening Panel results, due out later that month, determining whether she would have a chance to wear the moniker "Captain" in her next assignment or stay another junior officer in the mix.

Glancing at the navigation display, Haley noted she would be at her destination with an hour and twenty minutes to spare. She also noted that automated navigation systems tended to go wonky on military bases with their seemingly random building numbers. It was best to have a time buffer to allow for the search at the end. Additionally, her route included a seventeen-mile stretch on Interstate 95, a nexus of stupidity where just about anything could happen. Haley did not know what lay ahead of her, but she infinitely preferred to be waiting around for it to happen to being late.

As it happened, the I-95 stretch was an uneventful fifteen minutes, as was the short drive on 404 through Palm Shores, across the Indian River, and through South Patrick Shores to the Patrick SFB South Gate. After a brief wait in line, she presented her CAC to a Specialist4 in combat utilities and held her sunglasses up while he compared the image on his scanner to her face. Satisfied, he returned her card and said, "Welcome to Patrick, Lieutenant. Are you carrying any weapons today?"

As she always did when asked this question, Haley suppressed a smile and answered, "No."

The specialist rendered a crisp salute and said, "Have a nice day, ma'am."

"Thank you," Haley replied with a nod as she drove through. *I wonder if anyone ever answered, "Why, yes, I am!" to that question.* The navigation system worked this time, and she quickly located the 45th's HQ building and the associated parking. She glanced again at the clock: 11:13. *Where's the Exchange? There's plenty of time for a salad at the inevitable Charley's to hold down the stomach growls.*

After a quick meal at the Base Exchange, Haley returned to the 45th HQ, parked, and presented her CAC at the checkpoint. The Technical Sergeant manning the desk scanned the card and returned it with a visitor's badge. "Please wear this above your waist, ma'am. If you have any smart devices, drop them off before entry, please," he said, gesturing to a set of lockboxes on the wall. "Specialist Jinks will escort you to the room."

"Thank you," Haley said as she attached the badge to the pocket flap of her light blue uniform shirt. After dropping her cellphone, Fitbit, and key fob in a lockbox, she followed the young specialist through the security door. After a short walk, she was shown into a small room with a round table and four chairs.

"Bathrooms are down the hall to the right. Is there anything else I can do for you, ma'am?" the specialist asked.

"No, thank you very much," Haley replied and then sat at the table as the specialist closed the door behind him on leaving. The room had the usual décor proper to the service, in this case, the Air Force: large pictures of aircraft and rockets lifting off on standard military cream-colored wallpaper, with the standard military Berber carpet and 12:19 displayed on the standard military twelve-hour clock in the center of one wall. *Oh, good. At least eleven more minutes to wonder what this is about.*

It was actually eighteen minutes later when the door opened after a brief knock, and a woman in her mid-forties, stoutly built and one or two inches shorter than Haley, with short graying brown hair, stepped into the room. She was wearing the same Coast Guard tropical blue uniform as Haley, except for the four stripes of a captain on her shoulder boards. Haley jumped to attention and said, "Good afternoon, Captain!"

The woman waved her hand and said, "Carry on, please." She held her right hand out and continued, "Lieutenant Reardon? Jane Mercier. It's good to meet you."

"Likewise, ma'am," Haley said, shaking her hand. *The District Chief of Staff? What the <u>Hell</u> is going on here?* She instinctively completed the flash scan of the captain's uniform all officers did on their first meeting. Mercier had aviator wings above a stack of ribbons topped with the Legion of Merit, Distinguished Flying Cross, and Meritorious Service Medal, over her left breast pocket with a Command Ashore pin on the flap.

"Please, have a seat," Mercier said, sitting in one of the chairs. After Haley was seated in the opposite chair, she continued. "I'm sorry for all the close-hold associated with this trip. I imagine you're wondering WTF, am I right?"

"Something like that, ma'am," Haley replied with a smile.

"I think you'll be happy to hear you are being considered for a mid-season transfer to your own patrol boat command. The selection is outside the normal command screening process because of the time element and the unique mission profile of the boat. Is that something you'd be interested in?"

Haley's heart skipped a beat—*a PB command!* "Hell, yes! Oh, I beg your pardon, ma'am."

"No, that's OK," Mercier replied. "You don't have to decide at this moment. In fact, we dragged you over here for some frank talk about this unit and to observe an awards ceremony for the crew. After that, if you have reservations, you can turn this down with nothing going on the record."

Uh-Oh. "Captain, what unit are we talking about here?"

"*Kauai,*" Mercier replied, staring intently into Haley's gray eyes.

Ka-thunk! Haley tried to maintain an indifferent expression as her heart fell. *Talk about a poisoned chalice! A beat-up old one-ten consigned to be range safety cutter at the Cape until they could shitcan her? A mid-season assignment, too—they're probably yanking the CO for cause. Awesome!* "Um, ma'am...."

"Hold on a bit," Mercier interrupted. "I can see in your face that you've heard things, and I'll start by saying that there are official and unofficial versions of this boat's history."

"Yes, ma'am?" Haley said. *My God! Could it be* worse *than everyone says?*

"I'll start at the beginning. A couple of years ago, *Kauai* was a troubled unit with a buttload of discipline and operational issues. We finally relieved the CO after he almost lost the boat in a mishap on a routine migrant operation. It was quite a mess, and we considered washing our hands of her and advancing her decommissioning date. But she was in pretty good material shape, and with the FRC deliveries going slower than we hoped, it was killing us to give up a viable hull voluntarily. So, we decided to try something wild. We put on the best guys we could find for CO and XO—the previous exec was injured in the mishap—and let them build a solid team with the good folks they had and swap out the deadbeats.

"After a few months, the new cadre had completely turned things around, and *Kauai* was the go-to boat for any really outside-the-box stuff that could come along. The first test of that capability came last January. I can't give you details of that mission—there are only about a dozen people in the *world* who are totally in the loop on that one. All I can tell you is in the aftermath, both the officers ended up with the Coast Guard Medal, *Kauai* got a serious upgrade paid for by the Director of National In-telligence, and four of her crew got special combat tactical training."

Haley's earlier gloom vanished. "What sort of upgrades, ma'am?"

Mercier smiled at the change in Haley's expression. "She already had a prototype installation of the new Mod 2 Mark 38 twenty-five-millimeter gun we are putting on the FRCs. We updated the command-and-control sys-tems and sensors and rehab-ed the Bridge. The existing diesels were swapped out with a diesel-electric-battery plant that supports the increased electronic load and silent operations for short periods. Round that off with the addition of some light armor and stealth coatings, and you have a hull resistant to everything short of twenty-millimeter with the radar cross-section of a Response Boat, Small."

Haley leaned forward. "So, I take it the range safety cutter stuff is just a cover, ma'am?"

"No, if there's a launch from the Cape, *Kauai* is hon-estly doing that job. At other times, though, she is doing more-or-less normal PB operations, with the caveat that she must be made available immediately whenever needed for any 'off the books' operations. As a result, we keep *Kauai* within a radius that will allow us to turn her around quickly onto anything hairy that comes up."

"I see, ma'am. And *has* anything really hairy come up?"

"Yes. Last April, we sent her on a mission off Hon-duras, another hyper-secret one. You're about to get what details can be shared at the Top Secret level in the awards ceremony. The rest is codeword-classified."

Haley blinked in surprise. Codeword-classified referred to information and programs so secret that access could be granted only to specific individuals on a case-by-case basis after special vetting and read-in. She had worked at the highest classification levels on *Wasche* but saw no codeword-classified material there. The idea of a tiny one-ten caught up in a codeword program was mindboggling.

There was just one more thing, and it could make the difference between Haley stepping into an elite team or a demoralized mess. "Ma'am, why the hurry of a mid-season relief? Is there a problem with the current CO?"

"On the contrary," Mercier replied. "He has just been deep-selected for lieutenant commander and advanced to the top of the promotion list. No, this one is weird because of his and the XO's arrival timing. Do you remember I said they came on together to replace the old command? That would be two years ago in January. We don't want to pull them both simultaneously—we want continuity in the command. We also don't want to leave the XO on there for three or three-and-a-half years because it might hurt him professionally. Finally, the CO has been in commission for eight years, six-and-half at sea and four in command. And the last two years have been hard, first pulling that crew out of the crapper and then putting them in harm's way big time. In that last mission, he had two wounded, one of them the XO, who damn near died and is a close friend.

"In short, we need to give the man a break and a reward for what he's done. We swung a Command and Staff Course slot for him at the Naval War College starting in January. It will do him right professionally, and Newport is close to his and his wife's families, so big win."

Haley was about to respond when there was a knock at the door, and Specialist Jinks poked his head in at Mercier's bidding.

"Excuse me, Captain. You wanted to be informed when the admiral arrived," Jinks said.

"Oh, yes. Thank you, Specialist. We'll be right along." After Jinks departed, they both stood, and then Mercier turned to Haley. "Have you met Admiral Pennington?"

"No, ma'am." Haley hadn't thought her mind could spin up any further. *Wrong. The Seventh District Commander traveled from Miami to Patrick Space Force Base to decorate a patrol boat crew for a mission so secret its name could not be spoken aloud? Incredible!*

"Well, he's the real deal. He knows why you are here and wanted to speak with you about this after the ceremony. He wants to make sure that you go in with your eyes open if you take this job," Mercier said as she led the way down the hall. "Oh, and close-hold on everything we have discussed regarding the CO coming off—we have not told him yet. We'll duck out at the end of the presentation, so you don't get buttonholed by anybody."

"Yes, ma'am," was all Haley could say. *Holy Shit!* was all she could think.

****

When Mercier and Haley entered the reception area, two men in Space Force utilities were chatting with a third in a Coast Guard tropical blue uniform with an admiral's all gold shoulder boards. Rear Admiral Horatio Pennington, U.S. Coast Guard, was commander of the Seventh Coast Guard District, which included all the units in South Carolina, Georgia, the Florida peninsula, and the Caribbean basin. He had only been in the job for a couple of months, taking over when his predecessor had been disabled in a car accident. Haley had not met nor seen the admiral before, but Pennington had a reputation of being one of the smartest and best leaders in the service. In his early fifties, he was of average height and build, with a full head of close-cropped graying hair and brown eyes looking through round, silver-rimmed glasses.

Pennington turned as they approached as said, "Ah, Jane. And you must be Lieutenant Reardon." He held out his hand. "I've read a lot of good things about you."

Haley flushed at the compliment and shook his hand. "Thank you, Admiral."

After introductions between the new arrivals and his Space Force companions, Pennington said, "Gentlemen, could you excuse us, please?" After exchanging salutes and handshakes, the two men departed, and Pennington turned to Mercier and Haley. "I am glad you could attend, Lieutenant. Do you go by Haley?"

"Yes, sir."

"Good. As I was saying, I am glad you're here. My aide is getting things set up right now. Did Captain Mercier tell you I want to chat with you afterward?"

"Yes, she did, sir."

"Right. How do you feel so far?"

"Pretty damn psyched, if you'll pardon me saying so, sir."

Pennington's smile broadened. "You might change your mind once you hear what's involved, but I like the enthusiasm."

Before Haley could reply, a young Coast Guard lieutenant junior grade wearing the gold aiguillette of an admiral's aide on his shoulder came through one door and said, "They're ready for you now, Admiral."

"Thank you," Pennington said, then turned to follow with Mercier and Haley in trail.

After a short walk, the four turned into an alcove leading to a small briefing room where a dozen Coast Guard personnel stood in line in front of a podium. They all snapped to attention as Pennington came through the door when the aide shouted, "Attention on Deck!"

Pennington announced, "Thank you, rest." Pennington continued after the people in line came to parade rest, with feet slightly apart and hands behind them. "The best thing about being a flag officer is the chance to shake hands with courageous people and award them the recognition they deserve, not just for special actions, but for being there every day at the tip of the spear. This is one of those times, and I want to say how proud I am to be here and of you. I'm sorry your families can't be here to see this and hear what I have to say to you firsthand. The nature of your work, important as it was to both the nation and world, is too sensitive to release, and I appreciate your discretion." He turned to his aide and nodded.

"Attention to orders," the young man said, and while everyone else in the room came to attention, Pennington and Mercier walked to and stood before a Seaman at the far left of the line. After they exchanged salutes, the aide continued reading from a folder. "Citation to accompany the award of the Coast Guard Achievement Medal to Seaman Mitchell L. Pickins, United States Coast Guard. Seaman Pickins is cited for exceptional performance of duty while serving on board USCGC *Kauai* on the night of five to six April in action against armed terrorist forces on the island of Barbello, Honduras...."

The awards were presented by the increasing precedence of the medal and increasing rank of the awardee. Haley noted that the most senior member of the award party, a lieutenant, presumably the CO, was third from the end on the right. To his left stood a diminutive female wearing second class petty officer collar devices and a coxswain's insignia that marked her as a boatswain's mate and a lieutenant junior grade Haley guessed was the XO. Through the award narratives, Haley could piece together the story of the action:

Intelligence sources had detected a weapon of mass destruction on a boat seized by a terrorist drug cartel and moored at their island stronghold off the coast of

Honduras. The nature of the weapon and its origin were not revealed, which Haley deduced was the codeword information. The need to secure the device before it was moved and maintain secrecy prevented the assembly of a strong military force—the job fell to *Kauai*, supported by a small SEAL team and air force reconnaissance aircraft.

While the SEAL team stealthily seized control of the vessel, *Kauai* penetrated the harbor under cover of a rainstorm. The XO led a boarding team of four to rig a towline and manage the boat under tow during the escape. The rain had passed by the time of *Kauai*'s egress, and the cartel forces detected and engaged the cutter with rockets and machine guns. *Kauai* was hit by a rocket, causing minor damage and wounding one crewman. Shortly afterward, the towed boat was hit, parting the towline and imperiling both vessels. The female boatswain's mate went into the open during the firefight to cut away the towline wreckage with an ax, saving the cutter.

Meanwhile, the XO's boarding team restored and started the seized boat's engines, which the cartel had disabled. They safely cleared the island, but the XO was felled when a stowaway cartel member emerged and opened fire as the vessel was about to be scuttled in deep water. The officer had suffered a near-fatal brain injury and had to be evacuated by helicopter to a Miami hospital.

Bronze Star Medals were awarded to a boatswain's mate first class who took over the boarding party after the XO was wounded, the chief operations specialist who helped plan the assault and conned *Kauai* during the action, and the CO for his leadership during the raid. The boatswain's mate second class and the XO each received the Silver Star Medal for their efforts, and the XO and a boatswain's mate third class received the Purple Heart Medal for the wounds they suffered.

Haley was amazed by the citations and awards, and for the first time, she was experiencing personal doubts about this assignment. *How in the hell will I have any credibility with these people after what they have been through?*

As Pennington gave his closing remarks, Mercier turned to Haley and said, "Why don't you push off back to that conference room? The admiral and I will join you as soon as I can pry him away."

"Yes, ma'am," Haley said, then stood and quietly left the room. She had never been as conflicted as she was at this moment. Haley wanted this command more than anything in her life, yet, could she lead this elite of the elite teams? She had fifteen minutes to stew on it before Pennington and Mercier arrived in the room.

After they were seated, Pennington smiled at Haley and said, "Now's your chance, Haley. You have the complete picture now, and if you would like to pass on this, it goes no further than this room."

"Admiral, may I speak freely here?"

"Of course."

"I really want this command, but I am not sure I am the right one for this."

"Your record disputes that, but I'm interested in why you think that might be the case."

Haley swallowed and pointed at her ribbons, the highest of which was the Coast Guard Commendation Medal. "How do I go in there with this and command people with Coast Guard Medals, Bronze Stars, and Silver Stars?"

"The same as any other lieutenant in the Coast Guard. You go in with orders to command, and you command. If the criteria for selecting a new CO were a personal award as high or higher than anyone else on board, we would be out of luck because there isn't a lieutenant in the Coast Guard with that qualification. Is there anything else?"

Haley shifted in her seat. "There is just one other thing, sir. It's a question of leadership style. I'm effective, but, to be frank, I'm not much for the touchy-feely stuff."

Pennington sat back. "You won't need to be. They needed that personal touch a couple of years ago, but they've grown beyond that. Sam Powell did you a big favor there. Moreover, you don't *want* to be. You can expect the missions to become more, not less risky, and the risk calculus will be based on national defense, not SAR or law enforcement. In those cases, there *are* acceptable losses on a successful mission. Getting too 'touchy-feely,' as you call it, would be too hard for *you*. Do you understand what I'm saying?"

The sobering thought brought a quote from World War II to Haley's mind. "Yes, sir. When they get in trouble, they send for the sons of bitches." Pennington's eyes widened in surprise, and Haley thought, *Oh, shit! Now you've done it.*

To Haley's relief, Pennington laughed and said, "Well, I would like to agree with that in concept, but would not apply that term to you."

"Yes, sir. Not the 'sons of' anyway."

"At ease, Lieutenant," Mercier growled.

"Sorry, sir," Haley said contritely. *Yes, there* was *a line you don't cross.*

"That's alright. So, would you like some time to think it over?"

"No need, sir. I can do the job for you if you still want me."

Pennington smiled and nodded at Mercier. "I guess that's it then. You can expect orders shortly."

"I'll take care of it, sir," Mercier said.

"Excellent." They all stood, and Pennington offered his hand to Haley again. As they shook hands, he said, "Thank you, Haley, and good luck!"

"Thank *you*, Admiral," Haley replied.

After Pennington departed, Mercier turned to Haley and said, "I'll give your CO a call and explain the situation. You should expect orders within a week to kick off the transfer process. We'll do our best to get you out on *Kauai* for at least one patrol for familiarization before the hand-off, so be flexible."

"I will. Thank you, ma'am."

Mercier started to leave and then paused. "One more thing. The admiral is a kind and patient man, virtues I do not share. If you pull any of that wiseass shit in front of me again, I'll squash you like a bug, clear?"

Haley swallowed hard. "Yes, ma'am."

✳✳✳✳✳✳✳✳✳✳✳✳✳✳✳✳✳✳✳✳✳✳

There was no way Haley would head back home without taking a peek at her prospective command. She punched "Coast Guard Station Port Canaveral" into her GPS and was immediately rewarded with a display of the route up A1A via Patrick's North Gate. Haley put the top down on the Miata and headed out. Traffic was heavy through Cocoa Beach, and she was cursing her poor judgment for not opting for the longer, but probably quicker, I-95 route when the traffic thinned. She followed A1A in a gradual left turn to the west, then took the exit for 401.

After passing the cruise ship terminals on her right, 401 curved to the east, and she exited on the side streets leading to the Coast Guard station. As Haley pulled up to the sliding security gate, she had a clear view of the station's pier. One of the new Fast Response Cutters was moored, but she could not see a one-ten.

Huh. Where the hell is she? Haley pressed the call button on the gate's control box.

"Quarterdeck, Seaman Davis, may I help you?" said a disembodied female voice from the speaker.

"This is Lieutenant Reardon. Could you tell me where to find *Kauai*, please?"

"Yes, ma'am. She ties up in the East Basin now, and you'll need to go through the gate at the Space Force Station. It's just half a mile east on 401."

"I see, thank you," Haley said. *I should have known there'd be some sort of Batcave for a secret squirrel unit like that.* She backed out of the driveway, hit the accelerator, and headed to the highway with dust kicking up from her spinning back wheels. The pantomime at the Space Force Station Cape Canaveral security checkpoint was the same as Patrick's gate. After avowing the absence of weapons, Haley proceeded through and onto the station.

About one thousand feet past the gate, Haley turned right onto South Petrol Road and, a few seconds later, cleared the trees on her right, revealing the East Basin of Port Canaveral. There, moored with her port side to the north end of the massive Trident Submarine Wharf, lay the Coast Guard Cutter *Kauai*. Haley's pulse quickened at first sight of the white-painted patrol boat, and she slowed to a stop on the roadside and stepped out to look, pulling on her white and blue combination cap.

There was no activity visible on the boat, just the U.S. flag drooping lazily from the flagstaff at the stern and the union jack similarly lolling on the bow's jackstaff. Haley could not see any significant difference in appearance from conventional one-tens resulting from *Kauai*'s special modifications, although she admitted it had been years since she had seen one of the older patrol boats. She longed to go aboard for a close look inside and out, but was still bound by Mercier's instruction to avoid disclosing her status as the prospective CO.

Haley was lost in thought, staring at her new command, when a voice from behind startled her.

"Ma'am, please keep your hands at your sides and turn around slowly."

Haley momentarily froze, then pivoted slowly to see a man in combat gear, hand resting on his sidearm, his partner standing behind him next to their vehicle with his M4 carbine unslung in the ready carry position. Between her captivation with *Kauai* and the harbor noise, she had not even heard the security vehicle arrive.

"I'll need you to pull out your ID, ma'am. One hand and nice and slow, please."

Haley reached into her left breast pocket and held out her CAC. The guard stepped forward, took the card, and scanned it with his handheld scanner. After verifying the image on the card and his scanner matched her face, he handed the card back.

He saluted and asked, "Can I help you find something, Lieutenant?"

Haley returned the salute and replied, "No, thank you, officer. I'm just looking at the boat."

"Ma'am, there's parking at the docks. Please don't stop along the roads unless you want to draw attention to yourself and a visit from us."

"I'm sorry, officer. I should have known better. Won't happen again."

"No problem, ma'am. You have a nice day."

After another exchange of salutes, Haley pocketed her CAC and turned to her car. The two security guards watched as Haley climbed into the Miata and started to the station exit. After clearing the station boundary, she pulled off onto the asphalt apron next to the rocket launch viewing area, shifted into park, and laughed until she was almost in tears. *That would have been the shortest command on record.* She tried to picture Captain Mercier getting a call to bail Haley out of a Space Force jail just an hour after smacking her down for being a smartass in front of a flag officer. *Hell, even I would say, "Just keep her!" and hang up.*

Haley wiped her eyes, shifted to drive, and headed out on the first leg of the long return drive to St. Petersburg.

Part II - Transition

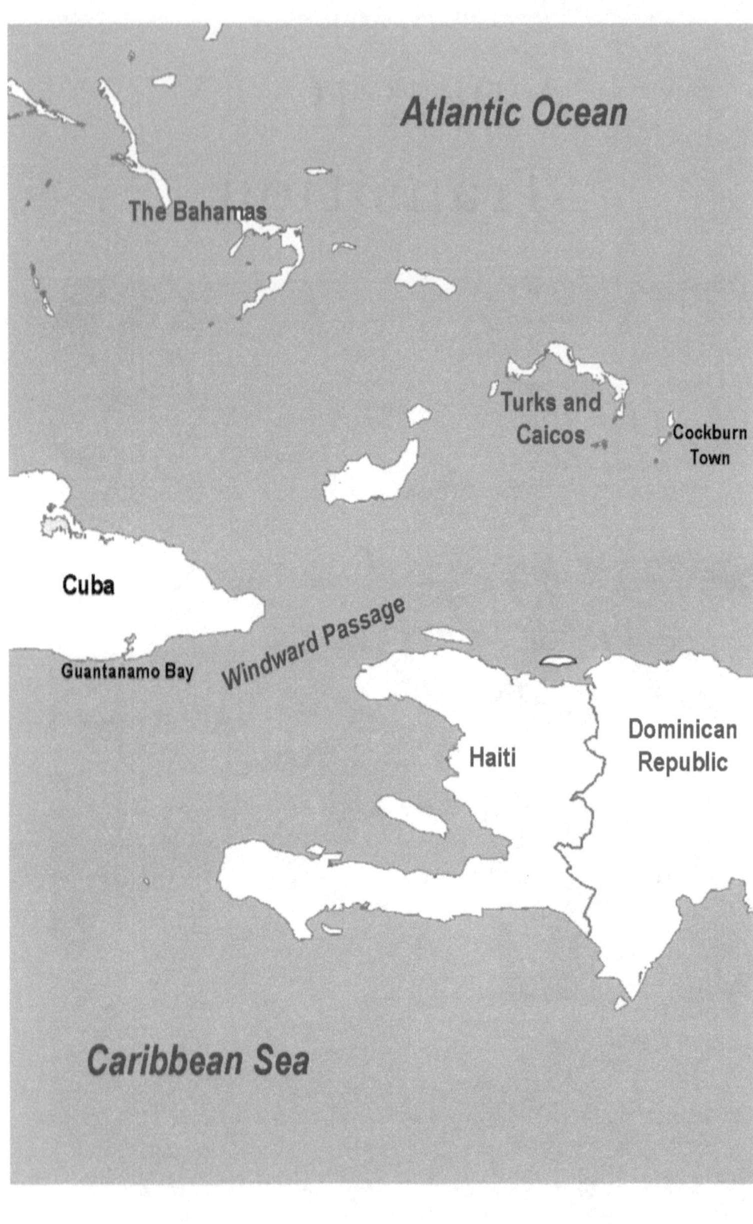

Atlantic Ocean
The Bahamas
Turks and Caicos
Cockburn Town
Cuba
Guantanamo Bay
Windward Passage
Haiti
Dominican Republic
Caribbean Sea

Chapter 6

Where There Is Life

Motor Vessel Miho Dujam, North Atlantic Ocean, sixty-two nautical miles northeast of Cockburn Town, Turks and Caicos
07:22 EST, 16 November

Anca

Anca Cazacu snapped awake as she lay on her mattress on the floor of the dimly lit room. She sensed it was morning from what she could hear outside the walls of the makeshift holding area she and eleven of her fellow captives shared. It was difficult to tell night from day in the windowless cargo hold of the ship in which they had been confined since their departure from Dubrovnik. *Days or weeks ago?* Anca honestly did not know. Time had no meaning waiting in this dark, stinking, awful place for a fate that would probably be worse.

It was only a month ago that Anca was in a different world, mid-way through the fall semester of her third year of medical school at Victor Babeș University of Medicine and Pharmacy, Timișoara, enjoying the challenges of school and the excitement of city life. Although brought up in a small town in the northern pastoral region of Romania known as Maramureș, Anca was no fool. She knew dangers were lurking beneath the façade of joy and sophistication of Timișoara, particularly for a young and attractive female college student. She took personal safety precautions when going out on the town: she stuck to public places, avoided drinking and drugs, and stayed with the group.

She did not expect to be betrayed by another woman.

Anca had befriended a barista in one of the coffee shops near the university campus. Karla was a city girl, funny and enjoyable to be with, who knew the ins and outs of Timișoara. Unlike many of her classmates and most campus locals, Karla did not look down on Anca for her provincial origin. Anca looked forward to the time she and Karla spent together. She did not think twice when Karla invited her to drinks and a meal at her apartment after several rendezvous at local restaurants and clubs.

Anca knew something was off as soon as Karla answered the door and invited her in. Once she stepped inside, powerful arms gripped Anca from behind and clamped a cloth over her nose and mouth that smelled of chloroform. The last thing she remembered seeing before passing out was the satisfied smile on Karla's face.

The indoctrination into the hell of sex slavery followed. Anca's captors hurried her out of Romania, from site to site in Bosnia and Croatia, where, even if she escaped, she would stand out and quickly be recaptured. There were no beatings, nothing that would mar her highly marketable body. Her captors were veterans of secret police goon squads with abundant tools and skills to inflict extreme pain while leaving no marks. Anca quickly realized the futility of resistance and instead concentrated on surviving, watching in the hope of the chance to escape, contact her parents, and hide out until they came to retrieve her.

That hope ended two weeks ago when she was handcuffed, hooded, and taken by van to Dubrovnik and loaded aboard the *Miho Dujam* with twenty-one other captives. No one knew where they were going, but the fact they were aboard a ship and not in the back of a van or truck told Anca they were likely being transported out of Europe. None of the guards spoke; they just showed the same icy contempt and demanded compliance, enforcing it with pain positions and electrified batons. The possibility of what awaited them filled her with dread.

Anca did her best to bond with her fellow captives when they were locked up. Meals comprised what Anca supposed were Russian army rations in boxes with Cyrillic lettering and water in plastic bottles. They were only allowed out of their confinement in small, easily controllable ones and twos for exercise and toilet use. Still, she learned there were twenty-two of them altogether, dispersed between the two rooms in the cargo hold. They were from several countries in central and southeastern Europe, and a network of translators evolved among the women to cope with the many languages and dialects in play. Some of Anca's fellow prisoners had been forcibly kidnapped, as she was, and others had been lured into servitude with promises of employment in housekeeping or au pair positions. The most tragic cases were the two young Moldavian girls, aged fourteen and fifteen, who their parents had sold to local pimps.

The two girls were the focus of the event that broke them all. Four days into the trip, one guard had cornered and was sexually assaulting the youngest of the girls when a young Polish woman intervened and physically struck him. The reaction was immediate—she was seized and held. After the women were assembled in the hold, the unfortunate woman was brought forward and given a paralyzing injection. Then, one by one, the seven guards raped her as the other women were made to watch.

After the ordeal, the head guard spoke in Russian, and he paused while his words were translated into the several languages spoken among the shocked and whimpering women. "The drug we gave her left her paralyzed but awake and able to feel everything. We will give her the antidote, and she will recover quickly. Know that we can repeat this with her or any of you as many times as we like without the risk of physical injury or death, although I am sure she and you would rather die. Do as you are told. Do not resist us, or you will suffer the same."

After the ghastly ritual was complete, the guards returned the women to the two rooms. The guards deposited the Polish woman on the floor in Anca's room, gave her an injection, left the room, and locked the door. After a minute, when none of the other women had moved, Anca stood and went to see if she could help. The head guard was wrong. The antidote may have counteracted the paralysis drug, but the woman had not "recovered." Instead, she lay unmoving, staring at the ceiling in a near-catatonic stupor.

Anca called over two other women, and together they moved the Polish woman to one of the sleeping pallets near the side of the room. She remained there, unmoving, since the ordeal. Anca became her caregiver, and she and the other women did their best for her, bringing her food and water and cleaning up after her since she could not use the toilet on her own. After a few days, Anca was convinced the woman would not recover without dedicated treatment, but she feared telling the guards. She knew they would simply throw the poor woman overboard. At least she was eating and drinking—as long as she was alive when they reached their destination, there was a chance, however slim, that she could be saved.

As hellish as their treatment had been, things became far worse once the weather turned. Unable to see outside, Anca sensed a change in the ship's motion that suggested they had moved into a different body of water. Remembering her high school geography, she speculated they had sailed the length of the Mediterranean and passed through the straits into the Atlantic. However, she could not guess where they were ultimately headed.

A couple of days after the sea change, the storm struck.

The ship's motion had been lively in the Mediterranean, a rolling that made it difficult to eat and walk, and the pitching up and down made some women sick for a day or two. In the Atlantic, it was different—the rolling and pitching were still there but slower. That changed when the storm arrived. As the motion increased, Anca and her companions tied down the Polish woman to keep her from being thrown around and then held on for dear life themselves. Everyone was deathly sick, and soon, every container in the room was filled with vomit.

After the second day of unrelenting violent motion and sickness, the guards stopped coming. Anca deduced they must be sick too, but their absence presented a fresh problem. No one was interested in eating, of course, but, from her limited medical training, Anca knew she and her fellow captives were becoming dehydrated. Without water, death was certain. She stood, made her way to the door, and started pounding on it whenever the deck was level enough for her to stand.

After what seemed like hours, the voice of one guard called out in slurred Polish, "Be quiet, bitch!"

Anca responded in rudimentary Polish, "We need water!"

"Fuck you, bitch!"

"We will all die without water! How will you profit from that?!"

There was a muffled response, then nothing. Anca huddled in despair beside the door for another half hour when she heard the lock removed. The door flew open, and the burly guard pushed two cardboard boxes into the room and slammed the door shut. Anca tore open the closest box, found three dozen water bottles, and shouted, "Thank you!"

Anca took two bottles out of the box and offered them to the women huddled on either side of her, getting dulled looks in return. "Drink! You have to drink, or you will die!" Finally, the two women took the offered bottles, and Anca moved on, dragging the box behind her. After handing each woman a bottle, she took one herself. Her stomach roiled as she drank the water, but she downed the entire bottle without vomiting. Anca turned to the Polish woman and, assisted by another captive, raised her into a sitting position and got her to drink.

The storm lasted for two more days, then the ship's motion settled to a still lively but tolerable level. The sea-sickness had passed, but Anca had to breathe through her mouth to avoid the nauseating smell of the room. Eventually, the door opened again, and two guards pushed in buckets and mops. One woman said something about being hungry, and the Polish guard said, "Clean room, then eat!"

Anca could not argue with the logic—she doubted she could keep any food down inside that room in its present state. Two women grabbed the mops and started swabbing the floor as Anca and another captive moved the Polish woman aside. Half an hour later, the guards returned, took out the buckets and mops, and pushed in boxes of food and water. Anca was ravenous by this time, and even the poorly made Russian rations tasted delicious.

The rest of the trip was the struggle of eating and sleeping, with occasional trips to the toilet being the only exercise. There was no night and day in the sealed, dark hold, but Anca could eventually make out the time of day by listening to the sounds around her.

On the fifth day after the storm, the routine suddenly changed. The ship's motion had settled down to almost nothing, and Anca supposed they must have moved into sheltered water. The ship's engine, which had been a low and steady thrum, became louder and picked up speed. Anca heard excited shouting but could not make out what was said. She had a glimmer of hope a naval or customs ship would stop the *Miho Dujam* and find them. Then she shook her head. There would be no rescue—if the inspectors could not be bribed to ignore them, their captors would simply kill them and drop them overboard.

The engine ran at high speed for a couple of hours when there was a tremendous bang, and it ground to a halt. There was more shouting and then silence. After several minutes, one woman shouted something and got to her feet. There was water leaking into the room from beyond the wall. Anca stood, dipped her hand in the water, then sniffed and tasted it. Saltwater! The ship was sinking! Anca stepped to the door and started beating on it as the other women began crying out in panic.

Anca's terror grew as the water level crept higher in the room. She frantically pounded on the door, then stopped when she heard a voice on the other side. She could not understand what the voice said, but she kept pounding on the door, shouting in Romanian, "We are in here! Please save us!" She heard the lock being smashed off, then the door flew open, and the light of a powerful flashlight blinded her. Anca stepped back involuntarily into the mass of huddling and whimpering women. She did not know who the men with the flashlights were, only that they were not the guards. For the first time since she left Romania, Anca dared to hope.

USCG Cutter Kauai, North Atlantic Ocean, twenty-three nautical miles north of Cockburn Town, Turks and Caicos
10:23 EST, 16 November

Ben

Ben was over halfway through his morning watch as the officer of the deck, also known as OOD. It was a typical mid-autumn day in the area, warm and humid with bright blue skies and puffy clouds over an azure sea. *Kauai* was gently pitching and rolling in the light seas as she motored along at a speed just high enough to hold a comfortable course.

Kauai was two weeks into what was euphemistically referred to as a "stretch patrol" at a location well off their usual beat between Florida and the Bahamas. They were holding a blocking position to intercept an expected uptick in illegal smuggling traffic skirting along the eastern side of the Lucayan Archipelago from the Caribbean to the southern U.S. It was a job better suited to a larger medium endurance cutter whose radar and embarked helicopter could surveil much more area per day, but these were in short supply.

There was a Coast Guard surge operation working to cope with a considerable upswing in illegal immigration from Haiti to the United States. On those rare occasions when economic conditions were particularly desperate in that miserable country, people sallied forth in every maritime conveyance available, from coastal freighters to rafts, even hollowed-out trees. The hope was to slip by unnoticed to land their human cargo in South Florida. Few made it. Some died en route, and the rest were intercepted by the Coast Guard and repatriated to Port Au Prince. With their ample flight deck space and more plentiful food and water, the larger cutters could readily support the hundreds of migrants interdicted each day while they awaited repatriation, and they were soon diverted from other duties.

Because of this migrant surge, the regular smuggling routes via the Windward Passage and Mona Passage on the western and eastern sides of Hispaniola were saturated with ships and surveillance aircraft. As the humanitarian crisis persisted, intelligence held that surpluses of illicit drugs would eventually push an increase in traffic along the longer but less crowded routes to the east. *Kauai* and other patrol boats had to pick up the slack with every available large cutter involved in surge operations.

Ben completed a round with the binoculars and stepped over to check the radar. They were idling about twenty miles north of Grand Turk Island, close enough to pick up any illicit traffic skirting the islands from the Lesser Antilles plus any Windward or Mona leakers sneaking through the Turks Island Passage. Commercial ship traffic was light through this area. The shortest routes from Europe to the Panama Canal were east of here through the Mona and Anegada Passages, and those from the Continental U.S. were west via the Windward Pass and Yucatan Channel. Anything passing where they were was either a local freighter or a target of interest.

Ben glanced at the left-hand console seat, where Chief Deffler monitored the UAVs. The UAV capability was limited—no radar and a narrow field of view camera that Deffler likened to "looking through a soda straw"—but it was far better than no aviation support. Ben, Hopkins, and Deffler had worked out a picket fence tactic with one or two UAVs orbiting at the edge of *Kauai*'s visual horizon, with cameras trained southeast along the threat axis. It was a simple solution that effectively quadrupled the ocean's width they could scan, allowing them to pick up anything between the shoreline and twenty-five miles seaward. But contacts were scarce, and some watches, like Ben's current one, had none. Warm, not hot weather, clear blue skies, and mostly calm seas made for a pleasant, uneventful watch. It was boring, but Ben would take boring any day over the soul-crushing grind of alien migrant interdiction operations.

Ben turned to look as Williams came through the door. "Joe, what's up?"

"I'm meeting Ms. Reardon to do soup-to-nuts on fire control, XO," he chirped. Williams was the expert on the integrated fire control/command and control or FC3 system. It was unique to *Kauai* in the Coast Guard but was being evaluated for retrofit in some form on the newer FRCs. Williams loved working on the system and showing it off.

"Right. Well, don't scare her off with the details. OK?" Ben said with a wink, returning to his watch.

Williams walked over to Electronics Technician Third Class Darryl Bunting, who had the navigation watch and was sitting at the console, and tapped him on the shoulder. "It's going to get crowded up here, bud. Let me take the watch for you, so you're not just standing around."

"Thanks, Joe!" Bunting said with a smile, then began a handoff brief.

The stretch patrol was an excellent opportunity for Haley to learn the ins and outs of the new command and get a feel for the boat. Ben felt odd working closely with Sam's replacement on an operational mission, but he liked what he had seen of her so far. She was leaning into

Williams, Hopkins, and Drake, soaking up knowledge of the new systems while she was just another officer and not yet the skipper.

Haley was close to Sam in terms of seniority, having graduated from the Academy about six months after Sam's graduation from OCS, but was closer to Ben in age. Despite this, their first meeting was a little awkward: it took several minutes for them to work out how to address each other to avoid hiccups after she took command. But they then settled into detailed discussions on Ben's unique dual role of second in command and tactical lead. Ben found her pretty different from Sam in terms of personality. Friendly enough, but not much for small talk, even when off the Bridge. Ben understood—working into a close-knit team like Kauai's had to be difficult.

Haley arrived soon after Williams. She was wearing the same dark blue operational utilities as everyone else, but still wore her Sector St. Petersburg ball cap. She scanned the Bridge, then came straight over to Ben. "Good morning, XO. How's it going?"

"Another quiet one, ma'am. No contacts."

"That's how it goes sometimes. If you have no objection, I asked Williams to give me the FC3 one-oh-one this morning."

"Not a problem, ma'am. If you like, I can clear it with the captain to spin up the main gun for dry runs."

"I'd appreciate that, thank you."

"No worries, ma'am." As Haley stepped over to Williams, Ben called Sam.

"Captain," Sam answered after two rings.

"OOD, sir. Nothing to report on the watch. Ms. Reardon is going through fam on the fire control, and I'd like your permission to power up and exercise the main gun."

"That's a good idea; permission granted. Anything else?"

"No, sir."

"Right. See you at chow."

"Yes, sir." Ben hung up the phone and turned to Williams. "Joe, the captain has OK-ed powering up the gun. Make the usual announcements."

"Will do. Thanks, XO." Williams nodded and went back to his instruction.

As Ben was relaying the permission to Williams, he noticed Haley giving him what he thought was a cool look. *I wonder what that's about?* He decided it was just his imagination and continued his rounds with the binoculars.

Chapter 7

Deliverance

***USCG Cutter Kauai, North Atlantic Ocean,
twenty-two nautical miles north of
Cockburn Town, Turks and Caicos
11:37 EST, 16 November***

Ben

Deffler straightened suddenly in his chair on the left-side station of the FC3 when an alert popped up on his screen. The artificial intelligence scanning the video feed from one UAV detected what it evaluated as an anomaly. It was a group of pixels different from its surroundings of sufficient size and duration that qualified for a notification to the human operator, who was otherwise unlikely to notice. Deffler switched to manual on the camera and activated the zoom. These were often items of no interest—a flock of seabirds or a patch of seaweed.

At first glance, Deffler could see nothing. He cranked the zoom using the vernier knob until the image became pixilated, then backed off slightly. "Ah, there you are," he murmured. It was a ship, alright, but it had a light-blue painted hull and dull white masts, making it challenging to pick out in the bright sea haze. He looked across the Bridge at Ben and said, "OOD, I have a visual contact with Bird Two. It's definitely a ship, but too far away right now to classify."

Ben walked over, looked at the screen, then smiled and said, "Well, that broke the monotony. Can you close on the target for a better look, Chief?"

"We have some margin, sir," Deffler replied. The UAVs had to stay within a certain distance of *Kauai* to maintain contact with their line-of-sight radios. At their current altitude, combined with the height of the ground control antenna on *Kauai*'s Flying Bridge, this distance was around twenty-one nautical miles.

"Right. Break the pattern. Close to the safety limit, and then we'll see if we want to move over," Ben said.

"Very good, sir." Deffler manipulated his controls. The UAV banked right and headed for the target, accelerating from its maximum endurance speed to its forty-five-knot long-range cruise speed.

"Are you going to call the captain?" Haley asked. She and Williams had paused their conversation on Deffler's first call to Ben.

"I can hold off for a couple of minutes, ma'am," Ben replied. "No sense pulling him off something important for what could be a supertanker. I've been down this road before."

"I see."

After a few minutes, the UAV closed sufficiently to firm up the electro-optical picture significantly. "OK, sir, I classify this target as a coastal freighter, heading southwest, twelve to fifteen knots."

Ben gazed intently at the image on the screen. Although it was still difficult to make out much detail, he agreed with Deffler on the classification: it was a small ship, not much over one-hundred-fifty feet long, with the pilothouse aft, clearly heading southwest. But that course made little sense for a ship of that size—a coastal freighter should parallel the shoreline. This ship's course was consistent with a transatlantic crossing, which you did not want to do with a small coastal freighter. Besides getting beat to hell in any rough weather, you could not carry a large enough cargo to make such a long trip worth the expense in fuel and time. He eyeballed a rough intercept course and then turned to Pickins on the helm. "Right ten degrees rudder, steer one-five-zero."

"Right ten degrees rudder, steer one-five-zero, aye, sir."

Ben picked up the phone and dialed Sam.

"Captain."

"OOD, sir. Could you come to the Bridge, please? A UAV has spotted a coastal freighter I am classifying as suspicious, and I have changed course to intercept."

"I'm on the way. Go ahead and spin up."

"Aye, aye, sir," Ben said, then dialed the engineering watchstander in Main Control.

"Main Control, Brown."

"Brown, OOD. Put one and three online. We're heading for a target."

"Put main engines one and three online, sir. Estimate two minutes."

"Very well, thanks." Ben hung up the phone. With the electric motors running at their slow patrol speed, there was only a small power demand on the ship's electrical grid. One of the three diesel generators was sufficient, and the other two were shut down to conserve fuel. With the high speed and maneuvering expected during an intercept, they needed the power from all three. Ben saw Sam coming through the bridge door and announced, "Captain on the Bridge!"

"Thank you. Carry on, please," Sam said. He stepped over next to Ben at the console and asked, "What have you got, XO?"

"Captain, we have a small coastal freighter, ID unknown, estimated bearing one-one-three at twenty-two point five, estimated speed twelve. This is still based on EO from UAV Two; the target is not above our radar horizon yet. MDEs one and three estimated online in one minute." As if in response, a muffled whirring followed by the grumble of a diesel engine sounded below.

"All good. Recommendations?"

"We'll need to increase speed to reach him before he enters the pass, sir, but I don't see a problem pacing him. I recommend having Bird Two light off Ghost and park it overhead when he's within twenty."

"That's good too. Make it so. Also, move the other bird in that direction at max endurance."

"Very good, sir." Ben bent over Deffler and gave the order as Sam stepped back and sat in the command chair.

Haley leaned close to Williams and whispered, "What is Ghost?"

"It's an active camouflage system, ma'am," Williams whispered in reply. "It senses the brightness and color of the sky above the UAV and projects it on the underside. The bird is almost invisible with a clear sky like we have now or a solid overcast."

"Cool!" Haley whispered.

"Yes, ma'am. There's a lot of stuff like that around here," Williams said with a nod.

The phone buzzed, and Ben answered. "Bridge, OOD."

"Main Control, sir. All MDEs are online, full power available on the grid." It was Drake's baritone voice.

"Thanks, COB. You're pretty quick to the scene today."

"When there are no guns, I ride to the sound of the starter, sir."

Ben chuckled. "You take what you can get, I guess. Thanks again." He hung up the phone. "All MDEs online, Captain. Full power is available. I'm coming up to twenty-four knots."

"Very well," Sam said with a smile. "I hope this one is interesting—I would hate to see all this enthusiasm wasted on another dud." He nodded at Williams and said, "Very fortuitous for you, Ms. Reardon: you get to see our top guy run through a suspicious contact procedure."

Kauai's bow lifted a few degrees as she started planing when approaching twenty-four knots. Fortunately, the seas were light, and they only had an occasional thump as the boat sped through the water. An alert notice drew Williams's eye to the navigation panel. "Radar contact, sir, at one-one-five and twenty point three. Running a plot now. Negative AIS." The target was not transmitting the Automatic Identification System, known as AIS, information required by international law.

After sharing an eyebrows-raised glance with Ben, Sam said, "Chief, I want to get a name and homeport as soon as possible. Coax the bird toward the stern, please."

"Will do, Captain," Deffler said. "Shouldn't be more than a couple of minutes now."

"Very well."

"Captain, target's course is two-four-zero, speed thirteen knots. He's heading for the center of the Turks Island Passage," Williams said, then turned to Ben. "Recommend one-five-two at twenty-four knots, XO."

"Very well. Helm, steer one-five-two."

"Steer one-five-two, sir."

"Ship's name coming into view, sir," Deffler said. "Um, not sure how to pronounce it. I spell: Mike, India, Hotel, Oscar, space, Delta, Uniform, Juliet, Alpha, Mike. Homeport says Dubrovnik. Where the hell is Dubrovnik?"

"Croatia," Haley answered. "He's a *long* way from home."

Sam leaned forward. "Agreed. Let's not take any chances. XO, sound Condition One, please."

"Aye, aye, sir," Ben said, then stepped over, grabbed the microphone, and activated the public address system known as the 1MC. "Now, General Quarters, General Quarters, set Condition One throughout the ship. This is not, repeat, not a drill." He hung up the microphone and pressed the paddle switch on the red general alarm box, starting a loud ringing gong sound over the 1MC lasting twenty seconds.

Williams stood, walked to and opened the locker at the rear of the Bridge, and took out Lightweight Helmets and Modular Tactical Vests. Haley appeared at his side and asked, "Can I help?"

"Yes, ma'am. Could you take these to the captain and XO, please?" Williams said, handing her two pairs of vests and helmets.

"On it."

Williams took out four more sets, handed one to Haley when she returned, stepped across the Bridge, and handed one each to Deffler and Pickins. Then he donned the last one himself and sat in the center seat of the console. Hopkins appeared next to Ben, pulling on a vest and helmet she picked up from the locker.

"What's going on, sir?" Hopkins was the OOD for Condition One and, after a quick rundown from Ben on the situation, relieved him of the duty. Ben took advantage of the break to get a good look at the *Miho Dujam* in the UAV video display. It was a small ship, a break-bulk carrier by the look of the cargo booms on the single mast and the size of the hatch covers on the holds. It was an old ship, or old-looking at least, with plenty of rust visible. Ben's suspicions were confirmed—there wasn't a chance in hell that ship would make a profit hauling any legitimate cargo across the Atlantic.

Ben noted the ship had an unusually large boat and davit system on the port side of the superstructure. *That is one hell of a lifeboat.* "Chief, can you get me a tight shot at their small boat, please?" he asked Deffler.

"Coming up, sir."

As the aircraft crossed behind the ship from the starboard side, Deffler manipulated the camera controls, and the image of the stowed boat filled the screen. It was a rigid hull inflatable like *Kauai*'s RHIB, but far larger, with a wide, flat deck and three outboard engines. Such a craft would have little purpose in the coastal trade in the ship's home territory of the Adriatic and Aegean Seas, but for running illicit cargoes ashore in out-of-the-way coves and bays, it would be perfect.

Haley had stepped beside Sam's chair to get out of the way of the console. She watched the action around her and was clearly impressed by the crew's quick transition from normal cruising to battle-ready. She turned and asked Sam, "Where do you want me, Captain?"

"Right there is good," Sam replied.

Ben stepped up on Sam's other side in his vest and helmet. "I've been relieved of the OOD by Chief Hopkins, sir. The ship has an unusually large RHIB on the port davits—looks like a runner for offloading cargo rather than a lifeboat."

"OK. Get with Zuccaro and set up a SIPR chat with JI-ATF South," Sam said, referring to Joint Interagency Task Force South, their operational commander on this mission. "Explain the situation and get any intel they have on the *Miho Dujam*."

"Very good, sir," Ben said. He stepped over to the console and kneeled beside Zuccaro.

Zuccaro glanced at Ben and said, "I heard him, sir. I'm working up a SATCOM link now."

He smiled back. "Nice. Let me know when you're ready, and I'll give you the details."

"Roger that, sir. Standby." After a brief period of concentration and furious typing, she said, "Alright, I'm ready, sir."

Ben dictated the details and timeline of the event and requested any information on the *Miho Dujam*. After more typing, Zuccaro uploaded the message and received an acknowledgment from JIATF-S. Ben's previous experience with intel requests was it took hours or days to get a response. *Hopefully, being in hot pursuit of the suspect will light a fire under somebody!*

"Looks like he's on to us, sir," Williams reported. "I'm picking up an increase in speed, now fifteen knots. No change in course; he's still heading for the pass." Ben glanced at the Tactical Situation or TACSIT screen. The red icon symbolizing the *Miho Dujam* included a line segment pointing southwest and a digital course and speed. The latter increased from fifteen to sixteen as Ben watched. *They can't get much more out of that bucket. She must be at least fifty years old!*

"I'm getting an update from JIATF South, sir," Zuccaro reported. "Nothing on EPIC or EID, and they're still waiting on DoD and Interpol."

Ben breathed a soft sigh of relief. He had expected nothing from EPIC, the El Paso Intelligence Center law enforcement database mainly dealt with drug smuggling from South and Central America—he doubted the *Miho Dujam* had ever ventured into the western hemisphere before now. On the other hand, EID, the Department of Homeland Security's Enforcement Integrated Database, would have any information about a terrorist threat associated with the ship. The fact there were no alerts was not conclusive. *Miho Dujam* wasn't likely to be loaded to the gunwales with suicide bombers, but there could still be a threat. He glanced again at the TACSIT readout and shook his head in wonder as the speed ticked up from seventeen to eighteen. *My God! Does he really think he can outrun a patrol boat?*

It took another fifteen minutes for *Kauai* to draw even with the freighter just as it drew abeam of the northern tip of Grand Turk, eight miles in the distance. Hopkins slowed *Kauai* to keep pace—nineteen knots—and gave minor course corrections to Pickins to maintain their position one-half mile abeam of the freighter. Ben could see no one on deck, just some shadowy figures on the Bridge.

"Incoming message from JIATF South, sir," Zuccaro said. "Negative on *Miho Dujam* from DoD, but Interpol has a TCO alert on them." TCO was the acronym for Transnational Criminal Organization, supranational organized crime groups that had become a plague in Europe after the collapse of communism. "Known association with the 252 Syndicate."

Ben whirled to look at Sam, who shook his head and said, "Damn. Not them again!"

Haley asked, "You have dealt with them before?"

Ben replied grimly, "Yes, ma'am. They're old friends who are always good for a few medals when you run into them. The kind of medals you earn by getting your head shot off."

Sam said, "Zuccaro, tell JIATF South we are keeping station with the subject at one-half mile and request instructions."

"Aye, aye, sir," the young petty officer replied and turned back to her panel.

"What do you think they're doing down here, XO?" Sam asked.

"Arms trafficking would be my bet, sir. It would not be drugs coming from Europe, although they might try carrying a load back. I'm not sure why they still have the pedal to the metal, though. They must know they can't outrun us."

"No, it makes sense. They know we won't stop and board without flag state clearance, and they probably have enough graft or intimidation in Croatia to tie that up until after they make port if they beat feet. After that, they'll be a ship in a bottle, but I imagine the profit from the guns would make it worth the trip. Any load of drugs or whatever on the return would be gravy."

"Sir, reply from JIATF South," Zuccaro said. "Maintain close contact only until further notice. Initiating flag state consultation now."

"Q.E.D.," Ben said with a frown.

"Suits me fine, XO," Sam said. "Let one of the big hulls handle a forced-entry boarding on these guys. Let's stand down from Condition One, but we'll keep an augmented FC3 watch to maintain contact. We may have to massage the OOD rotation—work it out with Chief Hopkins after she's relieved of the OOD."

"Will do, sir." Ben stepped over to the 1MC and announced, "Now, stand down from General Quarters, set the at-sea watch, afternoon watch on deck." Ben met with Hopkins after Lee relieved her of the OOD watch, and they worked out an augmented watch schedule. As it happened, the effort was academic.

A little over an hour later, Sam, Ben, and Haley were crowded in Sam's cabin discussing the morning's events when the phone above Sam's desk buzzed, and he answered it, "Captain. Yes, I'm on the way!" As they stood, Sam said, "There's been an explosion on the contact, and it's coming to a stop." Sam jogged to the bridge ladder with Ben and Haley close behind and strode through the door with the usual announcement. He stepped over to Lee, who was holding binoculars. Ben looked across at the contact and saw it was trailing oily black smoke from its smokestack, creating a large black cloud settling toward the water.

"I'm sorry, Captain," Lee said sheepishly. "It looks like their engine blew. I heard a big bang and saw the black cloud and thought it was a bomb or something."

"No, Lee, you did absolutely right," Sam said quickly, grabbing the binoculars. After gazing at the other vessel for half a minute, he offered the binoculars to Ben. "What do you think, XO?"

"It looks like the *Miho Dujam* just became a search and rescue case, sir," Ben replied with mock concern as he examined the other vessel. "I'll bet they're on the satellite phone dialing someone in the Balkans right now asking for instructions." He checked the TACSIT display—they were roughly in the center of the Turks Island Passage, about eight miles due west of Cockburn Town. "Shall we offer our help, sir?"

"Let them call us. When we go on board, I want it clean to avoid losing any evidence in exclusion. Lee, I want you to do an easy right three-sixty and bring us to about three hundred yards off their starboard beam. Can you handle that?"

"Yes, sir!"

"Good. Make it so. XO, set the Rescue and Assistance Bill. I want you to lead a boarding party with Drake, Bondurant, and Lopez if we can get them to give up without a fight. Have Drake look things over. I doubt he can do anything for the engine, but he can assess her fitness for a tow." As Ben stepped over to make the announcement,

Sam turned to Zuccaro and said, "Update JIATF South on what's happening. Be sure to include that the *Miho Dujam* has suffered an explosion and appears to be disabled. Explicitly request direction at the end of the message."

"Aye, aye, sir," Zuccaro replied.

As Lee gave the orders to the helmsman for the slow turn to the right, Sam climbed into the command chair, and Haley asked, "Is this the usual tactic?"

Sam smiled and said, "Usual? Like most things we seem to get involved with lately, we're making it up as we go along."

Zuccaro turned and said, "Incoming message from JIATF South, sir. Stand by vessel until further notice. Do not initiate boarding unless subject requests assistance."

"Now there's a big surprise. Thank you, Zuccaro."

Kauai took ten minutes to complete her circuit and stop alongside the *Miho Dujam*. Ben put on his boarding officer gear in his stateroom and made his way to the boat deck where the other three boarding party members waited. Lee trotted over a minute later in her boat crew gear—she would be coxswain for the boarding if there was one.

"Greetings, shipmates," Ben said with a mock stern expression. "I suppose you are all wondering why I called you together here in the sunshine of this lovely Turks and Caicos afternoon." After the chuckles subsided, he continued. "Well, I'll tell you. We are standing by to go onboard that disabled ship over there and help if they invite us. If they don't, we might do it anyway if we are sure they won't try to gun us down. This one looks dirty, and we have solid intel that the 252s might be involved, so the threat level is high."

"You don't think I'm going to be able to fix their engines, do you, sir?" Drake asked with one eyebrow raised.

"What, you don't 'know a guy' for that, COB?" Ben quipped. After more laughs, he continued. "No, I don't expect miracles, but we need to know if she's getting ready to go down from damage or might not take the tow. We'll need more of your damage controlman skill set than the machinery tech."

Drake was about to reply when a call came over Ben's headset, and he raised his hand. "LE-One, *Kauai*, *Miho Dujam* crew is abandoning ship via their RHIB, still no contact. Launch RHIB and board *Miho Dujam* ASAP."

Ben keyed his microphone and said, "*Kauai*, LE-One, roger, out." He then looked at the team. "OK, we are a go. The crew is abandoning ship. Let's get over there and take a look." They stood by as Jenkins craned the RHIB off its cradle and brought it even with the deck. "OK, let's go," Ben said.

Lee jumped on first and took her seat in the coxswain's chair. Once situated, she said, "Come on board!"

Ben stepped aboard, followed by Drake, Bondurant, and Lopez. Lee gave Jenkins a thumbs up, and he craned the RHIB off the side and then lowered it into the water. After starting the engine, Lee said, "Let go the fall!" After Bondurant released the crane hook block and guided it off the side, Lee said, "Release sea painter!"..Lopez took the line binding the RHIB to *Kauai* off the cleat on the bow and cast it over the side. Lee revved the engine, swung the RHIB toward the *Miho Dujam*, and then turned it alongside the ship's rusty, light-blue-painted hull.

The ship did not have a high freeboard, but the upper edge of the deck coaming was still at least ten feet above the water. Ben took out the grapnel and climbing rope and tossed the hook over the rail. After pulling it into place and checking it, he pulled himself up the rope, walking on the hull with his feet. After pulling himself over the coaming and scanning the deck, he gave the rest of his crew a thumbs up, then stepped over to the other side and watched as the ship's RHIB sped away with ten men on board. By the time Ben returned to the rope, Bondurant and Lopez were on board, giving Drake a hand over the side. He keyed his microphone and said, "*Kauai*, LE-One, boarding party on board and proceeding with the survey. Observed crew motoring off to the east."

"Copy LE-One, proceed. We are eyes on and in pursuit of the crew," Williams's voice replied.

Ben leaned over the rail and said, "Stay close, Shelley. We might want to get off this tub fast!"

"You've got it, sir!" Lee replied.

Ben turned to his crew. "Alright, let's head down below decks. COB, you take Lope and check out the engine space, and Boats and I will move forward in the hold. Stay paired up, please. I don't want anyone knocked out where we can't find them."

"Roger that, XO. Come on, son," Drake said to Lopez and then turned and walked toward a hatch under the pilothouse. Ben led the way through another door at the forward edge of the superstructure and then pulled off his sunglasses when they plunged into darkness. With the engine gone, there was no electrical power and no lights, so Ben and Bondurant pulled their large flashlights and started down a ladder to the cargo space. At the bottom, they turned and started moving forward in the hold.

With the hatch covers sealed, the hold was pitch dark, and Ben and Bondurant carefully stepped forward around stacks of boxes, many of which were annotated with Cyrillic lettering. He took out his waterproof camera, began snapping pictures every few feet, and whispered, "I don't suppose you can translate Russian, Boats?"

"You must be kidding, sir."

"It was worth a shot." Ben was mildly claustrophobic and joking to knock back the growing anxiety as they proceeded further into the dark cargo space and away from the door. Ben knew he couldn't last long in here between the fear of the enclosed space and the reeking atmosphere of diesel fuel, smoke, and stale vomit. If they were going to do a tow, he would first get those hatch covers open to let in the light and air things out. Then Ben heard a noise as he rounded another corner of a stack of boxes and froze.

It was the sound of running water.

"You hear that?" Ben asked in a normal tone.

"Yes, sir. I think we should get the hell out of here, XO."

"Concur. You lead the way," Ben agreed, and they turned around to make their way back. Suddenly, Ben's team radio squawked.

"Lead, this is COB. I'm encountering flooding in the engine space. Believe the crew has started scuttling!"

"Get topside, now. We are on the way.

"Understood."

They started walking again, and then Ben froze at another sound. It sounded like human voices and knocking. "Hello?" Ben shouted and heard muffled cries in response. "Keep shouting; we'll find you!" He knew it was unlikely the person crying out could speak English, but they'd get the drift. He keyed the team radio again. "COB, you and Lope join us in the hold. We can hear someone trapped."

"On the way, sir, " Drake responded.

The muffled cries were regularly coming now as Ben and Bondurant made their way through the obstructions in the hold. Ben could feel the ship listing to port. If they could hear the water running, the list would increase quickly. Beyond a certain angle, the cargo would shift toward the downward side and capsize the ship. They had to move fast!

They arrived at what appeared to be a temporary room built of wood with a padlocked door. Ben smashed off the hasp and lock with his heavy flashlight, yanked the door open, and shined his light into the dark interior. At least a dozen women were crying and cowering in terror on the other side of the space. Briefly shocked, Ben recovered and said, "Does anyone speak English?" No response.

Dammit, we don't have time for this! He tried his only other option, his high school German. *"Spreckt jemand Deutsch?"* [Does anyone speak German?]

"Ja, Ich spreckel" [Yes, I speak!] said a woman on the other side of the room.

"Ich bin Leutnant Wyporek von der amerikanischen...Seepolitzei." Ben stumbled on the correct German expression for "Coast Guard," and opted for "Sea Police," instead. *"Ihr schiffe versinkt schnell. Meine schiffe kommt. Sagen sie es ihnen sie müssen jetzt nach oben gehen!"* [Your ship is sinking quickly. My ship is coming. Tell them they must go topside now!]

"Ja, Ich sage." [Yes, I tell.] Rusty as he was, Ben could tell she wasn't a native speaker, but he was not in a position to complain.

"Wie viele sind sie?" [How many of you are there?]

"Zweiundzwanzig." [Twenty-two.]

Twenty-two! They can't all be in here! Ben shined his light around and found another locked door. "Boats, get that door open! Don't go in until we get this translator over there. We can't be chasing them all over the place!"

"Aye, aye, sir!" As Bondurant turned to comply, Drake and Lopez arrived.

"Holy shit, XO! What are they doing here?" Lopez exclaimed.

"Jesus, what do you think, Lope? As soon as the lady gets done talking, lead them topside. COB, recall *Kauai* as soon as you are clear of hull interference—there's no way we can save all twenty-two with just the RHIB."

"On it, sir!"

The woman had spoken her piece, and the other women were still huddling together and whimpering, but they stood and walked toward Drake and Lopez, except for one who remained motionless on the deck. Ben stepped over and saw she was alive, but her eyes stared upward at nothing. Ben turned to his interpreter. *"Sag es ihr noch einmal. Wir müssen gehen!"* [Tell her again. We must go!]

His translator shook her head. *"Sie hörte. Sie ist sehr traurig."* [She heard alright. She is very sad.]

Ben made a mental note, then said, *"Fräulein, komm mit mir."* [Come with me, Miss.] The woman followed him to the other door and into the room as Bondurant stood aside. *"Bitte, sagen Sie ihnen dasselbe."* [Tell them the same, please.]

"Ich, sage." [I tell.]

The situation was getting critical. There was now a perceptible tilt to the deck, and the ship could turn turtle any moment. When the translator had finished, all the women in the second compartment stood and filed out the door.

Ben said, "John, come with me."

"Yes, sir," Bondurant said as he followed Ben into the first room.

Ben could understand checking out after the horrors these women must have been through, but there was no time for therapy. "John, we have to carry this one. Can you give me a hand?"

Bondurant stepped over and said, "I've got her, XO. You go ahead."

"Thanks, Boats, I'll light your way."

The big boatswain's mate picked up and cradled the woman like a child, and followed Ben and his translator to the ladder and up onto the main deck. Ben blinked on emerging from the hatch and quickly donned his sunglasses. The hatch covers were covered with sitting, huddling, and crying women and girls, all looking down or shielding their eyes from the bright sun. Ben scanned aft and saw *Kauai* inbound about a mile away at full speed, her white bow wave spreading quickly from each side—she would be alongside in less than two minutes. He walked over to the grapnel and rope and called out to Lee. "Shelley, take Lope and stand off. We need you to pick up any leakers."

"Yes, sir!" Lee said, then moved the boat under the rope.

"Lope, get over here." After the young petty officer arrived, he said. "Get back on the RHIB and help Lee in case someone goes overboard."

"Yes, sir," Lopez said. Then he grabbed the rope, climbed over, and lowered himself into the RHIB. Once he was seated, Lee goosed the engine to clear the side for *Kauai*'s arrival.

Ben keyed his headset microphone. "*Kauai*, LE-One."

"LE-One, *Kauai*, go ahead."

"One survivor is catatonic. We'll need the litter to get her off."

"Understood, LE-One. Keep everyone clear—we're coming in hot." It was Sam's voice.

"Roger that, sir," Ben said. He looked around and caught the eye of his translator, who trotted over when he beckoned her.

"Vielen Dank für Ihre Hilfe, Fräulein. Wie heissen Sie?" [Thanks much for your help, Miss. What is your name?]

"Anca Cazacu, Herr Leutnant." [I am Anca Cazacu, sir.]

"Sehr gut, Anca. Das ist wichtig. Sag ihnen, dass sie zurückbleiben und darauf warten sollen, dass meine Männer ihnen an Bord helfen. Sie müssen sich aus dem Weg gehen und dürfen nicht versuchen, sich selbst zu hinübergehen. Verstehen Sie mich?" [Very good, Anca. Now, this is important. Tell them to stay back and wait for my men to help them aboard. They must stay out of the way and not try to cross over themselves. Understand?]

"Klar, Herr Leutnant," [I understand, sir,] the woman replied, then turned and trotted back to give instructions to the other women.

Ben keyed his microphone again. *"Kauai,* LE-One."

"Go ahead, LE-One."

"I'm down to three onboard, including me. Recommend we bring lines two and three straight over to the cargo deck."

"LE-One, roger that. I have everyone not on watch headed to the foredeck now. What's your status?"

"She's going fast, sir. We're already listing about ten degrees to port. The cargo is not loose, but it is in high stacks in the hold. If the bindings pop, she'll capsize in a heartbeat. Even if they don't, the water's coming up fast on the port side, and it will be all over when it tops the main hatches. I have the RHIB standing by if we have to jump for it, but the survivors have had it if they go in the water."

"Copy, LE-One. Have your guys stand by the hawseholes you want to use, so we have a reference."

"WILCO, sir."

Ben looked down the deck and could see Bondurant moving toward the aft hawsehole, the reinforced hole in the side they needed to pass *Kauai*'s mooring line through to tie the ships together. He had overheard the conversation and was moving to where he was required. Ben stepped over to Drake. "Try to keep them together, COB. John and I will handle the lines."

Drake smiled. "Roger that, sir. After all this time, my dream finally comes true—a SAR case with dozens of pretty young women."

"Yes, damn shame you're old enough to be their grandpa now."

"Watch it, XO," Drake smiled.

Ben turned and strode to his hawsehole, the smile fading quickly from his face.

Even if everything went right, it was going to be close.

Chapter 8

Calculated Risk

***USCG Cutter Kauai, Turks Island Passage,
eight nautical miles west of Cockburn Town,
Turks and Caicos
13:07 EST, 16 November***

Haley

What had started as just another low-key day on a quiet patrol had turned into the most exciting operation Haley had ever experienced. She was impressed with both the competence and confidence of the crew as they dealt with what Sam had said was a new challenge for all of them. She wanted to pitch in but realized that anything she did would disrupt the rhythm and likely hurt more than help.

Haley had been nervous as they closed on the fleeing cargo ship. If, as Ben speculated, they were smuggling arms, they could include man-portable rocket launchers that stood a good chance of sinking *Kauai* with one or two hits at her waterline. Sam admitted as much when she asked him about it privately in his cabin.

"That's a fact, but it wouldn't have come to that," Sam said with a completely blank expression.

"How so? I don't see the twenty-five-millimeter or the fifty-caliber being able to respond effectively in time," Haley said.

"We had eyes on with both the UAV and the EO camera. If I had seen anyone carrying anything looking like a launch tube, I would have green-lighted Guerrero on the Flying Bridge." During General Quarters, Gunner's Mate Second Class Deke Guerrero was stationed in a fortified position on the Flying Bridge. He was trained and equipped with a fifty-caliber M2010 enhanced sniper rifle. Anyone using a rocket would have to step into the open because of the backblast, and Guerrero could hit any target center mass from up to a mile away under the conditions they had today. Haley had not realized that kind of capability was in play.

The dispatch of the boarding team and the chase after *Miho Dujam*'s crew had also surprised Haley, who doubted she would have assumed that risk. She said as much to Sam on the Bridge as *Kauai* drove at full speed to cut off the crew's escape. Sam also had his worries, but answered frankly.

"It took me some time to accept it, but this is the job. The 252s are already a plague in Europe and are trying to establish themselves here with a ready narcotics supply and arms market. We have to keep them or any other TCO like them from linking up with the cartels, or we will have a war on our hands in our own backyard. This pushes beyond the standard law enforcement risk calculus.

"Ben and his team are combat-trained and can handle anyone left behind. They'll do a quick sweep and bail if they see anything sketchy. But if we can grab something, anything that leads us to whomever the 252s are working with over here, it'll be worth it. As for these mooks," Sam said, pointing at the fleeing boat on the video screen. "They're obviously not kamikazes, or they would have shot it out with us from a more defensible position."

The old expression that a stern chase is a long chase was coming true today. Even loaded down with ten people, the *Miho Dujam*'s RHIB was only a few knots slower than *Kauai*'s top speed. But they were closing the distance and were within minutes of heading off the villains' escape when the call came from Drake on the *Miho Dujam*.

"*Kauai*, COB, request immediate assistance."

Sam bolted out of his chair and grabbed the microphone. "COB, *Kauai* Actual, what's going on?"

"Sir, they set up scuttling before they beat feet. They also left twenty-two female trafficking victims and no PFDs or rafts."

"COB, we're on the way." Sam turned to Hopkins, "Chief, return to the ship. Fast as possible, please."

"Aye, Aye, sir," Hopkins replied and turned to the helmsman. "Left full rudder."

"Left full rudder," the helmsman repeated. "Chief, my rudder is left thirty degrees."

"Very well, steer two-six-five," Hopkins added as *Kauai* heeled to the right in reaction to the hard left turn.

Sam followed the fleeing RHIB with his binoculars after *Kauai* steadied on her new course, then slammed his right hand on the bridge railing. "Dammit! I should have known they would have done something like this." After a few seconds, his face returned to its regular calm expression, and he grabbed the microphone and switched to the 1MC. "All hands not on watch, don life vests and helmets and muster on the foredeck for rescue and assistance operation. Health Services Technician provide." He hung the microphone and called out the port bridge door, "Hebert!"

"Yes, Captain!" Hebert replied from his post on Mount 52, the port machine gun.

"Secure the mount, get to the foredeck, and take charge! We will have twenty-plus survivors coming on board in a few minutes!"

"Aye, aye, sir!"

Haley saw a chance to contribute and pounced. "Captain, those women have probably been through hell, and it can't hurt to have a female face down there."

Sam glanced at her, smiled, and said, "Go!"

Haley ran to the main deck, grabbed a boat helmet and life vest out of the ready locker, and continued to the foredeck. Hebert was already briefing the crew and turned to her. "Ma'am?"

"You're still in charge, Petty Officer Hebert. I'm just another pair of hands."

"Yes, thank ya', ma'am." Hebert nodded and then turned to the other crew.

Haley looked across the water at the *Miho Dujam*. There was wispy black smoke still drifting upward from her smokestack, and the bright colors of individual clothing were just becoming visible on the decks. Haley estimated about a mile to go. Two pairs of line handlers detailed by Hebert were already laying out mooring lines and attaching heaving lines to the ends, and Hebert himself was suspending three large fenders over the side.

Bryant stepped beside her, carrying a litter in one hand and his medical kit in the other. He placed both on the deck next to the superstructure and said, "Ma'am."

"Petty Officer Bryant." Haley stood silently for about half a minute. Bryant was one of the few people aboard *Kauai* who seemed less interested in small talk than she was. "Have you handled any human trafficking before?"

"When I was in the army, ma'am. Not here."

"I imagine communication might be a challenge. Do you speak any foreign languages?"

"Some German, Czech, and Polish, ma'am."

"Really, how much?"

Bryant turned to face her. "Enough to do the job. Do you speak any foreign languages, ma'am?"

"A little Spanish," Haley answered.

"Won't do much good with this crowd. Here's what you need to say: *Komm mit mir* is 'Come with me,' and *bleib hier* is 'Stay here.'"

"You think they speak German?"

"Enough of them will, ma'am," Bryant nodded and handed her a travel-sized jar of Vicks Vapor Rub.

"What's this for?" Haley asked as she looked at the jar.

"The smell, ma'am. Those gals have been locked in a box on that tub for two weeks on a North Atlantic crossing in November. I prescribe a swipe of that under your nose if you don't want to be hurling yourself."

They were within a quarter-mile now. Haley could clearly see the deck was crowded with individuals, and the ship had a visible list to port. They were still charging at full speed. *Hopkins had better hit the brakes if she doesn't want to overshoot.*

As if reading her mind, Hopkins's voice came over the 1MC, "All hands, prepare for crash-back!"

Haley observed the deck crew kneeling and grabbing a handhold. As she did the same, the bow suddenly dipped down, and the hull began the shudder Haley recognized as engines going full astern with a high forward speed. She almost fell forward in the deceleration as *Kauai* came to a halt about thirty feet off the *Miho Dujam*.

"Heaving lines, let fly!" Hebert shouted, and two small lines with weighted balls at the end streaked across the water to where Ben and Bondurant were standing. They hurriedly pulled over the two mooring lines, threading them through the hawseholes on the ship and giving a thumbs-up to show they had been attached. In the meantime, Hopkins was working motors and rudder to walk *Kauai* sideways into the larger vessel, with the crewmen pulling in the slack from the mooring lines. The two vessels came together with the loud squeak of compressing fenders. "Hold all lines!" Hebert shouted. "Second men, report to me!"

The second man at each position dropped his mooring line and trotted over as Hebert said, "Help Doc get the litter over there." As they assisted Bryant, Hebert turned to Haley. "Ma'am, it's gonna get mighty crowded mighty fast. Can you take them to the messdeck when we gather half a dozen? I have water bottles laid out for them."

"No problem!" Haley answered.

"Thank ya, ma'am."

The litter with the catatonic woman came across first, with Drake and Bondurant on each side handing it carefully across to their counterparts on *Kauai*, followed by Bryant. The men carried it aside, laid it on the deck for Bryant to do his work, and returned to their place on the rail. Like the litter, Drake and Bondurant handed off each survivor to the crewmen waiting on the patrol boat while Ben was herding the others into a single file for the transfer. Haley beckoned over each new arrival to keep the path clear. The fear they showed of the male crewmembers and the contrasting expressions of gratitude on their faces when they saw Haley almost made her tear up. As they huddled close to her, Haley was grateful for Bryant's gift—even in the open air and through the Vapor Rub smear she applied under her nose, the stench of waste and old sweat and vomit was almost overpowering.

When she hit the required critical mass of six victims, she led them aft to the open messdeck, sat them in the chairs, and handed out water bottles. There was concern among the women when she turned to leave, so Haley smiled, waved her hand, and said, *"Bleib hier."* as Bryant suggested. Those who had stood sat again, although their looks of concern remained until Haley returned with the second half dozen survivors. Some faces were more expressive than others, but the new arrivals brought signs of relief and hope.

On her second return to the foredeck, Haley noticed Ben was no longer herding the remaining women in line. In fact, he was nowhere to be seen, and she wondered if he had returned on board while she was shuttling survivors to the messdeck. After her third run, she remained on the foredeck and watched as the last survivor came aboard, followed by Drake and Bondurant after they cast off *Kauai*'s mooring lines. As the two vessels drifted apart, Haley walked directly to Drake and asked, "Chief, where's the XO?"

"He's inside looking for evidence, ma'am," Drake replied.

"He's *what*?"

"The XO told us to cast off and return on board after the last survivor crossed over. He's taking the RHIB back." Drake and Bondurant shared a worried look.

"How much longer will that ship last?"

"Ma'am, I'm surprised she's still upright."

Haley hated stepping in, but things seemed to be getting out of hand. "Chief, call the RHIB!"

"*Kauai*-One, COB, is the XO with you?"

"Negative," Lee's voice replied.

Drake lifted his radio again, but before he could speak, a series of loud bangs erupted from the *Miho Dujam*, and she quickly rolled to the left. He keyed the radio and shouted, "*Kauai*, COB, XO is still on board!"

The ship continued to roll with a cacophony of bangs and crashes and, within twenty seconds, had completely capsized with only her hull bottom visible. Haley, Drake, and Bondurant were transfixed in shock until the 1MC jolted them into motion.

"Man Overboard Port Side, repeat Man Overboard Port Side! This is no drill!"

Ben

Ben ducked as the heaving line came over, then grabbed it and started pulling over the mooring line. He seized the eye as soon as it came within reach and secured it to a nearby bitt after leading it through the hawsehole. Ben then returned to the crowd of women and, with Anca's help, herded them into a single file for the crossover. By the time he finished, the first few women had already transferred to *Kauai*.

Ben looked down the line of fearful women with despair, realizing that even if any of them were to come forward, their credibility in any American court would be almost nil. He had to get some tangible evidence of the 252's involvement. He strode over to Drake and said, "COB, I'm going to the Bridge to see if they left any logs or charts. If I'm not back when the last survivor goes over, cast off the lines and get aboard. I'll get off on the RHIB."

"Yes, sir," Drake said in distraction as he helped another woman over the rail into the hands of the crewman on *Kauai*.

Ben trotted over to the superstructure and darted inside. A series of cabins led to the Bridge, and although all were disorderly, he couldn't find any personal items, not even clothing. *Well, no one said these guys were dumb—they must have either taken everything with them or dumped it in weighted bags.* Ben stepped into the pilothouse and looked at the navigation table. No charts or notebooks were laid out, so he went through drawers. A quick scan revealed nothing with any marks. *They must have taken the ones they marked up.* He paused for a second. *And left the ones they weren't going to use!*

Ben started pulling open drawers looking for plastic trash bags and found some, along with an old laptop computer. They probably hadn't used it in a while and forgotten about it when they left. Ben wrapped the laptop in two trash bags and tucked it between his chest and life vest. He was stuffing charts into a trash bag when his world turned upside down and dark with a sudden lurch and bang.

Ben was floating and breathing and still inside the pilothouse. He knew he had not been swept anywhere by the water he could feel and hear rushing in. Ben grabbed the flashlight off of his belt and turned it on. Shining it upward, he could see the deck he had been standing on and the bottoms of the helm and binnacle. Everything else was floating around him or resting on what had once been the overhead. He was trapped inside a capsized, sinking ship.

Ben closed his eyes and took a deep breath to control the panic. The situation was literally his worst nightmare, and, between the shock and his claustrophobia, he was having great difficulty thinking. *OK, there's an air pocket, but it won't last. At least I'm not banged up.* He shined the light around and estimated about two feet between the surface of the water and deck, and the water was rising fast. Continuing around, he saw the bridge door and swam toward it. He tried to push it open, but it wouldn't budge. He briefly panicked, then realized the pressure differential would hold it closed until it was completely underwater.

As he did the last time he had faced death, Ben closed his eyes and thought of his first sight of Victoria on their first date. The memory of her smile in that beautiful green dress calmed him enough to think clearly. *When the door fully submerges, I can push it open and swim out. But the ship is above me now, and I have to swim far enough out that I don't get hung up under it. How far?* He closed his eyes again and tried to picture the ship in his mind. *Door on the starboard side, not much more than a walkway to the edge, almost no tumblehome. About ten feet should do it. Pull clear, swim like hell horizontally while counting to ten, then pop the inflation bottle and head toward the light.* He laughed. *No, DON'T head toward the light—float to the surface!*

The water finally closed over the former bottom, now the top of the door. Ben took and exhaled two deep breaths, then held the third, ducked underwater, and pushed on the door. It didn't move. Panic was returning when he realized hadn't turned the knob. He felt around, found and turned the knob, and pushed for all he was worth. The door opened slowly against the inrush of water—it was surprisingly cold this far beneath the surface. The pressure increase was tremendous, and Ben felt the pain he experienced in diving to the bottom of a swimming pool, only far more intense. It was like knives jamming in his ears, and it was all he could do not to cry out. Ben got the door open enough and pulled himself through the opening. He immediately collided with something, a lifeline. He felt his way around it, pushed off the ship, and began swimming. *One thousand one, one thousand two....*

He could see light now, sunlight attenuated and blue-tinted through the water. *One thousand nine, one thousand ten!* He reached for and pulled the tab for the CO_2 bottle and felt his vest inflate. It was pulling him up through the water. The stabbing pain in his ears was subsiding, replaced by the agonizing burning of his lungs. He knew he had to exhale, coming up from deep water, and started puffing air out his nose. The light got brighter, and he could now see the waves in the water as he looked upward. Then the light faded to gray and finally, black.

****

"Sir! Sir! Give me your hand!"

Ben opened his eyes and looked up in confusion. It was Lopez, reaching for him from the RHIB. Lee suddenly appeared beside Lopez and also reached for him. Ben put up his hand, then felt himself being pulled into the boat. He lay flat on his back, looking at the bright blue sky, and could hear Lee's voice as the engine revved and the boat turned and sped toward *Kauai*.

"*Kauai*, *Kauai*-One. XO is aboard and alive, returning to ship. Have Doc meet us at the rail with oh-two. Over."

It was hard to hear, and his ears hurt. *What's happening? What am I doing here?* Gradually, his confusion receded, and he could remember. *The ship, upside down, swimming out.* In a sudden flash of panic, he brought his hand over and felt for the laptop—it was still there, pressed against his chest by the inflated vest. He tried to sit up, was overwhelmed by dizziness, and slumped.

"Stay flat, XO," Lopez said as he rested his hand on Ben's shoulder. "We'll be on board the boat in a minute, and Doc can check you out."

Ben looked at Lopez, whose face was a mask of concern, and tried to nod. They were pulling up to *Kauai* now, and Lopez left him to tend to the sea painter while Lee grabbed and slammed the crane fall onto the RHIB's lift frame. Ben felt the boat lift from the water, and as it pulled even with the rail, Bondurant jumped in, and Ben was lifted out.

"Put him in the litter, John." It was Bryant's voice.

After being set down, Ben felt a plastic mask placed on his face and cool airflow. Someone was taking his pulse.

"OK, let's get him to his room." Bryant's voice again.

Ben felt himself being lifted and carried in the litter. He looked over and saw Bryant walking beside him, holding the mask on his face. They entered the boat, and after a couple of quick turns, they were in his stateroom, and he was lifted onto his bed. "Doc, what's happening to me?" Ben asked.

"You are pretty messed up from that deep dive of yours, XO. How do you feel?"

"Dizzy, and my ears hurt."

"Yes, I'm not surprised. You had what is called an ascent blackout. You were unconscious when Lopez and Lee found you. It has to do with the partial pressure of oxygen in the blood decreasing as you ascend from deep water. As for your ears, you have two ear blocks from the pressure underwater. It's the worst I've ever seen and might even be an eardrum rupture. That's probably the source of your dizziness too. I'm confining you sick-in-quarters until a real doctor can see you in Gitmo."

Guantanamo Bay, known as Gitmo, was the U.S. Naval Base on the island of Cuba and the closest resupply base for their operation in the Turks and Caicos. It would not be a long trip, only ten hours at their fast cruise speed of twenty-four knots. "Doc, where is the laptop I brought with me? It's important."

"Yes, we figured it had to be if you were willing to go down with the ship to get it. It's right here on your desk."

"Good, good," Ben said, then frowned as the old worry kicked in. "Will this deep dive blackout affect, you know, the other thing?"

"I'm sorry, sir, I don't know. I can tell you that the dizziness you are having now is far more likely from your inner ear mess than from your earlier injury, and that should mostly clear by tomorrow morning, as long as your eardrums aren't perforated. But they're going to have to do another no-shit neurological workup on you, I'm afraid."

"I figured as much," Ben said with sadness. He hated constantly hanging on the edge of losing his career.

"Try not to worry about it, XO. I can't run the whole battery, but your pupillary response is fine, and you don't have a headache or any other symptoms. As for your ears, I'd be worried if you had bleeding, but you don't, so surgery probably won't be necessary. No promises, though."

"Yeah, there never are. Thanks, Doc."

"Sure. Get some rest, sir," Bryant said as he stood.

Ben drifted to sleep shortly after Bryant had left and was startled awake by a knock on his door. He glanced at the clock on his wall—16:15—over two hours had passed. "Come in," Ben said.

Sam poked his head in and said, "How are you doing? Feel like talking?"

"Of course, sir." Ben started to rise, then settled when Sam waved his hand. Sam came in, shut the door, and sat in Ben's chair.

"You know, laddie, you really are doing your best to help me get over moving on from this job. If you weren't flat on your ass right now, you'd be braced-up in my cabin," Sam said with a warm smile. "Care to explain to me what you were thinking?"

"I'm sorry, sir. When I saw those women and what they were going through, I couldn't let those bastards get away with it. I figured I'd grab some charts or logs or something, but the laptop was all I could find."

"I saw those women too, and believe me, I'm as mad as you are. In fact, I'm glad I didn't know it during the chase—I'd have been tempted to blow their asses away with the twenty-five. That said, your decision is worrisome. Tell me something: if you had been unable to go yourself, would you have sent Bondurant, Lee, or Lopez?"

Ben dropped his head. "No, I wouldn't," he admitted.

"Why not?" He continued as Ben stayed silent. "Never mind, the question was rhetorical. The answer is because gathering evidence, even in this case, was not worth risking their lives." He paused for a second. "You took that decision out of my hands, but not the responsibility. Here's some CO perspective for you. It would've been devastating enough to have had to make a condolence call after Barbello or the *Aurora Mist*. Can you imagine what it would have been like for me telling Victoria or your parents you died trying to recover a *logbook*?"

Ben looked Sam in the eyes and tried to think of something worthy of the remorse he was feeling. "I don't know what to say, sir."

Sam reached over and squeezed his shoulder. "I won't say, 'forget about it.' Never forget about it. Let's take the W and consider ourselves lucky."

"Yes, sir. What's the plan? I understand we're headed for Gitmo."

"Yes, we need to get those survivors some attention. There are no English speakers among them, and, near as we can tell, they're from at least six different countries. Doc might be able to conn them through first aid and head calls with the German, Polish, and Czech he has, but he can't conduct a proper interview, and we wouldn't want him to, anyway.

"They have all been abused beyond human endurance sexually, psychologically, even hygienically. They're all scared shitless of any male right now. Thank God for Haley—she was spot on about a female face being therapeutic. She's keeping things calm on the messdeck right now. When we get to Gitmo, we'll hand them off to the people who can give them the proper care first and gather the facts later.

"As for you, the flight surgeon down there will also give you a going-over."

"Well, at least I didn't have to be medevac-ed off again."

"Not an option. Doc said any flight would blow out your eardrums if they aren't already. You're on the slow boat for the rest of this trip."

"Yes, sir."

"Also, that laptop is generating interest. We will be met at Gitmo by our buddies in the DIA, who will take possession.

"Pete Simmons again?"

"No, I'm happy to say we will not be renewing our acquaintance. Somebody named Frankle."

"Art Frankle?"

"I guess. His name is listed as Arthur."

"Yeah, that's Art. I met him on the Resolution Key op. You'll like him—very by-the-book."

"That will be nice for a change." Sam stood. "You rest easy. If you need anything, let me know."

"Thank you, Captain."

Chapter 9

Beginnings

USCG Cutter Kauai, moored, Pier B, Naval Station Guantanamo Bay, Cuba
14:18 EST, 17 November

Frankle

Arthur "Art" Frankle, Senior Case Officer, Defense Clandestine Service, Defense Intelligence Agency, stopped for a moment to take in the view down Pier B of the Naval Station. Frankle was tall for a field agent at six-foot-one and still remarkably fit for a man in his late fifties. Only his graying hair and the deepening wrinkles on his face hinted he was approaching the time for retirement. He had done his time in the field, trained dozens of junior agents, and still mentored many of them. His current assignment was mainly desk work, a well-earned break from stress and fear. Still, he enjoyed getting out of the building, even if it was only courier work.

It was feast or famine here at Gitmo: either the ships were few or, like today, the harbor was a beehive of activity. With the latest mass migration from Haiti in full swing, it was beehive time. Unlike the grim days of the Cold War, the ships crowding the docks were not haze gray-painted frigates and destroyers, but white-hulled Coast Guard cutters with their red "racing stripes" ducking in for fuel, replenishment, and what passed for recreation inside the forty-five square mile navy base parked on the coast of a hostile communist country.

Several smaller patrol boats were among the larger ships, sleek and fast compared to their larger sisters, but with shorter legs. The large, blunt ships were built for endurance and could hang offshore for two to three weeks at a time without replenishment. The most the patrol boats could endure was one week, and that was stretching it. In a high-tempo operation like this, darting back and forth at high speed in response to migrant vessels spotted by aircraft, their cycle time diminished to only three or four days.

Still, Frankle liked the patrol boats better. Their looks and speed appealed to him more as a former U.S. Marine Gunnery Sergeant than the larger ships. And, he admitted to himself, he was biased, having worked with one of those boats before. He scanned the dockside and picked her out. Her name was not visible from this perspective, but the number 1351 painted on her bow marked her as *Kauai*.

He had never set foot on the patrol boat, just seen her from a distance at the end of that near fiasco in the Florida Keys last January. Pete Simmons, a former mentee of Frankle's in the DSC, had sold the bosses that a Russian nuclear-tipped cruise missile accidentally fired after a midair collision between a Russian bomber and U.S. fighter hadn't flown harmlessly off into the Gulf of Mexico, but crashed somewhere in the Keys. The subsequent hunt for the live nuclear warhead overlapped a 252 Syndicate narcotics smuggling operation. After spending several days on *Kauai* during the search, Pete shifted ashore with the boat's young XO, Ben Wyporek, in tow as a liaison. The 252s launched a dandy snatch operation to grab Pete, tying down his backup in another location while they cornered him and Ben on the northern tip of Resolution Key. If it hadn't been for *Kauai*'s skipper driving the boat at flank speed through fog and shoal water to arrive in the nick of time to provide gunfire support, Pete and Ben would have been killed or captured. As usual, Pete's luck paid off, and, besides finding and securing the nuke, they disrupted a 252 scheme to import narcotics to the U.S. and wiped out a team of killers.

Frankle had only associated with Ben on two occasions on that operation, for a couple of hours during the first meeting after he and Pete had come ashore and for a few minutes after the fight on Resolution Key. He liked what he saw that first meeting—a bright, modest, and earnest young man. Frankle's esteem jumped an order of magnitude after Ben stood shoulder-to-shoulder with Pete in a fight to the death against five times their number of 252 soldiers. And when he saw how close Ben and Victoria had grown, he respected the man even more. Frankle and Victoria had worked together for several years, and he admired the woman's smarts and intuition. Since her resignation, he missed working with her and was delighted that Ben had seized the crucial laptop he had come to Gitmo to retrieve. Frankle looked forward to sitting with him to get the story and catch up with Victoria's life.

The TCO Section of the DIA, in which Frankle headed the 252 desk, had picked up a significant increase in chatter involving the setup of a major syndicate hub somewhere in the western hemisphere, but the location was a mystery. The chance meeting of the *Miho Dujam* with the Coast Guard confirmed these suspicions. It was regrettable that the crew could destroy the ship and its arms cargo and escape while the Coast Guard was occupied with saving the embarked sex trafficking victims. Frankle could not argue with the decision—although he would gladly break the rules to wipe any 252 member out of existence, he would not sacrifice innocent lives to do it. Saving twenty-two young women from death, or even worse fates, was a good day's work in anyone's book.

Frankle had arrived that morning on the daily logistics flight the Coast Guard ran from their air station at Miami-Opa Locka to Leeward Point Field across the bay from the piers. A twenty-minute ferry ride had brought him across to the deepwater part of the bay and resurfaced memories, good and bad, of the time he was posted here as a

Marine. He had hated it then, like everyone else stationed here. Now, it was a nice, warm place to visit while Washington descended into winter.

After arriving, Frankle's first stop had been the base hospital, where the women rescued by *Kauai* were being treated for their ordeal and processed by Immigration and Customs Enforcement. A couple of his people had come with him and were waiting to interview the women about their 252 captors. Frankle wasn't hopeful—even if they knew something, they were unlikely to share it out of fear for themselves or their families. The initial report from the ICE people was that the victims, some as young as fourteen, came from various backgrounds in Poland, Moldova, Croatia, Romania, and Bulgaria. Some had been abducted, others duped into thinking they were going to housekeeping or au pair jobs. Heartbreakingly, the two youngest girls had been sold to traffickers by their families. Frankle pulled his agents aside and directed that those two girls and anyone else in a comparable predicament be classified as government witnesses and detained in foster care. It was not by the book, but he was damn sure not going to let them be deported straight back into the situation that brought them here.

After reviewing the situation of the victims with the ICE agents and his people, Frankle drove his government vehicle loaner the four and a half miles over the rough base roads to the docks. He could not contact the ship and hoped the officers were not ashore, seeing to the many needs of turning around a warship during a short port break. He walked over to what passed for a quarter-deck, a small standup desk with a phone manned by a young seaman, and presented his ID. Within a minute, Ben and two other officers stepped out of the boat's superstructure and walked over to meet him.

"Art, it's good to see you again," Ben said, offering his hand.

"Likewise, Lieutenant," Frankle said, shaking his hand firmly.

"Senior Case Officer Arthur Frankle, this is my CO, Lieutenant Sam Powell, and our incoming CO, Lieutenant Haley Reardon," Ben said, introducing his companions.

"How do you do, Captain, Ma'am," Frankle said, shaking hands with each.

"Welcome aboard," Sam said. "It's pretty tight in my cabin for all of us. Will we be discussing anything too sensitive for the messdeck?"

"That should not be a problem, sir," Frankle said. After they were inside and seated at one of the mess tables, he continued. "I wanted to congratulate you on a magnificent piece of work yesterday. I stopped by the base hospital this morning, and those poor gals are still being treated and cleaned up, but their outlook has improved tremendously since yesterday."

"Yes, we were lucky we ran into them. That area is not regularly covered," Sam said with a nod. "Was it as bad as it looked?"

"At least. Some were near to losing their minds. Several of them were raped, that one you guys brought off on the stretcher repeatedly. She is still just staring at the ceiling right now. It seems she pushed back when one guard started getting fresh with the children, so they shot her with their paralysis drug. You know the one I'm talking about, Ben."

"Yes, that I do," Ben replied, his face darkening.

"As soon as she locked up with the drug, they took turns raping her while the other women were made to watch. No one pushed back after that. I didn't think I could hate those 252 guys any worse than I already did—I was wrong. Well, that's a few off their hook." He shook his head. "OK, I know you're busy, so we might as well get to it. What can you tell me about yesterday?"

Sam and Ben took turns relating the story, leaving out the details of Ben's near-fatal experience in the *Miho Dujam*'s capsizing. As they finished, Frankle said, "Yes, it's a pity they got away, since they had plenty of time to sanitize the boat before you guys got on board. Still, the laptop could be a gold mine for us."

"I'm not so sure," Ben said. "Given how thoroughly they were clearing up their personal items, it is surprising they would leave behind a PC. Could it be a red herring?"

"Possibly, but I think and hope they tucked it there at the beginning of the trip and forgot about it. Even if it is a ruse, the metadata in the files could offer opportunities for us to penetrate their networks, email, finances, *et cetera*. I'll get this over to the cyber-ninjas as soon as I get back to DC," Frankle said.

"I am surprised by the interest and quick response," Haley spoke for the first time. "What is going on that puts a senior DIA guy on a plane from DC?"

Frankle smiled in response. *This one is sharp. Good looking too.* "Good question. We've been picking up chatter that the 252s have worked a deal with someone over here to arrange a permanent depot for the transshipment of drugs and arms. That crowd you picked up yesterday was the staff for a new brothel there. After the Barbello deal, they realized they needed a base of their own to play over here. Our challenge is finding it.

"The problem for the 252s is that after they annihilated the Salinas Cartel, none of the other established outfits want to touch them. If they try to grab some territory of their own, the other gangs will do what it takes to evict them, even if it means working together to do it. So, we think they might try to work through one of the corrupt governments in the region. That's about all I can say outside of a secure space."

Haley nodded. "It seems strange that they didn't resist us, given what they had at stake on that ship. They could have caused actual harm during the boarding, maybe even sunk us if they carried any rockets."

"Not really," Frankle said. "Knocking you guys off would make it a whole new ballgame. Right now, they are a big law enforcement problem for Europol and a minor national security issue for us. They sink a Coast Guard cutter or other warship, and that's war. We would not only come down on them kinetically and financially but also put them on the Terrorist List and mess up every-one they do business with. They may eventually decide that's worth the risk if they can work a major government to cover for them, but not right now."

"Man, I hope I don't live to see that," Sam said, shaking his head.

"You and me both, brother," Frankle agreed. After a pause, he said, "I might as well grab the box and get going. Any chance of getting a tour while I'm here? I haven't seen the boat since Resolution, and that was from the beach."

"Not a problem," Sam said. "Haley and I will excuse ourselves to resume our handoff discussions if you don't mind. Ben can show you around and give you two a chance to catch up. It's worth your time—we've had quite an upgrade since Resolution."

"Excellent!" Frankle said as they all stood. After shaking hands with Sam and Haley, he turned to Ben and said, "After you, sir."

Frankle was surprised by what he found on the tour. He knew *Kauai* was among the last in her class still in commission and expected to see an aging, patched-up set of diesels in the engine room. With its clean and modern diesel generators and Ben's description of their new diesel-electric battery drive capabilities, *Kauai*'s powerplant was more like a modern conventional submarine than an obsolescent patrol boat. Now the account of the Barbello operation he had read made much more sense. The Bridge was another wonder, with capabilities beyond even the newest patrol boats coming into service. "I thought the Coast Guard was the mendicant of the federal government. How did you guys manage to get all this?" Frankle asked after Ben finished his presentation of the FC3 system.

"The DNI dug our performance at Resolution and wrote the Coast Guard a big check for upgrades; Barbello was the first payback."

"Wow. The DNI wasn't stingy, was he?"

"Nope, the total was at least four times what the Coast Guard originally paid to build the boat, even adjusted for inflation. Still, it was less than they're paying for the new ones."

"Nice," Frankle said. This was good information in his pocket, and he would know for whom to ask if they were ever facing another challenge like Resolution. "Well, this was fascinating. On a personal note, how are you doing? I heard you got roughed up at Barbello."

"Just shot in the head—no damage to anything of value," Ben joked.

"You're shitting me," Frankle said with astonishment.

"The bullet didn't penetrate my helmet, but it did mess me up badly enough that my parents almost got the dreaded 'we regret to inform you' call. On the whole, I was lucky, considering the DEA guy standing next to me was killed," Ben said, his smile disappearing.

"Man." Frankle shook his head. "That's rough."

"Yes, I *do* draw a lot of fire whenever I'm with you DIA guys."

"Hey, that's Pete. Most of us go our entire career without shooting outside of the gun range. Heard from him lately?"

"Not since I got hit at Barbello. Victoria says he's been detailed to the DNI's staff. Is that a promotion for him?"

Frankle shook his head. "More of a place of refuge. He tangled with the DIA director over how Barbello was run in front of the JUBILEE committee, and she does not forgive and forget. The DNI is giving him cover until she moves on to another job. It's a nice gig, but he can't wait to get back in the field."

"He seems to have a bug up his ass about the 252s."

"Yes, well, when it's that personal, even the hardest among us can get obsessive."

Ben looked at him with a raised eyebrow. "Personal? How so?"

"You know about Julie, right?" Frankle asked.

"His fiancée? She was Victoria's big sister. They've only mentioned that she died."

"Not exactly. The 252s murdered her."

"*What?*"

"Yep. Julie was 'collateral damage' in a car bomb assassination they pulled in Paris. Pete wasn't even in the service then, just a smart-alecky postdoc at Princeton with a talent for martial arts. It crushed him. He'd probably have killed himself if it hadn't been for Victoria. Pete hung on, but he's been on a crusade to eradicate them since joining us."

"He didn't tell me, and neither did Victoria, which is surprising considering she's an open book. I guess I should have asked about Julie, but I didn't want to dredge up painful memories for her." Ben said, hanging his head.

"Don't beat yourself up, kid," Frankle said as he patted his arm. "When she feels the need to talk about that, she will. We're all pretty happy she got hooked up with you, you know. Real-life Dudley Do-rights are rather rare these days."

Ben cocked his head and said, "I can't figure out if I should be pleased or insulted."

"Take your pick," Frankle said with a grin. "Now, how are you and Victoria doing? We sure miss having her around, both personally and professionally."

"I'll share that with her. Actually, we're awesome. She seems happy, and I can't believe my good luck."

"Better and better. So, will you make an honest woman out of her?"

"What, are you relieving Pete of the 'Dad Watch' or something? Please pass the word to call off the hit squads—I'm working up to it."

Frankle smiled warmly. "Good for you. And I mean that. Now, how about you hook me up with that laptop, and I'll let you get back to the regular job?"

"Suits me," Ben said.

After retrieving the laptop from Ben's safe and signing an evidence receipt, Frankle followed Ben to the quarter-deck and stepped ashore. Shaking hands with the young officer, he said, "Thanks again, Coast Guard. Take care of yourself and our girl."

"I will, Art. Stay safe."

As Frankle turned and started walking along the pier in the warm sunshine, he glanced at his watch: 16:18. He had time for a round of Gitmo Golf before sunset. Not that he was an avid golfer, he just wanted to tell the tale when he got home. The naval base had a nine-hole course of sorts. Its only grass was the artificial greens around each hole. The rest was rocky dirt—golfers carried a piece of Astroturf on which to drop and hit the ball for "fairway" shots. Gitmo Golf, iguanas, and the up to two-foot-long gray Hutias, known locally as "Banana Rats" wandering around, were part of the storied charm of Guantanamo Bay.

The truth was that Frankle needed the distraction before returning to the grind of Washington. The women from that 252 ship got to him, particularly that poor Polish woman who was raped into madness simply for standing up for a child. Maybe the laptop could provide something that would make a difference in the fight against the 252s, or maybe not. All he knew was that he needed to seriously consider pulling out of the game once this case concluded. He was beginning to hate too much, which can get you and your teammates killed.

**_USCG Cutter Kauai, Atlantic Ocean,
twenty-three nautical miles north of Grand_**

Turk Island
19:21 EST, 19 November

Haley

They had been on station for a full day, with three more to go. This time, it would be back home to Port Canaveral, not just another fuel, water, and food top off at Guantanamo Bay. This first day had been as uneventful as their patrol had been before the *Miho Dujam*'s arrival. Haley had used this respite to complete the last of her technical familiarization. A few frank, one-on-one discussions with Sam about individual crewmembers remained, a vital part of the handoff on a unit this small. The talks gave her essential insight into the strengths and weaknesses of each individual and how they understood, anticipated, and played off each other, much like a championship basketball squad.

Haley also used these sessions to benchmark herself against Sam, professionally and personally. Although they had come to this common point in their careers from different paths—Sam via the enlisted ranks and OCS and Haley through the Academy—they shared a similar worldview and upbringing. Both were highly intelligent and came from wealthy families who disapproved of their career choice. They were also aligned in their love for the Service and a desire to stay operational on ships if possible. But that was where the similarities ended.

Sam was a devoted family man, married with two young children, and, thanks to a very understanding wife, he successfully balanced the competing demands of job and family. His wife had been a navy brat and served as a navy petty officer before completing her bachelor's degree—Joana understood and embraced the nomadic life associated with being a military spouse and was Sam's partner in every sense. Haley could see that Sam missed his family terribly when he was on this long patrol, as much as he enjoyed the job and the company of his crew.

Haley could not have been more different in this respect. She'd had relationships at school and after getting her commission, but determined that the benefits did not cover the costs. Haley found out early that you didn't hook up with other officers in the Service—the job was too competitive for any relationship to work, and the wreckage afterward was bad for everyone, not just the couple. Likewise, she had no success with men outside the Service. The interesting ones moved on when they learned what her career entailed, and those who did not move on were inevitably needy. Haley was single and comfortable with the choice—the occasions when she missed having someone to unload on were rare. She treasured the freedom to go after opportunities wherever and whenever they presented themselves without worrying about pulling kids out of school or her partner's job or preferences.

In their two weeks together on this patrol, Haley grew to admire Sam and was impressed by his leadership talent and history. The crew liked and trusted Sam as a man and the captain. Haley suspected his having made his way up to chief petty officer before being commissioned lent him more credibility in their eyes than the typical junior officer. But it clearly went beyond that. Her brief exposure led her to believe Sam was one of those rare people possessing the total package: knowledge, judgment, experience, and "people sense." It wasn't just the crew—it was clear Ben's admiration for Sam was unbounded. The two men were the closest of friends, despite their superior-subordinate positions in the military hierarchy. Haley thought their talks would reveal insights into whatever secret sauce Sam used to build this much personal power.

Haley had hoped to get some detail on what was behind that last operation, but Sam had to decline, citing the codeword restrictions. He did share that the Resolution Key mission culminated with him driving *Kauai* at flank speed through fog and the shoal water north of the Florida Keys to rescue Ben and DIA Agent Simmons from a deadly 252 trap. Sam shared his intense dislike of Simmons for his recklessness that endangered Ben and his crew and warned Haley to be very wary whenever the agent was involved in an operation.

"I'm not saying he's corrupt or evil or anything like that," Sam said in summation. "He just has a different calculus for risking the lives of the people around him. You need to keep that thought in your mind whenever you work with him."

"Not much chance of that, is there?" Haley said.

"*Au contraire*," Sam replied. "He was behind the Barbello mission, too, although he wasn't responsible for the damage or injuries we suffered. Keep in mind this boat was practically rebuilt using DNI money, and the Intel Community will be looking for a return on investment. Simmons is one of those people."

"I see," Haley said. "So, does Ben share this view?"

Sam smiled sadly and said, "Yes and no. I think Ben was awed enough by Simmons to go along with some decisions he came to regret. That fight he was dragged into on Resolution scared the bejesus out of him. He's been much more cautious since then. I have to admit that I miss the old happy-go-lucky Ben sometimes." He paused and grinned. "But I treasure the new Ben."

Haley nodded. "Off the record; tell me about him."

Sam sat back and put his hands behind his head. "He's the XO of your dreams. Super smart and capable, but he doesn't seem to know it. At least, he is extraordinarily modest. Ben has an amazing grasp of what's needed and makes it happen with patience and humor. There isn't a member of the crew, from Drake on down, who wouldn't take a bullet for him or follow him straight into a hurricane. And he is as courageous as they come. Let me tell you a story that captures Ben to a tee.

"When he was on his way from Virginia during his transfer from *Dependable*, he called to tell me he had been held up by a traffic accident. His vehicle was not involved, but he was set back for a few hours. I told him to play it safe and report in the afternoon rather than driving all night. Good headwork, right? So he reports in the next day, and we're off to the races. Well, a few weeks later, the Sector Commander comes knocking to pin a Commendation Medal on him. He saw the accident alright, then climbed into an SUV about to fall off a cliff to rescue an unconscious woman and her two little kids. He stuck around long enough to give a statement to the cops and make sure the kids were safely in the hands of their aunt, then got back on the road. The only reason the Coast Guard learned of it was that the woman's husband was an army officer—he found out Ben was in the military and put him in for an award."

"What was Ben's reaction?"

"He was surprised and embarrassed. Ben saw the act as something that needed to be done, so he did it. He did not want to call attention to it because he did not want to admit how scared he was. It was the same way on the Resolution and Barbello deals—said all he did was get himself shot."

"Still off the record. Can Ben make the tough calls?"

"Yes," Sam said, then tilted his head. "Why would you ask that?"

"He strikes me as being too friendly for an XO, first names, touching, that sort of thing."

"Hmm. Ben plays by the rules in the ballpark. If you want to step things up, he'll make it happen.

"You disagree?"

"No, Haley. Even if I did, it will be your boat, not mine. We *have* been a little loose with things because of where we started and the lack of risk with the people here. I would probably play it tighter if I came on board now."

"I'm relieved it's not just me, and I'll break it in gently. Is there anything else I should know, as in personally?"

"Again, why would you ask that?"

"I have heard his girlfriend has 'issues.' Have you had any concerns about his focus?" She hated bringing this up, but Zuccaro had used the word "creepy" regarding Victoria in an informal discussion Haley had had with the women a few nights ago.

The meeting was one of those "seemed like a good idea at the time" mistakes. Haley wanted to get a read on the gender relations climate before her ascension to command would make that impracticable. The atmosphere had turned decidedly frosty when she asked point-blank whether any male crew had done anything to make them uncomfortable. Zuccaro had been the only one to say anything but an emphatic negative. Haley suspected it was cattiness based on the silent death stares Zuccaro received from Hopkins and Lee, but she had to be sure.

Sam leaned forward with a frown. "I won't ask who suggested that, but I recommend you consider them unreliable sources. Victoria is, I guess the polite word is 'neurodiverse.' She is a fully functioning adult with a genius IQ and an eidetic memory. I mean, this woman is world-class smart. She is also the warmest, most charming individual I have ever met. She does have an unusually formal way of speaking and an intense curiosity about whomever she is talking with that some may find a little odd. Victoria is the one net positive from our involvement with Simmons—she was his protégé, and Ben first met her on the Resolution op. About her effect on Ben, he is a better, more mature man because of her. Believe me; I've seen the before and after versions."

"Thank you. I suspected as much, but I had to make sure."

"I understand. There is one other thing I'll tell you off the record related to this topic. I hate doing it, but I'd prefer you get the straight story from me instead of someone spreading scurrilous rumors."

Uh-oh. Haley leaned forward. "OK, let's have it."

"Hopkins has hugged Ben on two occasions; both were as he was heading into those two fights. There was nothing sexual, just her matronly instinct overruling convention in extraordinary circumstances. I saw no harm in it and did not feel the need to make it an issue. If it would make you more comfortable, I can write a formal statement you can keep on file that I dealt with the matter appropriately."

Haley blinked and said, "No, that won't be necessary. I am going to put a stop to that, though."

Sam shrugged and said, "Your call. Is there anyone else you want to discuss?"

"No, I think that will do. If I come across anything else, mind if I pick your brain again?"

"Anytime. Please grab me for any questions. I've been at this for so long that there's stuff I don't even think of any more that might be important."

"Thanks, Sam. Good night."

"Good night, Haley."

Haley closed her notebook and stepped over to Ben's stateroom. She and Ben were "hot bunking"—alternating occupying the room for sleeping on this patrol. It was awkward, both in terms of the gender mixing and their soon-to-be respective positions.

This latest revelation regarding Hopkins was a particular concern. Haley was shocked that Hopkins found that kind of behavior appropriate, even more, that Ben did. And yet, Sam did not have a problem with it. *Is it just me? Am I "that guy," the one looking for an excuse to throw his weight around?* Haley shook her head. *No, I get now why Mercier wants to move Sam along. He's gotten too close to everyone. If he can't put a stop to something like this, how will he make the hard choice when the time comes?*

She spread her sleeping bag out on Ben's bunk and checked her watch—she needed to be dressed to turn the room over to Ben in just under six hours. As she disrobed, her mind went to how she would manage the transition from the current situation on board to the one that needed to be. *I'll break it in gently. Easier said than done.*

Chapter 10

Change of Command

**State Highway A1A, Port Canaveral, Florida
09:18 EST, 1 December**

Haley

It was shaping up to be a beautiful day, one of those late fall days in Central Florida when everything is perfect for an outdoor event. It was warm but not hot, with moderate humidity, a light sea breeze from the east, and a bright blue sky with just a few small cumulus clouds. Haley was smiling as she drove the blue Miata with the top down along the causeway bridge crossing the Banana River—she could not help smiling as this was the day she had trained and hoped for across her eleven years in the Coast Guard. When she crossed this bridge on the return trip to her apartment today, she would be Commanding Officer of the Coast Guard Cutter *Kauai*.

Haley got off at the cruise ship exit and followed route 401 around to the Coast Guard station on the West Basin. Unlike her earlier visit a little over a month ago, the gate was open and manned by two Coast Guard seamen in tropical blue uniforms to check for official identification or, for those without official ID, whether they were on the approved guest list. Haley had her CAC ready and presented it to one seaman, who saluted and directed her to the parking area. On her way to her parking spot, Haley passed *Kauai*, moored here instead of her usual berth on the Trident Wharf. The festivities were held here rather than on the Space Force station because it was far easier to get the guests through the more moderate security and the venue was more aesthetically pleasing than the shipyard-like grounds around the wharf. Haley almost teared up when she saw the boat in the full sun, gleaming white and "full dressed" with her signal flags hung in the prescribed rainbow pattern from a temporary cable leading from the jackstaff on her bow to the crosstree on the mast and then back down to the flagstaff on the stern.

Haley parked in her assigned spot, climbed out of the Miata, and donned her combination cap, running her eyes over her uniform for the hundredth time today. She was in dress whites, as were the other officers taking part in the ceremony. Haley hated the white uniform for its fragility—you could not bump into anything without leaving a glaring mar, and the need to avoid doing so distracted from everything you were doing. She retrieved her sword from the car boot and attached it to the belt hook protruding from her jacket. The sword was another anachronism Haley did not care for, but it was useful in that wearing one took skirts and pumps off the table.

Holding the sword loosely with her left hand to keep it from swinging around, Haley strolled to the grassy softball field, where a broad canopy covered a wooden platform on which a microphone-equipped podium and several folding chairs already stood. Hopkins was busy arranging items on a folding table to the side of the platform and came to attention and rendered a salute when she saw Haley approaching.

Haley returned the salute and said, "Chief, the boat looks wonderful. You've done a great job."

"Thank you, ma'am, but it was a team effort."

"Well, I appreciate it." Haley glanced at the table. "Anything I can do?"

"No, ma'am, we are pretty much ready to go."

"Right. I'll get out of your way then. See you later."

"Yes, ma'am."

Haley turned and walked toward the station's admin building, where the officials and guests gathered before the ceremony. Hopkins's cool demeanor made her uneasy—it had been that way between them throughout Haley's familiarization patrol. She wanted to attribute it to the natural wariness of someone new who was about to take over as CO, but the other enlisted personnel did not seem to share it, at least to that degree. Even the quiet Bondurant was downright chatty when compared to Hopkins. *I need to figure out what's going on there and fix it; that and the hugging thing.* She smiled again as she walked. *But that's for later. Now live for the day!*

Haley reached the admin building, stepped inside, and followed the "KAUAI COC" signs to the dayroom, where people were huddled in small groups and talking. Ben and Sam stood with Drake in one corner, chatting over various details of the ceremony. Ben had the harried, intense countenance that junior officers and XOs always had going into any highly choreographed ceremony. Drake towered above the two officers, calm and fatherly-looking, politely attentive and nodding in his tropical blue uniform. Sam was smiling at the interchange, confident and relaxed as ever.

Three women stood in another corner with Chief Deffler, talking and chuckling. Haley recognized Ben's girlfriend, Victoria, from the pictures on his stateroom wall. She was petite, with long auburn hair pulled back into a ponytail to reveal a heart-shaped face with large green eyes. Victoria was an attractive young woman, with a girl-next-door look in her sundress and sandals masking a formidable intellect.

Joana, Sam's wife, stood in a conservative white blouse and dark blue skirt to Victoria's left. She was a stunningly beautiful woman—the pictures in Sam's cabin did not do her justice. She was a couple of inches taller than Victoria, slender, with lightly tanned skin, dark eyes, and wavy raven-black hair cascading over her shoulders. Sam had related in passing they met when he was in OCS, and Joana had been the sister of one of his classmates.

She was a work-from-home computer graphic artist who shared Sam's gregarious nature and sense of humor.

Haley did not know the third woman, a medium-sized forty-ish woman with short, light brown hair, but guessed she was Drake's wife. Deffler's presence was curious—he was not a regular member of the crew, although Haley knew he deployed with them whenever they had a UAV detachment on board. She supposed he was invited and had accepted as a matter of courtesy.

As Haley walked over to the other officers, Ben and Drake came to attention, and she and Ben shared salutes. "Good morning, ma'am," Ben said.

"XO, Captain, Chief, good morning," Haley replied. "Everything going OK?"

"Same as usual, ma'am," Drake answered. "I'm keeping things running, the XO's sweating the small stuff, and the skipper's sitting back enjoying the day."

Ben smiled, and Sam rolled his eyes as Haley laughed and said, "That's one tradition we need to keep."

"Very sensible decision," Sam said. He glanced around the room and added, "Do you have any guests coming?"

"A few classmates and my parents," Haley said, glancing at her watch.

"I'll see they get seated in the front, ma'am," Ben said.

"Thank you," Haley replied with a neutral expression. She had mixed feelings about her father's and stepmother's attendance. Haley adored her father, Bradford Reardon, and, for that reason alone, tolerated her stepmother. Haley was an only child; her mother died of ovarian cancer when she was just ten years old. A few years later, Bradford met and married Margot Treadway, a beautiful and vibrant Newport socialite. She and Margot had the usual stepmother/stepdaughter friction, but Haley supposed it could have been worse. Over time, they settled into a truce for her father's sake, more or less ignoring each other as long as Haley kept her grades up and stayed clean.

They hit a rough patch when Haley joined the Coast Guard. Margot Reardon looked down on the military as she did any laborers, and was convinced Haley had selected the Coast Guard Academy over Brown or one of the other civilian schools just to spite her. Haley thought the notion that anyone would endure the rigors of the Academy and subsequent privations of military service simply to irritate someone else ludicrous and told her as much. After Haley completed her obligated service and elected to stay in the Coast Guard, Margot was finally convinced that this was neither a spiteful jab nor a passing whim, and the two resumed their peaceful coexistence. Haley had to admit that Margot loved her father dearly and made him happy; for that, she could forgive a lot.

Sam broke into her thoughts. "Let me introduce you to everybody." After they had walked over, he continued. "Chief Deffler, you already know."

"Ma'am," Deffler said.

"Lieutenant Haley Reardon, this is Trudy Drake, the long-suffering spouse of our beloved chief of the boat," Sam said.

"Don't get me started," Trudy joked as she shook hands with Haley.

"I'm pleased to meet you," Haley said.

"And this lovely lady is Ben's friend Victoria Carpenter," Sam said.

"How do you do?" Haley said, extending her hand.

Victoria took her hand and said, "I am doing quite well, thank you, Miss Reardon. I am pleased to meet you."

Haley wasn't sure what surprised her more, the formal language or the deep husky voice coming from such a small young woman. "Um, likewise," she said awkwardly.

"And, of course, my wife, Joana. This is Haley Reardon," Sam said.

"Haley, I don't know how to thank you for prying Sam loose for us," Joana said with a warm smile as she shook hands.

"Happy to take the hit for the team, Joana," Haley replied, drawing a puzzled look from Victoria and chuckles from everyone else.

The small talk continued until Lopez appeared in the doorway and hurried over to them. "Sirs, ma'am, Captain Mercier is coming through the gate now." Mercier would officiate the ceremony today, and the three officers were expected to greet her on her arrival.

"Thanks, Lope," Sam said, then turned to the others. "Folks, please excuse Haley, Ben, and me. We've got some eagle-stroking to do."

"Carry on, my brave captain," Joana said with a grin.

As the three officers followed Lopez out toward the parking lot, Haley felt her first pang of dread at the thought of encountering Mercier. They had had no occasion to speak since their last meeting, which ended with Mercier upbraiding her for being a smartass. *If she held a grudge, I wouldn't be here now. Right?* Haley thought, hopefully. A car pulled up, and Mercier and a lieutenant stepped out.

Mercier and the young officer returned Sam, Ben, and Haley's salutes as they walked up, and Mercier held out her hand to Sam. "Congratulations, Sam. How are you feeling this fine day?" she asked as she shook Sam's hand.

"Too many emotions to list, Captain," Sam replied.

"Yes, I know. It's always that way." She turned to shake Haley's hand. "Haley, last call to duck and run."

"Not a chance in Hell, ma'am," Haley replied with a smile. *OK, we're through that.*

Mercier turned and shook Ben's hand. "What do you say, Ben? Think you can get through the ceremony without getting banged up?"

Ben smiled and replied, "As long as your companion is not a closet DIA guy, I should be safe, ma'am."

Mercier chuckled and turned to the lieutenant. "Doug, you're not moonlighting with the DIA, are you?"

"I wouldn't dream of it, Captain."

"That's a relief. Everyone, this is Doug Liggett. He had the misfortune of not having enough work on his plate back home, so he gets to carry the box and listen to me trash talk ship drivers for three hours each way." After introductions and handshakes, she continued. "Doug, I'm sure Ben would like to get back at it, and he can show you where to put the stuff."

"Yes, ma'am," Liggett replied as he opened the car's boot. He handed Mercier her sword, hung his own on his belt, and grabbed a small cardboard box before closing the lid.

"Sam, Haley, how about you take me on a quick walkabout on the boat so I can impart some senior officer-type wisdom on you," Mercier said as she hung her sword on her belt.

"After you, ma'am," Sam said as they turned and began walking toward *Kauai*.

After crossing the parking lot out of earshot, Mercier said, "So, Sam, psyched for the move to Newport?"

"Not for the move, ma'am," Sam replied. "They seem to get harder every time, and I am trying to get my head in the frame for classes and paper writing after a fifteen-year hiatus. Jo is walking on air, though—her folks live only an hour away in Gales Ferry."

"Yes, well, you've both earned a breather after the last few years. Isn't Newport near your family as well?"

"Um, yes, ma'am. Enough said."

"Oh, sorry."

They reached the quarterdeck, exchanged salutes with the seaman on duty, went on board, and then up to the Bridge.

Mercier sat in the captain's chair, then gestured to the seats at the FC3 console. After the two junior officers sat, she said. "It looks like something's brewing regarding the laptop Ben looted from that smuggling ship. We got a warning order from the National Command Authority to put *Kauai* in readiness for an operation sometime in the next two weeks."

"What sort of operation, ma'am?" Sam asked.

"Unknown. The good news for you, Haley, is that you will not be headed to the Windward for migrant interdiction for a while. We need to keep you close."

"Does that mean we don't sail tomorrow, ma'am?" Haley asked.

"No, we'll put you to good use on the Bimini run. As you might imagine, things have picked up there since we've thrown nearly everything we have at mass migration out of Haiti. This op might come to nothing; if I had a dollar for every WARNO that got canceled, I could retire in splendor right now. But we need to go through the motions—cancel leaves and defer maintenance availabilities, yadda, yadda."

"Yes, ma'am," Haley said.

"I'll bet you're relieved you don't have to deal with another DIA-sponsored op, Sam."

"Again, ma'am, mixed emotions," Sam replied with a rueful smile.

Mercier glanced at her watch and said, "I guess we should get back before Ben and Doug melt down." She stood and said, "You two go ahead. Just be ready to catch me if I trip over this damn sword going down the ladder."

****

The trio broke up to mingle among the guests as they approached the venue. Haley saw her father standing in a dark three-piece suit chatting with one of the other guests and hastened to him. Bradford Reardon was a tall man, six-foot-one, lean with a full head of sandy, close-cropped hair, graying on his temples. He grinned as soon as he saw her, and they hugged warmly, and Haley kissed him on his cheek.

"You look wonderful, sweetie," Reardon said as he held her at arm's length and looked her over. "I am so proud of you."

"Thanks, Dad," Haley said, trying not to tear up. "It means everything to have you here." She looked around and asked, "Where's Margot?"

"She's inside arranging dinner."

"Yes, I'm sure it's quite a challenge to find one exclusive enough this side of the Hudson." The quip came out involuntarily, as if Haley had heard it spoken by another person. Her regret was instant, and the change in her father's expression from beaming to sad was the worst rebuke imaginable.

"That's a little uncalled for. You know she didn't have to come, but she wanted to, for you."

Actually, I think it was for you, not me, but that earns her just as much credit. "I know. I'm sorry, Dad. No more bitchiness today, I promise. Can I get a reset?"

"Sure." His proud smile returned, and he looked and nodded toward *Kauai*. "Your first command. She's a beauty! Can you show us around?"

"Let's do it after the ceremony, when we have more time. Besides, I want to be able to describe her as *my* ship!"

"Fair enough." They both turned as Margot Reardon arrived. She was Haley's height and still strikingly attractive, with graying brown hair and hazel eyes. Her stride and dark purple blouse and skirt radiated power. "Everything set, my dear?" Reardon asked.

"It took time, but I found a suitable place in Orlando," Margot answered, then turned and gave Haley an approving nod. "You look magnificent, dear!" After glancing at her uniform, she added, "A little late for white, isn't it?"

Haley grinned in return. "Perhaps, but it's Florida, Margot, not Rhode Island. The seasons are different here."

"Yes, I suppose they are." She looked around. "This is very...quaint. Will we have any role in the ceremony?"

"No, you get to sit back and enjoy it. Even my role is limited—the ceremony is mostly a celebration of the previous command."

"Oh, I see," Margot said with slight disappointment.

Haley glanced over at the stage and caught Ben's attention, motioning him over. As he stepped up, Haley said, "Dad, Margot, I'd like you to meet Lieutenant Junior Grade Ben Wyporek, Executive Officer, who will be my second in command. Ben, these are my parents, Bradford and Margot Reardon."

"Ma'am, Sir, I'm very pleased to meet you," Ben said as he shook their hands. He then said to Haley, "We're set to begin in two minutes, ma'am."

"Thanks, Ben. Carry on, please."

"Ma'am," Ben said, then spun on his heel and trudged off to the next crisis.

Haley turned back to see her father's smile had been replaced by a look of concern. "That young man, Haley. He was wearing the Silver Star and Purple Heart. Did he earn those on *Kauai*?"

Haley was stunned that Reardon recognized the medals, more so that he appeared to know what they implied. "Um, yes, he did." She gave him a look that said, "We can talk about that later."

As Reardon nodded, Margot piped up, "Don't worry, Bradford, I'm sure Haley will have just as many medals before long!"

The accidental humor of the well-intentioned comment struck both Haley and her father, and both smiled. "Thank you, Margot," Haley said. "I appreciate your confidence."

"Not at all, dear." Margot looked approvingly at them.

"Let me get you seated," Haley said, then led them to two folding chairs in the front row before the stage. "Please have a seat, and I'll see you again after the ceremony." Her father squeezed her upper arm, and then he and Margot sat. Haley turned, stepped up on the stage, and stood next to the chair on which she was to sit. *Kauai*'s crew was already standing in ranks next to the stage, and Sam gave Joana a last kiss, then stood beside Haley.

The ceremony began with the formal arrival of Mercier, then the presentation of colors—the honor guard parading the National and Coast Guard flags before the assembly and then off to one side. Ben narrated the purpose of the change of command ceremony and a brief history of Sam's tenure. Mercier presented the Coast Guard Unit Commendation jointly to Sam and Seaman Apprentice Nichols, the most junior crew member.

Next, Drake stepped forward and presented Sam with *Kauai*'s commissioning pennant. When Sam made to return to the stage, Drake said, "But wait, there's more." Joana was invited onto the stage, and Drake and Hopkins presented her with a small round mahogany navigator's box with an inlaid compass. Joana was reduced to tears and hugged the box to her chest after reading the inscription aloud: "To Our First Lady, Love Now and Always, Your Crew of *Kauai*." After Joana returned to her seat, Drake and Bondurant presented Sam with a beautifully framed collage of photos of each crew member during a funny moment. Sam was blinking back tears himself as he returned to his seat carrying the picture.

Sam's personal award came next—the Meritorious Service Medal pinned on by Mercier, with Ben reading the citation. His ceremonial "frocking" to lieutenant commander followed—he would not actually be promoted and paid until the summer, but could wear the insignia and be addressed by the higher rank. Per Sam's request, Ben and

Joana stepped onto the stage, and each replaced one of his two-stripe lieutenant shoulder boards with a new one having the two-and-a-half stripes of his new rank.

It was time for Sam's farewell speech. He had carried some papers Haley guessed held his prepared speech, but instead folded them up and placed them in his pocket. He then held the picture Drake and Bondurant presented and talked briefly about each crew member and the story behind their photos. It was a profoundly moving and personal tribute to his crew, and Haley was close to tears for the second time that day.

The big moment had come, the formal handover of command. Haley, Sam, and Mercier stood. Haley faced Sam, saluted, and said loudly, "Lieutenant Commander Powell, I offer my relief."

Sam saluted and replied loudly, "Lieutenant Reardon, I stand relieved." He grinned, shook Haley's hand warmly, and said quietly, "Congratulations, Captain!"

"Thank you, sir," Haley replied with scarcely concealed excitement. As Sam returned to his seat, Haley stepped over to the microphone. It was her chance to make a speech, but it was good form for the incoming CO to keep it short, and Haley intended to do just that.

"I want to thank you all for coming today, particularly my parents, who have made this wonderful day perfect for me by their attendance. I also want to thank Captain Mercier for her officiation today and the trust she and Admiral Pennington have shown in selecting me for this command. Last but certainly not least, I would like to thank Commander Powell for his outstanding leadership and attention to duty that have made *Kauai* and her crew the finest unit in the Coast Guard. No one could improve upon his eloquent expression of the crew's quality, and I can only endorse it with admiration. This is the proudest day of my life, and I will do my utmost to live up to the outstanding legacy of Commander Powell and *Kauai*." Haley turned to face Ben. "Executive Officer, all standing orders remain in effect until further notice. Dismiss the company at the conclusion of the ceremony."

Ben saluted and loudly replied, "Aye, aye, ma'am!"

The ceremony concluded after the formal retiring of the colors. After shaking hands with Sam and Mercier, Haley stepped off the stage to meet with her father and Margot. Reardon's beaming expression had returned, and he said, "Congratulations, *Captain*! What a day!"

Even Margot was red-eyed with the emotion of the event. "I have to admit the ceremony and the stories the commander told were quite inspirational. I think I begin to see what you find so compelling about all this, dear."

Margot's comment genuinely moved Haley. "Thank you, Margot." She said, "I know you would like to see the ship, but we need to attend the reception inside for a bit of schmoozing first."

Margot grinned. "Schmoozing is my strong suit, dear. Lead the way."

****

After an hour into the reception held in the station's dayroom, Mercier bade everyone farewell, and she and Liggett departed. It was the signal to wind down the reception, and as the crew and other guests filtered out, Haley bade farewell to Sam and Joana, then went to gather her parents. She was surprised to find Margot in a deep conversation with Victoria, with Reardon and Ben looking on. "Ben, Victoria, I hope you will excuse me, but I promised my parents a tour of the boat."

"Yes, ma'am," Ben said. "Will you be needing me to accompany you, or would you prefer I waited here?"

Haley blinked. *Duh! They're all standing around waiting for me to grant liberty. Pull your head out of your ass, Haley!* "Neither, XO. Please grant normal liberty. And by that, I mean you too. Beat feet, and I'll see you tomorrow."

"Very good, ma'am, and thank you," Ben said. He turned to Victoria. "Ready to go?"

"Yes, Benjamin. Mr. and Mrs. Reardon, it has been a distinct pleasure talking with you. I hope to do so again soon."

"Same here, Victoria. Good luck with your coding project," Margot said with a warm smile. After they had walked out of earshot, she turned to Haley and said, "What an extraordinarily charming young woman! I can see why your second is so taken with her."

Haley continued to be surprised by Margot's geniality toward everything going on. *Maybe we have have turned a corner here.* "Yes, I haven't talked to her myself, but she seems to have many fans. Shall we go now?"

"That would be fine. Will I be alright in these clothes?"

Haley hadn't even thought about that. "I wouldn't recommend going down into the engine room in those spike heels, but we should be OK everywhere else."

The tour was an eye-opener for Margot and her father, particularly her cabin, which, while the largest berthing space on the boat, was less than half the size of Margot's closet back in Newport. "Oh, Haley, you are expected to *live* here?" Margot asked in wonderment.

"Only when we are underway, Margot. Remember, *Kauai* is a patrol boat, not a large ship—space is at a premium here."

"Heavens!" Margot exclaimed, shaking her head.

As they completed the tour, Margot said to Reardon, "Will you excuse me while I make a few calls, dear? There are some things back home I need to see to."

"Yes, of course. I'll follow you soon."

Margot turned to Haley. "We'll see you for dinner, dear? I have a wonderful spot picked out."

"I am looking forward to it, Margot," Haley said.

After Margot had walked off, Haley turned to her father. "OK, Dad. What did you put in her coffee this morning?"

"I told you things have changed. She really was impressed by everything today."

"Well, it makes me feel even worse about my snotty comment earlier, but I'll take it."

"Glad to hear it." His smile faded. "Now, I think you owe me some honesty about what you will be doing here."

"I'm sorry, Dad. I would have shared more with you had I known you knew anything about this. Frankly, it comes as a surprise."

"What, you think I'm some sort of lefty brahmin? Maybe I was, but that changed when my little girl went into the service. Did you think I wouldn't learn all I could about your life? If you become a parent, you'll learn that you can't just send your kid off to college and not worry about them anymore. Now come clean—your XO and your predecessor have combat medals. Even I know that differs from the run-of-the-mill Coast Guard stuff you have been doing."

"Dad, the details are classified, but there is more to *Kauai* than meets the eye. I'm sorry, I can't elaborate, but what we do is vital."

He sighed. "And I thought I couldn't be prouder of you—wrong again. I hate employing such a cliché, but you will be careful, for me?" Although he did his best to conceal it with a forced smile, Haley could feel the concern in his voice.

"Dad, I will do my very best to take care of my crew and my ship." Haley smiled. "That covers me by default. Please don't worry about me."

"Sorry, can't comply. It's in the job description. But I guess I'll learn to live with it." He hugged her again.

"Alright, alright. Let's get back to the cars before I get weepy," Haley said. "I need to get back to the apartment and change before heading out on the town with you two."

Chapter 11

Evolutions

**Scotts on Fifth Restaurant, 141 5th Ave,
Indialantic, Florida
19:13 EST, 1 December**

Victoria

Victoria was troubled, even though they were sitting in this lovely little restaurant and eating some of the most delicious food she had ever tasted. They had a small two-person table in a relatively quiet corner of the dining room, next to the wall decorated with photos of some of the more famous people who had dined there. Although it was crowded, Victoria's agoraphobia was mostly dormant, overcome by the positive diversions around her. And yet something was going on with Benjamin, and she was frustrated by her inability to read him.

After the change of command event, Benjamin suggested they go out for a nice dinner. Victoria welcomed the distraction—the ceremony, moving as it was, was another step toward the transition of Joana out of her life. They had grown close over the past six months, and although they did not see each other every day, the thought that Joana was nearby was a great comfort to Victoria, particularly when Benjamin was at sea. She worried about how the loss would affect her, much as Benjamin was over the departure of the man who had become his best friend over the last two years. Victoria was grateful Benjamin recognized the need to step out of their routine, especially when he would head to sea again on *Kauai* the next day.

Benjamin had requested she wear the green dress she had worn on their first date but that she need not bother putting her hair up as on the earlier occasion. She reminded Benjamin this was a "hair up" dress, according to her friend Debbie. Like his uniform, it was essential to have things in proper order. He had smiled, raised his hands in mock surrender, and said, "I'll never resist a lady doing extra for me." She knew he liked the look and didn't mind the extra work it took. Still, something was off in Benjamin's unusually solicitous behavior—he was always thoughtful and accommodating of her unique needs, but this increased level usually preceded bad news.

She and Benjamin had had, what was for them, a fight after he returned from his last patrol. Victoria had been appalled by the risk he took that nearly killed him and told him as much. She was not buying the excuse that he sought justice for the women they rescued. Victoria knew from her DIA days the 252s had enslaved scores of women before these and were sure to enslave many more afterward—his sacrifice would make no difference. Then she foolishly demanded a promise that he not take any more chances with his life.

Benjamin was contrite—he admitted he had miscalculated the level of danger—but reminded her that his job entailed some risks. He could not make that promise. As they did with all their disagreements, they talked it out, then went to sleep in each other's arms. But Victoria feared Benjamin might rethink their relationship as a result.

Victoria was finishing her meal of Orange Ginger Salmon, baked potato, and sauteed zucchini served, she was delighted to see, on separate plates. She knew her need to keep her food separated was an irrational obsession, but she could not help it: the food items tasted better when they were not touching each other. Victoria observed that Benjamin's meal and everyone else's she could see in the restaurant was served on a single plate—he must have discreetly insisted her meal be served this way, perhaps even paid extra to make it so. She loved him even more for his cheerful acceptance of this and her other compulsions, but was worried compassion fatigue might appear at some point. This worry was magnified tonight, as Benjamin had repeatedly been lost in thought.

Their dinner plates had been removed, and they were enjoying an excellent dessert wine when Victoria finally decided to press the issue. "Benjamin, you seem distracted tonight. Is there something wrong?"

Benjamin smiled and said, "You are getting better at reading my moods, Victoria. I'm sorry. I was just working myself up for this. We have been living together for almost six months without a firm commitment. I know you did that to spare me from what you thought were personal quirks that I couldn't tolerate. At the same time, I know I put you through a great deal of uncertainty and worry about my job. I guess the change of command finally brought everything into focus, and, as much as I love you and treasure what we have, I need something more."

Victoria felt faint. *No! No, no, no! He is leaving me! That is what all this is about—he is trying to let me down easy.* She took a deep breath to calm herself, then asked, "Benjamin, are you breaking up with me?"

Benjamin's eyes widened in surprise, and he said, too loudly, "*What?*" He looked around self-consciously, then leaned forward and whispered, "My God! No, Victoria!" Then, he scrambled to his feet, came around the table, kneeled, and took her right hand in his left. "I know you set a condition that I would not ask for six months, and it won't be six months until next week, but we will probably be underway next week. You might say no, I hope not, but I could not wait any longer than necessary, and I needed to do this in person, not over the phone." He shook his head as if to clear it, then gave her a pleading look. "I'm screwing up the moment here, sorry. What I am saying is I love you, Victoria, and everything about you. I can't imagine being apart from you. Would you please consider marrying me?"

Victoria put her left hand to her mouth and gasped in shock. Her mind tumbled as it went between the extremes of emotion. She felt like she was about to cry and could only open, then close her mouth, saying nothing. Benjamin's expression became more desperate.

"Victoria, I realize this is a surprise. If you would like time to consider it, I'll understand."

No, I do not need time to consider it! I have been dreaming of this moment since we moved in together. What is wrong with me?! "No, Benjamin."

"No?" Benjamin asked, his face falling.

Oh no! He thinks I am turning down his proposal. "No, no, no! I mean, I do not need more time!" She took another deep breath before continuing. "Yes, yes, yes! Of course I will marry you, Benjamin!"

Benjamin's face flashed relief, and then he kissed her hand. He reached into his blazer pocket, brought out a black velvet ring box, and opened it to her, revealing a white gold ring with a pear-shaped emerald in a diamond halo setting. "I guess I should have had this out from the beginning, but I was worried it might put on too much pressure."

Victoria's eyes were fogging with tears that she blinked away quickly as she offered Benjamin her left hand. Now everything made sense: the subtle questions a few weeks ago on which gemstones she favored, his request for her to wear the green dress, and the quiet, romantic restaurant. He had cleverly created her most perfect vision of a marriage proposal. They had both comically blundered through the communication phase, making it even more special. She gazed at the gorgeous ring as Benjamin slipped it on her finger, then held it close to her heart. Only then did she notice the entire restaurant had fallen silent, and all the other diners were staring at them.

She saw Benjamin, still kneeling and smiling at her. She tilted her head toward the others, and Benjamin turned, noticing that they were the center of attention for the first time. Continuing to hold her right hand, he lifted his left hand over his head with a "thumbs up" and shouted, "She said yes!"

Victoria jumped in her seat as the restaurant erupted in applause and cheers. Normally, she would have been frozen in terror to be the center of attention of so many strangers. Instead, she stood and pulled Benjamin into a long, passionate kiss. She knew she would be safe with Benjamin for the rest of her life, and the noise and attention accompanying this moment seemed to be just about right.

Twenty minutes later, Victoria was still catching her breath. Several other couples had come to their table to congratulate them. Chef Scott himself came out from the kitchen in his cordon bleu uniform to wish them well and consented to a photo of the three of them the server took with Ben's phone. When they sat at the table again, Victoria held out her arm to gaze at her beautiful ring. "It is so wonderful, Benjamin. Everything you did was so perfect!"

"Everything but the comms." Ben looked guilty. "It's amazing that after researching to find the most romantic restaurant in Brevard County and all the other preparations, as soon as I opened my mouth, I convinced you I was giving you the heave-ho. Are you sure you still want to marry me?"

"Considering I have been dreaming of this moment for months, and my first response convinced *you* I was declining your proposal, I suggest we both have work to do."

"Well, Victoria, we'd better get on it. We only have the rest of our lives to get it fixed."

"I have every confidence we will succeed, my love!"

✳ ✳

Victoria lay next to Benjamin, tucked under his arm with her head on his chest as he slept. She listened to his slow and rhythmic heartbeat as her head lifted and fell with his breathing. She had been far too excited to sleep, but Benjamin had to report early in the morning for another patrol. He had been game to stay up with her, but Victoria did not want him to start another fatiguing patrol with a sleep deficit. She used a massaging technique she had researched, which, along with the wine from the dinner and the glass they shared on their return, put Benjamin to sleep.

They hardly talked after their return, just cuddled on the couch for an hour as Victoria admired the new ring on her finger. Although it was a simple design, she was captivated by the shape of the stone and its exquisite green color. As a rule, she did not wear jewelry other than a simple gold-inlaid pearl pendant her sister Julie had given her as a birthday present just before she died. She now had two treasures.

They had shared the news with Joana and Sam by phone on the way home from the restaurant. Both were ecstatic, and Victoria agreed to have dinner with them the following night to give Joana a chance to see the ring and talk about the future. After the call, she and Benjamin had a brief discussion, agreeing at once to ask Sam and Joana to stand as best man and matron of honor at their wedding. Victoria would ask them tomorrow.

There was much to plan and set up—at least Joana would be there at first to help her get started. Then there was communicating the news and sending out the invitations. *I have not even met Benjamin's parents yet. What will they think of me?* The thought they might disapprove disturbed her, and she turned her head slowly to look at Benjamin's face. He was sleeping soundly with a slight smile. It brought back the memory of when he was still in the hospital and, unsure of his future, asked her to reconsider her commitment to him. When she made it clear that would never happen, he had teased her that she was foolish, but they would figure things out somehow. *And here we are, dearest man! We will figure it out somehow, as we always do.*

Victoria nuzzled Benjamin's chest, careful not to wake him. She knew she would miss him while he was away, now more than ever. And the ever-present worry for his safety would be there as well. But that lingering background of fear that somehow she and Benjamin would not work out was gone. The happiness she had known for the past year would continue forever. It was with that sweet thought that Victoria finally fell asleep soon afterward.

USCG Cutter Kauai, moored, USCG Station, Port Canaveral, Florida
10:23 EST, 2 December

Ben

Ben was finished with the pre-patrol preparations. The crew was on board and hard at work, the fuel and water stores had been topped off, the container holding the squid projector had been moved from the storage building to the foredeck, and various systems were spooled up and tested. Haley requested a meeting with Ben and the two chiefs before setting the special sea detail and mooring stations. She had not told Ben the purpose, but he suspected it was to lay down the ground rules for the new command.

Ben was still riding high from the events of the previous night. He had been genuinely afraid that Victoria would have reservations about getting engaged, based on how upset she was about his last adventure with the *Miho Dujam*. His heart almost stopped when he mistook her no about not needing more time for a no to the engagement. His relief and joy were palpable, and the commitment, for some strange reason, made him less sad about leaving her for this patrol. There was no actual change in things, yet he felt a confidence in his future that before had been absent.

There was a knock, and Ben turned to see Drake and Hopkins standing in his doorway. "Ready for the big meeting, XO?" Drake asked.

"Damn straight. Let's get it done," Ben replied.

As they stepped over to the captain's cabin, Hopkins said, "You look like you just won the lottery, XO. What gives?"

"Big news. I'll share it when I get an opening," Ben replied as he knocked on the door.

"Yes?" Haley's voice called.

Ben opened the door and stuck in his head. "COB, Chief, and I are here as you requested, Captain."

"Excellent! Please come in and take a seat, as best you all can, anyway."

The three filed in, Ben grabbed the spare chair, and the two chiefs sat on Haley's bunk. Once they were all situated, Haley continued. "I wanted to get together to go over a few things before getting underway. First off, I'll repeat that it is an honor for me, and I'm super excited to be here. Considering where you all started, you have done a magnificent job, and you should be proud of everything you have achieved. We have all talked before, so you know my history and where I am in the power curve. I know I still have some learning to do, so if any of you see something you think might be a problem, you give me a nudge.

"By and large, I really like how everything is running here. I only have a couple of changes in mind. Chief, I want to get back on the Bridge to sharpen the edge a bit. I'd like to take the midwatch as OOD for this first patrol. Can you make that happen?

"Certainly, Captain," Hopkins replied.

"OK. The second thing might sting a little. I want us to tighten things concerning decorum. While I get why Commander Powell was a little looser, given the relief for cause and all, I am confident that everyone here is beyond that, and we can switch to a more conventional approach."

"Ma'am, can I ask you to specify what you mean by decorum, please?" Ben asked.

"Yes. No more first names when on duty, and we need to avoid unnecessary physical contact between the officers and enlisted. By that, I mean the occasional handshake is fine, and obviously, if someone needs help, you do what you need to do, but the other stuff is out. In particular, XO, I can't have officers hugging enlisted members under any circumstances."

Ben felt like he had just been punched in the stomach, but maintained a neutral expression. "Understood, ma'am. It won't happen again."

"Captain, I don't know what you heard, but I hugged Mr. Wyporek, not the other way around," Hopkins interrupted.

"Chief, I'm sure Mr. Wyporek doesn't need a translator," Haley said coolly.

"No, ma'am," Hopkins said equally coolly.

"Good. Now that's settled, how do we look to get underway, Chief Hopkins?"

"FC3 is warmed up with all codes loaded. The main gyro is spun up, and all sensors are checked and correct. Operations is ready for sea, Captain."

"Very well. Chief Drake?"

"Fully topped off with fuel and water, all main diesels blown down with the lube warmed up, ready for start and power grid cutover any time. Engineering ready for sea, Captain.

"Very well. XO?"

"All personnel on board. Full load of ammunition for the main gun, the fifties, and small arms. Squid projector is on board and ready for mounting. All lines singled-up. Deck, Weapons, and Ship ready for sea, Captain."

"Very well." She glanced at her desk clock. "Let's set the special sea detail in fifteen minutes. Questions?"

"No, ma'am," Ben replied.

"Thank you," Haley said and nodded.

Ben and the two chiefs stood and filed out the door. Once it was shut, Hopkins nodded toward the messdeck, and they turned and silently followed her there. Once out of earshot of the cabin, she turned to Ben and said, "I am so sorry, sir!"

"No harm done, Chief." Ben nodded. "I'm still on the Lieutenants List. This will take getting used to, for me, anyway. If I slip up, please give me a nudge, or throw something at me as needed."

"Will do, sir." Hopkins smiled warmly. "Oh, what is your big news?"

"Victoria and I got engaged last night."

"That's fantastic!" Hopkins took a step forward with her arms out, then stopped and dropped them to her sides. She held out her right hand and said, "Congratulations, sir."

Ben shook her hand and said, "Thank you, Chief."

Drake offered his hand. "That's wonderful news, sir. Congratulations!"

Ben shook his hand. "Thanks, COB. I guess we should go get'r done. Gotta send one last FIM, then I'll head out."

"FIM, sir?" Hopkins asked.

"Fiancée IM." Ben grinned.

"Oh, how the mighty have fallen!" Drake quipped as he turned to leave.

"See you on the Bridge, sir," Hopkins said.

"See you in a few," Ben said as he headed for his stateroom.

Haley

Haley looked at her hands folded in her lap. *Well, that sucked.* She had gone back and forth in her mind as to the best way to carry out the change and decided that ripping off the bandage would be the least painful. She knew Ben was an honorable man who probably never realized he was even giving all those back pats and arm squeezes or how an unscrupulous person could use that against him. *He just doesn't think like that.* Haley smiled. *I bet he's also a lousy poker player—he looked like I had slapped him when I gave him the hugging proscription.*

She was sure Ben would recover quickly and not show any effects in the meantime. Hopkins was a different story. Haley was caught off-guard by Hopkins's leap to Ben's defense, and her response to that had been unartful, to say the least. *Now Hopkins is madder than Hell at me. Sam was right: she does have a mother thing for Ben.* Haley shook her head sadly. *At least I don't have to worry about hugging anymore—she'd die before she put Ben on the spot again for that. I have to find a way to reach common ground with her.*

Haley looked around the cabin, which was stark except for a plaque with the ship's crest mounted on the wall opposite her small desk. She thought of decorations for the room. She had a picture of her and her father that she treasured, but she would never hang it in public view—it would be too weird. Margot had offered to help decorate the cabin when they were eating dinner last night. It was a kind offer, and Haley was tempted to accept, if for no other reason than to continue their sudden rapprochement. But chances were that Margot would find something proper for a cottage at the shore, but unacceptable for the CO's quarters on a warship. Haley did not want the risk of having to reject the suggestions and set their relationship back.

As the pipe to set the special sea detail came over the 1MC, Haley stood, grabbed her ball cap, brand new with a small "CO" embroidered with yellow thread above the back strap, and headed out toward the Bridge. The thought of Mercier's reaction if she heard of Haley and Margot "girly-ing up" the cabin brought an amused smile. Fortunately, she could be sure Drake and Hopkins would convey via the Chiefs-Net that it was quite the reverse—a true SOB had taken command of *Kauai*.

Chapter 12

One of Our Own

***USCG Cutter Kauai, Atlantic Ocean,
twenty-three nautical miles east-southeast
of Hollywood, Florida
01:14 EST, 3 December***

Haley

Kauai idled at her picket position, halfway between the Florida coast and the Bimini Islands. It was a high-tempo operation, and Haley was on the Bridge, standing a regular one-in-three OOD watch rotation with Ben and Hopkins, allowing Bondurant and Lee to rest when they were not involved in boardings. Haley supposed she would eventually tire of watchstanding and settle into the more traditional CO role of being on call, but not now. She was delighted to be back on the Bridge, conning the boat on this beautiful cool, calm night. There was no moon, only the stars and the soft yellow glow of the Miami-Fort

Lauderdale-West Palm Beach metroplex stretching across the western horizon.

It had started as a coordinated multi-unit interdiction operation designed to counter the increased fast-boat traffic between Bimini and the Florida coast. Smuggling gangs assumed a weakness in the Coast Guard coverage of the eastern approaches to Florida's Atlantic coast because of the ongoing Haitian migrant surge operation. They were taking advantage of this by pushing through more shipments of drugs and people by go-fast boats across the forty-five-mile strait between Miami and Bimini.

This assumption was in error. Operations south of the Bahamas *were* absorbing a considerable amount of the larger cutter resources, but the patrol boats and the speedy response boats at the individual Coast Guard stations were still present and available. The challenge lay in the eighty nautical miles of vulnerable coastline between Homestead and West Palm Beach; almost any point could be used to land an illicit cargo of contraband or illegal entrants.

Among the tactics in use this night was the classic "Hounds-to-Hunters" funnel operation, oriented east to west. Two patrol boats anchored the top of the funnel on the northern and southern ends, acting decidedly unstealthy in their operations, liberally using radios and lighting to make their presence known. Unladen scout boats sent by the smuggling organizations to reveal the positions of the Coast Guard patrols—places to be avoided during the actual smuggling runs—did their jobs. The locations of the two patrol boats were noted, as was the large coverage gap between them, and passed along to the coordinators who fed the routes to smuggling craft. Smugglers could scurry through the gaps without being detected for a quick run to shore, drop off the load, and make a carefree return to the east.

They did not know that five Coast Guard response boats were concentrated at the western end of the funnel, close enough together to be mutually supporting and well-covered from the air. The smuggling boats were faster than the patrol boats but slower and less maneuverable than the response boats. Those smugglers not stopped and apprehended would dump their loads in an attempt to escape. Either outcome counted as an interdiction, a win for law enforcement, although arrests and prosecution were preferred.

The smugglers knew there was a significant element of risk associated with the trade and losses of cargo. Even the loss of the occasional boat and crew was considered acceptable—part of the cost of doing business passed on to the customers. On the rare occasions they were found, the crew's modus operandi was simple: evade capture if practicable and submit to arrest without resistance otherwise. There was no advantage to fighting back, as the charges, if they could even be proven, were usually pled down to brief incarceration, provided resisting arrest was not included. If you fought back, the gloves came off and the prospect of hard prison time or being killed outright became a genuine possibility. Everyone understood that as long as this "gentleman's agreement" held, short-term consequences were mild and long-term prospects were unaffected.

On this night, someone did not get the memo.

A thirty-five-foot open panga with three outboard engines and a cargo of baled cocaine had launched from a boat landing in Alice Town on North Bimini, heading for a drop-off on Key Biscayne. The operators had been fed the latest intel on their Coast Guard opposition: two patrol boats separated so that only a slight course change was needed to evade them. Besides the usual three crew, a heavily armed drug gang member rode along to ensure delivery. This was not the standard procedure; customer ridealongs increased the risks if they were stopped, but the gang indulged no arguments.

The crew followed the planned track to evade the patrol boats, using GPS for navigation and keeping a moderate speed of twenty knots to conserve fuel. They breathed a sigh of relief upon clearing through the picket line and made a slight course change to the south.

Unbeknownst to the crew, they had been picked up by a U.S. Customs and Border Patrol long-range patrol aircraft shortly after they cleared Henry Bank and tracked throughout their journey. Based on the plane's information, one of the response boats from Coast Guard Station Miami Beach closed to intercept within territorial waters. It should have been easy: light up the target, and they either surrender or run. Everyone knew the rules; everyone but the gang member.

When the response boat's spotlight flooded over the panga, the gang member panicked and opened fire with his AK-47 on full automatic, wounding a coastguardsman and drawing return fire from the boat's 0.30 caliber machine gun. The panga's master, convinced they were about to be gunned down in a vicious crossfire, gunned the throttles to ram the stern of the response boat, hopefully crippling it enough to enable an escape. He smashed one of the boat's outboard engines, taking it out of the fight, but in doing so, the wounded crewman was thrown overboard and struck and killed by one of the panga's propellers.

Word went out instantly. The crew of the fleeing panga had attacked a Coast Guard boat with gunfire and ramming and had murdered a coastguardsman. The customs plane stuck to the boat like glue now, constantly relaying position, course, and speed to the other units on the net as the panga fled to the northeast. A Coastie had been murdered, one of their own, and all law enforcement in the area was determined to make sure this night did not end well for the panga crew.

Onboard *Kauai*, Haley had completed a round with the binoculars when the alert was received. Bunting had the FC3 watch and took the initial call from LE chat. "Emergency message, Captain," the young petty officer said.

Haley stepped over and read the chat message. "OK, Bunting, fire up all systems." She stepped over to the

1MC box and grabbed the microphone. "Now set Law Enforcement Condition One-Alpha, repeat set Law Enforcement Condition One-Alpha." She then pressed the buzzer used on *Kauai* for a law enforcement alert. Condition One-Alpha was law enforcement, where the suspects were considered armed and dangerous. It was essentially the same as General Quarters Condition One in terms of manning and equipment, but the law enforcement use-of-force continuum was still in play. *Kauai* could not engage a target with deadly force unless fired on or granted a statement of no objection from the command center.

Ben was on the Bridge within two minutes, followed by Hopkins and Williams, all grabbing body armor vests and helmets. Williams sat in the center seat of the console while Ben and Hopkins looked at the radar picture and the chat traffic. After a minute, they shared a grim glance, stepped over to Haley, and saluted.

Haley returned the salute and said, "You've seen the board. Do you have any questions about the situation?"

"No, Captain," they both replied.

"Alright. Coast Guard 28167 reported one shooter. We will assume that this is still the case. If it is still the one active shooter, I'll order the sniper to take him out. If it is multiple shooters, we will engage with whichever fifty caliber is unmasked until the gunfire is suppressed and proceed appropriately. Questions?"

"We need to make a general announcement about what is going on, ma'am," Ben replied.

"I intend to. Anything else?"

After both responded with head shakes, Hopkins saluted and said, "Captain, I offer to relieve you of the Deck and Conn."

Haley returned the salute and said, "I stand relieved." She then announced, "On the Bridge, this is the captain. Chief Hopkins has the Deck and Conn!"

After everyone on the Bridge responded with, "Aye!" Haley took the 1MC microphone again. "All hands, this is the captain. A thirty-five-foot panga believed to be carrying narcotics has just fired on and rammed a response boat from Station Miami Beach about twenty-three miles southwest of our current position. One Coast Guard member is confirmed dead. The suspect vessel is now under direct observation, heading zero-eight-eight at twenty-five knots. We will intercept this vessel, stop it, and take all persons onboard into custody. These suspects are considered armed and extremely dangerous.

"I know how you must feel about this. Believe me, I feel the same. Nonetheless, this remains a law enforcement mission, and we will observe the continuum of force rules of engagement. No one is authorized to fire without my direct order." Haley hung up the microphone, walked to the captain's chair, and sat.

Ben said, "All stations manned and ready, Captain. Mounts 51 and 52 are manned with rounds in the chamber. Mount 25 is ready with bore clear and HE in the chute. Overwatch is posted."

"Very well," Haley replied. "Williams, I need a course and time to intercept at twenty-eight knots."

"Aye, Captain," Williams said, typing in the query. After three seconds, he continued. "Recommend course one-eight-three at twenty-eight knots, estimated intercept time twenty-four minutes, ma'am."

"Chief, twenty-eight knots, please. Initial heading is one-eight-three."

"Very good, Captain," Hopkins said as she pushed the thrust levers forward to full speed. "Helm, come right, steer one-eight-three."

"Come right, steer one-eight-three," Pickins, the helmsman, replied. After about ten seconds, he reached the new course and reported, "Chief, steady on one-eight-three."

"Very well. Navigation, are there any contacts with a CPA within two miles?" Even in the pre-dawn hours, this was a heavily trafficked area, and Hopkins's principal responsibility was to keep *Kauai* from colliding with another vessel. Rather than get a series of reports on the dozen-odd targets on the scope, Hopkins requested those with a Closest Point of Approach, CPA, of two miles.

"Negative, Chief," Zuccaro responded. "The nearest CPA on current targets is three-point-eight."

Haley turned to Bunting, who had moved to the left FC3 seat, shifting communications to his screen. "Bunting, report to the command center. We are on an intercept vector for the suspect vessel. Estimate visual contact in thirteen minutes."

"Aye, aye, Captain," Bunting said and then began typing.

Haley turned to Ben. "XO, assuming we stop this target without sinking it, I want you to lead the boarding. Who do you want with you?"

"Bondurant and Lopez, ma'am. Lee on coxswain. Everyone with sidearms and Lopez with a shotgun."

"Agreed. Head down, make your assignments, and brief them. Boarding and deck crew to stay on the messdeck until we call all clear. Get back here as soon as you're done."

"Very good, Captain. By your leave?"

"Go."

Ben turned, stepped to the bridge ladder, and disappeared below.

Haley keyed her headset microphone and said, "Overwatch, Actual."

"Actual, Overwatch. Go ahead, ma'am," Guerrero replied from his sniper position on *Kauai*'s Flying Bridge.

"Overwatch, I don't know how this will play out, so I will give you a conditional. You are weapons tight unless you see someone firing directly at *Kauai*. In that case alone, you are cleared for deadly force on the shooter only. Copy?"

"Copy all, ma'am."

Guerrero was a skilled sniper, trained to hit targets on one moving boat while shooting from another. Sea and weather conditions were ideal, so he could theoretically kill any exposed shooter within seconds, provided the other vessel was not jinking too erratically.

"Alright. Post-shooter now. If needed, can you take out his engines?"

"Should be doable, ma'am, but the time of flight will be critical. I can't promise anything beyond seventy-five yards."

"Understood. I'll do my best to get you inside that."

"Copy, ma'am."

"Mount 51, Actual," Haley said, calling Hebert on the fifty-caliber machine gun on the starboard bridge wing.

"This in Mount 51. Go ahead, ma'am."

"Mount 51, you are weapons tight. Stay low unless you get the order to open up."

"WILCO, ma'am."

"Mount 52, Actual."

"Mount 52, ma'am," replied Fireman Connally, manning the counterpart to Hebert's gun on the port bridge wing.

"Mount 52, same deal for you. Stay low, weapons tight."

"Aye, aye, ma'am."

Haley looked at the bridge clock: 01:29—six minutes before the panga would come over the visual horizon. "Chief, let's darken ship."

"Aye, aye, Captain," Hopkins said. "Bunting, shut down navigation lights."

"Shut down nav lights, aye, Chief." Bunting flipped the switches labeled "Mast," "Side," and "Stern" to off and said, "Lighting off, Chief."

"Very well."

Running at twenty-eight knots without navigation lights was not something done lightly. In the event of a collision, the liability would be substantial, regardless of the other vessel's culpability. But the risk in this situation was negligible, and the gain from not alerting the panga of their presence was considerable.

Zuccaro leaned forward. "Radar contact, two-one-eight, eight-point-six, constant bearing decreasing range. Track position, course, and speed correlate with the suspect vessel, Chief."

"Very well." Hopkins did the math in her head: about forty knots closure, two and a half miles to go. "Williams, train the camera out to zero-three-zero relative. You should see them within three minutes."

"Yes, Chief," Williams said as he slewed the Electro-Optical Infrared camera around to that bearing. The monochrome screen showed the horizon and brightly glowing stars, but nothing else.

Haley leaned forward in her chair, scanning between the sensor/fire-control and navigation panels. *Now the wait. Is there anything I have overlooked?* She turned as Ben arrived beside her. He was decked out for the mission with body armor, a lightweight combat helmet, and an equipment belt with a holstered Sig P229 pistol.

"Deck and boarding parties are ready, Captain," Ben said.

"Thank you, XO. We should have a look at them in about one minute."

"Yes, ma'am."

Haley glanced at him. "Any advice, XO?"

"Ma'am, this is new for all of us. What's your plan?"

"Loop in to parallel him on his quarter at one hundred yards."

"Sounds right, ma'am. Recommend his port quarter. Hebert is steadier, and we'll be masked when we launch the RHIB."

"Good points. We'll do that. Thanks, XO."

"Yes, ma'am. And how do you intend to stop him, assuming we don't end up in a total shootout? I wouldn't plan on using the squid."

"Concur. I'll hit him with the locator light and put a burst over him with the fifty. If he doesn't heave to, I'll turn Guerrero loose on his outboards."

"Recommend you skip the light up and warning shot, ma'am."

Haley sat upright. "That's the protocol."

Ben shook his head. "With respect, ma'am, screw the protocol. Those bastards shouldn't get a reset just because they escaped the first boat they shot up. A warning shot will only tell them to start jinking if they haven't already, or worse, that they have nothing to lose by firing back. Same thing with the light. The engines on those outboards will glow like hot coals in Guerrero's night sight—he doesn't need any light."

Haley sighed. "I hate this, but you're right. We'll do it that way."

Ben nodded sympathetically. "Helluva break-in patrol for you, ma'am."

Haley nodded as she turned back to the panels. "Yea, verily."

Nicholas

Kenton Nicholas was a frightened man. There were three bullet holes in his windscreen from the firefight with the Americans. The closest was just to the right of where he stood at the helm. He had felt that bullet go by as it passed within an inch of him. His younger brother Nathan crouched beside him, staring straight ahead as the boat sped as quickly as possible with the bow partially caved in after the collision with the American.

His deckhand Jayden Wilson was forward, watching the makeshift patch plugging the tear in the hull. At least they had stopped taking on water—the hole in the hull was above the waterline, but gallons of seawater had poured in through the gap every time the bow dipped. The engines screaming at full power should push them at forty knots, but Nicholas would have been surprised if they were even reaching thirty, given the drag from the damage and the hundreds of pounds of seawater sloshing back and forth in the bilges. Fuel was also a worry; they were burning through it fast while traveling at a speed half of what they should be, thanks to that cargo, that damned cargo! Close to a ton of cocaine bales they had failed to deliver. What the hell good was it now? They were running for their lives on a damaged, overloaded boat, yet they could not jettison a ton of deadweight because of *him*.

That La Cantaña cartel monster was standing behind them, his AK-47 in his hands, ready to murder them if they stepped out of line. The man was not afraid, just stood there staring at them with gimlet eyes, his face and shaved head covered with tattoos. He was smoking a cig-arette, *smoking*! Their only hope was to make it back to North Bimini without being spotted by aircraft searching for them, and the fool was generating a glow that could be seen for miles! Nicholas had told him to put it out, and the man's only response was to flip the fire selector of his assault rifle off "safe."

He had warned his boss back home that they should not be dealing with these animals. They would bring what up to now had been a lucrative family business to ruin. But the boss would not listen; the money was too good. Then the customers insisted on including one of their men to oversee the trips—they had lost too many loads and wanted to make sure the crew did their job. Nicholas had pointed out how dangerous that was, but at this point, nothing mattered. The cartel owned the boss, and therefore, they owned them all.

Nicholas had tried his best for success this night. The scouts had nailed the positions of the American patrols; all he had to do was get past their picket line by crossing through a wide gap they had left. They didn't even have to land, just pull within twenty-five yards of the beach and dump the load for the La Cantaña cartel men to retrieve.

They were still a mile off the coast when, out of nowhere, came a blinding light and the call to heave-to.

It was unfortunate, but hardly the end of the world. Nicholas would turn away from the light and run while Nathan, Wilson, and the cartel man threw bales overboard. They were faster than the Americans when empty—they just had to stay ahead during the dump. The Americans would follow until they were confident the cargo was jettisoned and then stop to retrieve it. Even without arrests, it was a win for them, and no one wanted bloodshed. Lose cargoes? Even a boat or crew? No problem—part of the cost of doing business. He had explained this to their passenger before they left Bimini, and the man simply nodded without expression.

Nicholas was startled when the light hit them—there should not have been any Americans here. He recovered quickly and put the helm over when the cartel bastard started shooting. The Americans reacted at once, and the space between the boats was crisscrossed with 7.62-millimeter tracer fire. Nathan and Wilson flattened on the deck, and Nicholas instantly realized this was a new game. Their survival depended on getting out of range of the machine gun on the American boat. Even if they put down the cartel man, they would not stop shooting. Nicholas had to cripple them somehow and decided a glancing blow to the stern could take out one or both of the American's outboards without leaving his panga crippled. Then he had to run like hell.

It worked. After the jarring crash, they sped off into the night without pursuit. The Americans had stopped firing after the impact, perhaps with damage to their gun mount. Nicholas breathed a preliminary sigh of relief and ordered Wilson and his brother to dump the cargo. The cartel man turned his gun on them and said, "No!"

"You don't understand," Nicholas shouted over the engines. "We have to go fast to get home! This cargo slows us down!"

"No dump!" the man shouted back.

"What good is it when the Americans catch up with us?"

"They catch up, I shoot them too! No dump!"

That was thirty minutes ago, and Nicholas could see from the GPS they had at least another half hour before they reached the shoals of Henry Bank and safety. At least they had not seen any other boats. Nicholas thought luck might see them through when suddenly there was a bang, and the panga lurched to the right. He looked back to see the right-hand outboard spewing smoke. *Damn! Of all the times to blow an engine!* He put in some port helm to compensate for the loss of thrust and keep them on course and shouted, "Jayden, see if you can do something with it!"

The man was making his way back to the stern when there was a second bang, and the boat started drifting left. "It's been shot! They're shooting the engines!" Wilson shouted.

Nicholas's eyes widened in fear, and he spun the helm to the right—too late. There was a third bang, and the center engine, their last, ground to a halt. The boat, already slowing before the previous hit, coasted to a stop. Where only moments before the crew had to shout to be heard over the racing engines, wind, and water sluicing past, there was near silence, only the lapping and occasional thud of a wave striking the hull and the hissing and soft pings of the cooling engines. Nicholas looked around frantically in the darkness; there were no lights or sounds anywhere. The cartel man was training his AK-47 from beam to beam, searching for a target, any target.

Nicholas was dumbfounded. He had expected to hear the whine of a helicopter, one of those the Americans used to shoot out the engines of go-fast boats. At least he should hear boat motors if they were close enough to take out the engines with single shots. But there was nothing at all. Finally, a male voice pierced the darkness from their port quarter.

"This is the United States Coast Guard! You will surrender immediately or be fired upon!"

Nicholas, Nathan, and Wilson ducked behind the stacks of cocaine bales while the cartel man stood and began firing blindly in the voice's direction. There was a loud "crack," and the man's head snapped back, his arms spread out, and he collapsed backward with his assault rifle clattering to the deck beside Nicholas. *Now they'll kill us. That fool has done for us all!*

A moment later, the panga was bathed in a blinding white light originating from the port quarter. Nicholas looked at the sprawled cartel man, his mouth and eyes open and blood seeping from a large hole in his forehead. *Good riddance!* Nicholas reached out, grasped the AK-47, and clutched it against his chest. He had absolutely no idea what to do next.

"This is the United States Coast Guard! This is your last warning. You will discard all weapons and stand with your hands above your head. Anyone holding a weapon or not standing still with both hands in plain sight will be shot without warning."

"You are going to kill us anyway!" Nicholas shouted.

"No," the voice replied. "If you surrender peacefully, you will be placed under arrest and transported safely to the United States to stand trial. If you continue to resist, you will be killed."

"Kenton, what do we do?" Nathan whispered desperately.

Nicholas looked at the assault rifle in his arms, then over at the dead cartel man. *It's hopeless. Try to save Nathan and Jayden if you can.* "Coast Guard, it was the dead man that shot at you! None of us have fired a gun tonight!"

"If that is true, it might work to your advantage at trial. But you must surrender NOW!"

Nicholas tossed the AK-47 aside and shouted, "Coast Guard, we agree to surrender! Don't shoot!"

"Very well. Stand slowly with your hands in the air."

Nicholas nodded at the other men, and the three put their hands in the air and stood.

"Good call," the disembodied voice continued. "Now, stay exactly where you are with your hands in the air until the boarding officers direct you to do otherwise."

Now, Nicholas could hear a boat engine off the port side, and an orange RHIB emerged from the darkness and nudged gently into the panga. Three men in combat gear scrambled on board, two holding handguns, the third a shotgun. The men carrying the handguns had them pointed at the deck, Nicholas was relieved to see, but the man with the shotgun pointed it in the general direction of Nicholas and his crew.

The shorter handgun-holding man stepped over to the cartel man, picked up the AK-47 from the deck, repositioned the fire selector to safe, and then put the sling over his shoulder. He looked at Nicholas and said, "Are you the vessel's master?"

"Yes, sir," Nicholas answered.

"I am Lieutenant Junior Grade Wyporek. You are under arrest for violation of United States law. You have the right to remain silent, and you have a right to have an attorney present during questioning. If you desire an attorney and cannot afford one, the court will appoint one before questioning. Do you understand these rights?"

"Yes, sir."

"Very well. For our safety and yours, this man will search your person. Do you understand?"

"Yes, sir."

The officer nodded at his companion, a large black man who holstered his weapon and began a head-to-foot search. When that was complete, he leaned over and said, "I'm going to handcuff you now. Please put your left hand back." After placing Nicholas's hands in flex cuffs, the big man said, "OK, sit down."

The arrest process was repeated on the other crewmen, then the officer called back the orange RHIB, and the three panga crew were helped aboard. The officer and the large black man followed, and the shotgun man remained aboard the panga. It was a quick trip to get alongside the white-colored Coast Guard ship. When the RHIB had been craned to deck level, Nicholas and his crew were helped on board. Two crewmen took them to a side area on the ship's deck where their flex cuffs were removed, and they were manacled to the deck. The three men sat silently, watched carefully by another Coast Guard man holding a shotgun.

The Coast Guard crew rigged a hawser to tow the panga into port. By the time they had completed the linkup and started the tow, the eastern horizon was already aglow with the coming sunrise. A short time later, two Coast Guard men unshackled Nicholas and brought him into what looked like a dining area. The officer who led the boarding was seated at one of the two tables, some papers spread out before him, and Nicholas was brought to the table and seated opposite the officer. After reading him his rights again, the officer asked if Nicholas wished to answer questions or make a statement.

"Will this help me at my trial?" Nicholas asked.

"I can't promise that," the officer replied.

"Very well, I'll talk," Nicholas said with resignation.

The officer pushed a piece of paper and pen in front of him. "This is a written explanation of your rights and a statement that you are waiving them. You may reassert those rights at any time during the questioning. If these terms are agreeable, please sign on the line. Nicholas nodded and signed the paper, which was then signed by the officer and one of the other coastguardsmen.

"Thank you," the officer said. "Now describe in detail, please, your actions of last night, starting with your departure from Bimini."

Nicholas provided a lengthy commentary of the panga's activity and his role as the master, emphasizing the duress he and his crew felt from the cartel man. The officer nodded, took notes, and uttered an occasional acknowledgment throughout the interview. Finally, Nicholas completed his narrative and said, "That's all I know."

The officer nodded and said, "I have a few questions for clarification. You said the cartel man started the gunfight during your first encounter with the Coast Guard. Is that correct?"

"Yes," Nicholas answered.

"And you did not participate in the gunfight because you were driving the boat, correct?"

"That is correct, sir. Only the cartel man had a weapon, and he is the only one who shot at the Coast Guard."

"And you drove your boat into the Coast Guard boat, correct?"

"Yes, sir, but just to get away from the gunfight. I was not trying to sink the boat, only to keep it from chasing me."

"Very well. Is there anything else you wish to add?"

"No, sir. That is all."

"Very well, thank you," the officer said, then nodded toward the other crewmen. As they took Nicholas's arms and helped him from the seat, the officer said, "Oh, one more thing. Were you aware that a Coast Guard seaman was killed during your incident with the boat?"

Nicholas felt faint, took a breath, and said, "No. I am very sorry to hear that. But as I said, the cartel man did the shooting, not me."

"You just drove the boat."

"Yes, sir."

"As it happens, the man who died was wounded by gunfire...in his arm, a non-fatal wound. When you rammed that boat, deliberately, by your admission, he was thrown overboard. And when he was helpless in the water, one of your propellers took off the top of his head."

"Oh, God!"

"That man had a young wife and a baby girl at home. Now they are going to have to bury him. Most of him, anyway. All because you wanted to help import poison into this country *for money*. You think about that, you son-of-a-bitch!" He turned to the crewman. "Get him out of here and keep him separated from the others."

"Yes, sir," the crewman holding his right arm said. As they walked out on deck, he whispered to Nicholas, "Go ahead and try something. *Please!*"

Haley

Haley was still in her chair on the Bridge. She was tired, but far too keyed up to get any sleep or even eat. The tow of the panga was going well; they were making a steady eight knots toward the Coast Guard base in Miami Beach, where the vessel and their prisoners would be handed over to the appropriate authorities. It was slow going, as the northern set of the Gulf Stream reduced their speed over the ground to a plodding four knots.

Haley turned at the sound of footsteps on the ladder and saw Ben walking through the bridge door. He stood by Haley and saluted. "Interview complete, Captain."

Haley returned the salute and said, "How did it go?"

"About what we figured, ma'am. The dead guy was the only shooter, and the elder Nicholas was the driver. I must regretfully admit to being remiss in not having informed the suspect of the victim's cause of death prior to his admission of guilt in the act that caused it." Ben smiled.

"I'm shocked, SHOCKED at your inattention to detail, XO!" Haley grinned in return. Her earlier concerns about her ability to connect and get sound advice were gone. Ben, in particular, had come through quite well, standing up to her when he felt it was needed and delivering practical and effective suggestions. "Seriously, awesome job today. When we tracked the *Miho Dujam*, Sam told me you guys were often creating tactics on the fly. I'm a believer now."

The jury was still out on whether their not strictly by the book tactics would meet with official approval, but it would be hard to argue with the results: three arrests, one cartel shooter dead, a vessel seized along with what looked to be just under a ton of cocaine. And, hopefully, eventually, justice for Seaman Justin Demarest, the young man killed in the ramming. It warmed her heart that Drake had already hit her up to contribute to the collection he'd started for the seaman's young family. The crew and she were in the right hands.

Part III - The Mission

Atlantic Ocean
The Bahamas
Turks and Caicos
Great Inagua
Matthew Town
Cuba
Windward Passage
Ile Ste. Michel
Guantanamo Bay
Haiti
Dominican Republic
Caribbean Sea

Chapter 13

Realpolitik

Office of the Commander, U.S. Southern Command, Doral, Florida
0922 EST, 3 December

Pennington

Pennington had a sense of déjà vu as he sat at the conference room table. He had been sitting in this room last April when he had been briefed on the Barbello mission. Pennington was the Director of JIATF South then. Army General Lamont Miller, Commander of SOUTHCOM, was sitting at the head of the table now and led that earlier meeting. Vice Admiral Jennifer Irving, Director of the DIA, had been sitting across the table as she was this morning. Captain Mercier, sitting to his right, was also present at that meeting, where she had introduced Pennington to the upgrades the Coast Guard had made on *Kauai*.

"Well, Harry, here we are again," Miller said with a soft southern accent, echoing Pennington's thoughts. Miller was a tall, solid man at six-foot-four and 220. The only changes between his appearance now and back when he was a middle linebacker for the University of Tennessee were his shaved head and the wrinkles he had gathered from years of standing in the sun in the commander's cupola of M1A1 Abrams tanks and M2 Bradley fighting vehicles. "I'm coming cap in hand to borrow that nifty little patrol boat of yours."

"Yes, sir. I thought as much." Pennington nodded. He had a genuine fondness for Miller, acquired when he worked for the general during his last job. Pennington did not have the same affection for Irving, whom he regarded as a callous and conniving asshole. He turned an icy stare at her. "I presume this is another DIA operation?"

"Correct, Admiral," Irving replied with an expressionless face. She was an average-sized, graying blond woman in her early fifties. Like most career intelligence officers, she was also nondescript, wearing conservative business clothing rather than her U.S. Navy uniform. "We need the ability to insert and retrieve a team covertly onto foreign territory, and *Kauai* is our best option."

"What country?" Pennington asked.

"Haiti."

"You're joking," Pennington scoffed. "The country is an end-to-end basket case. You could land the entire 82nd Airborne in the middle of Port Au Prince with no one noticing."

"Not all of it is a basket case," Irving responded. "The island of Ile Ste. Michel, for instance."

"The one with the Chinese mine?" Pennington asked. "I suppose I would agree with that. As far as we know, the Chinese miners are the only living things on the island. I can see the irritation associated with a Chinese foothold in this hemisphere, but my understanding is that mine has been a bust. Am I in error?"

"Yes and no. You are correct that output is meager, but that is only because the Chinese need it to be. If they wanted, they could produce more out of that location than the rest of the world combined."

"They are leaving profit on the table? Why would they do that?"

"Admiral, you'll need some background. I brought my expert, Dr. Gregg Kenan, who can explain exactly why we are in a situation here. Doctor?"

Kenan stood and took a handheld remote control from the table. He was a balding, shorter-than-average man wearing a plain charcoal gray suit with a blue tie—more-or-less the stereotypic image of a college professor. He clicked a button on the remote and said, "Good morning, General, Admiral. I have a PowerPoint briefing prepared if I can direct your attention to the screen. I need to open by stating that this presentation is classified Secret, No Foreign."

"Understood," Pennington said.

"Thank you, sir," Kenan nodded. "I'll begin with a brief history leading to the current situation."

Kenan briefed that for most of human history, Ile Ste. Michel had been forty square miles of lifeless, windswept rock north of Cap Haitien on Haiti's north coast. It had no reliable water sources and thus none of the forests or arable land that many of the islands in the area possessed. There was no indigenous animal life; only mangroves and the hardiest rock-dwelling plants survived on the island. Neither did it have any natural harbors—even the pirates common to the region in the late 17th and early 18th centuries shunned it. It remained nothing more than a hazard to navigation until the late 1970s, when surveys detected one of the richest rare-earth elements deposits known. Even this elicited little interest at the time.

As electronic engineering evolved and the role rare-earths played in the manufacture of innovative technology burgeoned, the potential value of the Ile Ste. Michel deposit grew. Unfortunately, the upfront costs, which included the construction of a port and harbor, roads, housing for the workers, and fuel and water storage, were considerable. Several private corporations in North America and Europe examined and rejected the project as too risky with a government as unstable as Haiti. Government backing and financing were required, and no western government was willing to risk taxpayer funding on an engineering project principally benefitting a private corporation and Haiti.

However, the Chinese were game and made an agreement with the Haitian government to develop the island on a profit-sharing basis as part of their Belt and Road Initiative, or BRI. Western observers were puzzled by the move. China already controlled nearly all the rare-earth mining. Even on a profit-sharing basis, opening a vast new source in Haiti would only drive down the global market and cause significant pain to their suppliers at home. The true motive behind the Chinese move was revealed only after the mining operation opened.

Production from the mine was very low—less than a tenth of what most analysts and mining engineers had predicted, even after the construction was complete and the site was fully staffed. Observers wondered if the deposit was not as rich as initially thought, and they rechecked the surveys and samples but could find no errors. Worry that the mine was a cover for constructing a strategic base by the Chinese military spurred a CIA effort that "acquired" the documentation behind the deal. The terms of the agreement in these documents were astonishing.

The Chinese agreed to loan Haiti the funds required to build the mining facility and all supporting infrastructure in exchange for a thirty-year exclusive lease on Ile Ste. Michel by the Sino-American Mining Corporation. SAMC was one of the many Chinese Communist Party-owned companies working on engineering projects under the BRI aegis. By the lease terms, SAMC would share fifty percent of the profits from the mining activity with the Haitian government *after extracting whatever funding was required to service the debt.* The Haitian government also agreed to the presence of a small People's Liberation Army security force and to allow the port to service People's Liberation Army Navy warships without restrictions or even notification. The only caveats the Haitians insisted upon were that the port could not be used as an advance base for offensive military operations or any other activities contrary to international law. They did not want to get drawn into any wars or diplomatic sanctions.

The agreement was the most ingenious debt-trap diplomacy operation ever devised. Keeping mine production low artificially kept down the global supply of rare-earth elements, maintaining the profitability of China's domestic industry. It also allowed just enough profit to service Haiti's loan debt interest, keeping the nation servile in China's regional efforts. In effect, China had conned Haiti into funding both a mining operation that maintained China's near-monopoly on rare-earth elements and a Chinese military base on Haitian soil. The Haitian government officials familiar with the agreement's details either quietly went along in exchange for a generous stipend or suffered an unfortunate death in the endemic violence of the capital.

The details of the Sino-Haitian agreement were a closely guarded secret within U.S. diplomatic circles—the embarrassment of an agreement establishing a Chinese base practically in their backyard was too profound for any public release. Diplomatic efforts to induce Haiti to void the deal came to nothing. Although it proved a terrible bargain for Haiti, it was entirely legal under international law, and there was little incentive within the Haitian government to impose their sovereign rights on the island.

"That concludes my briefing, sirs. Do you have any questions?" Kenan asked.

"Yes," Pennington replied. "I'm as outraged by this as anyone else, but I cannot see what the U.S. can do about it, much less the Coast Guard. Why am I here?"

"That is outside my purview, sir. I'll need to refer you to Admiral Irving."

Pennington turned to Miller. "I have no more questions of the doctor, General."

"Neither have I. Thank you, Dr. Kenan," Miller said with a nod. After Kenan returned to his seat, Miller continued, "OK, Jenn. Now, what the hell *are* we doing here?"

"General, we think we might have the opportunity to show the Haitians the Chinese broke this agreement, which will allow us to come in, pay off the debt and open that mine for real. With that mine operating at full capacity, the breakeven point for the profit to pay off the investment would only be a few years. Then it's pure goodness: profit for both us and Haiti, removing a strategic threat from our hemisphere, not to mention a blow to the Chinese rare-earth monopoly and their international standing."

"Sounds fantastic. Exactly how do Harry and I fit into this opportunity?" Miller asked.

"A little more background is in order, General. You recall the last time we gathered together, it was to deal with a threat created by the 252 Syndicate?"

"How could I forget?" Miller answered.

"We have a laptop seized from one of their smuggling vessels." Irving nodded toward Pennington. "Thanks to the boldness of an officer from the very patrol boat that carried out the last operation, I might add."

Pennington nodded in return. He had been briefed on the rescue of the sex-trafficked women and the seized laptop.

Irving continued, "Our crypto techs went through it and found evidence of a linkage between that organization and the Chinese. There is nothing we can take to court yet, but the collateral information and metadata have allowed us to penetrate the 252's communications and data at a pretty high level. We know from these penetrations that a senior member of the 252s will come to Ile Ste. Michel for direct consultation with the Chinese director of mine operations about three days from now. He will fly by private jet into the Holguín airbase in Cuba, then to the Chinese port facility by seaplane. We intend to crash that meeting, grab the 252 man and any documents of the syndicate's collusion with the Chinese, and get out."

"Seems a little fishy to me, a higher-up taking that kind of risk when he can send a flunky. Are you sure this isn't some sort of spoof to embarrass us?" Pennington asked.

Irving nodded. "We thought of that too, but we think the probability is very low. We would see other indicators if that were the case. Why send a boss? They are building a brothel there to service the miners and a depot for arms smuggling. Those facilities were constructed at a suffi-cient distance from the Chinese port to maintain plausible deniability. The boss wants a look, plus check the feasibility of shipping cargo there by air to avoid our surface patrols, particularly the human cargo. The intercept of their freighter cost them a substantial amount of arms besides twenty-plus sex slaves, and he's on the hook to fix that supply chain for the next run."

"OK. I get why you want to grab him at the crime scene, so to speak, but why do you need *Kauai*?" Pennington asked.

"We can't use a helo in there without blowing the mission, and the ground is too rough to risk a parachute insertion. The narrow waters and shoals around the island make it too big a risk for a sub, even if we could get one there within three days. Our only chance is to close the coast and insert the team by small boat the night before in a remote cove near the 252 depot and then retrieve them by the same means after the snatch. *Kauai* can get in closer to shore than any gray hull and not attract any attention, given all the Coast Guard activity in the area."

Miller leaned forward. "How many do you intend to insert, and what opposition will they have?"

Irving replied, "We will have a team of four. We also have a special operations boat and cradle from Little Creek in the air now. It is a lightweight design that can carry the team plus three to four of your crew without overloading *Kauai*'s crane. Our best information is that the 252s are running light right now, about a dozen thugs with the usual small arms."

"And what about the Chinese?"

"One of their reinforced security platoons, about fifty men, supported by two VN-4 light armored personnel carriers. No other vehicles or aircraft that we are aware of."

"And their sea forces?" Pennington asked.

"A couple of tugs and small service boats and one Shanghai-IV class gunboat."

Pennington asked, "And what support will *Kauai* have?"

Irving glanced between Miller and Pennington. "None."

Pennington's jaw dropped. "*None*? Admiral Irving, I presume you know the capabilities of a Shanghai-IV. Do you know what a one-ten, even a souped-up one like *Kauai,* brings to the fight? One twenty-five-millimeter popgun." Pennington was familiar with the Chinese Shanghai-IV from his war college days. "The Shanghai-IV is faster and has radar-directed, twin thirty-seven-millimeter mounts fore and aft that can rip *Kauai* to shreds a mile before she can get in range with her twenty-five."

"We aren't sending *Kauai* into a fight with the Chinese. The operation will be miles from their base, and they are unlikely to rush to the defense of a criminal gang. We evaluate the chance *Kauai* would encounter Chinese forces as near zero. If we move a large support force down there, we will alert the opposition. We might as well not bother running the op."

Pennington was having difficulty controlling his fury. "If that's the level of backup we can expect, maybe we shouldn't!"

Irving's eyes narrowed. "I have my orders, Admiral Pennington. Soon, you will too."

Pennington put his hands on the table and began to stand when Miller reached over and gripped his arm. When Pennington glanced over, Miller shook his head, and he sat.

"Alright, Jenn," Miller said. "When do your boat and team arrive?"

"Their C-130 should land at Miami International in two hours. The boat is containerized for a tractor-trailer, so offload and hook up will be quick. Figure four hours tops to pier side at Base Miami Beach."

"Very well. We'll take it from here," Miller said.

Irving said, "I think I should be involved in the planning."

Miller stared back coldly. "I disagree. You delivered your tasking, and your role is at an end." When she returned the stare, Miller continued, "That will be all, thank you."

Irving stood and turned toward the door, with Kenan scrambling to his feet to follow. Once they had departed and the conference room door closed, Pennington turned to Miller. "My God, General! She really doesn't give a damn! I didn't think a human being could be that cold-blooded. You can't expect me to dish those kids up with no backup."

"Harry, I'd send a task group there if I had one, but I don't. She's right in that we need to take a shot at this if we can, but I have no intention of sending your folks in with no support." He pressed a button on his phone. "Chief, I need to talk to General Ryan at Air Combat Command ASAP. Thanks." He hung up the receiver and turned to Pennington. "Mick Ryan owes me a favor or two, and I'll get you some electronic attack backup and TACAIR if I can."

Pennington closed his eyes and shook his head. After a moment, he looked up again and said, "Thank you, sir. Are you going to tell Irving?"

"Are you kidding? Why do you think I booted her ass outta here? This is still my command, and if she wants to rat me out to the bosses, fine. I'll go out clean."

"Thank you, sir," Pennington repeated. "If you can excuse Jane and me, we need to get orders to *Kauai* to get this goat rodeo set up."

"Absolutely! Captain, coordinate rendezvous times and locations with my J3 staff as soon as your people have the op sketched out."

"Will do, General," Mercier replied.

"Good luck, you guys. You've got my number if you need me to knock any heads together."

"Thank you, General," Pennington said as he and Mercier got to their feet and shook hands with Miller. As they walked to the car after leaving the office, Pennington asked, "How long before *Kauai* pulls into BMB?"

Mercier checked her watch and said, "An hour, sir."

"Pass them a message for the CO, XO, and Ops Chief to report to my office by fourteen hundred. Tell them to bring the DIA team lead with them."

"Very good, sir."

USCG Cutter Kauai, moored, Coast Guard Base Miami Beach, Florida
12:47 EST, 3 December

Ben

Ben watched in deep concern as *Kauai*'s crane took the load of the special operations boat parked on the trailer next to the ship. It was engineered to be lightweight rather than durable but still weighed about twenty percent more than the cutter boat, medium *Kauai* customarily shipped. Drake had assured Ben the new crane could easily handle the load, but as XO, he needed to see for himself. The new crane was a significant improvement over *Kauai*'s original unit, cut in half by a rocket hit at Barbello. They had already installed the boat's cradle, actually more of an adapter to the existing cutter boat cradle.

The crane groaned slightly as the boat lifted from its trailer and rose to the height of the boat deck. Bondurant was operating the crane, his face frozen in concentration, watching the pivot and swing of the boat as the crane turned to bring it over the cradle. Drake stood behind Bondurant, scanning the crane and hydraulic connections. The boat descended onto the cradle, and Drake turned to give Ben a thumbs-up.

Lee, standing next to Ben throughout the evolution, grunted. "Looks like a real pig, XO."

"Need a pig to haul around nine guys, Petty Officer Lee." He turned toward her and added, "Think you can drive her?"

Lee turned toward Ben with a raised eyebrow. "*Really, sir? Puleeze!*"

Ben nodded. "Just the same, we'll get you some time on it before the mission to get the feel. Get together with the DIA guys to match pointers as soon as possible."

"WILCO, XO. Have fun downtown with the grownups."

"Yes, I'm sure," Ben said as he turned toward the ship and boarded. A short walk brought him to Haley's cabin, where she and Frankle conferred. "Special boat is safely aboard and being secured, Captain. There were no problems with the crane."

"Excellent," Haley said, then turned to Frankle. "Might as well push off in case there's traffic or other Miami B.S."

"Suits me," Frankle said. He was still wearing his suit and tie, forgoing a change to more casual clothes until after the meeting.

"I'll grab Chief and meet you at the car," Ben said, then started toward Hopkins's stateroom. He knocked on the door and stood as Hopkins emerged. "Ready for the fun, Chief?"

"Semper," Hopkins replied with a smile. "Lead on, sir."

It was a short drive to the Brickell Plaza Federal Building housing the Seventh Coast Guard District offices. After a brief delay through the metal detectors at the entrance, the three Coast Guard members and DIA agent made their way to the Chief of Staff's office to await their meeting with Pennington. Mercier smiled, stood from her desk as she saw them, and said, "Come in, please!" She shook hands with Haley and added, "That was a four-point-oh job with the panga, Haley."

"Thank you, ma'am," Haley said, beaming.

Mercier then moved to Frankle. "Agent Frankle, I'm Jane Mercier. It's a pleasure to meet you."

"Thank you, Captain," Frankle replied.

Mercier then turned to Ben and shook his hand, "Ben, seems you're teamed up with the DIA again."

"Yes, ma'am. I just updated my next of kin notification and servicemember's life insurance data."

She turned to Hopkins with a grin and shook her hand. "Chief, it's good to see you again. Are you keeping these two on the right path?"

"I'm doing my utmost to rise to the challenge, Captain."

"The world is in the right hands then. Please take a seat. The boss will be available in a few minutes. So, Agent Frankle, have you briefed them on what's going on?"

"No, ma'am. I had no orders to do so, and, as you might imagine, we're a fail-passive organization."

"Oh, my," Mercier said with a frown, then looked over at Hopkins. "Chief, could you shut the door, please?"

"Yes, ma'am," Hopkins replied, then closed the door and returned to her seat.

"Thank you. OK. Ben, that laptop you took off the *Miho Dujam* gave us a lot of information on the 252 organization and created quite a stir at the highest levels. In short, we're sending *Kauai* to the Haitian island of Ile Ste. Michel to seize one of their top guys and transport him here for interrogation. You'll close on the island, insert the DIA team, then wait offshore until the following night and return to pick them up."

Haley leaned forward and said, "Captain, I infer from the fact we are meeting with the District Commander that there is more to this than a snatch and grab of some criminal kingpin."

"Yes. The island is under the control of the Chinese."

Yikes! Ben thought, then said, "What kind of control, ma'am? Are we looking at a fight?"

"No, Ben." Mercier shook her head. "We'll discuss this in more detail in the meeting with the admiral, but our intention and belief are that we can avoid contact with the Chinese forces on the island." At that point, the phone on her desk buzzed, and she answered. "Yes, sir, they're here. Yes, sir." She hung up and said, "OK, we can go in now."

They all stood, and the four visitors followed Mercier into a conference room where Pennington was already standing. After introductions, they sat at the conference table with Pennington at the head, Haley, Ben, and Hopkins on one side, and Mercier and Frankle on the other.

"Thank you all for coming," Pennington said. "Agent Frankle, do you go by Arthur?"

"Art, Admiral," Frankle replied.

"Art it is. OK, folks, I know you're wondering why this is such a big deal. The fact is, we have an opportunity to not only nip a 252 incursion in this hemisphere in the bud, but maybe root out a Chinese one to boot. I'm not sure how into geopolitics you all are, but Ile Ste. Michel was a real black eye for us. While we were dithering over whether to invest in development and how much the taxpayers should be willing to risk, the Chinese swooped in and got a lock on what is probably the richest rare-earth element source in the world. At the same time, they built a port that could double as a small navy base right in our backyard.

"They have a thirty-year lease on that island they are maintaining using a debt-trap they laid on the Haitian government. The agreement is rock solid legally, but it has a provision we hope to exploit. Namely, the Chinese will not engage in any violations of international law. We have good intelligence that the Chinese are in cahoots with the 252s, at least locally on Ile Ste. Michel. What we need is evidence, and that is why we are having you take Art's team down there. There's no way to insert them by air and not enough time to develop the networks and cutouts to go in-country in Haiti to pull this off. So, we will send you down there to blend into the AMIO crowd during the day and insert and retrieve Art's team at night. This is the type of mission we designed *Kauai* to do. Any questions of me so far?"

"No, sir," all three of the *Kauai* personnel replied.

"Good. OK, Art, I'll turn it over to you for the next part."

"Thank you, Admiral," Frankle said as he stood and grabbed the remote. He clicked a button, and a topographical map of a landmass titled "Ile Ste. Michel" appeared on the large screen. Frankle put the remote down and walked over to the screen. He then hooked his left thumb in his belt and pointed at the far-right edge of the landmass on the screen with his right hand. "The Chinese constructed the port here on this headland. They concentrated all the admin buildings, warehouses, fuel and water storage, and residences in this area. Their method is to erect temporary buildings where they are actively processing to house the heavy equipment. As you can see, all Chinese activity is concentrated on the island's eastern half right of this ridge." He pointed to a zone of higher elevation, roughly bisecting the island.

"The 252s, with Chinese help, constructed a second site over here, west of the ridge, with residences, warehouses, water storage, and power generation. The site also includes a barracks serving as a brothel catering to the Chinese miners. Morale has been an enormous problem, and the Chinese are paying the 252s a premium to staff that brothel with European women as a worker perk." He glanced over at Haley, Ben, and Hopkins. "That group of women you intercepted was the first contingent.

"The *Miho Dujam*'s loss was a significant hit in terms of prostitution revenue, so the 252s are trying a more secure route by smuggling the women in by air. The 252 boss will pioneer this, flying by private jet into Holguín in Cuba and seaplane to the Chinese port. He plans to stay overnight to inspect the operation, confer with his Chinese counterpart, and return by the same route. We intend to grab him that night."

Frankle pointed at an indentation near the southwest corner of the island. "There is a small cove here, masked from both facilities by intervening high ground we can use for landing and pickup. You have good water to about two hundred yards from shore—I propose we launch the boat from five hundred just to be safe." He traced a path northeast on the map with his finger. "We have high-res satellite shots showing this as an optimal path to this high ground west of the 252 site. It has suitable cover for us to observe their pattern of life during the day and close to engage that night. Once we penetrate, we grab the big cheese and anything that looks like documentation and egress. If we're lucky, we can grab one of the SUVs they use to run around the island. If not, we should still have plenty of time to hoof it to the beach before first light." He turned to the group. "Any questions, Admiral?"

"Yes, Art. What are your rules of engagement?"

"Sir, we will kill any 252 members we meet other than the bigwig. If we run into any Chinese, they will be stunned and sedated, and the only one we take with us is the 252 bigwig. Do you have any other questions, sir?"

"Good here," Pennington answered.

"I have a question," Haley said. "What forces do the Chinese have, and what's the likelihood we will tangle with them?"

"They have a security force of about fifty men, supported by two VN-4 light armored personnel carriers, but no aircraft. The VN-4s have mounted 7.62-millimeter machine guns, but their armor is intended to protect against small arms—armor-piercing rounds from your twenty-five-millimeter will have no problem penetrating. There is a naval threat in the form of a Shanghai-IV class gunboat; its thirty-seven-millimeter guns will do you in before you can even get in range. That's the bad news. The good news is that we do not see them engaging to protect the 252s. As long as we stay west of the big ridge, we think they will leave us be."

"And what if they don't?" Haley asked.

"Um...." Frankle began.

"I'll take that one," Pennington interrupted. "SOUTHCOM is arranging for electronic warfare and tactical aircraft to cover your retreat if necessary."

"I see. Thank you, sir. And what are our rules of engagement?"

"Unless otherwise directed, you will operate independently under the national defense mission code. You will not engage in any other mission activity, even search and rescue, until this mission is complete. You will not engage or fire on any Chinese forces unless fired upon. Do you have any questions about that?"

"Yes, sir. What do we do if the risk of engaging the Chinese elevates during the retrieval phase?"

Pennington looked at her coldly. "You will use your best judgment informed by the principle of calculated risk, and you will not take *any* action likely to result in engagement with Chinese forces. Is that clear?"

"Very clear, sir."

Ben watched Haley exchange a glance with Frankle across the table. Pennington had just ordered her to abandon Frankle's team to their fate if she thought it necessary to avoid contact with the Chinese. The revelation appeared to have no effect on the agent's countenance. *Holy shit, he's OK with that!*

Pennington's face softened. "I want to emphasize that I have every confidence in you and your crew. I appreciate this is a hairy one, but I would not have agreed to it if I were not convinced you and your people would come back safely."

"Thank you, sir. To quote my XO, it is one helluva break-in patrol."

Chapter 14

Approaches

***USCG Cutter Kauai, Old Bahama Channel,
sixteen nautical miles north-northeast of
Guardalavaca, Cuba
08:12 EST, 4 December***

Ben

Ben and Hopkins sat in the messdeck with the four DIA team members for detailed planning of the expeditionary operation kicking off that night. As soon as the last breakfast meals were consumed and the remnants cleared away, the messdeck was placed off-limits, and Frankle and his team covered the tables with a large topographical map of Ile Ste. Michel and the latest satellite photos. The distance from the cove where the team would land and the high ground overseeing the 252 facilities was about two miles as the crow flies and probably half-again that distance over the intervening broken ground. The return route was shorter and more direct, thanks to the unimproved roads the Chinese had graded around the island's periphery and to the 252 facilities. Still, Ben couldn't imagine fleeing nearly two miles on foot while carrying an unconscious man.

The messdeck planning session reminded Ben of the special operations course he attended at Quantico the previous March. One exercise was an overland trek to a surprise assault on an insurgent position. The same types of terrain maps and satellite photos were employed, and the common considerations of time-distance, terrain, and contingencies had to be considered. That was where the comparison ended. Unlike Ben's group of novices fumbling through planning with instructors rolling their eyes or giving prompts ranging from "have you considered...?" to "are you really this stupid?!", Frankle and his team moved briskly through each step on the land op without hesitation or uncertainty.

Besides Frankle, another familiar face was at the table, his partner Lashon Bell. He had been on the DIA land team in the Resolution Key operation in January and had been present when Ben first met Victoria. Bell had been grievously wounded in a firefight with the 252s a day-and-a-half later and had been restored to full duty only months ago. He was very much like Bondurant, mid-thirties with a shaved head, powerfully built and quiet, although not as tall. Bell and Frankle were in their element in the planning meeting—they were both originally in Marine Corps recon units before being recruited into the DIA.

The other two members of Frankle's team were also involved in the January operation, but at a remote location. William "Billy" Gerard was a forty-ish, well-built man about Ben's height with light brown, close-cropped hair and a full, short-trimmed beard. He had also shipped aboard *Kauai* with Simmons on the Barbello mission. Steve Kelly was in his mid-thirties, a couple of inches taller, slim like Ben and clean-shaven, with black hair, close-cropped like Frankle and Gerard. This was the first time he and Ben had met. Unlike Frankle and Bell, Gerard and Kelly were not military veterans, but entered the clandestine service shortly after graduating from college.

After accounting for the route and terrain and the fact that they would navigate using GPS and night-vision equipment, the team calculated they would need between two-and-a-half and three hours to walk from the cove to the observation post and another half hour to dig in and camouflage themselves. They would need to be in place no later than first light, 05:17, meaning *Kauai* had to drop them off no later than 01:45. After observing the numbers and positions of the 252 personnel around the site and their patterns of patrol and movement, they would await the top dog. According to the itinerary, he would arrive at the Chinese port around 14:00 and, after a brief meeting with the lead Chinese administrator, leave for the gang's facility around 17:00. After spending the night, he was due to fly out on the seaplane around 09:00 the following day. Sometime between sunset, 17:09 local time, and 01:00, Frankle and his team would creep forward, silently kill any sentries, seize one of the gang's vehicles while disabling the others, grab the top dog and run to the beach to meet with *Kauai*. They would be over the horizon with their quarry by first light—a piece of cake.

The Chinese were the wild card. Everything depended on them staying put in their facilities across the ridge to the east. Several high-endurance reconnaissance UAVs had overflown the island in recent days, building a pattern of life. Everything seemed as expected—the Chinese were keen to avoid any apparent contact with their criminal neighbors and thus ran no land patrols or surveillance across the ridge. The gunboat showed no sign of movement during the observation period. Frankle was sure that a single sortie by the gunboat would burn through two to three months' worth of the diesel fuel used by the generators, vehicles, and equipment at the facility, so routine patrolling was unlikely.

Ben had no illusions about the gunboat—*Kauai* would be no match for her in any straight-up fight. Their only hope of survival was to avoid contact, and stealth was the order of the day. There was no sign of any radar facilities on the island beyond those organic to the gunboat. Any portable sets used by the Chinese or the 252s would have difficulty picking up *Kauai* beyond one mile. Within three miles of the shore, *Kauai* would maneuver on battery power only to avoid any dedicated or incidental listeners. The special operations boat they were carrying also had a low-power/low-noise signature mode if speed was not at a premium.

The four DIA men finished their discussion and noted the routes and timing in their notebooks. They all turned to Ben and Hopkins, and Frankle said, "OK, folks. You've heard the plan, and we're interested in your views and critiques."

Ben and Hopkins shared a glance, and then she said, "The shoreline is almost open, and the cove's position on the leeward side of the island pretty much guarantees a suitable sea state for operations. I don't see any problem from the maritime side. I'll leave any comments on the land ops to the XO—he's got the training, not me."

Ben turned to Frankle. "Art, you seem pretty confident you can grab a vehicle and knock out the rest. What happens if that doesn't work out? What if you miss one? These guys aren't idiots; they'll know you had to come by boat, and they'll move to cut you off from the only viable landing site: the south shore."

Frankle nodded. "Yes, that's probably the riskiest factor in the op. But we've seen nothing on the overflights indicating they're dispersing the vehicles or running any active patrols."

"Alright," Ben said as he reached for the topographical map and one of the aerial photographs. "I get you can get off the beach through this cut here," he said, pointing at the map showing a gentler slope off the beach to the shallow plateau that formed the island's base. "But looking at these photos, I don't see any way to get a vehicle through here without cutting a bunch of trees. What happens if you have armed pursuit?"

"Any chance *Kauai* could pick them off for us?"

"Nope. We can only do direct fire, and that foliage is too thick, and we can't just hose it down with the fifties without hitting you guys." Ben looked between the map and the photo. "What about this spot here?" he said, pointing at a gap between two copses of trees. "Good cover for an ambush and good fields of fire. A couple of us can set up and take out anyone on your tail after you pass. Once we stop them, we can hightail it to the boat. If your plan works and there's no pursuit, no harm done."

Frankle bent over, looking closely at the map. "What do you think, Billy? Can you find that hole while on the run?"

Gerard shook his head. "Not in the dark. At least, not without a marker." He looked at Ben. "You guys OK with chemlight markers?"

"Should be OK if we hold off lighting them until you get here, about five hundred yards away. It will serve them as well as you, but we want them coming into the crossfire, anyway. We'll set up with Mark 48s—that will cut through anything without armor. We want to be sure we stop them." The Mark 48 was a lightweight thirty caliber machine gun of Belgian design carried by special forces operators. Its larger round packed around twice the impact force of their standard M4 carbine bullets. Ben, Bondurant, Guerrero, and Lopez had special training to use the two carried by *Kauai.*

Frankle stared at Ben. "That will do it, alright."

After a pause, Ben asked, "What?"

"I don't know. Something this hardcore is a little out of character for you."

"I'm not itching for a fight, Art. I'd be a happy man never pulling a trigger again off the range. But Resolution and the *Miho Dujam* taught me these guys aren't playing soft and cuddly, and neither should I. It's their choice."

"Roger that." Frankle nodded.

"One more thing," Ben said. "You heard our orders. If the Chinese weigh-in, the boss has no choice but to leave you behind. Are you OK with that?"

"That's the way it is sometimes."

Ben shook his head. "Amazing. I'll take a hurricane rescue any day over your world of work."

Frankle grinned. "Oh, it's not that bad. We wouldn't be going if the odds weren't right."

Ben pushed the chart and photo away. "OK, I've got enough to brief the boss. Do you need anything more from us?"

"No, good to go here."

Ben checked his watch. "We'll be approaching Great Inagua in about two-and-a-half hours to train with the boat. You're welcome to watch."

"Thanks, I think we would," Frankle said.

Haley

Three days. Haley wondered at the realization that she had held this command for only three days. Her ship had pursued and stopped an armed and dangerous drug smuggler with gunfire during that time, killing a murderous suspect. Now, her XO and chief operations specialist were laying out plans for a covert operation on foreign soil that included the terms "ambush position" and "fields of fire." Haley stared at the chart while her brain came to grips with the reality of it.

"Ma'am?" Ben asked, snapping Haley out of her thoughts.

"Wha.... Oh, I'm sorry, XO. I guess I'm having difficulty taking it all in."

"Yes, ma'am. This is the worst case, naturally. If Frankle's team disables all the other vehicles, we'll be able to get out without firing a shot."

"No, XO, that isn't the worst case by a long shot. The worst case is that damn Chinese gunboat pins us to the shore."

"Yes, Captain. But nobody thinks that's going to happen, me included. Why would they stick their necks out for the 252s? It wouldn't make any sense."

"Crazier things have happened. Let's hope I don't have to make the hard choice. Now, as far as personnel, what are your recommendations?"

"Lee, Lopez, and me in the boat."

"If you are taking the Mark 48s, wouldn't it be better to have Guerrero with you?"

"We are all better off with him as Overwatch, ma'am. Lopez is fully up to speed on the gun."

"OK, why you instead of Bondurant?"

"That's kinda my job here, Captain," Ben answered with a tilt of his head. "Also, I'm pretty sure we're better off with him working the crane, and I'd rather have him around to pull someone out of the boat than the reverse." After a pause, he added, "Besides, he has a wife and two kids."

"That's true, but it's not the principal consideration. What happens if I go down?"

"I can't picture a scenario where you go down, and there's anything salvageable left behind, ma'am."

Holy shit! Are we really *talking like this?* "Very well. Do you see any problems with this new boat?"

"I don't think so. Lee thinks it's a pig, but she's trading a sports car for a family van in her view. The practice runs will definitely help; at least she can get a feel for it. I'd like to do a full load-out dress rehearsal at Great Inagua with your permission. I know COB said the crane would be fine, but I'd like to see it work before getting into dangerous waters."

Haley nodded. "Concur. You think we can get the DIA team to go along with it?"

"I don't think that will be a problem. Frankle has already expressed an interest in watching the try-outs. In any case, I can be *very* persuasive," Ben said with a grin.

"Very well, make it so." Haley smiled back. Ben's grin was infectious, and she was seeing why Sam had such faith in him. "Is there anything else?"

"No, ma'am, that about covers it."

Haley turned to Hopkins, whose face remained devoid of expression. "Chief, anything to add?"

"No, Captain," Hopkins answered.

OK, it ends here. "XO, this is a scary place, but you've made it easier. Thank you. Now, if you'll excuse us, I'd like to have a word with Chief Hopkins."

"Very good, ma'am," Ben said as he stood, then closed the door as he left.

Here goes. "Chief, Commander Powell said you were his ace in the hole, that he could count on you to give him straight advice and feedback. I'll be frank that I'm not getting that vibe from you."

"I'm sorry to hear that, Captain," Hopkins said.

"Perhaps you are. In any case, whatever this is between us, we need to get it sorted out before we go in harm's way. So, I'm offering you a free shot. For the next few minutes, no rank exists here. Lay out your issues with me, and I'll listen."

"Captain, I am a professional, and I will do whatever it takes to get through the mission and bring the crew and boat home safely. If I think you are making a mistake that threatens that outcome, I'll let you know."

"Good to hear. Now, I'll take a straight answer to my original question, if you please."

Hopkins raised her left eyebrow. "Right. Two issues, the biggest one first. It chaps me royally when someone else gets jammed up for something I did."

"You're referring to the XO?"

"I am. He's one of the finest men I have ever known. The dressing down you gave him in front of COB and me was just wrong, ma'am."

"Chief, Mr. Wyporek is not 'jammed up,' quite the contrary. And it was not a dressing down—I would have handled anything like that privately. My purpose was so that you and COB could help him with the transition. I'm pretty sure he would never dime me out to the crew or you as the reason he turned formal all of a sudden. You helped with that, I presume?"

"Yes, ma'am," Hopkins replied.

"Good. Mission accomplished. Now, what's the other beef?"

"That 'Girl Power' session you held before the change of command. I hope you don't plan on that being a regular thing."

Haley was surprised by both the subject and Hopkins's term for it, but kept a poker face. "No, that was not my intention."

"I'm relieved to hear it, ma'am. I realize you meant well, but it backfired badly. In case you haven't caught on to this already, Zuccaro is a troublemaker, and that little session empowered her. Don't get me wrong; she's good at her job, but I've had to come down on her before for being too flirty. Now she's smug, and the rest of the junior crew is wary of her, except for Lee, who, given a chance, would throw her ass overboard."

"Point taken. Is this an issue I need to take for action?"

For the first time, Hopkins smiled. "No, Captain. This one has two stops before it gets to you. I just needed to know I had support for a chief's intervention."

"Always. What's the second stop?"

"The XO, ma'am. He's young and amiable, but he's not a soft touch. You're really the last resort."

"His stock continues to rise. So, is there anything else? Now's the time to clear the air."

"That will do for me. Thank you for the chance to...."

"Bitch?"

"Yes, that's the word for it, Captain."

"Happy to oblige. Please keep us straight, Chief," Haley said as she stood and offered her hand.

"*Semper*, ma'am," Hopkins replied as she shook Haley's hand.

USCG Cutter Kauai, Atlantic Ocean, five nautical miles southeast of Matthew Town, Bahamas
13:27 EST, 4 December

Ben

They were cruising at an easy twenty-five knots in the special forces boat. Lee was at the helm, Frankle and his team distributed forward of the helm console, Ben and Lopez sitting aft, and five ten-gallon containers filled with seawater to simulate the weight of their arms and equipment, plus their expected passenger. The heavily loaded boat maneuvered as sluggishly as Lee expected, but its powerful engines still delivered a good turn of speed.

Ben keyed his radio. "*Kauai*, *Kauai*-One, stability checks complete. Ready for the high-speed run."

"*Kauai*-One, *Kauai*. We're ready here," Williams's voice replied.

"Petty Officer Lee, feel like opening her up?" Ben shouted.

"Hell, yes!" Lee replied. "In the boat, prepare for a speed run!"

Lee turned the boat to run parallel with *Kauai*, then pushed the throttle levers forward. The boat picked up speed quickly in the calm waters in the lee of Great Inagua island, creating a pleasant cooling breeze and the dazzling rainbows of spray as the boat slammed through the small waves. Ben looked aft, briefly watching their cream-white wake spreading on the dark blue sea behind them. The DIA men were grinning and looking out over the boat's sides, enjoying the warm sunshine. Ben remembered that just the previous day, the men had left the freezing temperatures of Washington, DC behind—for a while anyway, this was like a tropical vacation to them. Ben's smile faded when he remembered what they faced this evening. He checked his watch—three minutes—and keyed his radio again. "*Kauai*, *Kauai*-One. How's it looking?"

"*Kauai*-One, *Kauai*, thirty-four point six knots," Williams replied.

"Roger. Are you ready for practice approaches?"

"Affirmative. Cleared for approach and hookup."

"Petty Officer Lee, that's all we need—thirty-four point six! You can head back now!"

"Aye, aye, sir!" Lee brought the throttles to the twenty-five-knot cruise speed and then turned the boat to port to head for *Kauai*. Once the boat was steady on a heading to the ship, Lopez stood and made his way to the bow to handle the sea painter, a line from *Kauai* the boat would ride on while the crane falls were attached.

They were approaching *Kauai* quickly, too quickly, in Ben's opinion. He was about to say something when Lopez shouted, "Coming in a little hot, don't you think?"

"I've got this, Boot!" Lee replied as she took the throttles into reverse. The boat's waterjet engines, optimized for forward propulsion, dutifully went into full astern but lacked the thrust to save this approach. Lee realized they would not make it, took the right engine out of reverse to provide enough helm control for a turn, and shouted, "Hang on, everybody!"

The last-second correction was enough to alter the impact to a glancing blow and, with a tremendous "squeak" and lurch, the boat caromed off *Kauai*'s port side.

"Jesus, Shelley!" Lopez shouted.

"OK, sorry about that, everyone!" Lee shouted as she brought the other throttle up and continued turning to the left. She glanced at Ben and said less loudly, "I'll have a hard time living that one down, sir."

"Don't worry about it. That's why we're here."

The next approach was flawless, and after hooking up the sea painter, Lopez grabbed the fall when it came within reach and slammed the hook onto the boat's lift frame. Lee killed the engines and gave a thumb's up to Bondurant on the crane controls. As the crane took the load, its hydraulic motor screamed as the boat lifted slowly out of the water. The noise was unnervingly loud—Ben would have been concerned if Drake had not been monitoring the pressure gauges on the side of the crane and giving a thumbs-up. As the boat reached the main deck level, Bondurant held while the crew stepped out, carrying the water containers. He then lifted it onto the cradle.

Lee pulled off her helmet and said, "Got a little cocky. Sorry again, sir."

"Forget it, Lee," Ben replied. "That one is still a distant second compared to the 'Smurf Boat' incident!"

Lee rolled her eyes and said, "Yeah, I'll always have that one going for me. Thanks, sir!"

"Anytime. I'm all about morale, you know." Ben chuckled. The "Smurf Boat" event occurred when they were doing operational tests with the Squid, with Lee driving the RHIB in a series of tactical trials. One test squid canister detonated early and doused the RHIB and crew with blue paint. No one was hurt, but the video recording of the event and aftermath remained a crew favorite.

As Lee turned to head inside, Ben noticed Frankle was waiting for him forward of the crane. "You need anything else from us, XO?"

"No, that will do."

"Any changes to the plans?"

"Just for us. I didn't anticipate how loud the crane would be under this load. I'm going to recommend we launch at least a mile and a half offshore and ride the sea painter in and out. It should affect nothing you guys have planned."

"Cool."

USCG Cutter Kauai, Atlantic Ocean, one nautical mile south of the western end of Ile Ste. Michel, Haiti
00:18 EST, 5 December

Ben

It had been night for almost six hours. Ben looked at the cloudless and moonless sky, the stars painfully bright through his Night-Vision Goggles, called NVGs for short. The low growl of the boat's muffled diesel engines and the soft hiss of the water as they crept northward at twelve knots were the only audible sounds while *Kauai* was running on batteries. Ben glanced at the shoreline, then around the fully loaded boat, riding the sea painter as *Kauai* completed her approach to the island.

Their approach was later than planned—a result of a delay in the launch of their supporting UAV surveillance flight. They remained in position twelve miles offshore until the reconnaissance confirmed both the Chinese and the 252s occupying the island were tucked into their respective compounds, and the cove was clear. The boat held the same crew as the previous afternoon's foray, but the DIA team had all their equipment and were dressed out for expeditionary operations. Lee, Lopez, and Ben were dressed in full combat gear, body armor, and helmets with mounted NVGs. The three carried sidearms, and Lopez and Ben also carried M4 carbines.

Lee kept her eyes on *Kauai* and adjusted the helm and throttles to keep pace with the patrol boat. The sea painter was a tether only—it would part if they tried to use it to tow the boat. When they received the visual signal from the Bridge, an NVG-visible infrared light flashing the letter "L" in morse code, they would cast off and proceed independently to the shore. After dropping off the DIA team, the boat would rendezvous with the idling *Kauai*, and the two would proceed in company silently back offshore to the two-mile point, far enough that the crane could not be heard from shore. After craning the boat on board, *Kauai* would proceed offshore to her patrol box and await the team's signal to return.

Ben looked from the boat over to the shoreline—it was quite close now, and he could make out the outlines of individual trees through his NVGs. Finally, a pencil-thin beam of light shined down from the Bridge: dot-dash-dot-dot, the signal for launch. Lee said, "Release sea painter."

Lopez cast off the line, and Lee brought the boat into a left turn, crossed *Kauai*'s wake, and headed to shore at the slow speed of twelve knots. The quarter-mile journey took less than a minute. Lee cut the engines to idle as the boat gently nudged onto the shelving beach and said, "Go." The DIA men slipped over the side into the knee-deep water, and Ben and Lopez handed them their equipment. Once the handoff was complete, Frankle turned to Ben and reached out with his right hand.

"See you when we see you, Coast Guard," Frankle said as he shook Ben's hand.

"Godspeed, Art," Ben replied.

The DIA man gave the bow of the now floating boat a shove to help Lee pivot it around, then turned and began wading toward the shore. Ben scanned the shore with his finger near the M4's trigger until the four men passed into the treeline. He then turned to Lee. "OK, return to ship."

"Aye, aye, sir," Lee replied and pushed the throttles to ahead slow.

Ben looked away from shore, over the boat's bow, and noted that *Kauai* had already turned toward the open sea. She would hold bare steerageway until the boat caught up, then speed up to twelve knots to the recovery point. The journey and recovery of the boat took fifteen minutes. As *Kauai* continued offshore under battery power, Ben climbed to the Bridge, crossed over to the captain's chair, and saluted Haley. "Ingress complete. No issues, Captain."

Haley returned the salute. "Nicely done, XO. Now get some sleep. I expect tomorrow will be another interesting day."

"It is certainly trending that way, ma'am. Good night."

"Good night, Ben," Haley whispered.

Ben was slightly startled at Haley's use of his first name on the Bridge, but headed down without comment. He was suddenly exhausted, too tired to think about anything. Guerrero met him at the bottom of the bridge ladder.

"I'll take the heaters, sir," he said.

Ben had forgotten the M4 and the Sig pistol he was carrying—both would need to be locked in the armory. "Thanks, Gunner," he said as he handed them over, then took the short steps to his stateroom. As he stripped out of his combat gear, Ben heard the whirring of the diesel engine starter, followed by the low grumble as the engine turned over and started supplying power to the grid. Now that they were far enough offshore to be unheard, there was no further need to run on batteries.

He stared briefly at Victoria's green dress picture, smiling at the memory of her face when he slipped the ring on her finger. "Good night, my love," he said, touching the picture. He then flopped on his bunk and was asleep within a minute.

Chapter 15

Surveillance

Ile Ste. Michel, Haiti
00:25 EST, 5 December

Frankle

Frankle took a last look at the boat as it swung around and headed away from shore toward the larger patrol boat. They were committed, and the team's fate would depend on the accuracy of their intelligence, their choices and guesses during the planning, and their skills as operators. They arranged their equipment on the sand between them. During the offload from the boat, there was no time to make sure each man had the correct equipment items—they just needed to grab everything and sort it out on land. Each man removed his floatation vest; they were a useless encumbrance now and could be hidden within the tree line for use during the return trip. *Hopefully.*

Frankle grabbed the satchel he needed and slung it over his shoulder, then picked up and shouldered his personal weapon, in his case, a suppressed Uzi machine pistol. On his belt, he also carried a holstered Sig Sauer P228 and the Ka-Bar fighting knife issued to him when he was in the Marines. Bell also carried a Sig and Ka-Bar, but he favored a SOPMOD Block II-equipped M4 carbine that allowed for long- and short-range fighting. The other two men had standard M4s and Glock nine-millimeter pistols.

Frankle took out the Garman handheld GPS navigator pre-programmed with their route and slipped on the special hood as the others sorted themselves out. The screen would only light up when pressed to his eyes, which would prevent detection if anyone was looking their way. He turned the unit on and looked into the hood. The unit calibrated itself and then displayed a rough topographical map showing their current position and intended route. The Coasties did well: they were within a hundred feet of their planned drop-off point. Frankle looked from the navigator and, through his NVGs, located the gap in the trees that marked their route. He glanced at the others, standing ready with their equipment, and whispered, "Right, let's go."

The four men set out slowly with Frankle in the lead, walking from landmark to landmark, guided by the navigator. The lack of moonlight was a blessing in remaining undetected, but it forced them to find their way among the rocks using NVGs. Progress was slow but steady as they progressed north and climbed the sloping high ground to the west of the 252 facility. They reached the rally point three hours and forty-five minutes after landing, a good hour before first light. They each disbursed to their observation points and donned the ghillie suits that would camouflage them through the day.

As Frankle settled into his nook, he placed his Uzi in the satchel and, as the horizon grew light with the coming dawn, also tucked in his NVGs. He had binoculars and a rangefinder scope in the bag, and he would not use those until later when the chance of light reflecting off their lenses was eliminated. There would be plenty of time to make the final observations needed to complete the mission. Frankle adjusted his position to be as comfortable as possible and put his head down to get some sleep. Gerard had the first watch on the compound and would alert them via their encrypted headset radios if it looked like anyone was approaching their position.

As Frankle laid his head down, he noticed for the first time how quiet it was. With the lack of open freshwater sources, there was almost no non-human animal life on the island, so the usual crescendo of bird and terrestrial animal calls that came with the dawn was absent. Likewise, no mosquitos, Frankle thought with satisfaction—there was no blood to be had and nowhere for them to breed. *Always with the silver linings, old man*, he thought as he fell asleep.

Aeropuerto Frank País, Holguín, Cuba
09:38 EST, 5 December

Rostov

Yevgeny Vladimirovich Rostov adjusted his sunglasses and descended the stairs of the Gulfstream Five business jet leased to a Croatian shell corporation belonging to the 252 Syndicate. It had been a long flight from Zagreb, over ten hours, but an agreeably smooth one. Rostov yawned and stretched, taking in the wonderful warm sunshine under the cloudless sky, tempered by the cool breeze of the easterly trade winds blowing in from the Atlantic, thirty kilometers to the northeast. Not quite a sea breeze and no pleasant odors from the sea or flora, just the familiar stink of diesel and burned jet fuel.

Rostov glanced at the hangar about a hundred meters away and noted a white and green painted CD2 twin-turboprop amphibious seaplane being towed out. A former security officer in the *Voyenno-vozdushnye sily Rossii*, or Russian Air Force, he was familiar with most aircraft types, particularly those built in Russia. Still, this was the first example he had seen of the late production Chinese version of the Dornier Seastar. This would be the plane that would ferry him and his three companions the remaining hour and a half of their journey to the Chinese base on Ile Ste. Michel. It would be far less comfortable than the luxurious business jet he'd stepped out of, but after a busy night of drinking and sex, he was looking forward to getting some sleep on the way.

Rostov was one of the young turks of the 252 Syndicate, joining after being drummed out of the Air Force for *excessive* corruption. The founders, the first generation of secret police plotters and torturers turned out when the Warsaw Pact collapsed in the early 1990s, had largely passed from the scene, either through retirement or death. Present ruling cadre, the second generation, were the junior backroom heavies and assassins who rode in behind the founders to fill out the middle ranks of the new syndicate. Young and hungry movers and shakers like Rostov were moving up in the organization, searching for opportunities to shine, be recognized, and move into one of the coveted territory governing chairs. Rostov's chance came when he got close to Xiaotong Chen, a senior Chinese Communist Party official administering the BRI effort in Moldova. Each recognized a kindred spirit in the other: a rapacious and power-hungry sociopath with a knack for sensing and seizing opportunities for promotion. Their early partnership had cleared several bureaucrats out of the way of BRI projects via the go-to 252 tools of bribery, extortion, and murder.

Chen had been rewarded with a promotion and assignment to clean up a problem with morale on Ile Ste. Michel. The high rates of discipline problems and suicides among the miners assigned there were unacceptable. His predecessor employed the usual, often brutal, disciplinary actions but had failed—the mine was falling well short of even the artificially low targets set to keep the Haitians on the hook. Chen deduced the unrelenting boredom and physical isolation from normal civilization were to blame and evaluated that providing relief in recreational drugs and submissive women was the path out of the problem. He naturally turned to his erstwhile Moldovan partner, Rostov. The latter was quick to respond, negotiating not only an additional revenue stream for the syndicate but a strong base in the western hemisphere under the aegis of the BRI's Haiti project.

The *Miho Dujam*'s loss had been a significant setback, both in terms of the loss of revenue from the arms shipment and a blow to the syndicate's prestige in the late delivery of services to their new Chinese partners. At least the fools running the ship had sunk it rather than letting the cargo or any evidence linking it to the syndicate fall into the Americans' hands. The chief of the Croatian arm of the syndicate, who had been singing Rostov's praises before the loss, made it clear his future success in the organization, if not his very life, depended on him cleaning up the mess. Rostov got the message. The women could be delivered by air as soon as they were gathered, and the heavy cargoes of arms and drugs would come later, once the sex services were functional.

Rostov had seen to this first delivery himself, from selecting the women to the transport to the island. Knowing Chen's fondness for blondes, Rostov had scoured the syndicate-controlled brothels and, unable to find candidates of sufficient "purity," expedited a couple of ongoing abduction operations to obtain two worthy candidates, one each from Poland and Latvia. He oversaw their indoctrination into their new life and gave each a "test flight" on the trip across the Atlantic. They were still aboard the Gulfstream with his bodyguard, awaiting the call to board the CD2. Rostov was certain Chen would appreciate the personal touch he had put on this first delivery.

Rostov glanced to his right, where his assistant Dmitri was locked in an intense discussion with a local official beside a dated Peugeot sedan with "PNR" lettering. Two soldiers with shouldered AK-47s, also with the *Policía Nacional Revolucionaria,* watched from the side. Undoubtedly, the advance bribe the organization had paid for a smooth transition through Cuban jurisdiction proved insufficient. Rostov was used to corruption in government—it was a leading tool in the syndicate's business model—but Cuba was truly in a league of its own. Fortunately, a large cache of currency, both in Euros and U.S. Dollars, was locked in a concealed safe in the Gulfstream. After an appropriately vigorous but futile resistance, Dmitri would re-board the plane, supposedly to collect all the money the crew was carrying on their persons. He would grab a pile of odd dollar and euro bills from the safe and return to the official to learn the amount happened to be the exact shortage in the pre-paid arrival tax. It was comically venal and part of the cost of doing business.

After a few minutes, Dmitri turned, shook his head, and walked over to Rostov. "Time for some theater, Boss," he said.

Rostov affected an annoyed expression and put his hands on his hips. "Well, we'll make it look good, Dmitri," he said, shaking his finger in his assistant's face and getting a shrug in return. After a good show of indignation, Rostov took a wallet out of his pocket, pulled out 223 Euros in assorted bills, and, after handing the money over to Dmitri, made a significant gesture of shaking it upside down to the smiling Cubans. Dmitri took the bills, then trudged to the Gulfstream to complete the collection effort. Five minutes later, the official pocketed the money Dmitri handed him, and he and the soldiers climbed into the Peugeot and drove away.

As Dmitri stepped over, Rostov said, "Well done, my friend. You can tell the pilots it's safe to come out now." The CD2 pilots hid in a hangar storeroom to avoid getting caught up in the impromptu tax collection. They were Cubans running a charter service as a front for one of the 252's partners. The men were well-paid, and there was no risk of their blackmailing Rostov for more cash—the 252s were reluctant to risk acting against Cuban government agents but wouldn't hesitate to kill citizens and their families in brutal fashion. Dmitri returned with one man while another walked toward the plane.

"We are ready to depart whenever you wish, *señor*," the man said.

"No reason to delay," Rostov replied and turned to Dmitri. "Get them on board."

"I should come with you, Boss," Dmitri said.

"No, my friend, I need you to look after things here. Besides, Comrade Chen is a nervous man—the fewer of us there are, the better."

"Yes, Boss," Dmitri said, turning to walk to the Gulfstream.

Rostov followed the Cuban pilot to the CD2 and climbed aboard. It was configured for VIP transport, and Rostov had just sat in a comfortable rear-facing seat in the cabin's front when his bodyguard Vasili arrived, each of his massive fists with a firm grip on one woman. They were both lovely and well-dressed, but they were cowering in terror as Vasili dragged them on board and pushed them into two seats in the back. Dmitri followed with two suitcases and handed them to the pilot, who stored them in a baggage compartment, closed and locked the entry door, and then made his way to the cockpit.

As the CD2's two engines completed their start sequence, Rostov waved out the window at an obviously concerned Dmitri. He regretted leaving the man behind—Dmitri was a clever negotiator, and though Rostov did not expect any issues with Chen, you never knew. Neither man knew the decision had saved Dmitri's life.

The flight to Ile Ste. Michel took the advertised one-and-a-half hours, and with the beautiful weather and keeping over water absent of heated land updrafts, it was smooth enough for Rostov to nap the entire way. He was startled awake by the touch of the copilot, who said, "We are on final approach to the harbor."

Rostov stretched and said, "Thank you." Then he looked out the window to see the island's brown and tan landscape, surrounded by the deep blue of the Atlantic with the lighter shallows rimming the land. The plane descended and made a smooth landing in the sheltered waters just off the docks of the Chinese port facilities, then taxied ponderously to the boat landing, where the engines labored to push it up the incline. Once on level ground, the pilots shut down the engines, and Rostov watched as four armed Chinese men surrounded the plane.

The copilot stood, made his way to the cabin door, opened it, and stepped out onto the tarmac after showing he was empty-handed. After a moment, he poked his head in and said, "They wish to speak to you, *señor.*"

Rostov nodded and stood, then walked back and climbed out of the plane to face two armed Chinese soldiers. "Good morning, gentlemen," he said in English. "I'm here to see Comrade Chen."

"Comrade Chen is far too busy with government business to visit with wayfarers," one soldier said. "You may contact your associates to pick you up, but you will remain with the aircraft until they do so. After you depart, the aircraft must as well."

"Very well," Rostov said. The cold shoulder was expected—one of the caveats in the treaty establishing the Chinese presence on Ile Ste. Michel was the prohibition against association with international criminal activity.

He respected Chen could not be witnessed meeting with Rostov or any other syndicate members. Chen would make his way to the 252 compound after dark. "It will soon get hot within the aircraft with this sun. May my companions and I wait outside?"

The guard glanced inside and noticed the women for the first time. "Yes, but you will remain within five meters of the aircraft, and anyone straying outside that boundary will be arrested."

"Understood, thank you." Rostov turned and motioned to Vasili, who seized the women and pulled them through the door and under the shade of the CD2's narrow wing. The guards stared hungrily at the women, and Rostov was confident that if Chen weren't looking at them through binoculars from his office right now, he soon would be. Rostov pulled out a satellite phone and contacted the compound for a pickup.

Twenty minutes later, a large blue Chevy Tahoe pulled next to the plane, and, after one guard verified his identity, the driver climbed out and walked over to Rostov. It was Krupin, the supervisor of the compound. "Greetings, Mr. Rostov," the man said in Russian. "Welcome to our little tropical paradise." He glanced over at the women with a smile. "Our first attendants. Excellent choices, if I might say so. There is a considerable backlog of orders."

"They will remain unfilled for the time being, my friend," Rostov said. "These two lovelies are reserved for Comrade Chen and me tonight." He turned to Vasili and nodded, prompting him to move the women into the SUV.

"As it should be," Krupin said, grabbing Rostov's bag.

As they were driving away from the ramp, Rostov heard the CD2's engines start. He envied the pilots—they would fly to Puerto Plata in the Dominican Republic and stay overnight in a resort hotel, while he would have to make do with what passed for a VIP suite in a tropical brothel. *Such are the privations one has to sustain when you are the boss*, Rostov thought. He then glanced at the two women in the rearview mirror and smiled. *Of course, it could be worse.*

Frankle

Frankle stretched and rubbed his neck. He never liked this part of the job, laying prone and still for hours at a time, but at least the temperature was pleasant, not too hot or cold. The cold bothered him the most these days, yet another sign that it was time to hang it up. A glint of sunlight on glass caught his eye, and he trained his hooded binoculars on the road leading from the island's east side. It was the blue SUV returning, hopefully with their quarry on board. Frankle was a little surprised they were returning so quickly—he had noted the passage of a seaplane less than an hour ago he was sure carried Rostov and his bodyguard. He had expected a much longer meeting with the Chinese.

The overflights had tracked three SUVs associated with the 252 compound. Frankle's men had accounted for two, one sitting in front of the generator building and the other returning down the road. Frankle was disturbed by the fact they had not yet located that third vehicle—no other known 252 activity on the island could account for its absence. He supposed it could be off on the island's eastern side, working on some activity involving the Chinese. Another variable to be accounted for among too damn many.

He watched as the SUV continued down the coastal road, turned onto the side road leading to the 252 compound, and pulled to a stop beside the barracks/brothel. He moved his gaze to the forward passenger door and adjusted the focus as a man climbed out. It was Rostov, all right, looking like someone in a Sandals ad with his pastel blue shirt, white pants, and sunglasses. The rear door opened, and his hands tightened on the binoculars as another thug climbed out with two women. *Dammit, there wasn't anything about trafficking in the messages! Maybe they're volunteers; I'd rather be here than in a Croatian cesspool.* The thug answered his question by violently wrenching one woman's arm as he dragged both into the building. *Enjoy yourself, King Kong; you haven't long to live.*

Frankle's headset chirped, and he flipped it on. "Boss, did you see that?" said Bell's voice.

"Affirmative," Frankle replied.

"So, what are we going to do?" Bell asked.

"Our mission. Now get off the air."

Shit-shit-shit! As if it wasn't tricky enough to get into that compound and kidnap a security officer trained to resist. Bringing along two abused, traumatized, and likely hysterical women pushed it into the impossible category. He glanced over his shoulder south of the island. Although she couldn't be seen in the sea haze, *Kauai* was out there, somewhere within their radio range of fifteen miles, making like a typical Coast Guard cutter on a migrant interdiction patrol.

What would they think of a proposed mod to the mission to include the women? He knew what Ben would think, based on his performance on the *Miho Dujam*: Hell, yes! Reardon was another story—she was a cool customer, unlikely to react emotionally in a way that put the crew and boat at risk. Frankle nodded. *Yep, that's exactly what you need in a CO of a unit like this one.*

Frankle took out his tablet and typed a text message for encrypted burst transmission. "To Orchid From Delta, target on-site, observed in company of 2 captive women. Rpt, believe 2 women are prisoners. Unless otherwise directed, will attempt extract of prisoners during egress if willing. Ends." Frankle took the handheld directional antenna out of his bag, plugged it into the tablet, and scanned the southern horizon until it picked up *Kauai's* carrier signal. He tapped the send button, and the tablet did the network negotiation and sent the message in less than half a second. The tablet chat line said, "Msg rec'd OK," showing the checksum variable transmitted was valid for the message.

Frankle held the antenna pointed in the direction yielding the carrier tone, and, minutes later, received another chirp in his headset indicating an incoming text.

He glanced at the tablet. "To Delta From Orchid, prisoner extract approved. Window 2000-0030L. Req rndz time when able. Ends."

Frankle smiled, pleased but hardly surprised, as the risk to the boat was the same whether the women came along or not. Although it imposed a constraint, he was pleased to see the "window" times for the extract, for it meant Pennington had got them some air support. *Hopefully, we won't need it.* He put the antenna down and turned back to his observations of the compound. *The boat's big enough to carry the extra two passengers, but can that crane handle the added two hundred pounds?*

USCG Cutter Kauai, Atlantic Ocean, fourteen nautical miles south of the western end of Ile Ste. Michel, Haiti
12:05 EST, 5 December

Haley

Haley looked across her cabin at Ben and Drake. There had been minimal discussion about the response to Frankle's request to extract the women. There was no added risk to the mission if they wanted to come off, and Haley could hardly refuse, even if she was inclined to do so. The extra weight in the boat was a concern. During the full-load test, the howl of the crane's hydraulic motors had made her hair stand up, and she wanted assurance it could take the extra weight. "What do you think, COB?" she asked.

"I don't know, Captain," Drake answered. "We were nibbling at the red line throughout the lift, and I sure wouldn't bet a paycheck on it."

It was not the answer Haley wanted to hear. She looked at Ben.

"We could put a Jacob's Ladder over, ma'am. One or two DIA guys and I can climb out before the lift to take some of the load off. It will delay the recovery, but that has to be preferable to risking a complete breakdown."

"Why leave Lopez in the boat?" Haley asked.

"Can't take the chance of leaving Lee with no help in case we need a Plan B, ma'am."

"Agreed. OK, let's plan on that. Rig the ladder and brief your crew."

"Yes, ma'am," Ben replied as he and Drake stood.

After the two left, Haley sat alone in the cabin and contemplated the five-pound ice cube in her stomach. As she had a dozen times in the last couple of days, she went over her decisions relating to the upcoming operation. The message detailing the assignment of the Compass Call C-130 electronic warfare aircraft had been a tremendous relief, and at least they would have a good handle on what the Chinese were doing. It was bad enough to send Ben and Lopez ashore with machine guns *(machine guns!)* to support the extract. Sitting there ignorant of the actions of an enemy that could blow them all to hell would be unnerving.

She had only talked briefly with Lopez during her familiarization patrol, but found him bright and earnest. Sam had said they were lucky to have him, that Mercier had added an ME3 billet so that they could keep him on board after he graduated from the Maritime Law Enforcement Specialist A-school training. He was on the shortlist of crew members she needed to get to know better, and after this operation, she would make clearing that list a priority.

She pulled open the drawer and took out the picture of her with her father, taken on her graduation day from the Academy. He was wearing one of his finest suits, and she was in her dress whites, both of them smiling proudly. It had been the happiest day of her life until four days ago, when she had taken command of *Kauai*. She thought, *Oh, Daddy. Look at what your little girl is doing now!* She stood and put the picture back and closed the drawer.

She stopped on her way to the Bridge to glance in Ben's open door at the pictures of him and Victoria on his wall. Haley had been concerned when Ben told her they had become engaged the night after the change of command and remained convinced that emotional ties to the shore were liabilities officers could ill afford. Yet, despite this, Ben seemed to be as focused as before, if not more so, and Haley was wondering if it might be time to revisit her philosophy.

Chapter 16

Final March

Ile Ste. Michel, Haiti
19:07 EST, 5 December

Frankle

The sun had set almost two hours previously, and it was fully dark now. It was a new moon period, but their NVGs were fine in terms of visibility under the stars and clear skies. Not that they would need them for the approach to target—the 252 compound was lit up like Yankee Stadium in extra innings.

Right after sunset, the team had reformed on Frankle's position to compare notes and formulate the final assault plan. With Rostov's arrival, the 252s had stepped up their security patrolling, but Frankle and his men agreed it was more for show than any genuine security concern. The lazy way the guards held their weapons and the shortcuts they took on their rounds reflected complacency. It was not unexpected—there was nothing of value stored here yet, no indigenous population to guard against, and the Chinese were under orders not to deal with them. There was a fixed sentry post where the road entered the compound, but the guards posted there mostly sat around smoking and playing video games on their cell phones.

They debated whether it would be a net positive or negative to hit the powerhouse first and knock out the lights. While that would have the definite advantage of eliminating targeted shots from any of their opponents, it would also sound the alarm at the outset of the operation. Frankle decided there were too many risks in tipping their hand that early, and the powerhouse idea was shelved. The plan that evolved had Gerard and Kelly ambush the roving guard as he neared the vehicle parking area. They would kill the man with the silenced pistols they carried, hide the body, find the keys for one of the SUVs and slash the tires on the others. Frankle and Bell would await the success signal from the other team, then take out the entrance sentry and make their way to the barracks where Rostov and the women were housed. Anyone they encountered on the compound would be dispatched silently.

Finding the keys was another wildcard—given the lackadaisical approach to security, they expected to find them inside the vehicles, probably tucked into the driver's window shade. But they could be elsewhere, and a search for them might take minutes if they could be found at all. This was the worst case, as they would be on foot to the rendezvous, but so would what remained of the 252 staff. Not the preferred outcome, but still acceptable.

The tentative go-time for the assault was 21:00, time enough for whatever air support they were getting to get on station and build the tactical picture. The GO-NO-GO decision hinged upon a coded burst transmission from *Kauai* fifteen minutes before launch that she was in position and ready to retrieve them. If something prevented that, mechanical breakdown or activity by the Chinese, for instance, Frankle had a decision to make. He could either sit tight and let the opportunity pass by with a pickup by *Kauai* the following night or go in gunning to kill Rostov and then withdraw and evade as best as possible in the hope of an alternative rescue mode. His orders from Admiral Irving, known only to him, were the latter. He also had little doubt Irving would cut them loose rather than mount a risky rescue operation, and he was not about to throw away the lives of his team. If they had to abort tonight, he would order his team to lie low for another day, then contact *Kauai* for extraction, grabbing the captive women, if practicable.

Frankle smiled grimly. He knew before he started that this would be his last trip. He had maxed out his federal retirement and only held on as long as it stayed interesting. The past year's events, culminating with this op, had taken the shine off fieldwork. If he returned, *when he returned*, he corrected himself, he would put in for one of the instructor jobs at Quantico, Bragg, or Benning. He was jolted from his thoughts by the appearance of headlights on the coastal road off to his right. He took out his night scope and trained it on the oncoming vehicle. The glare of the headlights prevented him from making out any vehicle details. He would have to wait until it passed him. He knew the vehicle had to be Chinese—they had accounted for all three big SUVs the 252s were using in their work. His heart sank. What if it was one of their SUVs or, worse, one of the VN-4s? *What a time for those assholes to start their own patrols!*

He watched with interest as the vehicle slowed and then turned off onto the side road leading to the compound. As it entered a gentle curve to the right, the headlights were finally pointed away enough for him to get a vehicle profile. *My God! It's a sedan! A high-end one, by the looks of it.* The car stopped at the entry checkpoint, and the guard shined his flashlight in on the driver and passenger, then waved the car through. As it pulled into the bright lights in front of the barracks, Frankle could see that it was one of the latest generation BMW 5 series. He zoomed the scope on the passenger door as the driver jumped out, came around, and opened it. A portly man in a Hawaiian shirt, white pants, and sunglasses climbed out, hurried to the door, and then inside the barracks, his driver hurrying to catch up.

I'll be damned! That has to be Chen, the mine director. Only a high-up CCP prick would insist on having a status car on a Haitian island, and no boss would let a flunky use his wheels for a booty call! He chuckled at the comedic aspect of the entire event. *Dressed like Magnum P.I. and wearing Blues Brothers sunglasses at night for anonymity. Hilarious!* He keyed his microphone and whispered, "Bring it in, boys. We need to talk."

A minute later, the three other men had returned to Frankle's position. "OK, boys, here's the deal," he said. "Confidence is high that the *haole* who just arrived is the big CCP boss himself, which changes the objectives."

"Are we going to grab him instead or cap him?" Kelly asked.

"Absolutely not," Frankle replied. "We have strict orders, which I agree with for a change, that we do not kidnap or kill Chinese nationals. However, there's nothing in those orders about knocking one out and grabbing his biometrics. Please, one of you tell me you've brought a biometrics kit."

"Yo," Gerard answered.

"OK, give it to Lashon. Same plan for you guys as before—grab an SUV and bring it upfront after you disable the rest. You will also slash the BMW tires while you wait for us. Clear?"

"Roger, Boss," Gerard answered.

"Lashon, it's on us. We move in on the barracks, take out any guards and move on to the bedrooms. I'm pretty sure we'll find both our guys *in flagrante delicto*. We stun them, and while Lashon is hooking up Chen and grabbing his vitals, I'll be sedating Tovarisch Rostov and tossing clothes at the women. We load everyone and beat feet. Questions?"

"Yeah. How come you always get the girls?" Gerard asked.

"Two reasons. First, I'm the boss. Second, they will be pretty shook up and probably respond better to a grandpa type than the Incredible Hulk here or two other guys that look like the mooks who grabbed them from home."

"Ouch!" Gerard said, smiling.

"Deal with it," Frankle said. "Any questions?"

"Still want to go with 21:00?" Bell asked.

"Better push it back to 21:30 to give the sex, drugs, and wine a chance to take a firm hold. I'll tell the Coasties. Off you go." After the other three men disappeared into the darkness, Frankle took out the antenna and sent an update. After receiving an acknowledgment from the patrol boat out in the darkness, he tucked away the radio and turned to watch the compound. *This could be huge—documented evidence of Chinese collusion with the 252s at the highest level. All we need now is one damn set of keys!*

USCG Cutter Kauai, Atlantic Ocean, eight nautical miles south of the western end of Ile Ste. Michel, Haiti
20:03 EST, 5 December

Haley

They had gone to General Quarters Condition One half an hour earlier, with radar shut down, and moved from their daytime patrol position fifteen miles south of the is- land to half that distance. For now, Ben was on the Bridge, having briefed Lee and Lopez; he could be on the main deck and ready to launch in less than a minute. The FC3 panel was fully manned, Hopkins had the OOD, as usual, and everyone was in full combat gear.

An Air Force C-130 Compass Call plane, callsign Starfish One Seven, arrived precisely on time at 20:00, forty-five minutes after its launch from its forward base at Guantanamo Bay. On its arrival, the converted tactical transport made a slow pass along the island's north side, training its extremely sensitive passive sensors, electro-optical, infrared, and electronic surveillance inland. As ex- pected, these detected nothing along the north shore. As they swung in a wide arc around the island's eastern end on a westerly course off its south coast, the Chinese base was unmasked, and things got interesting.

"Orchid, Starfish One Seven," said the disembodied voice from the UHF radio speaker.

Haley plugged her headset into the microphone jack and keyed her press-to-talk switch. "Starfish One Seven, Orchid-Actual. Go ahead."

"Orchid, One Seven, initial sweep complete. No radars operating. Some encrypted traffic on UHF-FM band in the eight-hundred-megahertz range, probably handhelds. One warship dockside, one cargo ship dockside. Warship is active; we picked up a definite exhaust plume on in- frared. Over."

Haley's hand froze briefly, and then she pushed the transmit button again. "One Seven, can you tell if they are running generators, or is it the full plant?"

"Orchid, One Seven, unknown. We will pull in closer on the next pass."

"One Seven, Orchid. Roger, standing by." Haley dropped her hand and looked across at the navigation display. The screen showed *Kauai* as a pipper in the center, with a map display of Ile Ste. Michel stretching from directly north to the screen's edge to the east. *Kauai*'s radars were shut down to facilitate emissions control—they would navigate using GPS and bearings from the electro-optical camera. The heat plume from the gunboat was terrible news, and Haley hoped they were just running their generators for maintenance or normal engine turnover. None of the earlier nighttime overflights had shown any activity like this, and the conclusion was the ship usually ran on shore power when moored. The ten-minute wait for the following report was the longest of her life.

"Orchid, One Seven."

"Go ahead."

"I'm not an expert, Captain, but that ship is putting out an awful lot of heat for generators only. I've got a large exhaust plume around the stern. Over."

"Roger. Can you maintain contact? Over."

"Affirmative. We will maintain a port delta two klicks south of the island's eastern point."

"Thanks, One Seven. If that sucker moves, I need to know soonest. Over."

"WILCO, out."

Haley unplugged her headset and said, "Chief, the XO and I will be heading below for a minute."

"Very good, Captain," Hopkins replied.

Haley looked at Ben and said, "Let's chat."

"Very good, ma'am."

They stepped into Haley's cabin, and she shut the door. "Have a seat." After they both sat, she continued. "What do you think, Ben?"

"Things just got a whole lot iffier, ma'am," Ben said.

"No shit. All of a sudden, the Chinese are doing things they have never done before."

"We don't know why they are lighting off. I don't think they're expecting us to make a hit. If they thought we had an op going and wanted to intervene, they would be underway already. If I had to make a guess, it's a standing order to warm up the gunboat whenever the boss goes over the hill in case the 252s do something stupid. I imagine their armored car troops are on alert as well. If they roll when the shooting starts, I don't see how we avoid an engagement. But I think they'll try to get an order from the boss first."

"Do you think that would delay them more than a few minutes?"

"No, ma'am."

"Which means an engagement with the armored cars, the gunboat, or both would be likely. Something we were explicitly ordered to avoid."

"I would say so, ma'am."

"So you are saying I should follow the orders?" Haley asked.

Ben looked her in the eyes. "Ma'am, it's not my call to make."

"I know that. I'm asking what you would do if you were in my seat."

Ben's mouth tightened, and he said, "I would go in, ma'am."

"You know we wouldn't have a prayer if that gunboat pins us in that cove. Even if we break out, they have the speed to run us down, eight times our firepower, and the range to out-shoot us. Air support would be the only thing that could save us, and we can't count on that. You would take that risk for some abstract geopolitical gain?"

"No, ma'am, I don't give a crap about the price of rare-earth elements, but I would go in there to save four brave men and two innocent women. This is what we do, ma'am."

"At the cost of all sixteen of us?"

"I don't think it will come to that, ma'am."

"And if it did?"

"I would still go, ma'am. It's a big risk for us, but certain death for them otherwise. The SAR dilemma." Ben nodded.

"Very well, thank you for your candor. I need to think about this for a minute. I'll meet you on the Bridge."

"Yes, ma'am," Ben said, then turned and left.

Haley looked at her desk. *How can this be a choice? I obey orders, save my ship and crew, or disobey orders, and maybe get them both shot to hell. No brainer. But is it? Those four men and two women—can I really leave them to die, or worse, in the women's case? These are the choices you have to make,* Captain.

She looked from her desk and slowly glanced around the bare walls of her cabin. *Cold and sterile, like the mathematics of life and death.* Her gaze stopped on the ship's plaque mounted above her bunk. It was a smaller version of the one that hung on the messdeck, and she had to admit that, unlike the crests she had seen on other ships, she liked the design. It featured the escutcheon of the Kingdom of Hawaii, with a silver-colored fouled anchor in the background and the ship's motto on a golden scroll below: *Fortiter et Fideliter,* "Bravely and Faithfully" in Latin.

As the weight lifted from her shoulders, a sad smile crept over her face. *Of all the things, a plaque, for God's sake!* She stood, reached over to give the plaque a quick pat, then headed for the Bridge. "Carry on, please," Haley said as she emerged onto the Bridge to the usual call to attention. "Chief, start your approach. Secure MDEs at four nautical miles."

"Aye, aye, Captain," Hopkins replied.

Haley turned to Ben. "God help us all, XO."

"Indeed, ma'am. One helluva break-in patrol!"

Ben

The diesel engines shut down as Ben went below to the armory to check out his guns for this sortie. The eerie silence that followed gave him the shivers, as it always did. *Kauai*'s battery bank stored enough energy to propel her at twenty knots for two hours and progressively longer times at lower speeds. They had never put this endurance to the ultimate test, although they had come close at Barbello. They had six hours at their twelve-knot approach speed—plenty of time to roll in and out.

Lopez was already at the armory when Ben arrived, and Guerrero doled out the weapons and ammunition. The Mark 48 machine guns they were checking out were a little longer and three times heavier than the M4s they usually carried on expeditionary operations. It was one of the many factors Ben had to keep in mind tonight.

"Do you need a refresh, XO?" Guerrero asked.

Ben went through the standard checks from memory of his training six months ago. "Did I do alright, Gunner?"

"Spot on, XO." Guerrero held out his hand. "Good luck, sir."

"Same here," Ben said as he shook his hand. He slung the machine gun, grabbed the belt holding his pistol and other equipment, and followed Lopez out of the armory.

"Think we'll see action tonight, sir?" Lopez asked as they climbed the ladder to the main deck.

"I don't think you and I will. As far as the boat goes, just a little south of fifty-fifty."

"Right. Better make sure we get back then."

"That's the idea," Ben replied. They emerged on deck and walked aft to the special operations boat, already lifted from its cradle and positioned at the rail by Bondurant. "Gather 'round, folks," Ben said as he stood before them. "Plan is the same as we last briefed. The bad news is something is going on at that Chinese base, and we don't know what it is. This has dialed up the threat and our need to beat feet as soon as possible. So, the order of the day is expedite to the limit of safety—anything we break, lose over the side, etc., is the cost of doing business. Clear?"

"Got it, XO," Bondurant said.

"Any questions?" Ben asked. Seeing nothing but head shakes, he keyed his radio. "Orchid, Oscar-One, ready for launch."

"Oscar-One, Orchid, cleared for launch. Good luck, sir." Bunting's voice replied through his headset.

"OK, let's do it," Ben said, following after Lee and Lopez climbed into the boat. It was the same plan for approach as before, with the boat launched at two miles offshore and cruising silently on the sea painter until a quarter-mile and then on her own to the beach. Ben watched the shoreline through his NVGs as the two vessels approached, trying to pick out the agreed landing point. He looked across the boat at Lopez, who was also looking forward toward the island. He glanced at Lee, coolly scanning between her panel and *Kauai* to keep pace without putting too much tension on the sea painter.

A little under ten minutes after launch, the "L" signal flashed from the Bridge, and Lee said, "Cast off the sea painter."

Lopez pulled the marlinspike holding the line in place and, after it disappeared over the side, said, "Sea painter clear."

"Right, hang on," Lee said as she goosed the engine, scooting the boat forward along *Kauai*'s port side. It was a quick trip to the shore, where, unlike the previous night, Ben and Lopez pulled the boat's bow on the beach after they jumped out.

After slinging the gun over his shoulder with a grunt, Ben turned to Lee. "Now, no beach parties while I'm gone, Petty Officer Lee," he said, extending his hand.

"You are just so *Dad*," Lee replied as she shook his hand. "Come back safe, sir." She then grabbed Lopez's outstretched hand. "You too, Boot."

"See ya in a bit, Shelley," Lopez replied, plodding after Ben through the thick sand.

It took Ben a minute of scanning between the land-scape presented in his NVGs and the tablet with the GPS app to find the correct gap where he and Lopez would wait. Ben led them through the low brush to the gap, which extended about one-hundred-fifty yards to a pair of tree copses about fifty feet apart, beyond which was open ground. As they neared the mouth of the gap, Ben said, "Set up behind a good tree over there," pointing to the thicket on the left.

"How will they find us, XO?" Lopez asked.

"I'm going to pop a line of five chemlights running right along the center," Ben replied.

"Won't that bring the bad guys down on us?"

"I won't pop them until our guys are a minute out. If there are bad guys, they'll be following our guys. Anyway, we want them to come here instead of hitting us from the flank. Hopefully, there will be enough adrenaline in play to keep them from thinking too much."

"Hopefully, sir?"

"Hey, hope is my strategy for so many things these days."

As Lopez walked to his position, Ben turned and strolled to his. He found an excellent location to the left of a large tree and set up the gun, relieved to get the heavy weight off his shoulder. Once he had everything in place and a round chambered, he pressed the button on his tactical radio. "Delta-One, Oscar-One."

Seconds later, Frankle's voice replied. "Oscar-One, Delta-One, copy."

"Delta-One, Oscar-One, Uber's here. Call me one minute out so I can string the markers."

"WILCO, Oscar-One. We're stepping off now."

"Good luck, Delta," Ben said, getting a double-click in return. He then sat and tried to find a comfortable position on the hard ground. Like Frankle before him, Ben was struck by how quiet the island was, the absence of distraction leaving him with nothing to do but think about their situation. Ben thought back to Haley's decision to go ahead with the mission. It was a gutsy call—Ben didn't know if he could have made that decision, but he knew they would definitely be on the hot seat when they got back.

Chapter 17

A Fighting Retreat

Ile Ste. Michel, Haiti
22:03 EST, 5 December

Frankle

The silent trek down from the observation position had taken longer than the twenty minutes Frankle had expected, but both pairs of DIA men were in place. Bell lay beside him, sighting on the front sentry with his silenced M4 carbine. They would wait for Gerard's signal that he had killed the rover and seized an operable SUV, then pop the sentry to make their way among the buildings to the barracks, avoiding the lights whenever possible. It was no minor relief to hear Ben's voice an hour previously announcing they were in place, green-lighting the assault. *"Uber's here." That kid has a way with words,* Frankle thought with a smile.

Chen's driver had come out minutes after they had gone into the barracks and sat in the car, smoking and doing something with his cell phone. It would be handy if they could surprise him there with a Taser, followed by an ampule of the powerful sedative the DIA men all carried. Like his boss, the driver had to be left alive at all costs, and they couldn't afford to chase him all over the compound. Frankle scanned for any other stray 252s; a task made difficult in the alternating light and darkness of the compound. Nothing. He suspected the gang members not asleep were watching satellite TV in the crew section of the barracks at the opposite end of the brothel.

Not knowing the inside layout of the barracks was a real problem, hopefully one that wouldn't blow up in their faces. There would be no one near Rostov and Chen while they were "engaged" with the women—Chen had already evicted his driver, and Frankle suspected Rostov would have his bodyguard within shouting distance, but no closer. *He's probably near the front door where he could corral anyone blundering in. Hopefully, the "gotta pee" approach will work.*

Frankle's headset chirped. "Lead, I got a ride; others are dead," Gerard's voice said.

Thank God! Frankle clicked his transmit button twice, then reached out and tapped Bell on his right shoulder. After waiting for the guard to present an optimal aspect, Bell's finger tightened on the trigger. After a soft "pop" from the rifle, the guard slumped forward without another sound. Bell switched the fire selector to safe, raised to a kneeling position, and nodded. Frankle nodded, and they both stood and started toward the nearest building.

It took a few minutes to work their way around to the shaded side of the barracks behind the BMW. The Chinese driver was still sitting in the driver's seat with his hand out the window holding a cigarette, and Frankle could see he was still looking at his cell phone screen. When he began tapping his hand on the side of the car, apparently in time with some music or dance video, Frankle crept forward with his stunner handy. He jammed the weapon into the driver's shoulder on reaching the car and pulled the trigger. After a brief convulsion, the driver settled into a stupor, and Frankle injected an ampule of the quick-acting sedative. Within seconds, the driver was unconscious, and Frankle bound him to the seat using the seat belt.

Satisfied the driver was finished for the evening, Frankle stepped to the front door of the barracks and beckoned to Bell. When his partner was in position on the opposite side of the door, silenced pistol in hand, Frankle made what he hoped sounded like a timid knock. After a pause, he knocked again.

Behind the door, a deep voice intoned, *"Chego the khochesh*?" [what do you want?]

Affecting the highest voice he could, Frankle replied, *"Mne nuzno polzovatsya tualetom!"* [I need to use the lavatory].

"Po'shyol 'na hui!" [Go screw yourself!]

Frankle knocked again, holding in a laugh. "*Pojaluista, upustyte menia!*" [Please let me in!]

As expected, the door flew open, and Vasili's huge hand reached out to grab Frankle by the neck. The agent grabbed his arm and pulled the big man through the door in stunned surprise, where Bell killed him with a single shot to the back of his head. The two agents grabbed Vasili as he fell, dragged him into the barracks, and dropped him in an easy chair a short distance from the door.

Frankle nodded at Bell, and they each pulled a Taser, then crept forward to listen and peek in each door in the long hallway. Eventually, each found a target, and as Bell watched him, Frankle counted down on his fingers. Upon reaching zero, Frankle plunged through his door, shot a surprised and naked Chen with his Taser, then pounced on him with flex cuffs and a gag. The sedative was not an option with Chen, as they could not risk the man dying from an allergic reaction. He looked over to find a blond woman staring back wide-eyed and clutching bedsheets across her bare chest. "Do you speak English?" Frankle said. After getting no reaction, he tried German, "*Sprechen sie Deutsch?*" The woman nodded, and he continued, "*Ich bin ein Amerikaner, hier, um dich zu retten. Anziehen sich.*" [I am an American here to save you. Get dressed.]

Frankle had just finished tightening the gag on Chen when Bell appeared at the door and tossed him the bio-metrics kit. The agent took Chen's fingerprints, a blood sample, and digital photographs of his nude body at almost every angle. He flipped him on his stomach, patted him on the shoulder, and whispered in his ear, "Congratulations, Comrade. You are now the most biometrically documented man in history." He stood and gently took the now-dressed woman by the arm and keyed his microphone. "Billy, bring it in."

"On the way."

As the pair stepped out into the hallway, they almost ran into Bell, carrying the unconscious Rostov over his left shoulder, with the other woman following them. Glancing at Rostov's briefs, Frankle asked, "Not that far along, was he?"

"No, I have a weak stomach," Bell replied.

Frankle chuckled and peered out the front door. When an SUV pulled up, and Gerard jumped out, Frankle opened the door and said, "Billy, take care of the Beemer. Steve, help Lashon with Rostov." As Gerard pulled out his K-bar, Frankle led the two women to the SUV and helped them into the rear seat. As Bell and Kelly moved the unconscious Rostov into the middle seat, a shrill alarm sounded across the compound. "Shit! Let's go, let's go!" Frankle shouted, slammed the back door, and jumped into the forward passenger seat. He turned and shouted, *"Alles auf den boden!"* [Everybody, get down!]. Gerard jumped in, and the SUV hurtled toward the road, a cloud of dust spreading behind it. Frankle could hear automatic fire and the thuds of bullets striking the car's body. A burst shattered the rear window, and one woman huddled on the floor screamed. Through the smashed window, he saw headlights behind them on the road. "Billy, I thought you got all the cars!"

"I did! The damn Beemer has run-flats, and I didn't have time to do anything else!"

"Shit!" Frankle said, then keyed his microphone. "Oscar, this is Delta. We're three minutes out, and we've got a tail. Over!"

Ben

Ben was going over the mathematics of the gunboat's ETA when a strange sound got his attention. At first, he could not make out what it was, then came the unmistakable sound of automatic gunfire in the distance. Ben transmitted on his command set, "Orchid, Oscar-One, I'm hearing gunfire from the direction of the compound. Over."

"Oscar-One, Orchid, roger, out."

Ben jumped to his feet, grabbed a handful of chemical light sticks, trotted to the rear of the gap, activated, and dropped one. He ran ten yards up the middle of the gap, activated, and dropped another. After three more similar drops, he trotted back to his gun and reached it as Frankle's urgent call came.

"Oscar, this is Delta. We're three minutes out, and we've got a tail. Over!"

Ben keyed his microphone. "Delta from Oscar, we're ready. The path is lit!"

"Roger, out!"

"Lope!" Ben called across to Lopez.

"Yes, sir!"

"They've got a tail, and we're going to make sure we hit the driver. As soon as the first vehicle passes, open up on the second one with full auto. Aim at the lights, got it?"

"Copy, sir!"

Ben keyed his command set again. "Orchid, Oscar-one. Delta reports en route with pursuit. We are standing by to engage."

"Oscar, Orchid-Actual, roger, act at discretion, out."

Ben could see headlights now, bobbing on the graded road. He could intermittently see the second vehicle's headlights through the dust billowing behind the first vehicle. He watched as the headlights reached the coast road, then turned right toward their position. The second vehicle reached the road and followed, creeping up on the first. The lead vehicle reached a point where the driver could see Ben's chemlights and turned off the coast road, heading toward them. When the second car turned to follow, Ben shifted to the gunsight and watched in fascination as the target closed.

The first vehicle tore past them in a cloud of dust with a roar, and Ben and Lopez simultaneously pulled and held their triggers. After ten seconds of continuous firing, there was an eerie silence. Ben could see nothing through the smoke and dust at first. Then the light breeze from the northeast cleared the obscuration, and Ben could make out the car. Part of the car, anyway—their gunfire had killed the driver, and it had careened into a boulder, crushing the front half. Ben could make out something sticking out the smashed rear window. Ben stood for a better look and realized it was a human arm. Then next thing he knew, he was bending over and vomiting. He was still leaning over ten seconds later when Lopez shouted, "Sir, are you OK?"

Ben stood upright, shook himself, picked up the gun, and said, "Yes. Let's go!" He gave the car one last look, then trotted after Lopez down the gap. The SUV had effectively cleared the underbrush down to the beach, making the going a lot easier for Ben and Lopez on the return. They were halfway to the boat when Ben's command set buzzed.

"Oscar-One, Orchid-Actual, warning, Chinese vehicles approaching on the coast road. Expedite departure!"

"Orchid, Oscar-One, WILCO, out!" He turned to Lopez and said, "Move it. The Chinese are coming!" Then the two men took off in a dead run toward the boat where the DIA men and guests were already loading. As they got within twenty yards, Ben shouted, "Push off! The Chinese are coming!" When they arrived, everyone was on board but Kelly. After Ben and Lopez tossed their guns in the boat, the three men pushed it off the beach until they were thigh-deep and then pulled themselves on board. "The hell with stealth, Shelley, haul ass!" Ben shouted.

Lee slammed the right throttle forward with the helm hard over to the left, and the heavily loaded boat turned ponderously toward the sea and *Kauai*. Ben could see two sets of headlights approaching on the coast road. About the time the boat completed her turn and Lee had pushed both throttles to full ahead, the vehicles stopped near the gap with the still-glowing chemlights. A searchlight winked on and traced the path down to the SUV stopped by the water. *OK, you've found the SUV, now let it go, please!*

After pausing for a few seconds on the SUV, the searchlight began sweeping across the water off the beach. It passed over, then came back and fixed on the white wake and followed it up to the boat. When the light reached and settled on the boat, Ben shouted, "Hit the deck!" Two seconds later, the first burst of gunfire struck.

Haley

"Orchid, Oscar-One, I'm hearing gunfire from the direction of the compound. Over."

Haley wanted to jump from her chair but held herself in place and simply nodded at Bunting.

Bunting turned and transmitted, "Oscar-One, Orchid, roger, out."

"Captain, I have a vehicle. Make that two vehicles, moving down the side road from the compound on EO. Contact is intermittent because of land shadowing," Williams reported.

Haley swallowed. "Very well, track them as best as you can. Put it on the screen."

Ben's voice came from the command set speaker again moments later, "Orchid, Oscar-one. Delta reports en route with pursuit. We are standing by to engage."

"I'll take this one," Haley said, then keyed her microphone. "Oscar, Orchid-Actual, roger, act at discretion, out." Haley knew Ben would have done that anyway, but she didn't want him wasting a single thought on whether she approved. *This was what Sam was talking about. This is the agonizing part where you get to watch everything, with absolutely no ability to help. Those are your kids out there, and you have to trust them.*

Williams couldn't hold a fix on the vehicles with the ship's camera until they reached the coast road. Then the picture cleared, and Haley was surprised to see an SUV pursued by what looked like a luxury car—she would have expected the opposite. They lost the picture again when the vehicles turned off the road near the boat's landing site.

"Conn, Mount 52, sound of automatic gunfire, three-zero-zero relative, no visual target!" Connally reported through the open bridge door on the port side.

"Conn aye!" Hopkins replied.

Soon, Connally reported again, "Conn, Mount 52, sound of automatic gunfire has stopped!"

"Conn, aye!"

Lee's voice came over the command set, "Orchid, Orchid-One, SUV has arrived, passengers loading!"

Haley nodded to Bunting, who transmitted "Orchid-One, Orchid, roger, out."

Haley was about to ask for a report from Ben when the UHF speaker barked again. "Orchid, Starfish One Seven, I have movement from the Chinese base. Two vehicles, appear to be some kind of APC. Over."

APCs? Armored Personnel Carriers! It's the VN-4s! Haley changed to UHF on her radio selector and keyed the microphone. "Starfish One Seven, Orchid-Actual, please confirm two APCs headed west on the coast road. Over."

"Orchid, One Seven, confirmed. Over."

"One Seven, Orchid-Actual, roger. Keep an eye on that gunboat, out." Haley switched to the command set. "Oscar-One, Orchid-Actual, warning! Chinese vehicles approaching on the coast road, expedite departure!"

"Orchid, Oscar-One, WILCO, out!" Ben replied.

Haley balled her fists, then took a deep breath. "Williams, train the EO on the coast road from the east. Let me know when the VN-4s come into sight."

"Aye, aye, ma'am," Williams replied.

"Chief, no point in ultraquiet anymore. Light off the mains."

"Aye, aye, ma'am," Hopkins replied. She pressed the intercom and said, "Main Control, Conn, put all engines on line."

"Main Control, aye," Drake's voice replied. Within seconds came the whine of a diesel engine starter, followed by a grumble as the first engine caught and came up to speed.

Haley switched to intra-ship radio. "Overwatch, CO."

"Go ahead, ma'am," Guerrero replied.

"We have two Chinese armored vehicles approaching. Hopefully, they'll just have a look and go home. But, if not, we may have a fight. They have a mounted seven-point-six-two, but it is manually operated and will need target illumination. Your target will be that searchlight, but you will be weapons tight unless they fire on us or the small boat or I give a direct order. Do you copy?

"Ma'am, target searchlight, weapons tight. Engage only if the vehicle opens fire."

"That's correct. Good luck."

"Thank you, ma'am."

"Captain, I have headlights on the coast road, estimate one mile," Williams reported.

Haley turned and gazed at the EO screen. "Load APDS-T."

"Load APDS-T, aye," Williams said, then typed a command into the console. On the foredeck, the ship's gun emitted a series of clanking sounds audible on the Bridge as the automatic loader fed the first armor-piercing, discarding-sabot tracer round into the breech. "APDS-T loaded, Captain."

Haley gripped her chair and said, "Surface action port. Target the lead vehicle."

Williams said, "Target the lead vehicle, aye." Williams slewed the gun camera to the ship's EO, already locked on to the leading VN-4. After he typed in a few commands, the gun mount came alive and traversed left to align with the gunsight. Then the gun elevated automatically to account for the VN-4's height above the water and compensate for the slight ballistic drop over the measured distance. When the computer's AI was satisfied with the gun's alignment, the reticle on Williams's screen turned green. "Target identified. Target selected. On target and tracking, Captain."

"Very well, hold."

"Hold fire, ma'am," Williams said, eyes locked on the screen.

The Chinese vehicle stopped and, as Haley expected, turned on a searchlight and directed it down onto the beach. Williams repeated, "On target and tracking, ma'am."

"Hold."

"Yes, ma'am," Williams said, shifting in his seat. "They're sitting ducks in that boat, ma'am."

"Knock it off, Williams," Hopkins said, to Haley's surprise.

"Aye, Chief."

Haley watched in agony as the light swept out from the shore, and held her breath as it picked up the wake, then settled on the boat. Then the VN-4 opened fire, tracers reaching into the boat.

"Commence fire!"

Williams had already pressed the fire button at the beginning of the command, and the gun barked a loud bang and immediately loaded another APSD-T. The quarter-pound penetrator shed its sabot jacket on leaving the barrel, and its tracer tail made it look like a glowing red streak as it crossed the water at almost four times the speed of sound. At around seven hundred meters to the target, the flight time for the round was half a second. The round punched through the light armor in the empty troop compartment and filled the interior with fragments and dust. Guerrero's first shot arrived almost simultaneously, tearing the searchlight off the vehicle. The panicked gunner shifted from the boat and fired wildly toward *Kauai*'s muzzle flash while the drivers scrambled to put the vehicle in reverse. *Kauai*'s second and third rounds ended all that, cutting the gunner in half and bursting the vehicle's fuel tanks. The second VN-4's commander was no fool, backing away from his burning comrade at full speed without lights or gunfire.

"Second target disengaging, Captain," Williams reported.

"Ceasefire, but stay on him until he is out of sight," Haley said, then keyed her command set. "Orchid-One, Orchid-Actual, report!"

"Orchid, Orchid-One, three down: Kelly, Frankle, and Lopez," Lee replied. "Minor hull damage, but we should make it to the ship. Over."

Haley felt like she had been punched in the stomach. "Orchid-One, how bad? Over."

"Kelly is dead. Lopez is very bad; XO is working on him now. Frankle should be OK. Over."

"Roger, continue to ship. Out." Haley stared straight ahead, her mind reeling.

"Captain, shall I get underway?" Hopkins asked.

Haley turned and blinked. "Yes, minimum recovery speed, heading your discretion."

"Aye, aye, ma'am."

"Orchid, Starfish One Seven."

Haley looked at the UHF speaker and thought, *Oh God! Not now!* She nodded at Bunting.

"Starfish One Seven, Orchid, go ahead," the young petty officer transmitted.

"Orchid, One Seven. Your gunboat has left the pier and is heading your way. Estimated speed thirty-two knots. You need to get out of there, sir."

Haley said, "I'll take it." She switched her radio to UHF and said, "One Seven, Orchid-Actual, we have to recover our boat. Is there anything you can do to help us out? Over."

"Orchid, One Seven, I can jam his fire control radar and call for help. That's about it. Over."

"Do what you can, One Seven. Thank you. Orchid-Actual, out." She switched to intra-ship. "Boat deck, CO."

"Boat deck, ma'am," Bondurant replied.

"Boat deck. We have a Chinese gunboat bearing down on us at full speed. As soon as that small boat hull is out of the water, I need to know so we can start running."

"It's coming alongside now, ma'am. Stand by." Moments later, *Kauai* heeled a few degrees to port. "CO, boat deck, the small boat is clear of the water!"

Haley turned to Hopkins. "Chief, course three-zero-zero, maximum speed."

"Helm, right standard rudder, steer three-zero-zero!"

"My rudder is right fifteen degrees, coming to three-zero-zero, Chief!" Pickins replied.

Hopkins keyed the intercom. "Main Control, Conn. COB, we have an enemy gunboat coming after us at flank speed, and we need every knot you got. Take propulsion control."

"Conn, Main Control, I have propulsion control. I am by-passing safeties."

"Very well."

"Captain, I have the gunboat on EO/IR, bearing one-seven-eight relative, target angle zero," Williams said.

Haley glanced at the navigation panel in front of Zuccaro. It showed the island in the navigation chart function, but no radar overlay with all transmitters secured. Zuccaro was frozen, staring at the screen, and her hands were motionless over her keyboard. "Williams, I want you to ping that gunboat with the rangefinder long enough to get a single readout—don't leave it on."

"Aye, aye, ma'am."

"CO from boat deck." Bondurant's voice came over the intra-ship channel.

"Go ahead," Haley said.

"Small boat is cradled, and the crane is secure. Casualties and passengers have been transferred to the mess-deck. XO asked me to pass that he is assisting Doc with the wounded."

"Bondurant, relieve Mr. Wyporek of his medical duties. I need him on the Bridge ASAP."

"Aye, aye, ma'am."

"Captain, gunboat range is six thousand, three hundred fifty yards," Williams said.

"Very well, ping them once every thirty seconds."

"Aye, aye, ma'am."

Now it was a race. Haley hated to drag Ben to the Bridge when all he was likely to do was stand around, but they had to have a standby if she or Hopkins were incapacitated. *What has gotten into the Chinese? Are they going to start a war over a bunch of goddammed criminals?* She stepped over to the ship's telephone and dialed the messdeck.

After one ring, the phone answered, "Messdeck, Jenkins."

"Petty Officer Jenkins, Captain. Is Mr. Frankle able to talk?"

"Yes, ma'am. Standby, please."

After a couple of seconds, Frankle came on the phone. "Frankle."

"Agent Frankle, I've had one shootout with the Chinese, and now that I'm retiring, I've got a gunboat coming balls to the wall to catch us. What the HELL is going on here?!"

"I knew I should have killed that son of a bitch! It's Chen, the Chinese base leader. We caught him with his pants down, literally, in that brothel. He knows if we make it through, he's finished! When the APCs didn't do the job, he must have ordered the gunboat to destroy us at all costs. I'm sorry, Captain, I did not see this coming."

"Right. So much for negotiations. Chief Drake's pulling out the stops below, and maybe we can stay out of reach."

"Yes, ma'am. And again, my apologies."

Haley hung up the phone, turned to see Ben coming onto the Bridge, and was briefly shocked at his ghastly appearance. He was covered with dirt and blood and had the pale, vacant look of shock. She walked over, reached for his upper left arm, and squeezed it. "Ben, I can't tell you how relieved I am to see you," she whispered. "How's Lopez?"

"Doc is working on him, Captain. Bondurant, Gerard, and Lee are doing everything they can to help." He turned to look her in the eyes, then shook his head.

She led him to the command chair and said, "Have a seat."

"No, ma'am, I'll be OK...."

"Sit down. That's an order. We may need you again soon."

"Aye, aye, ma'am."

"Captain! The gunboat has opened fire!" Williams shouted.

Haley's gaze snapped to the camera display, where a line of four glowing balls climbed slowly into the air, seemed to stop, and then descended into the water, flashing when they hit.

"Ranging shot," Williams said. "Starfish has their radar jacked up, so they don't know our range."

"In other words, they're pinging us."

"Yes, ma'am. But they're already inside six thousand yards, and their pings will start reaching us any second."

Haley keyed her intra-ship transmitter. "Mount 51, Mount 52, and Overwatch, secure and shelter inside the

Bridge!" Then she turned and stared at the image of the gunboat on Williams's screen. As if on cue, the image emitted another string of four balls. These landed much closer, and Haley could feel the taps from the shock waves of the detonating shells through the balls of her feet, although the sounds of the explosions were masked by the roar of *Kauai*'s diesel generators.

Hopkins stepped beside her and said, "Captain, you should let the crew know what to expect."

Haley looked at her and received a sad smile in return. "You're right. Thank you, Chief." Haley stepped over to the 1MC and picked up the microphone. "Folks, this is the captain. I'm sure you've heard we have a Chinese gunboat on our tail, and he's closing fast. We are within his thirty-seven-millimeter range, and I expect him to start send-ing HE shells our way, hoping for a lucky hit. We have an electronic warfare bird who has knocked back his radar, so his shooting will be wild until he gets closer. Our bird is calling in air support, and it will hopefully be here before then. Our armor should keep out the shell fragments, so hang tough and stay inside and away from the windows. Good luck to us all." *Yeah, and when he gets close enough for direct fire with armor-piercing rounds, what then?*

Guerrero was coming through the door with his rifle, with Hebert and Connally right behind him as she re-placed the microphone. "Hunker down, guys, and prepare for incoming."

"You don't need to tell us twice, ma'am," Hebert said as he and the other two grabbed spots in the Bridge's rear.

Ben stood from the command chair and held it for Haley. She had just taken her seat when Williams said, "Here it comes!" The gunboat had fired a burst of four shells, which landed even with *Kauai* about fifty yards to port and detonated on contact with the water. These were close enough to hear the loud bang of the explosions.

"Chase salvos, Chief!" Haley ordered. *Kauai* was a difficult target at this distance, and the gunboat was trying to conserve ammunition using short bursts rather than continuous fire. Without radar, the gunboat would have to correct its aim based on where the last burst landed. "Chase salvos" meant turn toward that side and foil the correction.

"Aye, aye, Captain. Helm, left to two-nine-five."

"Left to two-nine-five," Pickins repeated.

Another burst landed and detonated off the starboard side, and Hopkins ordered a course change to the right. Haley knew their luck would not hold for long—as soon as the gunboat captain realized what they were doing, he would go to rapid-fire. She selected UHF and keyed her microphone. "Starfish One Seven, Orchid Actual. Where's that help? Over."

"Orchid, Starfish One Seven. I'm on with a flight of F-16s from the 93rd. They're three minutes out. Over."

"One Seven, Orchid Actual, roger, tell them to step on it! Out."

Hopkins had just altered course to the left again, and the game went on for two more salvos. Then, as Haley feared, the Chinese captain tried a long burst. The twelve shells missed, falling on both sides. Two were close enough to pepper *Kauai* with shrapnel, sharp pings ringing through the Bridge like hail on a tin roof.

Their luck ran out on the next burst: one shell exploded on the left side of the mast, knocking out the EO camera and showering the Flying Bridge with shrapnel. Another struck the special operations boat and started a small fire. The fire itself was not an immediate danger to the ship, but it provided a beacon that brought hell down on them. Shells were bursting on the rear of the superstructure and in the water around *Kauai.* The bridge crew huddled behind what cover they could find as the windows in the rear doors shattered and debris scattered around them. As they kneeled together between the command chair and the FC3 console, Haley looked into Ben's face and, seeing the same fear she had, reached out and gripped his hand.

The bombardment ended abruptly with an ear-shattering double boom that shook the deck beneath them. Haley's first thought was, *Shit! Now they're using rockets!* Then a second double boom shook the ship, and, after a brief delay, another pair of double booms.

"It's the F-16s! They're thumping the gunboat!" Ben cried.

Haley smiled with relief, gave Ben's hand a last squeeze, then let go. They both stood and looked at the chaos of the Bridge. As the others stood, Haley called out. "Chief! Are you OK?"

"Pickins and I are tolerable, ma'am! Still on heading three-zero-zero."

"Thank God. Ben, are you alright?"

"Yes, ma'am."

She glanced at the FC3 crew, Hebert, Guerrero, and Connally. "Anyone hurt?" After getting mumbles of "OK" and thumbs-up from the rest, she nodded and turned to Ben.

"What the hell does 'thumping' mean?"

"They were buzzing the gunboat at a hundred feet and Mach One-plus. My dad told me they used to do it when he was flying F/A-18s in Iraq, and they needed to provide close support but couldn't drop bombs or shoot. That double boom was the shock wave. If it shook us at two miles, you can imagine what it must be like a hundred feet away. It's non-lethal, but you can be sure there isn't an intact window, light bulb, or glass lens on that gunboat anymore."

Haley nodded, plugged into her command chair, and selected UHF. *Please let this be working.* "Starfish One Seven, Orchid Actual.

"Orchid, One Seven, good to hear your voice, ma'am!"

"One Seven, Orchid, Backatcha. We're blind here. What's going on?"

"Orchid, One Seven. Your gunboat is bugging out. He's heading zero eight zero at thirty-four knots. The thumper element has bingo-ed for the tanker, but the two shooters are holding on station until he heads into port."

"One Seven, Orchid, roger. Please pass a huge thanks from us."

"WILCO. And, for the record, none of us were ever here. Copy?"

"One Seven, roger that. Never heard of you. Thanks for everything. Out." She turned to Ben. "Nothing like a 'Back Off or we'll kill you' gesture to give a captain a moment of pause. He probably thought he was chasing some pirates until the attack aircraft showed up."

Ben nodded. "Yes, ma'am. The boat is still burning, Captain. I'll head down to deal with that now."

"Yes, good luck. Call me when you can."

"Yes, ma'am. Hebert and Guerrero, let's go!" Ben said, then turned and left with the two petty officers, their feet crunching on broken glass and ceiling fragments covering the deck.

"Petty Officer Williams, see if any bridge systems are still working," Haley said.

"Aye, aye, ma'am. Bunting, Zuccaro, give me a hand!"

Haley tried the intra-ship radio without a result. She stepped over and pressed the call button for the intercom. "Main Control, CO."

"Main Control, COB here."

"Report, COB."

"No damage in Main Control, ma'am. I have Brown checking the hull forward for leaks."

"Thank you, COB. Carry on, please."

"Yes, ma'am."

Hopkins stepped beside her. "Ma'am, we need to throttle back and post a lookout."

Haley put her hand to her forehead. "Yes, thank you, Chief. Come back to ten knots for now."

"Aye, aye, ma'am. Connally, grab a handheld radio and binoculars and get up to the Flying Bridge. No, wait, it's probably trashed. Go on down to the bow. See if you can remember how to be a lookout."

"On it, Chief!"

Hopkins pulled the throttles back, and *Kauai*'s hull ceased planing and settled back into the water. Haley grabbed the bridge railing for support and shook her head. *Wouldn't that be ironic, surviving two gun battles and then sinking after smacking into another boat?*

Ben

Ben led the two petty officers down the ladder, carefully hugging the ship's side with their boots crunching on broken glass, shrapnel, and other debris. The fire hose nearest the boat deck was shredded, and Hebert had to make two stops before finding one still intact. The fire proved easy to extinguish, as it was confined to the boat, having started when the shell shattered the engines. Ben posted Guerrero as a re-flash watch and did a quick tour around the hull—there were plenty of black marks from blast scoring, but no penetrations from what he could see.

Ben dreaded what he would find on the messdeck. He would never forget that awful moment of chaos on the boat when the Chinese machine gun fire laced across the bow. It was only the one burst that hit home. *Kauai*'s return fire, each round looking almost like red laser fire accompanied by a loud crack from the shock wave, silenced the Chinese vehicle. But the damage had been done.

Ben had cried out when he saw Lopez was down and crawled over to find him bleeding profusely from two wounds—the bullets must have been armor-piercing as they punched right through his vest. Lopez was writhing in pain as Ben pulled open his vest and applied pressure to the wounds with his bare hands. Lopez quickly passed out and remained unconscious for the rest of the boat's return to *Kauai*. Ben looked around the bow to find Kelly face down, unmoving, and Frankle, his arm a bloody mess, being attended by Gerard.

Bryant was waiting with the litter when they arrived, and Ben helped carry Lopez into the makeshift surgery on the messdeck. Bryant worked quickly—he had performed gunshot wound first aid frequently in Iraq and Afghanistan while in the army. Ben bent to the task of assistant, helping with surgical equipment and I.V.s until Bondurant tapped him out.

"You're needed on the Bridge, sir."

"Screw that!" Ben muttered, turning to Lopez.

Bondurant grasped his arm and gently turned him around. "*We* need you on the Bridge, sir."

Ben looked at the big boatswain's mate and blinked. "Right."

That was only twenty minutes ago, Ben thought as he looked at the clock when he came into the messdeck. His gaze fell on the mess table, where Bryant, Bondurant, Lee, and Jenkins were clustered—a bloody white sheet covered Lopez's upper body and head, and no one was moving. Ben blinked in disbelief. His chest tightened, and when he could finally take a breath, he blurted out, "No!"

They all turned, and Lee walked over, embraced him, and buried her face in his chest. "No," Ben said again, more quietly, putting his arms around Lee and holding her as she sobbed.

Chapter 18

Tristitia Victoriae

USCG Cutter Kauai, moored, Pier C, Naval Station Guantanamo Bay, Cuba
13:29 EST, 6 December

Haley

Haley was exhausted, physically and emotionally. She was waiting in her cabin to be called to give her statement to the commander sent by the Seventh District headquarters, who had met them when they arrived at 07:30 that morning. He had eyed the vessel coolly, saluted respectfully when Lopez's and Kelly's bodies were brought ashore, then informed Haley and Ben he was sent to get statements from the crew about the mission. One by one, the senior members of the enlisted personnel had been called in, and Ben was with him now.

Haley expected to be relieved of command by day's end. She had checked every block required: violated orders, banged the shit out of her command, and got one of her crew killed. Haley knew she should go over her account in her head, if not on paper, but she couldn't work up the motivation. She felt empty and, for the first time in her life, utterly alone.

She thought back to last night, shortly after the battle. They were hard at work restoring functionality to the bridge systems when the news of Lopez's death brought everything to a stop. Haley stood in shock, staring silently out into the darkness. She did not know how long she stood there before she felt Hopkins's hand gently laid on her shoulder.

"I'm sorry, Captain, but you need to say something," Hopkins said.

Haley turned to look and could tell, even in the darkness, that Hopkins had been crying. Haley walked stiffly to the 1MC and reached for the microphone. "Attention, all hands. I have just learned that our shipmate Juan Lopez has died from his wounds. If I could give you time now to pause and think of him, I would, but we need to look to the boat right now. I know that is what Juan would have wanted. We will take the time to grieve for him as soon as we are out of danger, but I must ask you to continue with the repairs for now. Thank you." She hung up the microphone, turned, and returned to the command chair.

Williams, Bunting, and Zaccaro quickly restored communications and the auxiliary navigation radar—the primary multi-mode radar had taken a direct hit and was finished. At least, with an active navigation radar, they could travel safely. Haley made her initial report of the damage, Lopez's and Kelly's deaths, and her intent to dock at Gitmo as quickly as possible. Shortly after Ben returned to the Bridge, they received confirmation orders to Gitmo and were informed resources for emergency repairs were being sent.

There was a knock at her door, and Haley called, "Come in."

Ben opened the door and stepped in. "Commander Lewis wants to see you, ma'am."

"Thank you. How did it go?" Haley was almost afraid to ask.

"He's thorough. But he seemed just interested in the facts."

"I see."

As she stood, Ben said, "It's going to be OK, ma'am."

"Thank you for that," she said resignedly.

"No, ma'am, you don't understand. I have been in exactly this situation before, at Resolution. Sam thought he would get canned and came out with a medal. It's the same. You'll see."

Haley gave his shoulder a soft squeeze. "Thank you, Ben. Whatever happens, you sure earned your pay this week."

"Thank you, Captain," he said, then stepped aside to let her pass.

It was a short walk to Drake's stateroom, where Commander Charles P. Lewis conducted the interviews. Lewis was the Coast Guard Liaison Officer for the Guantanamo

Bay Naval Base and had been detailed to put together a formal report of the action. Drake's quarters were cramped for such an effort, but the Bridge was under emergency repair, and the messdeck was still being cleaned. Haley knocked on the door and entered when Lewis bade her come in.

"You wanted to see me, Commander?" Haley said with as little emotion as possible.

"Yes, Captain. Please take a seat." After Haley sat, he said, "I apologize for adding to your stress after the hell you all have been through, but orders were to get statements while the events were still fresh in everyone's mind." He then explained her rights against self-incrimination and asked if she wanted counsel.

"No, sir. Let's get it done," Haley replied.

"Good. Now take me through the action from when you put the DIA team ashore on the 4th."

Haley told the story to the best of her recollection and then answered several questions, none of which were the "gotcha" kind she expected. After she answered the last question, Lewis said, "That about does it for me. Do you have any questions?"

"Yes, sir. Will they decide soon? I would like to get my folks home."

"Decide what?"

"Whether I'm to continue in command."

He sat back in astonishment. "*What?* That is not a question on anyone's mind, to the best of my knowledge. I was sent here to help you transfer your 'guests,' get patched up and on your way, and relieve you and your XO of the burden of writing an official report. I apologize if you were given any other impression. The reading of rights is standard procedure for any inquiry."

"I see. Thank you, sir."

"Look, it's not my place to tell a captain what to do on her ship, but I strongly recommend you and your XO get some rest. You've both been through hell. Let us take the load off you while you're here, at least."

"I'm grateful to you, sir."

"Not at all."

USCG Cutter Kauai, Port Canaveral Ship Channel, two nautical miles east of the Trident Access Channel, Port Canaveral, Florida
09:03 EST, 8 December

Haley

This was an easy transit for Haley. This time, Lee was doing the mooring, with Hopkins doing the coaching. Lee was a nervous wreck, of course. Haley shook her head in wonder—Lee was fearless when it came to danger and a master with a small boat, but she was almost a basket case on a special sea detail with the CO looking over her shoulder.

Ben was standing beside her, ostensibly assisting with oversight. In fact, he was there so that Haley could keep an eye on him. Ben looked like hell, and Haley was sure he had slept little, if at all, since the engagement with the Chinese. Despite her insistence to the contrary, she knew he blamed himself for Lopez's death and was genuinely worried that he would end up another casualty of the action. Haley called Victoria when they came under cell-phone coverage and asked her to meet them at the dock. Hopefully, she could reach him and pull him back. At the very least, there was no way Haley would let Ben drive in his current state.

Lee's mooring was flawless, and as Haley was finishing a very positive critique, Ben strolled onto the port bridge wing, as usual, to watch as the deck crew doubled the mooring lines and rigged the brow. Haley followed a moment later and saw him looking at a woman approaching. It was Victoria, walking toward the ship in her white sundress with her red hair pulled into her customary ponytail. She saw Ben and waved.

"XO, aren't you going to wave back?" Haley asked from behind him.

Ben, startled, then waved at Victoria. "How?"

"I called her once I got a cell signal," Haley answered. "I told her you had a rough trip, best discussed once you two were home. She agreed. Now, you are done for this patrol. Beat feet."

Ben blinked away tears and said, "Aye, aye, ma'am."

Haley watched from the Bridge thirty seconds later as Ben strode over the brow and swept Victoria into his arms. *You're a lucky man, Ben Wyporek. Don't screw it up.*

Haley went inside the Bridge, nodded to Hopkins, who was busy securing the FC3 with Williams, and went to her cabin. She was only there a minute when her telephone rang, and she answered, "Captain."

"Seaman Pickins on the quarterdeck, ma'am. You have a phone call on Line 2."

"Thank you, Pickins," she said, then pressed the Line 2 button on her phone. "Lieutenant Reardon."

"Haley, it's Sam Powell. I heard about what happened and wondered if you would like to talk."

"Thank you for your consideration, Commander. I'll be fine."

"It's still Sam, and if you'll forgive me for saying so, I don't see how anyone coming off what you just went through would be fine."

Haley was conflicted, as she really *did* need to talk to someone right now. The clichéd term "loneliness of command" was suddenly very real for her, and her choice to stay unattached was rapidly losing its appeal. Still, she didn't know if she could share with the man who brought this ship and crew through two years of challenging operations when she balled it up and lost a man in her first week.

"OK, Sam. What have you been told?"

"Mercier shared the gist and asked me to call. She's seen this sort of thing before and is worried about you. She knew she couldn't help, so she called me."

"To straighten me out and get things back on track?" Haley asked bitterly.

"Not hardly. She knew you were on your own, going through an experience that would have cracked *me* when I had the two best partners in the world to lean on, Jo and Ben."

"You got everyone through two years. I got Lopez killed before I completed my first week."

Sam sighed audibly. "There, but for the grace of God. I was lucky, Haley, luckier than I deserved. I lie awake sometimes thinking of how bad Resolution and Barbello could have gone, maybe should have gone."

"Maybe, maybe not. All I know is that Ben will have his hands full with transfer requests when he returns. If he returns, that is. You should have seen him this morning."

"Victoria will put Ben back together, and he'll be on board in a day or two—don't sell either of them short. And he won't come back to any transfer requests. Do you think the crew will lose faith in you because you took a calculated risk that didn't work out? With respect, you're wrong. The mistake would have been leaving that DIA team and those two women to their fate, and they would never have forgiven you for THAT."

"And what about Lopez?"

"He would feel the same. And he would have gone, too, even if he knew things would go south. Did Ben tell you the Lopez/Barbello story?"

"No."

"He was coming to the tail-end of his ME A-school when we got the call. He was supposed to meet us over at AUTEC in the Bahamas the following week, so Hoppy called and told him to hang out in PC instead. Not Lope. He wrangled an early graduation and drove a rental down to Key West to jump on with us before we stepped off. There was no way he was going to sit around while his family was mixing it up."

"Is that supposed to make me feel better?"

"No, just point out what the crew has transcends you and me. They know the risks and are on *Kauai* because they want to be. They don't expect miracles from you, only that you keep the faith, and you've proven that."

"*Fortiter et Fideliter.*" She glanced across the room at the small plaque, but could only see a blur through the tears.

"Exactly. I'm not here to pump sunshine up your behind, just to tell you that you are what and where the crew and the Coast Guard need you to be."

Haley took a breath to steady herself, then said, "Thank you, Sam."

"Not at all. Could you come over for dinner tonight?"

"No, I know you are busy getting ready for the move."

"Nonsense. We need a break, and Jo needs an excuse to whip up her Ropa Vieja. You'd be doing me a favor—she's been on my ass for weeks to drag you over here. Please, take another hit for the team."

"Well, when you put it that way, how can I say no?"

"That's the spirit. Go Bears! See you at six?"

"Sounds good."

"Excellent! 5630 Breakers Lane on Patrick."

Haley jotted the address on her notepad. "5630. Got it. Thank you."

"No worries. You have my number. Any time you need to talk, I'm here."

"Thank you, Sam. I'm looking forward to dinner."

"Take care, Haley."

He really is a good man. She thought as she replaced the phone. She felt rather silly now, thinking that Sam would try some cheap psychological bullshit on her. *You haven't been right about anybody lately.* Then she smiled sadly, pulled her cellphone out of her desk drawer, and dialed a number she hadn't in a long time.

"Haley!" the voice said, answering after two rings.

"Hi, Dad."

Victoria

Victoria did not recognize the phone number when the call came at 7:30 that morning, but remembered the area code as one of the two in Hillsborough County, Florida. She knew no one in Hillsborough County and was inclined to let it roll over to voice mail. However, the software on her phone did not indicate spam or a telemarketer, so she took a chance. "Hello?"

"Hello, Victoria? This is Haley Reardon."

"Oh, hello, Miss Reardon!" Then the realization set in. *Why is she calling me and not Benjamin?* "Has something happened to Benjamin?" she blurted out.

"No, no, he's fine," Haley had answered quickly. "Sorry, I should have led with that. And I wish you would call me Haley."

"Very well, thank you, Haley. Is there something I can do for you?" Victoria asked, trying to conceal her relief. She was afraid of appearing "clingy," particularly in front of Benjamin's new commanding officer.

"Yes, we'll be entering port this morning, around nine o'clock. I hope you'll excuse me. I try not to meddle in my subordinates' personal business, but I wonder if you would mind meeting us at the dock when we arrive."

"Oh, I do not mind at all, Miss... Haley. Is there something wrong?"

"Not to worry you, Victoria, but it has been a difficult patrol, particularly for Ben, and I'd feel better if he did not drive himself home this time."

"I am grateful for your concern for Benjamin. Can you tell me anything about what happened? I appreciate there might be things you must hold back because of security concerns."

"No, Victoria, it's not security. It's that I'm pretty far out on a limb just calling you, and Ben should tell you about things in his own way."

"I understand, and I will be there in time to meet *Kauai* when she arrives."

"Thank you, Victoria. I hope to see you soon. Good-bye."

"Goodbye, Haley," Victoria said as she hung up.

For the next hour, ending when she left for the harbor, Victoria scoured the Internet for some clue of what had happened over the past few days that would involve Benjamin. Nothing. She was tempted to call Joana for advice, but decided she had to learn to do these things herself. Her need to focus on her driving as she made her way to the base was a welcome distraction.

She recognized the guard at the gate of the Space Force Station—he was one of her favorites. "Hello, Sergeant Timms. It is good to see you again!" She handed over her ID and the special pass that allowed her on base.

"Good morning, Victoria. Likewise. How's it going?"

"Quite well, thank you. Benjamin and I are engaged."

"Wow, that's terrific! Those Coasties have all the luck," he said as he returned her documents.

"Thank you, Sergeant."

"Take care, Miss."

It was a short drive from the gate to the Trident Wharf. When she cleared the trees, Victoria's heart jumped when she caught sight of *Kauai*, already in the Trident Access Channel, after passing the security barrier. She parked and walked through a gap in the warehouses to watch the mooring. The process involved in the mooring and un-mooring of a large vessel like *Kauai* was always fascinating to Victoria. Using asymmetric thrust from the engines, turning moment from rudders and mooring lines, and the direction and speed of the wind were all factors in a delicate ballet that brought *Kauai* into the exact desired spot along the wharf. Benjamin said that Emilia Hopkins was the best at this—Victoria wondered if she was in control just now.

Something was off about *Kauai* this morning. As the ship got closer, Victoria ran her eye carefully over the boat's lines and noted some discrepancies from her memory. Several of the lifelines and stanchions were missing, as was the RHIB. The large radar antenna atop the mast had been removed, and tarps covered the large electro-optical camera below it and the entire Flying Bridge. As the boat pivoted to moor pointed outbound in the channel, Victoria could see the windows in the doors at the rear of the Bridge were also covered. *It looks something like the damage from Hurricane Jacob, but there was no storm anywhere in the vicinity. What could have happened?*

Victoria saw Benjamin come out onto the bridge wing to watch the line handlers, followed by a female officer she took to be Haley. Victoria waved when Benjamin looked in her direction, but he did not wave back at first. Most unusual. He had some sort of discussion with Haley, then disappeared into the Bridge. Less than a minute later, he emerged and crossed over onto the dock. Victoria ran to meet him and pulled up in shock as he approached.

Victoria had never seen Benjamin look like this. His face was pale, eyes red with dark periorbital circles, and he looked haggard. Victoria had seen him fatigued before, but this was something altogether different. He dropped his bag and took her into his arms, and, like always, she squeezed him tightly, feeling the strength of his arms and immersing herself in his scent.

"Victoria, thank God. I'm so happy to see you," he said.

Even his voice seemed drained. It was apparent now why Haley had been concerned. "I need to get you home, Benjamin."

"But my car..." he said distractedly.

"Your car has sat here for five days, Benjamin. One more day will not matter," she replied firmly.

"Yes, Boss," he said with a sad smile.

Victoria reached up to caress his face, gave him a quick kiss, then took his arm and led him to her car. They traveled home in silence. Benjamin knew she did not like to be distracted by conversation while driving, but his complete silence was unusual. He stared vacantly out the window the entire trip, almost without moving.

When they reached the apartment, Victoria led Benjamin inside and over to the couch, sat beside him, took his hands, and said, "Benjamin, I know something is wrong. I can see that *Kauai* was seriously damaged, and even I can tell something is affecting you inside. I know you want to spare me, but we are formal partners now, and you need to tell me when something is wrong."

Benjamin nodded and began a narration of the story from the beginning. This was the first time Victoria had to deal with a serious emotional event with Benjamin—she was terrified of doing something wrong and adding to his distress. She rigorously applied Joana's advice: just listen; don't guide him, inquire deeper, offer suggestions, or tell him he's wrong to feel the way he does. Just let it flow.

Benjamin broke down and started crying when he got to Juan Lopez's death and his sense of responsibility for it. Victoria desperately wanted to tell him he was not to blame and should not feel that way, but held her tongue. She was beating back tears herself—she had talked to Juan at one of the unit gatherings and was fond of him—she would save her grief for later. Benjamin had finished and was quietly sobbing, his face buried in her chest. She leaned her cheek on his head, stroking his back and nape.

The moment had cleared away the last remaining barrier between them. During this terrible time, Victoria knew Benjamin needed her very badly and felt confident at last that she was precisely where she needed to be, doing exactly what she needed to do. *My brave, good, and kind man, I finally have a chance to give back what you have always given me.*

Robbery-Homicide Division Commander's Office, Police Administration Building, 100 West First Street, 5th floor, Los Angeles,

California
09:05 PST, 14 December

Haley

The Condolence Call. This was the other hard part they tell you about in CO school, but nobody seemed to know anyone who has had to do it—line-of-duty deaths were that rare in the Coast Guard despite the extreme hazards of the work. Lopez had not listed any next of kin or emergency contact information, and they were at a loss as to what to do with his personal effects. Then Ben remembered Lopez talking about knocking around in the foster care system, teetering on the edge of becoming just another victim or victimizer, when an LAPD detective stepped up and changed his life. Lopez could not say what motivated the detective and his wife to take him on as a foster child, just that they gave him an excuse to do good. Ben pulled Lopez's Servicemembers' Group Life Insurance forms and found a name—Reuben S. Vasquez—then, after a little more research, found a Captain Reuben S. Vasquez in command of the Robbery-Homicide Division at LAPD Headquarters. There was no doubt this was the same man.

It was cool in Los Angeles that morning, with the typical bright sunshine but a rare on-shore breeze that brought a sense of freshness to the city. The weather was a small blessing during the short walk from the hotel to the Police Headquarters Building in her service dress dark blue uniform. Haley had flown in the night before, a non-stop from Orlando, leaving Ben in acting command of *Kauai* in her absence.

Ben had returned after three days of quasi-convalescent leave, with a worried-looking Victoria dropping him off with a kiss. He was changed, less light-hearted, and more focused than before. Like Sam before her, Haley had mixed feelings about what was arguably a professional improvement. Haley was stunned and moved a couple of days later when he submitted a request to extend for a year as Kauai's XO. "You need looking after, ma'am," he said semi-seriously when she had asked why. It was the most expeditiously approved extension request in Coast Guard history.

Ben had offered to make this trip for her, and Haley had been tempted to accept—Ben had known Lopez for over a year instead of Haley's few weeks. She was also not looking forward to blowing up the lives of Lopez's beloved foster parents with the devastating news. In the end, she knew this was one duty a CO could not delegate.

Haley waited in the outer office with the beautiful mahogany box holding Lopez's personal awards and keepsakes. Haley had been surprised when Drake had brought it in before her departure, expecting a simple cardboard box. Her question of where he got hold of it received the standard Drake reply: "I know a guy." Fortunately, he stepped out before she opened it and found the inscription on the brass plate inside the hinged lid—In Memory of Maritime Law Enforcement Specialist Second Class

Juan Lopez, Our Shipmate Forever, the Crew of USCGC *Kauai* (WPB-1351). She had cried for ten minutes after reading it.

"Lieutenant, Captain Vasquez can see you now," Vasquez's administrative assistant said as she held open the office door. After seeing Haley fumble with her combination cap, the middle-aged woman continued, "I can take care of that for you, miss."

"Thank you," Haley replied as she stepped through the door, and it closed behind her.

"Good morning, Lieutenant!" Vasquez said, standing to come around his desk with an outstretched hand. He was a fit and handsome man, an inch or two taller than Haley, with short salt-and-pepper hair and a mustache in his late fifties. Vasquez was in shirt sleeves, tie, charcoal-colored vest, the matching jacket hanging on a clothes tree in the office corner. "I am always psyched to meet another Coastie." He smiled as he shook her hand. "My foster son is a petty officer in the service."

"Yes, sir. I know. I ... was Juan's commanding officer," Haley said. Vasquez's hand froze, and his smile vanished.

"When?"

"A little over a week ago. I am terribly sorry, Captain, both for your loss and the delay we had in informing you. Juan didn't list you as next of kin or emergency contact."

"No, that's Juan for you. Please sit down," he said, gesturing to one of the guest chairs by the coffee table. "I'm sorry, I didn't get your first name," he added as he sat in the chair facing her.

"Haley, sir."

"Thank you, Haley. I appreciate you coming to see me. Is there anything you can tell me?" he asked, looking into her eyes.

"Yes, sir. He was badly wounded helping rescue two women from a transnational criminal gang and died on the operating table. Last week, his remains were buried with full military honors at Arlington National Cemetery. Again, I'm sorry we didn't get word to you, but I promise everything was properly done. We have put Juan's awards and some of his personal items we thought you might want in this box," she said as she carefully handed it to him.

"Awards?"

"Yes, Juan was awarded the Coast Guard Commendation Medal with the Valor device for a classified action last April and the Coast Guard Medal for saving a couple and their two little girls during Hurricane Jacob in September at great peril of his life. The others are the Bronze Star and Purple Heart for his last action." She paused when he put his head down, and a tear fell on his lap.

He regained control before he straightened up and gazed into her eyes again. "Is there anything else?" he asked, placing his hand on the box's lid.

"Yes, sir. A few pictures, his collar devices for petty officer second class—he was promoted posthumously—and a beat-up copy of *The Black Echo*."

Vasquez nodded. "Yes, that was the first book I ever gave him. He wanted stories about what I did—Connelly's novels captured the gist and are good reads." His eyes welled again. "He was a wonderful kid who became one of the best men I've ever known."

"I can name sixteen Coasties who would say the same, sir. I had only known him myself for a few weeks as I had just taken command, but his loss was the most terrible one I have ever faced. You should know that he thought the world of you and your wife. He said he could have easily gone very wrong. There was so much peer pressure, but you two gave him something he could grab on to and hold close."

He looked down and shook his head. "I wonder why we bother. Medals and no difference to the drugs, crime, and misery. Is that what Juan died for?"

"Sir, if I may, I think you'll find this a more substantial legacy." She pulled an envelope out of her pocket and handed it to him.

Vasquez took a piece of paper out of the envelope, glanced at it, then at Haley.

"Those twenty-eight names are people whose lives Juan had a direct role in saving. The first four are the family I told you of, the next twenty-two were human trafficking victims he saved from a sinking ship, and the last two were the ones from his last action. Those people are alive today because of Juan—he made a difference."

Vasquez read through the sheet, then folded it and put it in the envelope. "Thank you, Haley. That does help."

"I'm glad of that, sir. Is there anything else I can do for you? Anything that you need?"

Vasquez stood, walked over, and placed the box in the center of his desk. "No. Thank you for coming."

They shook hands, and Haley stepped out of the office. She could hear Vasquez quietly sniffle as she closed the door. As Vasquez's assistant handed over her cap, Haley asked, "Where is the restroom, please?"

"Turn right, then the second door on the right," she said, pointing across the room.

"Thank you, ma'am," Haley said. She barely made it inside before she started crying again.

Chapter 19

Coda

Interrogation Room 3C, United States Penitentiary, Administrative Maximum Facility, Florence, Colorado
11:07 MST, 27 December

Rostov

This was his sixth visit to the interrogation room in the three weeks he had been incarcerated. On each previous occasion, he had been frog-marched the two hundred meters by two burly guards and chained to a fixed table and chair in the middle of the room. There he sat for close to an hour awaiting the arrival of a government lawyer, who would read the charges against him and ask him if he wanted to give a statement. He would say no, he wanted an attorney, and then the government lawyer would pack up and leave. He would be returned to solitary confinement in his 3.5-meter by 2-meter cell. Rostov was unfamiliar with this interrogation technique. It was certainly not one he would have used when he was a security officer—the process took far too long and had none of the ancillary benefits of inflicting pain on the victim.

This trip held an immediate surprise: someone was already seated at the table when he arrived. Rostov looked him over carefully as he was brought into the room and shackled to the table. He was of average height and stature in his mid-30s, with a plain face, brown medium-short hair, and a scruffy beard. He wore a plain navy blue suit with a white shirt and plain maroon tie. Everything about the man was plain. He was obviously no lawyer—this man was an intelligence officer.

After the guards had secured him to the table, the man said, "That will be all, thank you." The guards departed without speaking and closed the door. He then sat staring at Rostov without speaking or moving for what must have been five minutes. It might have been another novel interrogation technique—bore your opponent into submission—but Rostov decided to bring it to an end.

"Aren't you going to lay a panoply of my alleged crimes before me and threaten me with millennia of incarceration unless I confess and betray all my comrades?" Rostov asked.

"Yevgeny Vladimirovich, why on earth would I waste my time with such a useless gesture?" the man replied in perfect, northern-accented Russian.

"My compliments, you speak passable Russian," Rostov replied in Russian.

"Hell, if one hundred forty-five million Russians can do it, how hard can it be, eh?" the man said in English with a broad grin. After allowing the insult to set in, he continued. "I sense you believe that my government needs something from you, something that we would be willing to make a deal for, perhaps to include your freedom. If that is what you genuinely believe, please let me set you straight. We know everything about your organization, from top to bottom. There is nothing you can tell us about the 252 Syndicate we do not already know. How do we know these things? Let me explain.

"About two months ago, a ship operated by one of your front companies, the motor vessel *Miho Dujam*, was detected and pursued by U.S. law enforcement agents in the Bahamas. The crew scuttled the ship, which prevented the seizure of a large quantity of illegal armaments but failed in the murder of the twenty-two female captives on board who were destined for sexual servitude. I am delighted to say these women have been or soon will be returned to their families or another safe environment. Before the *Miho Dujam* sank, our officers found, aside from the women, a laptop computer containing enough data and metadata for us to penetrate your IT systems at all levels. That is how we learned of your travel itinerary and could position forces to apprehend you.

"Your organization wisely ditched all their current passwords when you were taken, but it was far too late by then—we were in everywhere. As we speak, forensic accountants across the northern hemisphere are tracing every bank account you use, every property you own, and every bent politician and policeman on your payroll. The days of expansion are over for the 252 Syndicate. Now, I'm not saying we can extirpate you. There will always be those countries where most of the ruling class is corrupt, and a vile organization like yours can flourish. You are welcome to them. So, Yevgeny Vladimirovich, there is nothing the United States needs from you to sink the 252s."

"You lie! If that were true, why go to the trouble of kidnapping me? Several of your men were killed, and was that for nothing?"

"Ah, now you *are* thinking, Yev. Yes, we thought you would be of value along with documentation of your organization's involvement with the Chinese government, particularly involving the Ile Ste. Michel operation. So we went after you while you were there. But wait, right in the middle of our operation, the Chinese base's big Lǎo Bǎn himself shows up! There to dip his wick with two more victims you provided, whom we also rescued. We got every biometric known to man from that guy while he was in your brothel. So, once again, your utility to the United States has vanished. Unless...."

The man leaned forward. "Are you familiar with the expression 'icing on the cake,' Yev? No? It means something a little extra on top of an excellent thing. In your case, it means you give a detailed account of your involvement with Xiaotong Chen and any other Chinese officials working the BRI efforts in Europe. We already have a slam-dunk case of conspiracy in international crime that we can use to help the Haitians break out of that God-awful lease they signed. However, the Chinese can tie things up for years in World Trade Organization litigation. It would be nice to drop some hints that the smart play for them would be to let it go, lest *things* get out into the press. Things that make other BRI clients, past and future, stroke their chins and say, 'Hmm, I wonder if....'"

Rostov started to fold his arms, but then the rattle of chains reminded him the gesture was impossible. Instead, he grinned and said, "Sounds like I have a powerful hand to play after all. Suppose I tell you I have quite a dossier on Comrade Chen and several other colleagues. Depending on what I get in return, I might share that treasure. Now, what are you offering *me*?"

The man sat back with a grim smile and said, "Your life."

"My life?"

"Yes, you get to live. You see, Yev, if you don't give us everything you have, you are quite useless to us. It is expensive to keep a prisoner in a supermax facility like this. With no return on investment, why would we? This is your one and only deal, and the offer, if not accepted, expires when I leave this room. You answer every question we ask about the Chinese, wholly and truthfully, whenever we ask, and we'll keep you alive. Otherwise, we'll cut you loose for a public demonstration of the criminal justice system and find out who wins the race to kill you, the Chinese or your erstwhile chums in the 252 Syndicate. My money will be on the latter, by the way—I'm sure they have a stronger presence in our prison system than the Chinese."

Rostov opened his mouth silently, his mind racing. This was the endgame, and he had no cards he could play. Rostov ached to reach across the table and snap this *Amerikanski mu'dak*'s scrawny neck. He looked down at his shackled hands, trying to keep the frustration off his face.

"Tick, tock, Yev. I haven't got all day here. And don't think I have any investment in keeping you alive for a second. I'm sure there will be plenty of action around my office in *your* death pool."

Rostov glared at the smug little man with all the hatred he had. *Someday, I'll pay you back with interest for this. But I must be alive to do it.*

The man shook his head, stood, and said, "So be it. Good luck in Hell, Yev."

As he turned toward the door, Rostov said, "Wait. I agree. What do you want to know?"

The man shook his head. "That's for someone else. No, Yev, our association ends here. Another officer and lawyer will be with you shortly to get your signature on the usual waiver documents and start your interrogation. I will drop these clothes in a burn bag and go for a long, scalding hot shower in bleach to try to get your stench off me."

As the man reached the door, Rostov spat, "Who the hell are you to talk to me like that?"

"Doctor Peter Simmons, DIA," he said, then stepped through and closed the door.

Harbour House, 1901 Highway A1A, Indian Harbour Beach, Florida
20:07 EDT, 20 May

Haley

It had been a beautiful ceremony, with Victoria and Ben standing beneath the floral arch on the beach overlooking the Atlantic Ocean. Victoria was radiant in her elegant white dress, with her hair up and her long veil lightly stirred by the gentle on-shore breeze. Ben looked every bit the dazzling hero in his dress white uniform with medals, sword, and his brand new shoulder boards holding the two full stripes of a lieutenant. The nondenominational ceremony was conducted by a young Air Force chaplain from Patrick, whom Ben and Victoria had befriended shortly after moving to the area. Even the vows were memorable, with the nervous Victoria delivering flawlessly in her beautiful low voice while the confident Ben actually stumbled with emotion in a couple of amusing places. Overall, Haley rated it a four-Awww! performance.

Kauai's crew, past and present, was heavily represented in the wedding party. Sam Powell stood up for Ben in dress whites as best man, and Joana was a resplendent matron of honor in a long, v-neck, cranberry-colored dress. Hopkins and Lee were almost unrecognizable in their matching dresses, with their hair down and, in Hopkins's case, glasses laid aside for the day. The only "foreigners" in the wedding party were the two groomsmen, two of Ben's friends from the Academy, also in dress whites.

Haley attended as a guest, happy to be spared the awkwardness of appearing in either her uniform or a bridesmaid's dress. She had used the event as an excuse to go shopping with Margot on her last visit home. The strapless blue cocktail dress they picked out was rather stunning compared to Haley's usual choice and made the most of her athletic build. It had been a simple, but significant bonding event that had cleared the remaining bad air with her stepmother.

The reception venue was also first-class and conveniently next to the beach altar, while the reception itself was on the low-key side, with about fifty guests and a DJ. The food was excellent for a mass service, and Sam's wedding toast to the bride and groom did not disappoint. Pleasant as the ceremony and reception were, the most exciting factor for Haley was the man standing in as the father of the bride.

Victoria's parents had been killed in a car crash when she was only eight. Her older sister had filled in as a surrogate parent until she died, shortly before Victoria's graduation from high school. Victoria and her late sister's fiancée helped each other through their grief, and then he, a post-doctorate astrophysicist, helped her through her undergraduate studies at Princeton. When he entered the DIA, he arranged for a data scientist position for Victoria, an arrangement of considerable mutual benefit for her and the organization. This was the famous, or, from Sam's point of view, infamous, Dr. Peter Simmons.

She was intrigued by her first sight of the man as he escorted Victoria to the altar. He was only average height, maybe an inch taller than Haley, but he had a nice build—athletic without being over-muscular. He looked a few years older than she was, maybe mid-thirties, with medium-length dark hair, a close-cropped beard, and a youthful face that reminded her of one of her favorite actors, Joseph Gordon-Levitt. Obviously reveling in his current role, he was beaming as he walked Victoria to the altar and shared a warm look and handshake with Ben when they arrived.

The contrast between Ben's dynamic with Simmons and the latter's with Sam and Hopkins was fascinating. Haley knew Sam was not a fan of Simmons from their conversations in the command handoff, but the depth of the animus surprised her. On the one occasion she saw them shake hands, Sam's bearing and expression were what she would expect from a man forced to shake hands with his soon-to-be-ex-wife's slimy divorce attorney. Hopkins didn't even make a pretense of civility, just turned and walked away the one time Simmons approached her. And yet, he and Ben were clearly friends.

Haley got her chance to inquire later in the evening as she took a stroll on the deck outside the venue overlooking the beach. She was gazing at the stars, surprisingly bright in the cloudless sky, when a voice from behind startled her.

"A rather boring selection this time of year."

She turned to find Simmons looking at her with interest. "I mean the constellations, of course."

"Of course," Haley replied, turning again to look. "Good for navigation, though. I can see at least eight first magnitude stars."

"Six, actually. Antares, Vega, Capella, Arcturus, Spica, and Procyon. Although Castor, Pollux, and Regulus are close. I'm Peter Simmons, by the way."

"Really? I seem to have heard of you."

"And I of you, Captain Reardon. Am I what you had expected?"

"Fewer tentacles and less brimstone than my predecessor would have me believe."

"Well, we all have our supply chain issues these days."

After a chuckle, she said, "You can call me Haley if you like."

"Thanks, Haley. Pete."

Haley nodded, glanced toward the venue, and said, "So, is this a happy day for you?"

His smile became warm. "Honestly, yes, one of the happiest I have experienced in quite some time. The woman I love like a little sister has just married the finest man I've ever known. It would be an enormous challenge to improve on that score."

"I understand you were the one who brought them together."

"Yes, that's true. I would love to claim it as a stroke of genius, but it was dumb luck."

"Sounds like an interesting story."

"You can pry it out of me with a drink."

"I'm game. Let's go."

A short time and several drinks later, Haley got round to the question she had been dying to ask all night. "So, what is the deal between you and Sam? I mean, he and Ben are so tight, I can't get my head around his hostility to you."

"*Mea culpa*. We started bad, and I haven't been able to make it up since. We almost came to blows at one point."

Haley glanced across the room at Sam, sharing a dance with Hopkins. "With Sam? Really?"

"No shit. Ben had to get in between us to prevent a fist-fight in the Key West SCIF, of all places. Then I got suckered by the 252s into a kill box with Ben along for the ride, and Sam had to throw away the book to save our asses with *Kauai*. That's how I got added to Hoppy's death list, by the way," he said with a rueful glance.

"Hmm. I guess I can understand the hostility."

He grinned. "And yet, we are still here sharing drinks."

"Yeah, I like to live dangerously. A bad boy geek from the intel community sounds like an interesting way to burnish my badass cred."

"*Bad boy geek?*" Simmons grinned. "Now that's a moniker I can work with." He raised his glass. "Here's to the beginning of a beautiful friendship, the Bad Boy Intel Geek and the Badass PB CO."

Haley clicked his glass with hers and said, "Cheers. One thing, though, before we get too far along on this epic relationship: if you get any of *my* kids in a jam, I *will* kill you."

USCG Cutter Kauai, moored, Trident Wharf, Port Canaveral, Florida
08:13 EDT, 31 May

Haley

It was Ben's first day back from his and Victoria's honeymoon to Yellowstone, an interesting choice for a venue, although understandable given Victoria's curiosity for anything and everything scientific. The trip was apparently quite a success, as the man who returned was much more like the original Ben she had met. It was another tally on her personal ledger's "time to hookup" side.

Haley herself had had a long sojourn with Simmons—three days and nights. He was a remarkable man, entirely unlike anyone she had ever been with before in many respects. Besides his physical prowess, he had an exceptional intellect combined with a wonderful sense of humor that made him exciting and fun to be around. She looked forward to the next time they could get together.

There was a knock on the door, and Haley turned to see Ben standing there with a smile. "Come in, XO. Let's catch up. Tell me about your trip." Ben settled in his stateroom/office to plow through the physical and electronic inboxes for an hour after the initial hello. As usual, Hopkins had monitored things in Ben's world of work to make sure nothing important was overlooked in his absence, so it was not a heavy lift coming back.

"It was a wonderful time, ma'am. We ended up with quite an adventure, although not exactly what we planned."

"Really? What, the flights didn't work out or something?"

"No, we got there all right. But instead of touring for a week as we planned, we pitched in on a no-shit mystery."

"No way!"

"Way. They had never met a data scientist before, much less employed one. Victoria was over the moon. And I can cross 'run with a posse' off my bucket list."

"You're serious?"

"Yes, ma'am. On the whole, they were pretty happy with our contributions, and the sheriff said they more than made up for the squad room windows."

"The squad room windows?"

"Yes, ma'am. And the gazebo."

"The *gazebo*. XO, is this a story I want to dig in on?"

He paused, deep in thought. "No, come to think of it. You probably don't. How about I just say we had a fantastic honeymoon and leave it at that?"

"I'm very OK with that, XO."

"Very good, ma'am. I've gone over the check-off lists on all the work orders. There are some outstanding items on this availability, but I think I can get those knocked out today."

"Super. No problem heading out to AUTEC next week?"

"None, ma'am."

"OK, let's get it done, then."

"Roger that. Excuse me, Captain."

After he stood and headed to the door, Haley said, "XO?"

He turned and said, "Yes, ma'am?"

She smiled warmly at him. "I'm glad you're back, Ben."

"Thank you, ma'am. Me too." He nodded and closed the door on his way out.

Extract from the Canadian monthly periodical Financial Journal, published 5 June.
"Canada-U.S. Joint Venture to Take Over Haitian Mine Lease."
By: Edmond L. Peterson

TORONTO. Quesnel Mining & Development Corp [QMD | TSX] revealed the formation of a joint venture today with the American firm Penobscot Engineering Ltd. [PEL | AMEX] to succeed Sino-American Mining Corporation [SMC | SGX] in the long-term lease of Ile Ste. Michel, Haiti, for Rare-Earth Element (REE) mining, effective 1 July. The new venture, called Pan-Antilles Development Ltd., headquartered in Toronto, is scheduled to begin operations within 60 days of the lease transfer. The announcement coincides with the formal approval of financing by the U.S. Export-Import Bank (EIB) to clear the outstanding balance of the Haitian government's debt to the Silk Highway Fund, a state-owned investment fund of the People's Republic of China, headquartered in Shanghai. This financing will be repaid via profit sharing between the EIB, Pan-Antilles, and the Haitian government.

Industry experts were surprised by both the formation of the new enterprise and the swift approval of financing by the U.S. government. The annual outputs of the REE mining operations on the island of Ile Ste. Michel, located 25 miles north of Haiti's northern coast, have consistently fallen far below predicted levels, leading to speculation that original assessments of the richness of the REE find were flawed or fraudulent. The rapidity with which the lease was terminated by mutual consent of the Haitian government and SAMC has further stoked the speculation that China is seeking to cut its losses.

Responding to inquiries on whether filings estimating output at 8-11 times the current levels might be overly optimistic, Pan-Antilles CEO Lloyd Dunnington-Smith cited next-generation equipment, techniques, and management as making these forecasts readily achievable....

USCGC KAUAI
Fortiter et Fideliter
WPB 1351

Author's Notes

None of the characters in this book represent any particular person (you got that, all you lawyers out there?). However, some of the best qualities of the fictional crew members of *Kauai* were inspired by many of the fine people with whom I had the honor and pleasure to serve while I was a part of the Coast Guard.

USCGC *Kauai* is fictional. There is no "D Class" of the 110-foot patrol boat series, and the last of those built was USCGC *Galveston Island* (WPB-1349). I created a fictitious D-Class to buy some extra margin of verisimilitude and get the nit-pickers off my back. The cutters *Dependable* and *Joseph Napier* are genuine and still in service as of this writing.

The island of Ile Ste. Michel, Haiti, is fictional. The geography illustrations at the beginnings of Parts II and III of this story were altered to show it off the northeast coast of Haiti.

The lethal encounter between the panga and the Coast Guard response boat is based on an actual event occurring on 2 December 2012. USCGC *Halibut* was operating in the Channel Islands off Ventura, California, when it detected a Mexican panga loitering off Santa Cruz Island. A boarding party led by Chief Boatswain's Mate Terrell Edwin Horne III was dispatched in the cutter's RHIB. When directed to stop, the panga rammed the Coast Guard RHIB, ejecting Chief Horne, who was struck by the panga's propellers and died of his injuries. Horne was posthumously promoted to Senior Chief Petty Officer and awarded the Coast Guard Medal. The new Sentinel-Class cutter USCGC *Terrell Horne* (WPC-1131) is named after him. The suspect vessel was pursued by other Coast Guard units and stopped four hours after the ramming, and the two men on board were arrested. They were convicted in the death of Chief Horne on 5 February 2014.

The dialog between the Coast Guard people and in radio transmissions depicted in this story has much more "plain language" than what you would hear during actual operations. Including all the acronyms, jargon, and formal protocols vital for clarity and brevity in real life would have been more authentic. However, it would also be a great deal more tedious or confusing for the average reader. I ask all veterans and any other purists' forgiveness for this compromise for the sake of readability.

Request a Review

First of all, thank you for purchasing *Bravely and Faith-fully*! I know you could have picked any number of books to read, but you chose this book, and I am incredibly grateful for that. I hope it gave you what you were seeking, be it a little extra enjoyment or just a chance to escape the trials and tribulations of life for a while.

If you enjoyed this story, I'd like to hear from you and hope you could take some time to post a review or at least a rating on your bookseller's website, Bookbub, or Goodreads (URL/QRCs provided below).

Bookbub:
https://www.bookbub.com/books/bravely-and-faithfully-cutter-kauai-sea-adventures-book-3-by-edward-m-hochsmann

Goodreads:
https://www.goodreads.com/book/show/210968278-bravely-and-faithfully

My Website:
https://www.edwardhochsmann.com/

Read the Next
Book in the Series

**A covert mission. A Caribbean volcano.
And a race to save an island.**

The USCGC *Kauai* is assigned to a straightforward job—on paper. She'll provide cover and transport for a volcanology survey on the island of Saint Ignatius while quietly shielding a deeper DIA operation in the region. To the outside world, Ben Wyporek's crew are just Coast Guardsmen watching a sleepy mountain.

The mountain doesn't stay sleepy.

As volcanic activity spikes and the survey's warnings turn urgent, the "cover story" becomes the one crisis no one can ignore. When Saint Ignatius finally erupts, evacuation plans fail, evacuees are scattered, and a handful of survivors are stranded in the path of fire and ash. With fuel low and orders pulling them the other way, the *Kauai*'s crew must choose between the safety of their ship and the lives of people who were never supposed to be their problem.

Against this backdrop, the crew's personal lives are tested as harshly as their seamanship. Ben, newly married and serving as executive officer, struggles to balance a high-risk career with supporting his neurodiverse soulmate Victoria. Captain Haley Reardon discovers that command doesn't have to mean isolation when her connection with DIA officer Peter Simmons deepens under pressure. Cadet Marcus Porter's routine Academy internship becomes a fight for survival—and an unexpected bond with island administrator Isabelle Jones—when the volcano blows.

Excerpt from *Indies Inferno*

Haley had been watching the maneuver from the bridge wing, willing it to go faster. Hopkins had just completed the turn and was bringing *Kauai* up to speed when a colossal blast from the volcano, far louder than any they experienced before, shook the ship. A few seconds later, Haley's attention was drawn skyward by a strange ripping sound, as if someone were tearing a giant bedsheet. The sound became louder until Haley caught a glimpse of a large rock, perhaps thirty feet across, an instant before it plunged into *Kauai*'s wake with a tremendous splash.

Haley stood frozen in shock. Had that rock fallen just five seconds earlier, it would have disintegrated the patrol boat.

"What was that, Captain?" Hopkins shouted from inside the bridge.

Haley turned slowly and reeled onto the bridge. "You don't want to know, Chief," she said, shaking her head. She stepped over to the command chair and was sitting down when Ben called up from the messdeck on the tactical radio net.

"Captain, all survivors are on board and being settled in. Final count is seventeen, including all the UAV team. Two of the ferry crew and two civilians were killed during the eruption, and we have four minor injuries among the civilians we are dealing with now," Ben reported.

"Well done, XO!" Haley said. "Keep me informed." After getting two clicks in acknowledgement, she turned to Williams. "New message, report 'Have cleared Jamestown harbor with seventeen survivors.' Keep repeating that until it's acknowledged."

"Yes, Captain," Williams said.

Haley nodded and turned to Hopkins. "Chief. Just confirmed by the XO, the UAV team are all aboard and unhurt."

Hopkins exhaled with relief, then said, "Captain, our fuel is critical. We're down to ten percent. I recommend we throttle back."

Haley shook her head and said, "No, we need to put some distance between ourselves and the island. I expect a pyroclastic flow anytime now."

"It will stop when it hits the sea, right?" Chief asked.

"Dr. Hernandez told us it may, but they have also been known to travel for miles over water, borne by a cushion of steam from the seawater heated to boiling."

"But we'll be OK as long as we're inside the ship, won't we?" Hopkins asked.

"Chief, the temperature inside a pyroclastic flow can top a thousand degrees Celsius. It will ignite our paint and melt the windows. By the time the fuel and ammunition explode, we'll all be roasted alive. So keep her wide open for now."

"No problem, ma'am," a wide-eyed Hopkins replied.

"Captain, I'm picking up something on radar. Moving off the island fast," Williams called out in alarm.

They crowded around the console to look at the screen. What looked like an enormous bulge was hurtling off the island, thrusting eastward along a line to the north of their position, but spreading rapidly. "That's it! That's the pyroclastic flow! Turn thirty degrees to starboard, Chief!" Haley ordered, guessing turning perpendicular to the wave front gave them the best chance of escape. As Hopkins gave the order, Haley stepped to the closed starboard bridge door and gazed aft out the window. The flow was coming into sight now—a great, roiling mass of black and gray clouds, with flashes of glowing red within, like Hell itself was boiling out of the Earth. Haley could only gape speechlessly at this vast, monstrous horror, rushing in from behind to consume them, wanting to run, yet unable to look away.

Buy *Indies Inferno* today!

https://www.edwardhochsmann.com/books/kauaiseaadventures/indies-inferno/

Dagger Quest

In this first novel of the series, the world is standing on the brink in an Eastern Europe showdown between NATO and Russia. Meanwhile, a mid-air collision between a Russian bomber and an American fighter triggers a nuclear-tipped Russian hypersonic missile launch. The missile immediately disappears from radar and is lost in the Florida Keys. Can *Kauai* and her crew find and retrieve the warhead before it is discovered and triggers World War III?

Available in Ebook, Paperback, and Audiobook. Follow this link to find your retailer of choice:

https://bit.ly/DaggerQuest

Caribbean Counterstrike

In the series' second novel, the 252 Syndicate has created a new nerve gas far more dangerous than any in existence. But a vicious drug gang/cult has grabbed it along with their converted supply ship lab during a drug war. Can *Kauai* and her crew seize the ship from the gang's heavily fortified base before the 252s retrieve it and market the weapon?

Available in Ebook, Paperback, and Audiobook. Follow this link to find your retailer of choice:

https://bit.ly/CaribbeanCounterstrike